❧ FIENDISH SCHEMES ❧

FIENDISH SCHEMES

K. W. JETER

TOR®

·*· A TOM DOHERTY ASSOCIATES BOOK ·*·

New York

This is a work of fiction. All of the characters, organizations, and events portrayed in this novel are either products of the author's imagination or are used fictitiously.

FIENDISH SCHEMES

Edited by James Frenkel

Book design by Heather Saunders

A Tor Book
Published by Tom Doherty Associates, LLC
175 Fifth Avenue
New York, NY 10010

www.tor-forge.com

Tor® is a registered trademark of Tom Doherty Associates, LLC.

Library of Congress Cataloging-in-Publication Data

Jeter, K. W.
    Fiendish schemes / K. W. Jeter.—First Edition.
        p. cm.
    ISBN 978-0-7653-7402-8 (hardcover)
    ISBN 978-0-7653-3094-9 (trade paperback)
    ISBN 978-1-4299-9290-9 (e-book)
    1. Steampunk fiction.   2. Science fiction.   I. Title.
PS3560.E85F53 2013
813'.54—dc23

2013018478

Tor books may be purchased for educational, business, or promotional use. For information on bulk purchases, please contact Macmillan Corporate and Premium Sales Department at 1-800-221-7945, extension 5442, or write specialmarkets@macmillan.com.

First Edition: October 2013

Printed in the United States of America

0 9 8 7 6 5 4 3 2 1

To Geri, my wife & co-conspirator

CONTENTS

PART ONE: BY THE SEASIDE

PART TWO: OF MATTERS URBANE

PART THREE: TO THE DEPTHS

PART FOUR: THE AFTERLIFE AND BEYOND

Dead on their sense fall marches hymeneal,
Triumphal odes, hymns, symphonies sonorous;
They crave one shrill vibration, tense, ideal,
Transcending and surpassing the world's chorus.

— JOHN ADDINGTON SYMONDS (1840–1893),
"The Vanishing Point"

PART ONE

⚓ BY THE SEASIDE ⚓

CHAPTER
1

In Which a Grand Enterprise Sets Forth

AFFORDS there a sight more evocative of joy and triumph than the sun upon the sea? If my weary, battered heart responded thus, how much more inspiring it must be to those younger than I, whose hopes and desires still course strong within their unbowed forms.

"Does this aspect lay hold upon your imagination?" My companion spoke expansively, as might have befitted the commander of a navy's grand flagship, however landbound his actual vessel. "My understanding was that you are of London born and bred. A man of the city; surely the promenades of Mayfair and the dome of St. Paul's are more to your liking."

"I have learned to appreciate the rural life." Standing at the great curved windows of the lighthouse's cockpit, I swirled the dregs of claret in my glass. "It is a somewhat quieter, more contemplative existence I lead now, than any of which you might have heard rumour."

The same wine reddened Captain Crowcroft's visage, so much admired by the distaff readership of the broadsheets hawked throughout the land. "I expect so," he replied before turning his gaze from me, out toward the same vista that had momentarily brightened my thoughts. Churning waves threw themselves upon the sharp-edged rocks of the coast of Cornwall; gale winds caught the upflung spray, streaming mist along the southwestern extremities of the British mainland. The fancy caught me—I confess myself unused to this extent of imbibing—that the daylit ghosts of drowned sailors had been resurrected from their watery graves, as though the lighthouse were some luminous Saviour newly arrived amongst them. Now they swirled about and dispersed to air, haunting no longer the tides and stones that had ripped open the bellies of storm-driven ships, filling their crews' mouths with brine. *No more, no bluidy more,* those coarse-voiced angels seemed to chorus above the ocean's heaving *ostinato.* No more sodden, tattooed corpses washing up on the strand; no more bales undone, crates pried open, salvage fingered and value estimated by Cornwall's eager wreckers. A twist of a hissing stopcock and Newton's *Fiat Lux* would be cast to the damp horizon, the lighthouse's beam spangled over those crests that even now gleamed as sun-coppered as a victorious army's upraised shields.

"This is magnificent." The words stumbled over my wine-leadened tongue. I looked away from the sight that had inspired such lofty meditations, as unfamiliar to me as the expensive vintages that had filled my glass, one after another. "How I envy you—"

"Indeed, Mr. Dower? How so?"

I blinked in confusion. Instead of Captain Crowcroft's face, with its rectilinear jaw and brow as unfurrowed as that of Grecian statuary, I found myself gazing—once I had tilted my sightline down a bit—into a mustachioed assemblage of red-mapped nasal veins and eyes rheumy with indulgence.

"Excuse me." I managed to recognize the host of the launch party to which I had been invited. "I seem to have mislaid the course of my thoughts—"

"Never you mind, old boy." Hooking a broad thumb in the sleevehole of his waistcoat, Lord Fusible clapped his other hand on my shoulder with sufficient force to embed a row of boltheads into my opposite ribs. Pinned between the iron window frame and my gregarious interlocutor, I endured his ripely alcoholic breath. " 'Tis not a moment for *thinking*—your father was man enough for all that! We're the fortunate heirs to his genius. Our task is but to celebrate!"

"You're too kind." Above his balding head, I could see over to where Captain Crowcroft had enlisted about himself the party's female regiment, their sly chatter and admiring, lash-fringed glances obviously more congenial than my ruminations. "In a construct such as this—" Fortunately my glass was empty as I indicated the lighthouse's bridge with a wide sweep of my hand. "My father's contribution is, you must admit, only a small fraction of an ambitious sum."

Fusible nodded, lower lip jutting out in approval of my familial modesty. "Nevertheless." He raised a spatulate finger in front of my eyes. "An *essential* contribution."

"I appreciate your saying as much." A few of the women had overheard the braying compliment—in the circular confines of the bridge, it would have been impossible not to—and directed a mute, mildly curious enquiry toward me. "Of course, the only thing I might have appreciated even more—"

My tongue tasted salt as I bit my lip, sealing the words behind it. The wine had seemingly ebbed far enough in my brain to restore a degree of circumspection to my speech. It would have been rash to point out to Lord Fusible that the limited corporation he headed had not yet seen fit to honour my father's memory with a cash payment to his son, for the use of whatever clever device had been posthumously fitted to the lighthouse's navigational systems. From my previous encounters with the wealthy and powerful, I knew the delicacy with which they needed to be approached on all matters remunerative. One of the fond conceits of those with a lavishment of money is to imagine that all whom they encounter love them for themselves alone.

"And that's why you're here with us today!" Fusible's bullish enthusiasm allowed little notice of whatever I might have said or not said. He grabbed my arm with both his hands and tugged me toward the center of the bridge. "Make way," he shouted, "for the guest of honor!" The fashionable crowd parted for us as though the others were a glittering Red Sea and Fusible a Moses with a single strolling Israelite to ferry from Migdol to Baal-zephon.

"This is an excellent spot." Fusible turned me about in front of the intimidating devices at the rear of the bridge, a thicket of polished brass levers and pipes, the latter branching and connecting at all angles, seemingly for no other purpose than to confuse the eye and intimidate the mind. A constellation of gauges surrounded me, the red needles quivering and darting across the numbered dials like the slender beaks of hummingbirds. "Ladies and gentlemen—distinguished officers of Phototrope Limited—if I may request your indulgence . . ."

The jumbled conversations dwindled to murmurs, then silence. All faces turned toward us, the motion distressingly similar to that of an artillery battalion directing its cannons toward its target.

"So good of you to take the time," cooed a female voice at my side. Lady Fusible was of even more diminutive stature than her husband, but possessed of one of those intimidating bosoms upon which a diamond necklace rested as horizontal as though displayed upon a jeweler's velvet cushion. She took my arm in both her kid-gloved hands. "Your invitation was my idea, you know."

"Oh." I gave a nod, unsure as to what other noise I should make. "Very kind of you."

Lord Fusible pressed on: "I believe none would disagree with me . . ." He arched his back, presumably to expand his lungs for full stentorian effect. "That the limits of Man's creativity have been reached, here and now in our good Victoria's reign." I could see a slip of paper tucked inside his jacket cuff, with minutely scrawled prompts upon it. "For proof of that assertion, one need but look around oneself!" The paper assumed its own fluttering trajectory as Fusible cast his arms wide. "That of which men have dreamt . . . men have conceived . . . or invented . . ." Without his *aide-mémoire,* now lying like a dead moth at the toe of his boot, he wandered past the vaguely recalled signposts of his speech, before abandoning the path altogether. "Whatever they damn well did," blustered Fusible, "we've done it even better, with this ungodly great thing! Cost a packet, too, I can tell you."

"Hear, hear," murmured a Phototrope Limited officer, with the hunched back and spidery fingers of one who kept account ledgers.

"Of course, we'll make a packet on it as well." Behind the twin apertures in his amply padded face, Lord Fusible's eyes glistened with a piratical twinkle, as though he stood upon a galleon deck strewn with pound notes. "Our underwriters will be squealing with glee about that soon enough, I wager! Oh . . . just a moment . . ." He suddenly seemed to have recalled why he had dragged me up before his friends and business partners. "I'd like you to make the acquaintance of somebody who had absolutely nothing to do with any of this—but his father did. Clever bastard, from all I've heard of him. What did he invent?"

Another of the Phototrope Limited coterie spoke up. "The gyroscopic tourbillon. That bit's his."

"The deuce you say." Fusible's shoulders lifted in a shrug, indicating that he wouldn't have known my father's navigational device from a ditching spade. "Howsoever be it. Here's Mr. George Dower, the son of that prodigy."

A smattering of polite applause came from people who had no conception of whom they gazed upon and self-evidently cared less.

"Do say something." Lady Fusible pushed me forward. "I know they're all dying to hear you."

I would rather have been cast down a tin flue to the bowels of the earth. But instead, I waited a few seconds, as though the clapping of hands had not already died away, then cleared my throat. "Your flattering attention, I must confess, seems a source of both pride and confusion to me. Pride, in that being connected, or being thought to be so, in any manner however ephemeral, with such an heroic enterprise as this—naturally one finds one's blood stirring at even the prospect. Confusion, in that the certainty is manifest that there are many individuals other than myself, more suited to cast an encompassing reflection upon such an auspicious—"

"For God's sake, man." If I had no idea of what I was blathering on about—impromptu oratory had always been more of an occasion for panic than inspiration—then Lord Fusible had even less. He shook his head with such dismayed force that the surfeit of alcohol could almost be heard sloshing in his whiskered jowls. "Let's just get on with it. Crowcroft! Damn it all, where's Captain Crowcroft?"

Less chagrined than relieved by Fusible's outburst, I watched as the crowd's faces mercifully swung away from me, the guests searching in their own midst for the lighthouse's commander. Who in fact had taken advantage of the momentary distraction afforded by my discomfiture and was now stationed at the far reach of the bridge, leaning with apparent fond attention over the fairest of the young women. It was the very scene of two lovers exchanging those foolish smiles and whispers, the words of which no doubt meant little more than the ones I had just spoken, but which obviously were more happily received. And while a beguiling blush tinged the young lady's cheek at being so discovered, little if any impropriety could be imputed by even the most envious gossipers; she had been introduced to me as not just Lord and Lady Fusible's daughter, but also Captain Crowcroft's announced *fiancée*, Evangeline. Whatever advantage might accrue to him by marrying into the fortune that constructed the same lighthouses that he so famously helmed, it was surely outweighed in his thoughts by the girl's swan-necked charm and delicate features. A fair brow made whiter by its frame of unruly brunette curls, she—while not as tall as he whose arm her hand lightly rested upon—still towered above her squatty parents. Indeed, the difference between generations gave credibility to the folkish tales of changeling infants, though in this case the Fusibles would seem to have done rather better in the exchange than was generally the case. Even in the heart of as resigned an old bachelor as myself, the sight of such a handsome affianced pair evoked a sweetly melancholic pang, the notion of all that might have happened in a more accommodating world, but that had instead passed me by.

"Do your job, man!" Lord Fusible shouted across the bridge. "Not *that* one! Get over here and put this beast in motion."

Bearing a one-cornered smile, the self-congratulatory emblem of a man who had just been spotted in the company of an unusually pretty girl, Crowcroft made his way over to where we stood. Fusible stepped back and gestured at the incomprehensible levers. "Go to it," he snapped.

Crowcroft reached for the greatest lever, an imposing construct of brass inlaid with ivory and mother-of-pearl, surmounted with an effigy of mythical Britannia, seated with a lion's head in her lap. He hesitated, fingertips just short of the device, then turned toward me. "Perhaps you would be so kind, Mr. Dower?"

"I'm . . . not sure what's required . . ."

"Just pull it forward." He indicated the limited arc through which the lever would travel. "Nothing more than that."

Warily, I wrapped both perspiring hands about it. I tugged, but nothing happened.

"Perhaps," said Crowcroft, "with just a bit more force applied."

I braced myself and, with teeth clenched, drew the lever toward my chest.

Not for the first time did I feel that awed sensation—half fear, half exhilaration—that comes with the unleashing of great machines. Many years ago, before all those events that had left me a broken and chastened man, I had fumbled about in the back room of my watchmaker's shop in the London district of Clerkenwell, poking and prodding the mysterious assemblages that had been my father's legacy to me. On rare occasion, I had even managed to set a few of their coiled mainsprings into life and had leapt back to avoid being snared by the sudden fury of intermeshing gears and cogs, spherical balance weights sweeping toward my head as though they were a schoolboy's prankish conker made lethal by mass and velocity. Younger then, and not yet laden with grim experience to come, I would stand transfixed by the spectacle, as Galileo might have when first peering through his telescope at the similar workings of an unexplained Cosmos.

A subtle vibration transmitted itself through the lever's gleaming surface. It grew stronger, traveling through the bones of my arms as I brought the brass goddess closer to me. At the same time, an excited murmur swept through the launch party's attendees, as the bolted floor and walls shook about them. From below came the groaning of immense engines, roused from slumber. The shouts of the lighthouse crew could be heard on the tower's lower decks, as they scurried to their duties, attendant upon the pistons sheathed in oil and the sharp-toothed gears they drove, larger and fiercer than the smouldering altars that Moloch's ancient priests had fed with human sacrifice.

"That's fine. Thank you very much." The lever, unleashing such hidden but undeniable forces, had reached its lower stop. Captain Crowcroft managed to peel my white-knuckled grip from it. "I'll take over from here."

I stood back, my thoughts now more topsy-turvied than any amount of wine could have made them, and watched as the lighthouse's commander set to work. The position of smaller controls he set precisely, as a violinist might trim his instrument's tuning pegs by hair-thin degrees. Other levers appeared to be for the purpose of signaling both the engine room below and various other compartments of the lighthouse's operations; Crowcroft rapidly pulled those back and forth to the toll of clanging bells, evoking further alterations in the mechanical noises emanating beneath the feet of the guests. His labours were assisted by a pair of subordinates clad in the red-trimmed livery of Phototrope Limited's working legions. They set about monitoring the navigational apparatus' well-being with ears laid to various sections of its brass-clad anatomy, then making subtle adjustments with the handspanners they wielded. The eldest of the bridge crew crouched near his commander, finessing care to a brace of reciprocating rods with a microscopic screwdriver and the spout of an oil-pump flexed between his thumb and forefinger.

"We're off!" Lord Fusible barked his cry across the heads of the crowd.

"Not quite yet," noted Crowcroft mildly. "First we need to deploy our basal extremities." He turned back and set to work on another section of levers and gauges.

"This is a sight worth seeing! Come along!" Laying hold of my arm, Fusible dragged me over to the bridge's windows, pushing aside those who had already positioned themselves at the most advantageous spots. "Have yourself a gander at that."

As my host directed, I laid my forehead against the wind-chilled glass, the better to gaze down the length of the lighthouse tower.

Around its base thronged an even larger congregation of merrymakers, comprising the residents of the local fishing villages, as well as a motlier assortment of layabouts and their disorderly wives and children, carted out at Phototrope Limited's expense from the nearest towns. Plied with as much free beer as they could consume, down to the infants swaddled in their careless mothers' arms, they had devolved into an army of riot, intent on flailing fisticuffs and as much public debauchery as the British in their cups could enact before falling headfirst in their own spew. The beflagged pavilion from which drink had been dispensed was already demolished, with various comatose or perhaps even deceased figures sprawled amongst the stoved-in hogsheads.

"Will those people be gone when it's time for us to leave?" The thought of stepping from the lighthouse's relative security into the midst of such a mob filled me with terror.

"What?" The scarcely more sober Fusible glared at me. "For God's sake, man, concentrate! There—look there!"

Even as he spoke, Captain Crowcroft pulled a tapered wooden knob dangling from an arm of the machinery his men serviced. Gouts of steam burst from the pipe organ–like whistles that studded the lighthouse's flanks. The discordant screeches were loud enough to draw the attention of even the most marginally conscious of the revelers on the ground. A squadron of police, too few to tamp down the rolling mayhem, set about with their truncheons, endeavouring to drive the crush away from the base of the tower.

"Well enough," judged Fusible after a moment. "That lot can watch out for themselves."

Our captain had made the same assessment. I could discern Crowcroft and his bridge crew, reflected in the window glass before me, throw a further set of levers. One such was so stiff and unwieldy that it required the efforts of two men, one pulling and the other ramming his shoulder against its length, to bring it to the desired position. The resulting increase in the transmitted vibration was enough to elicit quick screams from the female guests, as well as some of the more delicate men.

I might have been amongst the latter, had my breath not already been taken away by the sight below, of great iron appendages unfolding from beneath the base of the lighthouse. Details of such a walking lighthouse's perambulatory operations had been explicated to me previously, and I had even perused a set of copper engravings arrayed along the tower's central spiraling staircase that depicted such, but nothing had yet prepared me for the actuality of the event. The reader of these lines will, I hope, pardon my ignorance about such things that have become everyday occurrences for so many. During my self-imposed exile from the bustling modern world, my tranquility had been obtained at the price of becoming a relic from a previous age, where such marvels had not yet bestridden the captivated world.

Picture, then, if you have the patience, my wide-eyed apprehension of six bolted and hinged crescents of iron, widest where joined directly beneath the tower's base, tapering to pointed claws yet bigger than a draughthorse where dug into the soil and rock. Other historians of this our mechanical age, blessed with more descriptive fluency than myself, have compared the construction to those crabs seen scuttling through shallow tidal pools, housing their tender parts inside the abandoned shells of other aquatic creatures, the spiraling points of such assumed habiliments wobbling above them like the awninged *howdahs* strapped to the backs of Indian elephants. If the spidered legs below had been fronted by a pair of eyes waggling on bristly stalks, the resemblance to such crustaceans would have been complete.

The bridge chamber tilted for a moment as the massive claws found purchase, digging a yard or more into the ground as they straightened and reared the tower's weight from where it had rested. A few of the unsteadier guests were knocked sprawling into each other by the sudden motion, before Crowcroft and his men made the necessary adjustments to bring the lighthouse perfectly vertical again.

"Marvelous!" Lord Fusible enthused beside me, as though he himself had lifted the tower into air. "Bloody marvelous!"

Below, roiling clouds pushed the hysterical roisterers farther back, as though they were in danger of being scalded by the exhaust from the lighthouse's engines. The pistons and gimbaled rods—thicker about than century oaks—that formed the legs' motive anatomy, glistened in the sunlight. One by one, each claw lifted in precise order and fell again, thunderously penetrating the earth a little farther on. Thus did the device, with myself bracing to keep balance far above, begin its ponderous trek to the sea's edge.

Of course, Phototrope Limited could have stationed their latest venture at its destination to begin with, rather than a quarter mile inland. But by doing so, the corporation's officers would have deprived themselves of the lusty cheers of the groundling onlookers, the crowd now completely enthralled by this armless giant lumbering onward in their midst. I knew how little ever happened in such remote parishes. A break in the soul-numbing monotony such as this would no doubt be sung and storied for generations to come, if for no other reason than the epic quantity of free beer that had accompanied it.

With the more incapacitated straggling behind, the lighthouse led the shouting parade toward a typically craggy Cornish promontory. As Captain Crowcroft steered his landbound vessel past a bend in its path, I was able to lay the corner of my brow against the window glass and peer back whence the lighthouse had progressed. In the middle of the holes gouged by the iron claws, a segmented pipe—greater in diameter than a man's height—trailed behind, steam hissing from its joints. Such was another of the day's sights, common enough to those who had stayed *au courant* with innovation and discovery, but not seen before by me.

"I hope you have found this excursion to be of interest."

Turning from the window, I saw that the lighthouse's commander had left his station and joined us.

"Exceedingly," I replied. "I had no idea."

Crowcroft laughed, finding my simple words to be praise greater than a thousand orators might have summoned. "Take a degree of credit for yourself," he said, "or at least your lineage. I have skill enough to steer this craft to its port, but its workings are far beyond my comprehension. Not the least of which is that devised by your father, hidden away though it might be."

I nodded, having heard similar before, though never to my comfort.

"If you'll excuse me—" Crowcroft reached past me to a latched compartment mounted beneath the window. "This is a tricky bit."

He opened the compartment and I perceived a set of levers inside, similar in arrangement to those manned behind us, though lesser in scale. With an eye on the rugged seascape ahead, Crowcroft began a series of delicate adjustments.

The fury of the waves dashing against the rocks kept the straggling crowd at a respectful distance, watching as the lighthouse picked its way over the seaweed-festooned boulders. What had been felt as tolerable rocking and swaying amongst those of us on the bridge, while the lighthouse had crept over level ground, now transmuted to a harsher jostling. That, combined with the sight of the watery horizon, turned green some of our party's faces, as though their bearers were trapped aboard an actual ship heaving from crest to trough.

Captain Crowcroft at last brought the lighthouse to its appointed berth, a great angled outcropping the width of the tower's base. The iron legs, having transported their burden this far, now grappled the stone, splitting apart its brine-soaked crevices until the claws were so embedded that no storm tide could have swept us from this perch.

"That should do." Crowcroft signaled to his men, who began returning the various levers and controls to their starting positions. The last, the one that my own hands had been set upon, was brought upright again, the lighthouse shuddering with the expulsion of pressure from its boilers. As one who tires from strenuous exertions, the tower settled into its resting place. The sheer tonnage of its construction deflected the rocky promontory by a few degrees, the bridge's floor once comfortably leveled as Captain Crowcroft tapped the controls with a gentle fingertip.

The clouds of steam were vast enough to momentarily occlude the bridge's windows. All was at peace once more. Wind dissipated the white mist, the long roll of the breakers the only sound that came to our ears. As the ocean lapped at the tower's base, I brought my face close to the windows again, looked up, and saw the sentinel gulls wheeling in the purpling sky, heralds to this prodigy that Man's craft and cleverness had erected amongst them.

⊷⟊◉⟊⊶

"WOULD it be inopportune of me—I realize, of course, that you have weightier matters to attend—but might I enquire as to whether you've had a moment to consider the subject of our previous conversation?"

Lord Fusible peered at me, as those do whose memories as well as vision are befogged with intemperance. But desperation had prompted me to put my question to him. As one such as I had but rare occasion to enter his lordship's concentric circles of power and influence, I had no idea as to when a similar opportunity for supplication might arise.

"Arrhghmm." With a deep phlegmy rattle, Fusible cleared his throat. "Much to consider. Much to consider, my dear chap." He nodded, sinking his chin into the wattle of fat protruding above his collar. "But you can be assured—with every confidence—that those matters of which we spoke . . ." He swayed a bit, as though bringing forth words from his sotted brain were an effort epic in scope. "Soon as I get back to London—the absolute soonest I arrive, I promise you—all of that will receive my undivided attention. Have no fear."

Naturally, every fear rushed upon me, at least in regard to receiving any assistance from Lord Fusible and his Phototrope Limited partners. I could see that Fusible now had not the faintest idea who I was, and even when eventually sober, would have no greater idea then. Having been paraded before his guests at the lighthouse's launch party, I had concluded my usefulness to him. This was not the first time I had opportunity for the morose reflection that wealth so elevates men, that the rest of their species appears to them but as ants scuttling about on the ground. Indeed, Lord Fusible could have had no more withering and dismissive a regard for me if he were still ensconced in the bridge of the lighthouse, now looming above us.

Those for whom he did have a use were his personal attendants, now draping a fur-collared cloak about his shoulders. The Atlantic wind, that had so picturesquely lofted spray above the rocks, bitterly sliced through my own unseasonal coat. A thread of scarlet at the horizon marked the sun's last diminishment and the advent of night. I would have a bone-chilling trek back to the seaside inn that was my temporary abode, without even the spark of hope to warm me.

Only a few carriages were left on the narrow dirt road, a few yards from the coastal rocks. As the lighthouse's beam swept across the ocean, I could hear Fusible's wife snoring inside the gilt-and-lacquered brougham that had carried them hence and would return them to the urbane comforts that constituted that life to which their bank accounts had accustomed them. Their other guests had already departed, their transports ferrying them past the prostrate figures of villagers sleeping off the effects of their merriment. I had dallied to the last, specifically for the purpose of these few and useless words. Now, as Lord Fusible was assisted in clambering into his conveyance, I brought my gaze up to the lighthouse tower's topmost point.

Above its bridge, other crew concerned themselves with the operation of the light-casting apparatus. They appeared to me as moths, shortly to be consumed by the dazzling glare of the flames magnified by the curved reflector mirror behind and focused by the immense Fresnel lens before them.

Shielding my eyes with an uplifted hand, I caught a glimpse of the lighthouse's commander. The cheering party having gone, Captain Crowcroft set his profile and narrowed his vision, looking out from the bridge to the world's farthest reaches, as might one who had planted the flag of Empire amongst savages and deserts of barren stone.

Behind me, I heard the snap of the carriage driver's whip, bringing about the matched pair of horses and setting them toward the Fusibles' destination. But there had been two carriages, I knew, and the second had not stirred.

I glanced over my shoulder. Sufficient moonlight slid from behind the night clouds that I could recognize Lord Fusible's daughter,

Evangeline, a knotted shawl wrapped about her shoulders, leaning forward from where she sat. She also gazed up toward the height of the tower, her gaze fervent upon the distant visage of her *fiancé*.

No surprise, that she should display such tender concern for the man to whom she had given her heart—

What struck me with dismaying force, though, was the expression she displayed to me, when she saw that I still remained, only partially obscured by the roadside shadows.

Rarely have I been the recipient of admiring glances from young women, especially the beautiful amongst them, but not before this had such an eye-slitted mask of pure loathing been tossed my way. The girl Evangeline's features tightened as she gazed upon me with murderous contempt. Indeed, if the force of such hatred-fueled regard had been transmuted into an actual weapon, I would have been struck down, a dagger through my heart.

I could not breathe, until she gave a quiet command to her driver. My heart still pounding from this unexpected event, I watched as the carriage vanished down the road.

Of the cause of such disdain, I had no idea. I had scarce exchanged more than half a dozen words with the young lady, upon being introduced to her at the commencement of the launch party. My life might have been such that many have wished me ill, but never upon such short acquaintance as this.

Perhaps it was an omen, and no more than the world's general assessment of my worth. I turned away from the lighthouse and began making my way along the path upon which I had come that morning. Seeking some advantage from Lord Fusible and his friends had always been but an alternate plan, a wistful and idle hope. Once I had returned to the inn at which I was staying, I could set about with an unencumbered conscience on the course which I had already determined. To wit, that of killing myself with a merciful bullet to the head.

Mr. Dower Examines a Lethal Device

A S with so many endeavours in my life, the intent was more easily formed than the deed accomplished.

Footsore, dispirited, and damp—during one of the Cornish coast's inevitable rain squalls, I had lost the narrow footpath and had nearly toppled from a cliff's edge in the resultant dark—I returned to the inn where I had taken lodging for the sole purpose of attending the lighthouse launch party. It would have been difficult to devise any other reason for doing so: travelers more impecunious than myself might well have balked at its mean and shabby aspect. Ill-favoured with a roof so sway-backed that the floor and ceiling of its verminous attic met in the middle, in silhouette the establishment resembled nothing so much as a loaf of bread fallen from a provisioner's cart and run over in the mud by one of its wheels. Its proximity to the sea—lying in my equally concave bed upstairs, I could hear the waves crashing against the shore with their dullish, unending drumbeat—allowed the full wrack of the saline winds to have warped every timber embedded in the wattle-and-daub structure. One might as comfortably have dined in the horseyard outside, so large and numerous were the gaps in the walls.

The landlord appeared similarly to have suffered from the harsh locale. Invariably clad in vest and apron so spotted with ancient, unattended stains that he might have been mistaken for one of the encrusted rocks at the sea's edge, the man was suited to his position in the like degree of his decay. As the inn grew more round-shouldered and slovenly, without ever completely collapsing upon itself—though the rooms above the stable were now but naked beams, scrabbled by owl and rat—so had its keeper, as though the constant damp had mildewed his bones as well. However dismal it might have been to contemplate the extent to which the inn would devolve into the mouldy earth through the coming years, it was even less cheering to imagine into what state its proprietor would be transformed.

So late was my return from the launch party that the public rooms' hearth was nothing but cold ashes, the candles extinguished upon the rickety, beer-soaked tables. The inn managed to turn a small business amongst the few sodden locals, who nightly hunched over their tankards, growling in a dialect as coarse as dogs barking; I preferred to take meals in my room. Though that arrangement appeared to have come to an end. The landlord had initially been content enough to deposit upon the dresser a battered pewter plate bearing a greasy chop and some squat root ostensibly boiled to edibility, but he had ceased this practice on the previous evening. From the squint-eyed glare he bestowed on me, I deduced he had formed the suspicion that he would be somehow illuded of full settlement of his bill.

In which uncharitable notion, alas, he would have been completely correct. As I mounted the stairs toward the room housing my meager luggage, the few coins rattling in my trousers pocket represented nearly my entire worldly capital. If I had been able to wangle some sort of commission from Lord Fusible, my first act would have been to plead for an advance against my wages. Approaching the landing, I heard a door creak partway open below and could feel the innkeeper's darkly assessing glare upon my spine. I unlatched the door to the room I had engaged and silently slipped inside, grateful for what little refuge it provided.

The bed groaned beneath my weight as I extracted the half-empty packet of Swan Vestas from inside my waistcoat. I managed to coax to life the lantern on the small deal table, turning the flame as low as possible, not for reasons of economy but to spare myself a brighter examination of the circumstances to which I had been reduced. The room's wobbling chair was fit for nothing but draping my rain-soaked coat upon. I leaned back against a thin pillow and contemplated the speckled copperplate etching that hung framed upon the opposite wall, its depiction of the bombardment of Taganrog being the room's only decoration.

"I rather suppose," I murmured aloud, "that I should not have returned here at all."

Speaking aloud is, of course, a sign of derangement. That I had lapsed into such came as little surprise to me, nor did I make any great effort to abstain from the practice. What skills or even desire for sociability that I might ever have possessed, my rural exile had eroded. But my journey here to Cornwall had placed me amongst natives whose dialect seemed to possess even fewer and odder vowels than did the Welsh. The innkeeper, for purposes of trade, no doubt, managed to emit a few sounds resembling the Queen's English; but that much had been the limit of my spoken intercourse with others until I had arrived amongst Lord Fusible's guests.

"Having gotten away without confrontation—" An intelligible voice, even though my own, provided a measure of comfort. "I should have taken advantage of that." My nod was emphatic, however late my decisiveness. That the landlord was brooding upon the demand of payment from me, I had already been sure; thus my departure before the sun's rising. I had naturally not wished to carry my slight luggage with me to the launch party, my arrival on foot rather than by carriage being unprepossessing enough. Taking a bunk, as low slang expressed the notion, would have entailed abandoning the one bag that now sat at the foot of the bed. "No great loss," I judged. What garments I had that could be described as other than threadbare, I had worn upon my back this day.

It had hardly been for the comb and mirror and other gentleman's accessories, arranged beside the room's bowl and pitcher, that I had returned to the inn. But there was one other object, of sinister but needful purpose, that weighted my luggage.

"Now's the time."

Sitting cross-legged upon the bed, I unlocked the bag, threw it open, and drew out the final article of my father's legacy to me.

That the device was a pistol, I had no doubt, though of typically eccentric design. Guns of every size and variety could be manufactured in the rudest foundry, comprising the simplest workings, and they would all be roughly equal in lethality. Such would never have been sufficient for an inventor and craftsman such as my father. The weighty metal contraption now resting in both my hands was of an intricacy that rivaled what one might have viewed upon prying open a *montre à secousses* from the clever cantons of the Jura Mountains, with all of its whirring, ticking escapements and complications. As to why a pistol would require that much clockwork for the elementary task of propelling a bit of lead toward its target—as ever before, the cogs and wheels of my father's mind remained equally as baffling.

However elusive its design might be, that the weapon was capable of accomplishing that which I would ask—namely, propelling the aforementioned lead through my skull—I also had little doubt. It possessed a fearsome *gravitas,* as fine guns often do, combining their etched beauty with the darkly oiled scent of those machines which so easily throw open the doors of Eternity for all comers.

My father had seen fit to craft curved plates of Gaboon ebony-wood for the pistol's checked grip, which added to its fatal allure in the way that mourning jewelry carved of black jet, draped about the snowy throats of certain smiling widows, makes its owners the objects of men's desire. Two barrels—one octagonal in cross section, the other rounded—extended nearly a foot in length, similar in arrangement to the nine-shot LeMat revolver I had briefly glimpsed in the offices of the London Arms Company, while making a minor mainspring adjustment to the corporate treasurer's wall clock. The functions of the miniature engagement rods and piston-like mechanisms festooning the barrels were lost on me, as were those of the interlinked constellation of escapements and ratchet-mounted balances extending through and above the central rotating cylinder. Even the cartridges inside the cylinder were of intricate design;

though unable to find a method of removing them for closer inspection, I was still able to peer through a circular lens mounted before the hinge of the cocking hammer and marvel at the exquisite details just as would an entomologist dissecting a scarab beetle beneath a microscope.

Technically, by letter of the law, the device did not properly belong to me. Years before, at the conclusion of those travails that had once made my name a popular synonym for disaster and iniquity, I had turned over all the creations of my father still in my possession to the Royal Society of London for the Improvement of Natural Knowledge, that august scientific body having pledged to make a complete examination of them, with the hope of benefiting society by a revelation of those secrets that had been my father's stock-in-trade. In exchange, I had received a not inconsiderable sum of money. It had only been some time later, after the last of the carts laden with the boxes and hammered crates of these treasures had rumbled off to the Society's Collection of Curiosities, lately relocated from Crane Court, that I discovered the pistol. In gathering up the few sentimental items I wished to take with me in my flight from London, I had accidentally put my elbow through what I had always assumed to be a solid wall in the storeroom of what had been my Clerkenwell watch shop, and before that my father's shuttered laboratory. After examining the revealed hole more closely, I had soon extracted the pistol, my breath blowing the dust from its surfaces and my sleeve burnishing the metal to its original gleaming.

While I possessed no more of the virtue of honesty than the average man, thievery was still not a vice that could be attributed to me, likely due to cowardice more than stern morality. Yet even while initiating a communication to the Society's officers, requesting them to return to the now abandoned shop and claim this last bit of the properties they had purchased, I found myself instead laying down my pen and picking up the heavy, hand-filling device from the desk before me.

Some magic in its silent gears had lured me, and thus had made the decision, separate from the ratiocinating centers of my brain. It wasn't thieving, I had reasoned, in that the Royal Society had received more than ample value for their money, carting away a collection that generations of their Newtons and Babbages might analyze and tinker with, before answering all its riddles. What was one more piece to that grand, inexhaustible puzzle? Surely a loving son—or as close to one as I could simulate being—was entitled to one memento of the man whose name I bore.

Thus I thought, and thus I sealed my fate.

Which I had unlocked now and weighed in my hands.

Granted, I had had no notion of suicide at that time, when I had removed myself and my few belongings to that remote rural village, where I had hoped to live unnoticed while enduring the slow ebb of my infamy. My affairs had been in order then, or at least their financial aspect. A stuporous future had been laid out for me, much desired in that regard after all I had endured. But Man—or at least George Dower, it seems—cannot evade his destiny. However innocent of cause I had been in my first ruination, the second one was all the result of my own folly. The thought provided scant satisfaction.

Now, in this bleak Cornish inn, I raised my father's pistol and examined it with care greater than that which I had undertaken upon previous occasions. I had made attempts before to fire the thing, aiming it at some bottle placed upon a countryside boulder. Some subtlety in its operation eluded me, though. I had discovered a tiny key that could be withdrawn from a repository in the pistol's black grip and had further discerned that this simple gilded piece, not much bigger than a mouse's forelimb, could be inserted into various points about the device and used to wind its coils and mainsprings to readiness, much as one attended to the single driving force in one's pocket watch. On the occasions when I had done so, the pistol's inner gears and escapements had immediately begun their busy whirrings and tickings, just as would similarly be the result with the aforementioned timepiece. A perceptible vibration had coursed out of the supposedly dead metal, as though my hand had seized upon a living creature, the pulse of its minute heart racing faster than my own. The first time I had experienced this sensation,

I had immediately dropped the pistol, so startled was I by the impression of it having sprung to the same vibrant animation Man shares with the beasts of field and branch. And if brass and tin and iron could be possessed of life, it also seemed that they could own that degree of mulish stubbornness that Man has heightened to the level of Principle. For try as I might, forefinger tightening upon what was self-evidently the pistol's trigger, I could not get the blasted device to fire. Various latches and levers protruded from the mechanism, all of which I had prodded and adjusted, singly and in combination, but to no avail. The shivering release of the clockwork pistol's wound-up mainspring was as much liveliness as it had been willing to display. The cartridges had remained entombed inside, rather than bursting forth with a martial roar to spang upon the nearest stone wall.

That had been frustrating, but only to the idle curiosity I had roused to break the monotony of the agrarian existence to which I had resigned myself. Now, I was rather more motivated.

Having once again wound the pistol's various springs and coils, I returned the key to its niche. Optimism is a desirable virtue in all pursuits, but never so much as in suicide. A host of considerations form impediments to the wished result, from the dreaded pain of the bullet's impact, however brief, to a vision of the ungainliness of one's body, limbs splayed at the sort of comical angles that would provide amusement to callous onlookers. (No doubt the latter prompts the enthusiasm for quick-acting poisons amongst women committed to self-annihilation, the efficacy of such compounds allowing for a more decorous arrangement of the corporeal remains, free of repulsive gore. The last scene of the Bard's *Tragedy of Romeo & Juliet* would hardly have seemed so tragic, though perhaps a bit more exciting to the groundling rabble, if it had included a gunshot to the head rather than a maidenly swoon upon the sarcophagus—though my fragmentary memory of the classics does recall something about a dagger as well.) If the *soi-disant* suicide entertains notions of failure in the attempt, he is likely to give up altogether and pessimistically resign himself to his miserable life.

Having decided my course, I was determined to see it through. I had never conceived of myself as a figure of heroic resolve, but then, better late than never.

I swung my legs over the sagging bed's edge, the better to bring the clockwork pistol close to the lantern's illumination. My experience in the past had always been, as others wiser than myself have remarked upon, that a problem's solution might elude the enquirer upon first and most forceful application, as a drop of mercury darts away from a fingertip brought square upon it. Whereas inattention—a skill I had seemingly developed to a high degree—often brings the answer unbidden. Such proved to be the case in this event, or so I assumed. It had been some time since last I occupied myself with my father's eccentric clockwork pistol. The same small levers and catch-points that I had manipulated before to vain effect, I now pushed and prodded in differing order. This produced some edifying results: one such lever, the largest and most prominently situated behind the pistol's rotating cylinder, swung through its arc to a position unobtained on previous occasions. Other novelties seemed to ensue thereby: the pistol's ticking and whirring grew louder, as might a small captured animal's heart beat faster and breath pant with more avidity, perhaps upon spying some route of escape. I instinctively tightened my grip upon the device, some fanciful part of me apprehending that it would indeed bolt from my hand.

"Yes!" These developments gratified me enormously. I continued my addled soliloquy. "You haven't taken the better of me this time." Though my words might better be considered as a dialogue, in that I seemed to be addressing my dead father. "Now I've got you!"

I have no surety that all suicides experience the same emotions I did, those having succeeded in their attempts being no longer available for interview, and the failures hardly reliable in this regard. But excitement surged in my breast as I sensed the opening of that escape I had imagined for some trembling hypothetical creature. I raised the pistol, now the most gratefully received portion of my father's estate, and brought its cold circular snout to my temple—

Just then, someone knocked at the room's door.

An expletive escaped from my lips, which I immediately regret-
ted. Not that I feared any lapse in polite vocabulary might offend the
overhearing party, but that the mere act of speaking would confirm
my presence to this unfortunate visitor. At times such as these, one
values one's privacy—understandably, given the delicacy of the procedure at hand. There's precious little opportunity to acquire practice at killing oneself, at least if one is serious about it.

If the person on the other side of the door's thin panels were the
inn's landlord, arisen from his own bed and re-trousered for the
mere purpose of demanding his payment, I could hardly put him
off—if for no other reason than that he could unlock the door and
enter at his pleasure. In such a situation, waving about a pistol—
however remarkable its design—would scarcely improve my prospects. If he snatched it from my hand—and he was thug enough to do
so—I would have little recourse for carrying out my self-destructive
intent, other than rushing from the inn and casting myself from the
nearest cliff. The prospect of drowning in Cornwall's cold and
mucky waters filled me with justifiable distaste.

With my mind racing from corner to corner of my hemmed-in
thoughts, I found it difficult to conjecture who else might be at the
door of the shabby, slant-floored room. Whatever business I might
have had with Lord Fusible and his Phototrope Limited associates,
which had brought me to this terminal extension of the British Isles,
had come to a conclusion once their lighthouse's launch party had
ended. Fusible was hardly more likely to have considered offering
me a position with his firm when he was sober than when drunk—
and in either state, the chances of his sending for me in the middle of
the night were virtually nil.

As I pondered, the knock sounded again. "Mr. Dower? Are you
there?"

So not the landlord, as the person enquiring had sufficient teeth
to enunciate consonants and diphthongs, a dental condition not often encountered outside London, and rarely enough there. I decided
to accept a temporary hiatus in the course of the project upon which

I had embarked and slid the clockwork pistol beneath the bed-pillow.

"A moment, please." The room was so cramped that I had but to stand in order to reach the door. I shifted the latch and pulled it toward me—

At that moment, the past surged over me. As though I had indeed wandered down to the moonlit shore, and one of those tidal monsters that the Japanese term *tsunami* had towered above me like a shimmering wall, then struck me full force.

So many trials I had endured! Abyss of violence and deceit, so narrowly escaped!—as might one crawl over the lip of that fiery Pit into which one had been cast, blameless before, castigated and reviled afterward. I gaped at the swarthy visage of the apparition in front of me and heard again the long-forgotten voice of my man-servant, Creff, speaking those words which had initiated my fall from Grace, headlong into Chaos and Despair:

Mr. Dower, sir, there is a crazed Ethiope at the door, presumably to buy a watch.

For indeed it was that author of my misfortunes who stood there in the glow cast by the room's lantern, the figure I had once known only as the Brown Leather Man.

CHAPTER
3

On the Ecclesiastical
Tendencies of
Sea-Going Mammals

O R perhaps not.

As I regained consciousness—for I had swooned in a dead faint and fallen backward—I discerned a fairer face hovering above me, possessing thin, blondish whiskers and skin no darker than my own or any other Englishman's. He seemed at least a few years younger than me.

"Are you all right, Mr. Dower? Here, let me help you up."

I took the gentleman's hand and allowed him to assist me into a sitting position at the edge of the bed. The back of my skull felt a little tender as I rubbed it, though a glance downward indicated that the rotting floorboards had suffered more damage from the impact than had I myself.

"I appear to have taken you by surprise," spoke my visitor. "You have my apologies."

"Quite all right." With an upraised hand, I waved off further attention. "Accept my apology, instead. I have been lately . . . stressed."

He smiled. "That comes as no surprise to me. I am rather more familiar with your affairs than you might imagine possible of a stranger."

I let that remark pass. At one time, the whole world had seemed concerned about my comings and goings; if only one person was so caught up in them now, that was an improvement.

As my vision cleared, I examined more closely my unexpected visitor. My senses were still confused by the persistence of the briny odour in the room, but that mystery was partly dispelled by the sight of the pool of sea-water spreading out from where he stood, its diameter increased by the rivulets still trickling from the dark, rubbery garment in which he was clad from neck to toe. Such had been the cause of my mistaking the gentleman for that rather less human creature, in origin if not form, who had come wetly traipsing to my Clerkenwell watch shop years ago. Of course, for he whom I had named in my mind as the Brown Leather Man, the function of the similarly encasing attire had been to keep the sea-water inside, as one of his aquatic origin could not survive without. (Though if any of his breed were still alive now, in their submerged habitat off the remote Orkney Islands, that would have come as equal surprise; a degree of this latest shock came from the apprehension that one dead had turned up on the room's door sill, enquiring after its tenant, as though the Angel of Death had decided to meet me halfway.) Whereas for this gentleman, more recognizably of English stock, the garment's purpose was to fend off the ocean. I had read of such enthusiasts, and even seen representations of the distinctive gear they had crafted for themselves, which made possible deep immersion in our nation's chilly coastal waters. The diving garment's hood, which I had taken for that which had hidden the Brown Leather Man's true and unimaginable face from me, was now pulled loose from the matching seam at his throat, so that it might dangle flaccid at his back. A narrow tube of black India rubber hung coiled at his belt. This was undoubtedly a necessary part of the apparatus which allowed him to breathe while submerged, a perforated float carrying the open end to the water's surface.

While relieved that I had been accosted by neither the dead or one other than human, I remained of a perplexity as to why someone garbed for marine exploration would want to talk to me. Conversations with strangers were always initiated by some interest in my father's creations; I knew of none that could be successfully operated in sea-water.

"I'm afraid," I said, "that if we've met before, the occasion has slipped from my memory."

"We haven't, in fact." My visitor reached into a pouch next to the coiled tube and extracted a calling card, which he then proffered from his extended hand. "I could scarcely expect you to know any- one as obscure as myself."

Whether that was a sly dig at my past notoriety, I could not tell. Examining the card, I saw that it was coated in some translucent wax, presumably to keep it safe of the salt-water from which the gentleman had so obviously arisen. The card read:

HAMUEL STONEBRAKE

Senior Vicar

The Mission to the Cetaceans

Is there anyone whose heart does not sink upon meeting an evan- gelist? And of course, the obscurer the sect, the more persistent and troublesome such a person was likely to be. What wise street poet was he, whose doggerel stated that nothing frightened him more than religion at his door? Whoever it had been, he had had the right of it. Annoying enough when some traveling proselytizer, demented with godly revelations, turned up at one's home, where peace and comfort could be restored simply by turning him away; I thought it rude of him to accost me here, where I was so obviously adrift amongst strangers. And if this Stonebrake fellow knew so much about me, as he claimed, couldn't he have reasonably inferred that before his interruption I had been busily attempting to kill myself?

"May I?" He gestured toward the room's single chair.

"By all means." I pulled my jacket, still somewhat moist, from the back of the chair and draped it across the bed. If I had been more charitably disposed toward the man, I would have warned him of the chair's fragility. He managed to lower himself upon it without incident, the diving garment squelching upon the wood.

"You are perhaps wondering as to the purpose of my calling upon you. At such a late hour, and in such, I admit—" He smiled and ges- tured with both hands toward himself. "Unusual circumstances."

"Not at all," I replied. "I imagine that the Lord's work—which appears to be your business—requires any number of unusual exertions. In this case, however, your efforts are somewhat futile. If you've come to ask me for a donation to this—worthy, I'm sure—Mission of yours, I have to inform you that my funds are limited at the moment."

"Then it's well that I did not come to make any such request." He leaned back in the creaking chair, evidently amused by the description of my finances. "Nor would I have needed to—the Mission is well funded by its benefactors. A certain gentleman named MacDuff has been most generous in this regard."

"I'm sure he will receive his appropriate reward in the next life. But as I indicated, at the moment I can make no similar investment."

"Your inability to do so comes as no surprise, Mr. Dower. Believe me, I know close to the exact shilling the extent of your straitened condition."

Perhaps the man did, perhaps he didn't. I didn't care to pursue the point. For a dreadful suspicion had seized me. If he had not come here to solicit money—

"Good Lord." I stared at him in horror. "Please don't tell me that you actually come here out of concern for my immortal soul. I hope that I'm not one of these—" I glanced again at the card he had handed me. "These 'Cetaceans' to which you minister."

My words drew a quick laugh from him. Then he leaned toward me, his elbows on his knees. "Do you know what a Cetacean is?"

"No more than I care, sir." I drew myself upright. "I was not churched as a child; I am not versed in Bibles and Testaments and Prophets. My father, who had the sole rearing of me, was of the iconoclastic persuasion. I am aware, through common schooling, that certain Christian notables spent a great deal of time in correspondence with others; how they found time to be martyred, I can scarce imagine. The result being stacks of letters to Ephesians, and Thessalonians, and every Hebrew wandering about the Dead Sea. I have not read such letters—inasmuch as none were addressed to me personally—but I am sure they are edifying, if not diverting.

Doubtless these Cetaceans of which you speak are similar recipients of such missives, full of good advice and moral nagging. Perhaps the original Cetaceans were of some distinct national character, so that their collective name became a metaphor, a general spiritual descriptor, as did *Pharisee* and *Samaritan*." The fellow's cheerful impertinence had roused me to unusual eloquence. "If you can find Cetaceans in London, or Hull, or Birmingham, all in need of your Mission's care, then please, do so. However, I am confident that I am not one of these Cetacean fellows, so I could be safely left alone by you and your brethren, without your feeling that you had failed somehow."

"Spoken well, Mr. Dower." A single clap came from Stonebrake's dark-gloved hands. "You do your slender faith proud. If ever nonbelievers required a preacher, I would nominate you to ascend their pulpit. Your logic, however, exceeds your knowledge."

"I have never been accused of possessing a surfeit of either."

"As that might be," said Stonebrake. "But let me assure you that Cetaceans are not to be found in London, or any other city—at least not in living form, though sometimes their bones are put on display."

"How barbaric." I had no idea what the man was going on about.

"It could hardly be otherwise. For Cetaceans are not found there, but here." He pointed to the room's one crooked window.

"I was not aware that Paul or the other Church fathers wrote to anyone in Cornwall. This puts a new light on early Christian history."

"Droll, Mr. Dower. But I meant you to look farther."

"Very well." Perhaps if I indulged the fellow, he would go away and leave me to the final task to which I had appointed myself. I obediently glanced once more at the night-filled window, then back to him. "There is nothing farther, Mr. Stonebrake, but the sea."

"Exactly. That is where you would find a Cetacean, if you were seeking one. For a Cetacean is but a whale, sir. That aquatic wonderment, of immense size and appetite—that is, if you are speaking of the suborder *Odontoceti,* or the toothed whales. Their kin the *Mysticeti,* the baleen whales, are content to feed upon the tiny creatures that swill about in the ocean currents. Fascinating creatures, all of them, once you make their acquaintance."

"Which I take it you have."

"On many occasions, Mr. Dower."

I raised an eyebrow. "And on these 'occasions,' sir, you somehow minister to these whales? Discharging your pastoral duties toward them, I mean. By, say, preaching sermons to them?"

"Not quite." Stonebrake gave a shake of his head. "I am but a vicar in our organization. The head of our Mission is quite a fiery orator, though, and a godly man. He preaches to them."

"Where?" A sudden, unbidden vision came to me, of some church vaster than York Minster, its magnified size necessary to accommodate the pews for such creatures, their fins awkwardly turning over the pages of the hymnals.

"As I told you." My visitor was all patience as he pointed again to the window. "At sea. Our Mission is an ocean-going one, with a ship that serves as its headquarters and pulpit. I'm sure that you'd agree that a general rule of operation for all Christian missionary work, in Africa or the Atlantic, is to go where there are ears to listen to one's teachings, rather than drag the heathens back to the home country for instruction."

"Ah. Yes. Of course." This was not the first time I had noted that when one conversed with the insane, their responses often seemed outwardly sensible and logical. "And are there other duties involved in this ministry that you and friends have undertaken? Does the head of the order, when not preaching to these whales, also hear their confessions and forgive them their sins?"

"That is a theological point that has not yet been established." Stonebrake continued displaying his surface rationality. "We are a relatively new order, and as such, we do not have the lengthy history of disquisition that the ancient branches of the faith so obviously have. Thus, there are some matters on which we have disagreement with other Christians—"

"You could say that. I'm not aware of many Anglican priests, say, having lengthy discussions with fish."

"Mammals, sir; whales are mammals. And that is where the ontological debate begins. Convinced of these creatures' intelligence—and they are cunning beasts, I may assure you; very admirable in that respect—we are not yet sure if the species were participants in that antediluvian fall from grace that gave rise to Man's condition of original sin."

"Right." I gave a nod. "I would expect that whales have a more favourable opinion of the great Flood mentioned in the Bible, than we do."

"They might," judged Stonebrake. "Be that as it may, the question remains: If whales are not of the same sinful nature as Man, does the sacrament of forgiveness of sins have any application to them? Myself, I could go either way. The Mission as a whole is still pondering the matter."

"I've heard enough." I dug under the pillow for my father's clockwork pistol, having formed the intent to employ it immediately, rather than waiting for my guest's departure. Whatever distress he might experience upon the sight of my blowing my brains out, such was of limited concern to me at this point. "I hope you'll excuse me while I attend to some personal business, long delayed—"

The pistol's whirring and ticking sounds had been muted by the pillow, but were now clearly audible as I raised it to my head, a finger crooked upon its trigger. A blow struck me, but to my chest, knocking the wind from my lungs. Dazed, I found myself sprawled upon the room's floor, one of Stonebrake's hands at my throat, the other prying the pistol device from my grip.

"You fool!" All affability had disappeared from the other man's expression. Stonebrake's face darkened with fury, eyes narrowed to slits as he glared into mine. "Do you believe I came all this way to discuss maritime theology with you?" He glanced for a split second at the pistol he had wrested from me, then tossed it aside. Rising to his feet, he hauled me upright with him. "Do you really think that whales are so important?"

"You were . . ." I gasped for breath, his fist hard at my throat. "The one who . . . brought them up—"

"Desist!" His other hand struck me across the face, hard enough to send me flying onto the bed, which collapsed beneath me. "You and I have other business to attend to—"

"Wuttin blazes garn thar?"

Both Stonebrake and I looked over at the door, which had flown open to reveal the innkeeper, clad in a flannel nightshirt. Our voices had no doubt roused him from his slumbers, his concern heightened by the audible eruption of violence.

I could see the room's chaos reflected in the man's eyes. The broken timbers of the bed frame were scattered about, with myself prostrate on the mattress, Stonebrake's knee pressed against my chest, his fist raised above my bloodied head.

"This man—"

The landlord was not interested in hearing me out, or in coming to my aid. He remained unflustered, having assessed the details before him. Such scenes apparently occurred on a frequent and casual basis in these lodgings.

"Thar'll be charge far thet," he said, nodding toward the bed's splintered debris as he retreated, pulling the door shut once again.

Though not alleviated, my situation was to a small degree improved, this distraction having given Stonebrake an opportunity to regain his composure. A simmering anger still hardened his features, but he no longer seemed intent on murdering me. He released me and stood back, attending to various fastenings of his diving garment that had become disarranged in our one-sided scuffle. For my part, I managed to push myself into a sitting posture against the wall, as I wiped the blood from my mouth.

"Do you know what this is?"

I looked at the bright bit of metal caught between the other's thumb and forefinger. "A crown," I said. My ability to speak was restored to a small degree. "Coin of the realm."

"Indeed." Stonebrake returned the item to the pouch on his belt. "You need such. Don't attempt to deny it. And I want such. A great many of them."

"I thought you were a man of the cloth. Or at least affiliated—"

"That might be," spoke Stonebrake grimly. "But I am not a bloody idiot. An opportunity has arisen to garner wealth beyond your dreams—though not beyond my desires. The mere fact that you are essential to that acquisition will not deter me from the pursuit. You will aid me, and profit thereby, whether you choose to or not."

His words baffled me. "What assistance can I provide?"

"I have come to tell you as much. The relation will take some time, as the matter is unusually complicated, with aspects I anticipate will be unfamiliar to you. We had best begin at once, as my journey here was accomplished in secret, and I must return before the morning light reveals my absence."

"Indeed." I was thankful that my lip had stopped bleeding, though the side of my jaw still ached a bit. "Matters of which I know nothing, yet to which I am essential—can you provide a reason I should believe you about this?"

"You will find my exposition convincing, I assure you." Stonebrake brushed his hair, disarranged during his attack upon my person, back from his brow. A thin smile flitted to one corner of his mouth, signaling the resumption of his pretense to gentility. "Or convincing enough. You have a skeptic trait about you—not a bad thing at all; I share as much—so I anticipate that you will not believe completely until you have a letter of credit at the Bank of England that can levitate itself and raise the dead, so great are its powers."

The passion with which he spoke I found both intimidating and oddly beguiling. As I had indicated previously to the reader of these lines, my thoughts had become somewhat disordered due to my trying circumstances. The speaking aloud to myself was one telling indicator. But there were others, more serious—as a rule, self-destruction is not embarked upon with a cheerful demeanour, nor with everything perfectly straightened and in place within one's mind.

"Hear me out, at least." Stonebrake discerned the direction of my thoughts. "Set aside your plans of suicide for the balance of the night. I would sooner have you willingly offer your aid, than force your coöperation in this glorious scheme."

That seemed a point reasonable enough. What was there for me to lose, that I had not already determined to discard forever? The prospect of my annihilation, achieved by my own initiative, had the liberating effect of placing me beyond the usual earthly cares. If nothing the man had to say was of interest, then I could simply proceed upon my previous course of action without qualm.

"Very well," I said. "Tell me what you will."

"Not here." Stonebrake reached his hand down toward mine, to draw me to my feet. "Let us go for a little walk."

*A Low Proposition Is Offered,
Then Accepted*

I NSPIRING—don't you think?"
I wrapped my arms more tightly about myself, shivering inside my thin jacket. The offshore winds had quickened, driving away the rain clouds, but also chilling the flesh on one's bones.

"To a certain degree," I replied to Stonebrake. "But as with so much of Nature, I would appreciate it even more from indoors, gazing out through a window."

"You'll soon have all the windows you could ever desire—a townhouse replete with them." Stonebrake turned to look back at me, the waves surging to the height of his knees. "The only Nature you'll likely see would be your manicured gardens."

He had led me out from the inn, to a sandy cove bulwarked with craggy rocks. Leaving me a few yards behind, he had plunged out into the foaming surf, seemingly deriving some obscure pleasure from the pull of the tide against his legs. Above us, the stars glittered with icy crystallinity, dimming when the brighter glow of the distant lighthouse swept past us.

"I hope you'll forgive my enthusiasms." Stonebrake trod back across the sand and sat himself beside me on a rounded bank. He leaned forward to brush the salt-water from his diving garment. "I've rarely been considered to be of an excitable temperament, but the contemplation of vast fortunes has had, I admit, an unsettling effect."

"You might have murdered me." My jaw still ached to a degree, from the blow I had received.

"And thereby saved you a spot of bother. It would seem your gratitude would be more in order."

"You said you had something important to tell me." Pressed to annoyance, I looked away from the man. "Important in the sense of profitable. Very well, you have my attention. But then, you had my attention back in the relative comfort of my room. The necessity of removing to this place eludes me."

"Ah." Stonebrake nodded. "Perhaps I have been too long at sea. I forget that not everyone is equally charmed by the great roll and surge of the waters. That was in fact one of the attractions to me of the Mission—I fear I would have been of little value to the Royal Navy, coming from too poor a family to have purchased a commission as an officer, and not inclined to happily follow orders from those of more fortunate circumstance. But to walk the decks of a ship and do the Lord's work at the same time . . ." He raised one hand in a beneficent gesture. "What could be finer than that?"

"Obviously, to make a great deal of money. I suspect that the Lord is not greatly involved in that other ambition of yours."

"You wound me, Mr. Dower. I have done rather more on His behalf than you have. If God now sees fit to reward me with this munificent opportunity, let us consider it merely as payment for services rendered."

"Very well," I replied. "However you wish. I can assure you that matters of conscience do not weigh heavily on my soul."

Stonebrake smiled. "I knew we would get along."

I ignored his insinuation. "And so what would be the exact nature of this opportunity?"

"Hush." He held a finger to his lips. "We must be careful." A sidelong glance was cast toward the ocean. "They might be listening!"

"Who might? These precious whales of yours?"

"No . . ." Stonebrake gave a slow shake of his head, then leaned closer toward me, the very personification of intimate conspiracy. "The seas!"

I was not taken greatly by surprise by his words, nor did they give rise to greater doubts about his sanity than those I already entertained. I knew whereof he spoke.

"You refer, I take it, to that notion which has been so much discussed of late, of the ocean itself being an intelligent organism, as capable of thought as we ourselves?"

"Not *an* intelligent organism," corrected Stonebrake. "But many such. There might be as many about this island nation as there are parishes within it."

His point was well taken, at least in regard to those details of the conjecture which had so gripped both the official and the popular mind of Britain. Even I had heard of it, as deeply buried in the uncouth countryside as I had been. Somehow the news had traveled to my remote and rural corner, that the surrounding oceans had been discovered to be not just living, but thinking creatures, capable of independent decision and subsequent action. Two schools of thought had developed, debated even by the ignorant villagers amongst whom I dwelt: to wit, that the oceans had always been alive, from the dawn of time, but either they had never had the opportunity to display this aspect of their nature or oblivious Man had just simply never noticed when they did; or that the oceans had just recently undergone the transformation from large, unconscious, and inanimate bodies of water into vast creatures who appeared just as before, but now had the ability to think and move. Not even the controversied theories of Mr. Charles Darwin could account for an event such as the latter supposition, though a number of atheistic scholars, spurning the biblical account of Man's creation, maintained that the soup of organic compounds coursing through our veins and sloshing about inside our skulls was but the simmering counterpart of the salts and other chemicals filling the sea-beds to their brims. If some portions of that great primordial ocean had had the notion to separate themselves from the larger aquatic body, evolving from gelatinous, tendrilled jelly-fish to the sort with eyes and fins, and then on through that grand procession of lizards and scurrying rat-like things, then monkeys and apes and other foreigners, culminating at last in those sturdy

English yeomen who were just as we are today, except for their habits of wearing furs without undergarments and eating their meat raw—then why not other divergent possibilities? Perhaps the development of Life and Reason had occurred before all that jelly-fish folderol, and the bits of coalesced ocean that had stumbled dripping up onto the land, *en route* to becoming Mankind, had been cast-offs from the great thinking and living stew that had spawned them?

Such were the matters being debated even now, in shabby pubs and learned parlours alike. I supposed that if I had desired the most scholarly opinion on the subject, I might have applied to those few distinguished persons who might still have remembered me, in connection with my father's creations. But for me to initiate such a request, it would have been necessary for me to—frankly—even care about the issue, at least in regard to how and when the oceans had acquired these hitherto unremarked characteristics. In this regard, I fancy I had much in common with other Englishmen: all very fine to while away an evening over one's pints, going in one door of the controversy and then, as the Arab poet puts it, leaving by the same. It was the practical aspects, however, that demanded the attention of both sailors and the landbound.

"Continue with your exposition." I suspected that Stonebrake was of the same mind. "To this point, you have only told me that which I already knew."

"Then I can assume," said Stonebrake, "that you know much else besides. You are no doubt aware that here in Britain, we find ourselves surrounded not by a single sentient, active ocean, as might be the case if we were some small speck out in the tropical Pacific. We are instead swarmed about by waters composed of many sentient, liquid organisms. The currents off the Outer Hebrides islands are apparently one organism, as reported by both mariners and coastal observers. The Irish Sea is another organism, and so forth."

"So I have heard."

"You heard correctly." He pointed to the dark, rolling waters before us. "What we see here is as separate a creature from its brethren off East Anglia and Humberside as you and I are separate examples of the human species. That these living seas appear to

merge at their edges does not alter that fact. As with all living organisms, they might be coöperative with each other or antagonistic." He
smiled as he gestured between the two of us. "Just as it is with us."

"The bulk of Humanity has displayed more hostility than kindness toward me."

"All that will change," insisted Stonebrake, "when you have the
ready jingling in your pocket. That's the music to which people
listen—and applaud. But let me proceed. I take it that you are also
familiar with the complications, in regard to navigation, that have
arisen from the oceans being living creatures?"

"Who is not?" I shrugged. "As you say, these living seas have
been observed to act on their own initiative and agenda, in ways that
might not be convenient for Mankind. An ocean strait that might
have been deep enough for ships to sail through before, now might
suddenly become shallow enough to rip a ship's hull open with the
exposed rocks below." In relating that which the entire civilized
world knew already, I could be as pedantic as him. "Or similarly, a
passage that was previously too dangerous for ships because of its
strong currents might now be safely calm and navigable—the task
for sailors being to find those new, safe routes, without losing one's
ship and crew in the process."

"Well said." Stonebrake's smile was as irritatingly patronizing as
before. "And what assists them in so doing?"

Nothing would do for the man, apparently, except a complete
recitation of the information with which we were both familiar.
"The lighthouses, of course."

"Ah, but we had lighthouses before we had to deal with animate
oceans. And it took a good deal of effort and entrepreneurial capital
to construct them. To what avail? A lighthouse that was previously a
valuable navigational aid, might find itself miles from the rocky shore-
line that it had helped ships sail past, or be completely submerged
and its light extinguished by an ocean that had decided on its own to
shift its position but a couple of miles east or west. What would be
the point of even constructing a lighthouse if its usefulness could be
unpredictably ended the day after it goes into operation?"

"Now I am perplexed." I regarded the other man with a more incisive appraisal, as though in the darkness more had been revealed than by the room's lantern. "You make claim to know my affairs—and so you initially seemed to—but these tiny *lacunae* crop up. Are you aware that just this day I attended a launch party for Phototrope Limited's most recent venture?"

"Of course I know. I observed you there."

"How odd. I don't recall seeing you amongst the guests."

"The festivities up in the lighthouse's bridge chamber?" Stonebrake shook his head. "No, not there. I observed you later, after the lighthouse had grappled its perch upon the rocks, and after Lord Fusible's other guests had departed. Outside—that is where." With one hand, he indicated his diving garment. "You were so intent upon your conversation with Lord Fusible—though I could have told you beforehand that importuning him for some type of commission would be pointless—that you didn't see anything out amongst the waves. You didn't see me, to be precise."

His words nettled me. However little I cared for being spied upon, I took even less comfort in knowing which ungracious moments had come under his scrutiny.

"Very well." I straightened, as though to gather the tattered rags of my dignity about me. "Then you must be fully versed as well in the nature of an enterprise such as Phototrope Limited. Being as it is, of course, one of several such limited corporations that have sprung up since the advent of the living oceans has come upon us. Faced with a dilemma that might well have put the builders of the original, stationary lighthouses out of business, these new corporations' engineers have developed the solution."

"Yes," said Stonebrake. "The *walking lights*."

"Exactly. Lighthouses that are capable of auto-locomotion; that is, lighthouses that can move under their own power from place to place. The same massive mechanized legs at the base of such lighthouses, that enable them to crawl spider-like across various terrain, also allow them to grapple a perch onto the rocky crags of a new location. Of course, the drawback to such cleverness is the expense of both construction and operation: such complexity is not cheaply devised or maintained." I knew that Lord Fusible's comments at the launch party, however coarsely made, were accurate enough. I continued my own exposition, as if there were some advantage to be gained in demonstrating to Stonebrake that I was not a complete fool. "The walking lights are obviously much more complicated than a simple tower with a rotating light source at the top; with engine rooms and steam boilers for power, they need entire crews to move from place to place, along with skilled captains to steer them to various remote and often dangerous locations."

"Bravo!" Stonebrake seemed exhilarated rather than intimidated. "You exceed my expectations, sir; I couldn't have done better myself."

"I'm glad you feel that way. The only thing of which I appear to be still ignorant—a matter which you promised you could rectify—is how all this translates into wealth for us."

"That part is simple." Stonebrake leaned closer toward me. His voice lowered, as though there were indeed some risk of the envious ocean overhearing our secrets. "We wager, Mr. Dower; we wager upon the Sea and Light Book."

The reader may imagine the arc of emotions that rocketed through my breast upon hearing the man's words. Yes, I had already contemplated suicide, and decided upon it as a reasonable course of action, given my desperate situation; and yes, I thought this Stonebrake at best a lunatic, but most likely a charlatan. Nevertheless, even at this extremity, a flicker of hope had been aroused in me. Not just to escape the sentence of death I had decreed upon myself, but to transport myself to the giddy financial heights of which he had spoken so passionately. The prospect was like that of those children's fairy-stories, in which the peasant straps on the fabled seven-league boots, and strides from abyss to mountain-top in one go.

How cruel to have one's hopes raised, only to have them dashed at one's feet. This time, the violent reaction was mine. I sprung from the rock, my fist cocked, but did not let fly at my tormentor. Instead, I turned and strode away, the waves' pounding drowned out by the roaring of the blood inside my head.

"Dower! Wait!" the other called after me. "Where are you going?"

I made no reply. I kept walking, blinded by rage and disappointment. Toward no destination—the night was so dark, this spot so far from any human habitation, that all I could see was the faint blue phosphorescence of the waves splashing near my path. If any plan resided in my thoughts, it would have been no more than to somehow stumble my way back to the squalid inn, retrieve my father's clockwork pistol, and finish the task for which I had kept it; or to climb to the top of one of the rocky bluffs surrounding this bit of sand and from there hurl myself into the ocean. Given the fury that sent my blood hammering at my temples, the effect would no doubt have been similar to dropping a red-hot ingot into a blacksmith's cooling bucket, a burst of steam mounting skyward to mark my demise.

"For God's sake, man—" A hand grasped my shoulder and pulled me about. I found myself looking into Stonebrake's face again. "What is wrong with you?"

"Oh, that's a fine question, all right." My white-knuckled hand remained balled into a fist, the muscles of my arm aching to drive a blow between his eyes. "After all your easy boasting about how much you know about me, and about my circumstances."

"And so I do. Haven't I indicated as much? You're valuable to me, Mr. Dower; I'd be a fool not to have made a study of you."

"And fool you are, then." I spat out my words. "If in all your picking at another man's private affairs, you managed to overlook as salient a fact as this."

He blinked in confusion. "I'm not following you . . ."

"Evidently not. You come to me with some daft plan, spinning fantastic reveries about the vast sums in which we'll soon be wallowing. I admit I was intrigued, more fool I. You caught me at a weak moment, when my thoughts were easily beguiled. But then, having thus ensnared me, when pressed as to the actual details of this grand scheme of yours, all that you can tell me is that it centers upon laying bets with those bookmakers who track who's up and who's down amongst the lighthouse corporations."

"So it does," admitted Stonebrake. "If you'd but allow me to impart the full details to you—"

"What need is there? As God is my witness, your opacity astounds me. Are you not aware that wagering with the Sea and Light Book is what reduced me to these wretched circumstances?"

The reader's forbearance is requested. If, in the furious pace of my narrative, I write of matters unfamiliar to those whose lives have been more circumspect than mine—which I assume would encompass most of the population, there being so little effort or good fortune required to achieve that happy condition—my apologies are extended. So sunk in misery had I become, that it would be only natural to assume that everyone was as acquainted with such sordid matters as myself. No great charitableness is needed to recognize that others lead, in general, more virtuous lives than mine.

To elucidate, in pursuit of understanding amongst those curious about such things:

For the British nation, so thoroughly dependent upon ocean-going trade as we are, the awareness of the surrounding oceans as living creatures—with its accompanying effect upon navigation—gave rise to more than Phototrope Limited and its competitors. Scarcely a bale or crate of goods is loaded or unloaded at a British port, but that one of the lighthouse corporations receives a share of the merchants' proceeds, for having guided their vessels safely about the hazards that ring our island. No business as large as that can stride upon the scene, like some valiant commercial hero, without other money-making endeavours trailing behind. The opportunity to profit from the activities of the new lighthouse corporations is not limited to those who had invested so wisely in them.

The rivalry amongst the different lighthouse corporations, and between the walking lights and their celebrity captains, such as the much-admired Captain Crowcroft whom I had so recently met, is so exciting to certain easily impressionable minds that it is little wonder that interest in such matters has swept through so much of our society. The more genteel of our households limit their indulgence to reading about the latest exploits of Crowcroft *et al.* in the popular

journals of the day. No doubt there are many tender-hearted maidens who catch their breath at the portraits that accompany such
deathless prose, and who murderously envy Lord and Lady Fusible's
daughter, Evangeline, for her betrothal to the heroic lighthouse captain who had captured her heart. Such diversions are essentially innocent. The darker aspect to enthusiasm for walking lighthouse
exploits is to be found in the betting shops and bookmakers' parlours, in particular that constellation of the same that has become
known under the general rubric of the Sea & Light Book.

Perhaps the reader has heard of such things, but has spared himself intimate acquaintanceship. I wish I could speak the same of
myself. For I had allowed myself to become caught up in the betting
mania, to my moral chagrin and financial detriment, the combination seemingly terminal.

In the remote English village in which I had established my
abode, there had been little opportunity to lay a bet upon the out-
comes of the various corporations as their landbound fleets of walking lights competed against each other, pursuing those coastal
locations where they could render the most navigational assistance
to the ships at sea. In this, their captains' decisions were much like
those made by players at a game of chess, though one on a colossal
scale and whose squares shifted about at the whim of the surrounding oceans, moving their depths and shallows and sweeping currents from place to place at but a moment's notice. Word had reached
my ear, though, of this grand sport, and of the gains that could be
made from the bookmakers' purses, by one who could correctly
guess the winners amongst this ongoing struggle. Rumour had it
that some such lighthouse gamblers had managed to enrich themselves to fortunes greater than those of captains of industry such as
Lord Fusible and the other owners of Phototrope Limited and its
competitors.

Perhaps it had been mere folly on my part, that I had thought I
could emulate the success of those sporting types. Certainly I had
never been given to placing a bet on the turn of a card or on which
horse could nose out another at the race-course.

"But you thought—" Stonebrake's voice forced its way amongst my bitter memories. "That since you were your father's son, and that one of his creations had been found to possess utility in the operations of the walking lights—therefore you had some particular insight that would assist you in your wagering."

I turned from my brooding regard of the ocean, and coldly regarded him; I found his ability to discern the course of my thoughts to be irksome in the extreme. "Yes," I said. "So I had thought. I soon learned that I was wrong about that."

Even more embittering was the knowledge that I had been warned, before ever I had placed a wager. The last words of my aged servant, Creff, as I nursed him upon his death-bed, was such: *Please, Mr. Dower . . . don't bet on them unnatural things. 'Twill be the ruination of you . . .* He had been aware of the interest that had been sparked in me by various overheard accounts, and had been perceptive enough to see past all my disavowals. To my shame, I heeded him not; scarcely had I thrown a handful of earth upon the lid of his coffin, than I had turned from his newly dug grave and headed to the nearest town large enough for a betting shop that met my requirements. I had returned that evening; loath to enter the now cheerless cottage that we had shared, I had come again to the churchyard and sat down beside the mounded dirt, packed tight with the flat of the gravedigger's shovel. Another had been there, though its spirit had likewise gone before me. Greyed head upon its paws, the small dog whose master, my servant, had named Abel—the companion through so many of my own trials—slept the unwaking sleep of one whose devotion had earned such rest. I had gathered the cold form into my arms and had wept into its fur, realizing how friendless and abandoned I had at last become.

"Wretch—" I spoke aloud, unsure whether I was castigating Stonebrake or myself. "Have you no human sympathy? Would that kindness have been beyond you, to let me be? If ruin I achieved, then perhaps it was ruin I pursued. And deserved."

"You are too hard upon yourself." Stonebrake stood unperturbed by my wrath. The dark waves continued rolling toward us.

"If you wish to grovel before the immensity of your self-assumed sins, you might as well do so in comfort. Which you would have achieved, if you had not insisted upon betting 'wrong,' as the bookmakers term the practice."

I stared at him. "You are aware of the nature of my wagers?"

"As I have said, to the last shilling."

"I made those wagers in confidence!"

"And in so doing, you trusted a bookmaker to keep your secrets. Imagine," marveled Stonebrake, "an oddsman who would divulge his client's account, for no more than a pound note in exchange. Whoever heard of such a thing?"

"Sarcasm scarcely serves one who seeks another as his ally. As to my wagers, I merely laid down what I believed, at the time, had the best chance of succeeding."

"And in every case," he replied, "you wagered against Phototrope Limited and its walking lights, and any other corporation that had seen fit to use your father's creations. And in every case, Phototrope and those others went on to glory, pipping their competitors past the post, as it were. If all you had wanted to achieve was to sneer at your father's posthumous success, you might easily have found a less costly way than throwing your capital down a betting shop's gullet!"

I had no desire to debate the matter. The initial flush of my anger had ebbed, and the wind off the ocean resumed setting ice in my flesh.

"This is a useless discussion," I pointed out. "Whatever the motive or other details of my involvement with the Sea and Light Book, the result is the same. Destitution, simply put. I gambled away every penny of that modest sum, which with modest husbandry might have maintained me to my demise. And somehow you believe that you can inveigle me into some scheme that revolves around more of the same?"

"Ah, but you see, Dower—before, you wagered foolishly. You believed that you had some particular insight, sufficient to make you wiser than the other bettors. In that, you were incorrect."

"You tell me nothing of which I am not already aware."

Stonebrake's sly smile appeared again. "But this time, in league with my associates, you and I would actually be the possessors of that information, which would make sure things of all our wagers. Thus we would decimate the bookmakers, and reap those fortunes that those clever as we deserve."

"This," I said, "sounds dishonest."

"Only to a slight degree, and not one easily discovered. Criminality is in the eye of the beholder."

"And when the beholders are the police, the consequences can be serious. I speak of imprisonment."

He dismissed my concerns with a wave of his hand. "Have no fear. My backers are rich and powerful men, who—as with all such—merely wish to become even richer. Your value to them will protect you."

"And what value would that be?"

"You see? You're interested, aren't you? Despite yourself."

"Merely curious," I insisted.

"That is how it begins. But allow me to explain. The Sea and Light Book, as you have learned some time ago, accepts wagers on the operations of the various lighthouse corporations, the successes or failures of their various endeavours, and the profits earned or losses suffered thereby. And of course, those operations reflect the lighthouse corporations' best efforts to anticipate and accommodate the actions of the living, active seas by which we now find ourselves surrounded. Agreed? Very well. Obviously, a lighthouse corporation that could acquire advance knowledge of how and where the oceans might shift would have a competitive advantage over its rivals. If Phototrope Limited or any other lighthouse corporation knew ahead of time that the ocean waters were going to recede from a certain section of the Scottish coast, and flood another area so that passing ships would need navigational assistance, it could have one of its lighthouses immediately uproot itself and head off for the newly desirable location, beating out the other corporations. Similarly, I am confident you would also allow that anyone who knew ahead of time about where the sentient ocean organisms would be shifting and moving, as well as having information about how much the various lighthouse corporations knew about that, would be able to make the seemingly riskiest bets—the type that the bookmakers describe as 'long shots'—

yet be absolutely sure of winning vast sums of money. Such a person would in fact be undertaking no risk at all, for his wagers would be based on that reliably predictive information."

"If such information existed," I said. "Which would seem to be the problem."

"Granted." Stonebrake gave a nod. "But bear with me. I have come all this way to inform you that this possibility of beating the Sea and Light Book has become real—or tantalizingly close to real—due to the means having been developed to actually communicate with the sentient oceans. That worthy organization of which I had previously informed you I am a member, the Lord's Mission to the Cetaceans, was originally created to minister to sailors on board ocean-going ships. But now the organization has an altered name and a different purpose: having determined that whales are intelligent enough to convert to Christianity, Father Jonah—our Mission's leader—believes as well that since whales are actually mammals, complete with vestigial legbones inside their rear flukes, they might actually be one of the lost tribes of Israel mentioned in the Bible."

"This Father Jonah individual seems to be a lunatic."

"He might well be," conceded Stonebrake. "I have been associated with him for some time, and many of the things he proclaims have begun to give me pause. So much so that I and others have come to believe that there is not much future for us in the Mission. Its operations had been funded in the past by certain wealthy and pious patrons in Clapham Common, who had been swayed to open their purses by the Father's charismatic fervour. However, his notions about the whales have, quite frankly, put some of those people off. Many of them feel that their moneys might better underwrite charitable endeavours such as transporting hundreds of indigent families to some place known as Borrioboola-Gha, on the left bank of the Niger, there to cultivate coffee and educate the natives in the Church of England's basic catechism."

"If I had funds for charity, I would be more likely to give it for that purpose than for Christianizing whales."

"Exactly. As other Mission members have decided in concert

with me, high-minded pursuits are all very fine, but at a certain point one must look out for one's self. I do not intend to starve to death aboard Father Jonah's evangelical ship; that being the case, I might as well be rich."

A frown set upon my face. "I still don't see how that is to be accomplished."

"Simply enough. The Mission's leader is something of a naturalist as well as preacher, and rather better at the former than the latter. You are aware, I hope, that whales are capable of emitting extended sequences of noises, that some even describe as songs?"

"They might be capable of singing Italian operas, for all I know."

"Take it on faith, then. Using a variety of devices, similar to those ear trumpets used by the incipient deaf—but modified to be lowered into the water—Father Jonah has made an exhaustive study of these songs and other sounds performed by the whales. He claims—and I have ample reason to believe this to be true—that he is at last able to understand what the whales are saying."

"Indeed," I said. "So both you and he have taken leave of your senses."

"Not so." Stonebrake's retort was emphatic. "I have heard and seen the proof of these assertions. And more—Father Jonah has modified the pipe organ installed aboard the Mission's ship, that before was used for the accompaniment of hymn-singing. With it, he is able to produce noises similar to the whales' songs, and thus communicate back to them."

"Really? And what do he and the whales talk about? Theology, or just the events of the day?"

"Mock as you will, but what I say is true."

"I neither doubt it or accept it. For the time being, I will take an agnostic opinion on the matter."

"Fair enough," allowed Stonebrake. "As to the subject of their conversations, I fear that Father Jonah, due to his advanced age, has grown a bit senile. He seems only interested in preaching to the whales. Perhaps that is only to be expected. But I and other members of the Mission are more intrigued by another discovery made by the Father."

"There seems to be no end to such."

"But this is the most important one. The key to our fortunes. And it is this: The whales speak to others beside themselves. *They speak to the oceans.*"

I could see at last where his discourse was taking him. "And that is what intrigues you and your associates. You realize some speculative value in having the whales serve as emissaries between yourselves and the intelligent, active seas in which the whales swim. You might enlist the whales' aid in obtaining clews about the impending actions and movements of the sentient ocean organisms—which information you could then provide to the various rival lighthouse corporations."

"You have it in a nutshell, Mr. Dower. I can tell that you see the potential for profiting upon these discoveries."

"Of course." I shrugged. "You learn from the whales what the oceans will be up to, and Phototrope Limited or another lighthouse corporation learns the same from you. Then you rush off to the betting shop to wager everything with the Sea and Light Book, confident that your bets will prove true."

"Genius, eh?" Stonebrake's smile grew wider.

"I have but one question. If all these marvels are true, why are you revealing them to me? What do I have to do about it? You should just go and talk to your gossipy whales—I presume you do so behind this Father Jonah's back—then make your wagers, collect your winnings, and leave me blessedly alone."

"Ah. There's the rub." His expression turned to something more rueful. "That is what we've been doing—and we have not made our fortunes. And it's not for lack of the appropriate stakes to put up; we have some of the wealthiest—and greediest—individuals in the nation as our backers. Alas, though, the information we obtain from the whales is often fragmentary and unreliable. Sometimes we win our wagers, and other times we still lose."

"How regrettable. But still no concern of mine."

"Bear with me," said Stonebrake. "A number of our group, myself included, have determined that what we must do is not just employ the whales to communicate with the oceans, but *negotiate* with them. If we could find a way to enduce the oceans to act and move in certain ways, we would clean up on the Sea and Light Book."

"I fail to see how I could assist you with that. My powers of persuasion are minimal, at best."

"It would be a conundrum for the most eloquent. None of our party has come close enough to understanding the nature of the sentient oceans, so as to be able to determine exactly what they might want from human beings, so that they would agree to do anything for them. For us."

"Perhaps they also wish to be left in peace."

Stonebrake rubbed his chin in a musing fashion. "The person to crack that puzzle will be in a powerful and lucrative position . . ."

"If you say so." I could do nothing other than lift my shoulders in a shrug. "My best wishes to him."

"How appropriate that such is your desire. For that person is none other than George Dower, Esquire."

"Me?" I gaped at him in amazement. "Now I am certain you are insane. I have neither the desire nor the ability to negotiate with whales and oceans—or moonbeams either, for that matter."

"You underestimate yourself." Stonebrake placed a fingertip against my chest. "You are your father's son, and that quality is what makes you the man of this hour. One of the category of devices invented by the senior Dower were intricate clockwork systems of violin-like strings and rosined wheels that could, when properly tuned and arranged, simulate human voices. Do you recall any of those?"

I could barely forget one of the damnable things, try as I might. In an abandoned London chapel, years before, I had had an unsettling experience with a pack of automaton figures crafted by my father, a mechanical clergyman and accompanying choir all given voice by the mechanisms described by Stonebrake. Their creaking and groaning blasphemies still had the power to evoke nightmares.

"Such devices created by my father have, with any luck, been dismantled. Even if any were still intact, I don't see what value one could be to you and your fellow conspirators."

"Use your imagination, man. If human voices could be so simulated, then why not whale voices? The pipe organ that Father Jonah modified to communicate with the whales doesn't do a good job of it, quite frankly. This has no doubt led to the erratic and undependable nature of the information that we have received from them. What hope would we have then of plying the whales to negotiate with the oceans on our behalf?"

"You're right," I said. "Best to give up this whole mad scheme."

"And lose the fortunes that are almost within our grasp? Never!" Stonebrake's previous steely resolve displayed itself again. "We have reason to believe that your father created a larger and more versatile device for simulating voices, capable of infinite degrees of adjustment. This *Vox Universalis* machine would be exactly what is required for the successful furtherance of our plans."

"*Would be,* you say?" I peered more closely at him. "The implication is that you don't actually have the device in your possession."

"We soon shall. You may rest assured on that point. A matter of days, at most. And when we have it, we shall then need the assistance of the creator's son—you, to be precise—to adjust it as needed for our purposes."

I could feel the blood draining from my face. "I rather think . . . you overestimate my facility in that regard."

"How so? Who more fitted than the living progeny of that great inventor? Surely you inherited at least a modicum of his skills."

"You would probably be better off taking a bash at it yourself."

"Nonsense," insisted Stonebrake. "Gather your courage, man. An hour or so before, you were about to put a bullet through your brain. I offer not only wealth to you, but your life itself. Would you refuse it?"

"If I were as intelligent as you believe me to be, I probably would. This is madness."

"Again the admirable skeptic." He gave an approving nod. "I did not anticipate that I would be able to cozen you into acceptance with mere words. But perhaps I can purchase—or at least rent—your interest."

As I watched, he reached into the pouch fastened to the belt of his diving garment and extracted a leather packet. As soon as I received it in my hand, I knew from its weight and muffled clinking noises that it contained a sizable sum of money.

"There is more than enough," said Stonebrake, "to settle your bill at the inn. And provide for comfortable transportation to London. You will find as well a card with an address inscribed upon it."

I had managed to undo the packet's watertight fastenings, and discovered all those things inside it, though the sliver of moonlight was too dim to read the exact words.

"Of course," he continued, "you are free to make what use of the funds you will. You might, for instance, pay out your landlord here . . . then use the remainder to scurry off to some other cheap and wretched hiding-place, scraping out a few more weeks of cheese-paring existence."

The thought had already occurred to me.

"And when those days have inevitably wound down to their end, you would be exactly where you were before. In a shabby room, with a gun pressed to your brow."

To that bleak observation, I could make no reply.

"Decide as you see fit, Mr. Dower." Reaching behind himself, Stonebrake pulled the hood of his diving garment onto his head. He then uncoiled the rubber tube of the breathing apparatus. "I hope to see you again."

I heard but did not observe him splashing through the oncoming waves, then disappearing beneath the roiling water. I stood in silent contemplation of the small but weighty packet in my hand. And remained so, until the first reddish light of dawn tinged the cliffsides above me.

The innkeeper was already up and about when I returned to my temporary lodgings. "Thar be summat maun say yer bill—"

"Will this suffice?" Standing on the inn's doorstep, I handed him one of the larger-denominated coins that had been bestowed on me. The man's eyes widened at the sight of it in his grubby fingers.

I gave him another. "Hire me a carriage," I told him. "I must go to London."

PART TWO

⚜ OF MATTERS URBANE ⚜

CHAPTER
5

Mr. Dower Observes
Giant Serpents
in the English Countryside

AS I was jounced over country roads so rutted as to seem extended representations in scale, crafted in mud, of the distant Kashypamaran mountain ranges, my thoughts turned to foxes and proverbs.

To be mired in unprofitable meditations was a deep-grained failing of mine, often commented upon by my late servant, Creff, the more so as he approached the afterlife and its dreaded account books. Before his death, he had apparently come to believe that a ruthless attention to his employer's faults might be regarded by the Recording Angel as instances of a laudable devotion to honesty, and thus entered in the credits column of his personal ledger, outweighing at least a few of the debits of his own picayune sins.

Mark my words, Mr. Dower— An unwished image entered my mind, of Creff's age-withered hand reaching from his death-bed, to clutch my sleeve. *Leave off all yer daft brooding and scheming. If the Lord Our Maker had wanted us other than fools, He'd put clockwork brains in our skulls, rather'n these soft, spongy tripes He gave us instead.*

As with all such valuable warnings in my life, this one had gone unheeded. Which left me gazing out the carriage window at a sodden rural landscape, attempting to reconstruct the exact wording of the hoary adage about a fox having more than one exit to his burrow, such foresight being considered clever on his part. At some point in my sketchy formal education, I had access to a massive leather-bound compendium of the unlettered world's vernacular wisdom—more trite than pithy, it had seemed to me even at a young age—and a number of its ungraceful mottoes still rattled about in my head. But at this moment, the only one that came to mind, dealing with creatures of the vulpine persuasion, was one presumably bandied about by the primitive Serbs, to the effect that *A foolish fox is caught by one leg, but a wise one by all four.* The applicability of this to my current situation seemed remote.

The carriage vaulted into an even deeper crevass, of such vertical extent that the driver was obliged to colourfully encourage the horses to greater effort, accompanied by a paroxysm of lashing with the whip. Above me, I could hear the one small trunk that held my diminished worldly possessions, bouncing about in the baggage rack. I imagined that if it were to fly across the hedge and into the nearest boggy field, the driver would feel little urgency to go and fetch it, but would instead merely continue urging our rickety transport toward its destination.

Thus my thoughts seemed to trudge forward on their own accord as well. The proverb about foxes—that which I could recall only hazily, not the Serbian one—was self-evidently an admonition in regard to avoiding those circumstances best termed blind alleys, without more than a single way of extricating oneself. Such was sage advice, the consequences of my own repeated failures to heed it being proof enough of its wisdom. The bleak vista upon which my gaze rested, my plodding thoughts as measured as the carriage's passage through the same, seemed consistent with the assessment I had made of my current situation. Through no great forethought on my part, I did indeed have as much a second exit from my burrow as the crafty fox possessed. I could take comfort in the knowledge that if things did not uncoil as hoped with the schemes in which I had been convinced by my new acquaintance Stonebrake to enlist, my situation would be scarcely worse than it had been before our dampish meeting. And the escape from it would similarly be no worse than that upon which I had taken the first tentative steps. Even now, the second egress from my burrow nestled its considerable weight close to my heart, as though it were one of those great iron keys that required both hands of some medieval gaol-keeper to turn, to free the prisoner held in some dank stone cell. As though I had been expecting the worst of the carriage driver's dismissive handling of my admittedly less-than-prepossessing trunk, I had stowed upon my own person the single most valuable object still remaining to me. My father's intricate clockwork pistol would yield its fiery mysteries the next time I laid its cold muzzle upon the corner of my brow; of this much I was darkly confident. How much cleverer a creature Man is than a Fox, I mused, that he could devise and carry with him such a convenient and portable exit to whatever circumstances in which he might find himself encumbered.

A hard, violent shock traveled the length of my spine as the carriage's wheels found the bottom of another ravine. My eyes sprang open, and for a moment I conjectured futilely as to my location and to the nature of this cramped, double-benched cabinet that confined my stiffening limbs. I realized that I had fallen asleep, lulled by the prospective comforts that would attend my own self-annihilation. Bit by bit, as children assemble puzzles upon the carpet-decked floors of their nurseries, the nature of my journeying returned to memory. Returning to London, upon the behest of some shabby confidence trickster—there to find my fortune, without even the benefit of Bow Bells to advise me. If God adores fools, as I had once been instructed by the village priest, then I was apparently *en route* to salvation as well.

Rain had commenced, of the sort more mistily annoying than torrential, to further blur and haze the uninhabited landscape revealed through the carriage's window. Another few seconds passed before I realized that the surrounding countryside was not quite so monotonous as I had first assumed, but that my hired conveyance had in fact ceased its forward progress. Investigation was called for; I pushed open the door beside me and stepped down to the ground, my boots instantly mired to the ankles in mud.

Slogging to the front of the carriage, I discovered that the driver had released the horses from the yoke and limbers, leading them by their harnesses to the roadside trough in which the thirsting beasts now thrust their muzzles.

"Best to gie thum a brayther and a drink, sir." The driver tugged the brim of his cap. "Yon hill's a steep 'un." He pointed ahead, to where the road slanted toward a crest ringed with bare-branched trees, more skeletal than vernal. "We'll mek good speed on t'arterside, though."

"I expect we shall." Reminding him not to leave the spot without me, I availed myself of the opportunity to stretch my own legs and take care of the other needs that a long journey impresses upon one's body.

A few yards away from the road, yellow thickets of bracken screened me above the waist, affording me sufficient privacy in which to unfasten the front of my trousers. Winter had so recently lain upon the ground that ice crystals still glittered in the mire at my feet. These dissolved into hissing steam as I expressed the nature of my urgent business upon them. Re-doing my garments with cold-numbed fingers, I was bemused to note that the hissing sounds continued even as the small puddle I had created now chilled and seeped into the weedy soil. More intriguingly, the hiss seemed to come from some more distant point, on the opposite side of the low earthen rise before me. To my concern, through the inclement weather's mist I perceived white clouds roiling upward, as though an otherwise silent army had just completed *en masse* the same corporeal duties with which I had tasked myself.

In my previous modes of existence, caution had been my watchword. The alley behind my watchmaker's shop in the district of Clerkenwell, the business premises being an inheritance from my father, had been infested with that breed of lean and feral cat native to London's squalid dens and nooks. Having the opportunity to observe the species at close range, due to Creff's incorrigible habit of scraping the breakfast and dinner plates into their yowling mouths, I had noted that the creatures exhibiting the most courage, the first to investigate every rubbish bin and splintered crate, flourished for a time but were ultimately outlived by their more timid brethren. If so in untutored Nature, I had reasoned, how much more so in the crueler and less caring drawing-rooms of Civilization? As with those felines who survived the few more years that constituted old age amongst their kind, I placed a higher value on my skin than on my curiosity.

Or so, as I have indicated, I had before. Little I had experienced in this life had served to alter my attitude in this regard; indeed, the majority of my supposed adventures, if not the entirety, had reinforced my tremulous predispositions. At least until now. Perhaps enlistment in my recent acquaintance Stonebrake's hare-brained schemes had rent the veil of discretion through which I had previously viewed the world, and left me a subscriber to that decrepit maxim—*In for a penny, in for a pound*—by which so many of my own species had come to ruin. In any event, I found myself climbing up the low rise, in order to discover the source of the cumulus-like phenomenon mounting into the grey skies.

At first, as I planted my boots upon the highest ground I could conveniently reach, I thought that I was dreaming, yet asleep in the carriage. A monstrous vision lay before me—literally monstrous, in the sense of loathsome creatures having taken possession of the Earth. The scaly, elongated bosoms of great serpents pressed upon the sodden fields, their vermiform bodies of such lengthy dimension that both their tails and heads were hidden beyond the horizons to the north and south of where I stood. The dull, crepuscular sunlight of an English noon glinted from the reptiles' metallic hides. So possessed of venom and general ill temper were they, that billowing vapours seethed from every crook and curve of their forms, the noise of hissing that came to my ears now as loud as though I had been standing underneath a Mancunian factory whistle. Even more disgusting to my perception was the evidence that I had stumbled upon the immense snakes as they had been engaged in that unseemly act of *coitus* by which rudely fertile Nature multiplies all its creeping, crawling progeny; as I gazed forward at the scene, unable to tear my appalled sight away, I discerned that several of the immense serpents were not merely intertwined with or lying across each other, but actually connected at various points, the junctures leaking a presumably poisonous steam with even greater ferocity.

"Ay, 'tis a contemp'ble slew, ain' it? Ye've ne'er seen it before?"

Startled by the unanticipated words, I turned and saw the driver standing next to me. Across the distance I had traversed, I spied the carriage, its brace of horses harnessed in position once more. The man had evidently come to fetch his passenger, in order to resume our journey.

"No—" I gave a shake of my head. "I have not." It had been a comfort to believe that the oppressing vision had been but a nightmare shaken by my conveyance's violent motions into the daytime hours. My heart crawled downward through my viscera, as though it were some woodland vermin seeking desperate refuge from the hunt's baying hounds, at the prospect that I had encountered one more aspect of Reality with which I could gratefully have gone unacquainted to my dying day. "What manner of beast," I enquired of the coachman, "are these?"

"'Beast'? No bluidy beast're they." His laugh rattled congenital phlegm in his neckerchiefed throat. "'Tis but pipes ye see."

I stared at him in noncomprehension. "What do you mean, *pipes*? Are they not snakes? Giant serpents?"

"Get a bluidy clew, man." He pointed toward the fields. "D'ye see them movin' about?"

"No—" In this, the carriage driver was correct. Other than the hissing emissions from their flanks, no animate sign was visible. "I do not."

"Hardly be bluidy snakes, then, would they?" Gleeful scorn brightened his visage, of the variety relished by the unlettered, when they catch their educated betters in some apparent foolishness. "Snakes be writhin' about, all wriggly like. 'Less they be daid, of course." His self-congratulatory logic continued to its conclusion. "So these be pipes, ye maun admit."

"Pipes." I mused over the baffling possibilities. The landscape being so marshy, as though our route had brought us to the edge of the infamously dismal Chat Moss, it hardly seemed likely that there was any need to convey water from one point to another across it. "Pipes bearing what?"

"Aye, steam, of course." His black-nailed index finger pointed again. "D'ye not see it?"

Understanding broke behind my brow, as dams are riven by burrowing sappers' sudden gunpowder charges. My habitation of the last few years had been so rural that I had read and heard gossip of these engineering marvels—so termed by their enthusiastic adherents—that had gripped the English countryside, but I had not witnessed them. Until now.

This was my understanding, previously unconfirmed by observation: The country's journals and broadsheets had been lavish in their printed adoration of that *coterie* of British entrepreneurs, men of wealth and influence who wished to become even wealthier and more influential by bringing the alleged benefits of steam power to society at large. The heat of the vast fires churning at the Earth's core, conjectured by the more advanced thinkers in the scientific community, evidenced by the molten rock spewed forth by the Italian peninsula's Mount Aetna and other, more distant volcanic apertures, would warm our hearths and furnish propulsive force to our factories. The slight disadvantage of there being few if any volcanoes and vaulting geysers in the British Isles would be addressed by the simple if arduous expedient of digging straight down to where these seething thermal channels were believed to run. Once tapped, the same red-hot, sluggish magma from which the overly excitable Romans had fled, would just as readily fire the boilers of our own newly created *steam mines,* as their inventors called them.

More than mere heat being required to generate steam, though, the precise location of the steam mines was a pressing issue. While much of the English countryside was as perennially damp as the fields on the edge of which stood myself and my carriage driver, even greater and more easily channeled quantities of water were required to service this grand scheme. Thus the locating of the mines in what had previously been known as the Lake District. The idyllic, romantic shores of Windermere and Buttermere and Ullswater, and all the rest extolled by the enraptured poets, were transformed to muddy bogs as their liquid contents were funneled to the grim, grey powerhouses erected in the surrounding fells and valleys. That sable night, once lit by only the slowly wheeling constellations and the moon's mensural caravanserai, was now reddened to a furious near-day by the lava-fed furnaces, their glow reflected by the now perpetual clouds pressing heavily from above. Gouts of fire, the inevitable accidents of industry, scorched the hillsides bare of trees and foliage, leaving only blackened rock where poetical daffodils had once nodded.

"Aye, this be naught, compared." The carriage driver was able to discern my thoughts. "Ye still see a bit o' green, here'bouts, when springtime comes. And the birds be nesting, where they can. Up north, all's baked hard as the bricks o' a farrier's furnace."

"But not everywhere." I amended his observation, based upon the accounts I had read, of the transformations wrought by the steam entrepreneurs. "I have heard tell, that those towns and cities, whose factories had been driven by coal, are now abandoned for such usage. Pleasure excursions to idyllic Birmingham and Newcastle are now in vogue; such is my understanding."

"Mebbe," admitted the driver. "I'd ken but a mickle of sech grand doin's. Them places might be veritable Gardens of Eden these days. All's knowed by me is that they've made a right dog's breakfast frae these parts."

I could scarcely gainsay his comment. Whatever heaps of grey ash and clinkers that had been produced by our previous stoves and manufactures, the coal that fired them had the advantage of being relatively portable. A lump dug up in the north of England could be carried by canal boats to London and set alight, there to emit its pent-up heat. To convey the force of steam to its desirous recipients required the construction across the nation of a vast web of pipes, the very ones that I had mistaken for giant serpents.

Controversy, some part of which I perused in the journals that found their way to my remote village, accompanied this development.

My carriage driver was of that unschooled mind that grizzled at all disturbances to long-established ways of life. And perhaps he had the right of it: the *Steam Barons,* as the popular press referred to these colluding businessmen, might have both over-extolled the beneficent wonders of this newly devised power source and belittled its possible disadvantages, the better to vanquish any objections to their schemes.

Not only was the English landscape disfigured by the enormous pipes and conduits that had been laid about its surface—though to certain sentimental types that would have been injury enough— there was apparently as well the constant danger of fatally scalding explosions, a risk magnified by the greater and greater pressures of steam forced through the web of pipes, to feed the increasing demand of populace and industry. I say *apparently,* as knowledge of such occasional explosions was ruthlessly suppressed by the Barons, their amassed wealth having been sufficient to purchase controlling interests in every publication to come rolling from the presses.

"Right bastards, they are." The carriage driver's gaze narrowed to slits as he surveyed the invasive pipeworks, as though he could trace their mazing course back to the manicured, beringed hands that turned the valves at their source. "Got us all by the bollocks, they have." I knew he referred to the stranglehold the Steam Barons had upon our collective lives, in all but the remotest and least developed parishes, as the one I had just left. "Fancy themselves lords, they do! And sech they are, damn their eyes! Ye can scarce bile a pertato these days, without payin' them a penny for the priv'lege."

"Perhaps we had best be on our way." I had seen my fill of what changes had come to modern society during my absence from it. "I was rather hoping we might reach a traveler's inn before nightfall."

"So we shall. Have nae fear o' that." The driver turned and headed back down to the road.

I followed him. In silence; given the dark, anarchic disposition he had revealed, I assumed that it would have scarcely improved his mood for me to disclose that the address to which I was bound was the palatial townhouse of exactly one of the powerful, world-bestriding Steam Barons he so murderously despised.

CHAPTER

6

Mr. Dower Returns to That City from Which He Once Had Fled

MY familiarity with the habitations of the wealthy and powerful was a product of my own unfortunate practices. I have already written here of the too-frequent visits to the local betting shops, which had so effectively reduced me to penury. Such financial wisdom as I possess was purchased dearly. Certain other information was thrown in *gratis*.

The lust for riches is often spurred by the comparison between our own mean estates and those upon whom the gods have more beneficently smiled. As at many bookmakers' dens, the one to which I had brought my dwindling capital encouraged such envy by adorning its walls with framed lithographs of the townhouses in which opulently luxurious existences were maintained by their deep-pocketed owners. No doubt, the attitude to be encouraged was that in which bettors assured themselves, in their silent hearts, that they were well on the way to living in similar fashion, as though the wagers laid down on the cash-worn counters were but small payments on their own elegant residences, soon to be bought outright with their amassed winnings.

One such architectural portrait, which I often contemplated as I fingered the most recent betting slip in my coat pocket, had been that of an immense edifice, fronted with marble columns and, above its portico, a *bas relief* representation of the Battle of Stenyclarus. A legend at the picture's lower margin helpfully noted that Featherwhite House—the name being a fanciful reference to the plume emitted from a steam engine's safety valves—was located in a fashionable district near London's Strand. With that picture in mind, it was a facile process to note, in the various publications that purported to advise those who set wagers in the Sea & Light Book, the frequent mentions of the Honourable Marston Dredgecock of exactly the same Featherwhite House. Whatever considerable fortune had been his inheritance, that sum of cash and lands had evidently been augmented by his speculations in various commercial fields. Dark hints flitted through the smudgily printed pages, to the effect that Dredgecock's kid-gloved hand might be found pulling the strings of a vast web of controlling interests, not the least of them including the purveyance of the steam power upon which the lighthouse corporations depended for the mobility and functioning of their luminous enterprises. There was every possibility that if I had more closely examined the massive pipes that I had spotted knitting up the fields by which my carriage had passed, I might very well have found somewhere upon their hissing flanks the insignia of one of Dredgecock's interlocking corporations.

With that likelihood in my thoughts, I had hesitated to have the carriage driver deliver me directly to the front door of the famous—or, no doubt to some, infamous—Featherwhite House. A reasonable caution foresaw that the coachman, having already muttered scowling imprecations upon the oppressive Steam Barons—of which plutocratic band the aforementioned Dredgecock was so prominent a member—might well be spurred to some violent action upon seeing that he had delivered his passenger right to his sworn enemy's abode, as it were. A vision came unbidden to me of my alighting from the carriage, only to have my trunk heaved directly upon my head. Small as my luggage might be, it still possessed enough weight to flatten me upon the London pavement, given sufficient accuracy as a projectile.

As a prudent compromise, I had the driver deposit me at a coaching inn on the outskirts of the great city. My funds had been significantly lightened by payment for the lengthy journey, but were still sufficient to have my luggage transferred to a hansom cab summoned for the purpose and directed to my ultimate destination.

Soon enough, I was engulfed by the sights and sounds of that urban conglomeration, the districts of which had once constituted my daily existence. It seemed to have changed but little during my long rural exile, the streets surrounding the hansom being as crowded and noisy as I remembered them. All about me, as I leaned forward to peer from the hansom cab's small window, surged the clamouring tides and breakers of an ocean seemingly as large as that Atlantic, upon whose rocky Cornish coast I had so recently stood. Perhaps it was all the talk of evangelized whales and brooding, sentient seas that had been poured into my ears, that had resulted in my thoughts taking on a distinct aquatic cast; the result was that the crush and press of London's citizenry, with its carts and bales, costermongers' cries and jumbled coaxings and curses, struck my staggered senses like one of those monstrous waves reputed to lift ships upon their crests and tumble them to their capsized dooms.

The impression was heightened by the clarity with which I was able to view the city's inhabitants and buildings, all the way to the great dome of St. Paul's, looming above its less impressive neighbours as though it were some snow-capped Alp pried from its station upon the Continent and transposed to this metropolitan locale. A moment of puzzlement elapsed before I realized that the perpetual haze I associated with London, the smoky reek from its chimneys and furnaces that previously had filled its air with oft-times blinding soot, was absent from my view. Indeed, I could draw in a deep breath and not feel as if my lungs had just been the depository of a dustbin shaken of its contents. This apparent change seemed to have had a salutary effect upon the health of the city's natives: turning my ear toward the hansom's window, I could not detect in the mingled human roar any of that consumptive hacking and wheezing that had before divided virtually every spoken syllable from the next.

If the London air had been as murky as I recalled it being, I might not have perceived at last the actual change that had been wrought in the city's streets and lanes. The phenomenon had been obscured by the throngs of people and their attendant conveyances, but as though a final obscuring veil had been lifted in my brain, I saw amongst them the same glistening metallic shapes that I had witnessed crossing in static place over the distant rural countryside, on my coach journey to this point. The immense vermiform constructions, the function of which was to convey the pressurized force from the even more remote steam mines to the north, laced themselves along the lengths of the streets and to either side, the human population forced thereby to divide themselves to left and right as they sought to achieve their own destinations. If the public areas of the city had indeed been the great ocean of which my fancy had briefly conceived, the steam pipes might very well have served as those whales and dolphins and other large aquatic creatures whose glistening backs are glimpsed breaking the surface of the waters or rearing even higher into the disclosing sunlight.

But this alteration to the city's appearance was not confined to the level of the streets. From my vantage point inside the hansom cab, I lifted my gaze, following the course of the glistening pipes as they snaked up the sides of the buildings. Smaller pipes branched from the larger, penetrating the brickwork as a snake might plunge its tapering head into an earthen crevice in search of its furry prey, or creeping in through windows stripped of their glass panes in order to facilitate the entry of the steam conduits. As my memories of the London that had been before faded from my recall, I saw with appalled clarity that the entire city, as far as my gaze could reach, was tangled about with the interconnected pipes, as a child's play house might be embraced by creeper vines, both inside and out, were it left abandoned in an unkempt garden for a sufficient period of time.

Nostalgia's blindfold having thus been stripped from my sight, my other senses were freed as well, to more accurately discern the urban reality that had been erected in my absence. Through the hubbub of the clamorous voices, I heard now the perpetual underlying hiss from the pipes, as well as the occasional yowl of pain and surprise from an infant whose careless mother had brought him too

close to one of the scalding white gouts from a leaky join or patch.
These were of such frequency along the serpentine course of the
pipes that the clouds overhead were, I realized now, merely the con-
densed emissions rising from below. The warm, damp flush upon
my face, that I had glumly supposed to be the first symptom of an
advancing fever, was similarly revealed to be the oppressively sultry
atmosphere in which all the city's inhabitants were caught, as though
the entirety of London had been transformed into one of those steam
baths of which various Asiatic cultures are reputedly so fond.

As the hansom made its slow progress through the crowd, I settled back in its leather seat. My mind was oddly at peace; having
been initially appalled at the transformation that had been wrought
in the city which had once been my home, I took a degree of comfort
in knowing that I bore no responsibility for these changes. My earlier experiences, by which I had discovered the exact nature of the
devices engineered by my greatly clever and overly heedless father,
had left me as no great enthusiast for the various technological advances touted by those who so eagerly plunge toward some glad-
some Future, the benefits of which are more often than not as elusive
as their proponents' ardour is frenzied. Indeed, my retreat to one of
the most rural corners of the nation was prompted by the desire to
evade as long as possible the encroachment of those dismal prospects to come, the outlines of which I had glimpsed in my father's
inventions. That mine was an opinion embraced by few, I was well
aware; even in the distant village from which I had now removed,
that which was most commonly labeled Progress was anticipated
with the same heartfelt longing with which a child might view an
unopened birthday gift, the bright delusive wrappings of which conceal delights yet to be realized.

Very well, I thought smugly to myself. *Here upon you is that Future you so desired, in all its hissing, clanking glory. If your fingers
are burnt as you grasp hold of it, don't blame George Dower, Esquire.*

Preoccupied with such self-congratulatory meditations, I was
taken by surprise when the cab came to a halt. I had been made
aware, by its hastening forward motion, that the crowds had become

less numerous in composition as we left the more commercial thoroughfares behind us. Now at a standstill, I perceived complete silence about the vehicle, other than the horse's wetly mumbling breath and the heel of the cabdriver's whip stamping upon the floor of his seat above.

"Here ye be, sir." The overhead hatch had slid open; the top-hatted, bewhiskered face peered in at me. "I'd be most 'preciative if ye'd be of some haste in yer disembarking, as I'm not abs'lutely comfortable tarrying 'bout these parts."

The cabdriver's comment puzzled me. What sinister manner of event did he anticipate, in as fashionable a district as that in which my destination of Featherwhite House was located?

"Is there something amiss, my good man?"

"Oh, it's not fer my skin I'm 'feared," he hastily assured me. "It's Molly—the horse, I mean. She's a sociable creature, she is; seen naught but London streets 'er whole life. So she considers the 'ustle and bustle to be natural-like, and gets 'erself skittish when there's no-one 'bout."

The framed engraving on the wall of the village betting shop had shown elegantly parasoled women and their escorts promenading before the townhouse's gates; I expected as much when I turned and gazed out the hansom's window. Instead, I was greeted with a sight fully consistent with the assessment I had just been given. The street was empty, stones missing from its paving in such quantity as to render it impassable without the skill the cabdriver had shown in steering around the jagged chasms. On either side, the once palatial residences now appeared abandoned by all save ghosts and whatever homeless transients might choose to find temporary abode behind the broken windows and boarded-up doors.

Beyond a rusting, spike-topped fence, the anticipated outlines of Featherwhite House were recognizable, albeit only after a long moment of squinting study on my part. It appeared equally as disinhabited as the forlorn structures of its neighbours.

A sloping rise visible at the rear of the grounds shielded a view of the Thames. I was aware from my previous familiarity with the city that we were but a short distance from the hub of governmental powers, housed at Westminster Palace.

"Was there someone as was meeting you 'ere, sir?" The cabdriver's query intruded upon my survey of the area's dismal aspect. "Doesn't seem as anyone's waiting on your 'rival, though."

I pushed open the cab's door and stepped down to the pavement. "Wait here," I instructed the driver after I paid him the fare which we had previously negotiated. "I might require further transportation."

"At your bidding, sir." He touched the handle of the whip to his hat and eased the horse's leads.

The sagging gate creaked as I laid my weight against it. At the same moment, I heard a heavy thump behind me. I turned and saw the hansom cab speeding off, in the direction from which we had journeyed, its driver having yielded to his tender concern for the feelings of his draughthorse. No doubt reluctant to be considered a thief, he at least had the courtesy to deposit my small trunk upon the pavement, albeit from the height upon which he perched.

I returned to the roadside and secured my luggage, then carried it with me toward the darkened, unwelcoming *façade* of Featherwhite House. The path of my approach ran straight, bordered by gardens that had reverted through neglect to bramble and lichen-covered stone. One side of animation remained: one of the hissing steam pipes, those great serpents that had come to interlace the city with their endlessly uncoiling lengths, ran through a breach in the fence and across the grounds, penetrating the townhouse at its farther aspect.

Mounting the wide steps, my trunk still in hand, I glanced up past the capitals of the marble columns to the *bas relief* above. Humorous vandals had taken advantage of the townhouse's vacancy, daubing with paint and tar the sculpted representation of battle, so that the Grecian warriors seemed less intent upon bringing their swords down upon each other's heads than upon embracing and inserting the crude procreative organs with which they had been adorned. Some motto of plebeian disdain had been scrawled across the formerly heroic scene, but I scarce had opportunity to decipher its exact wording before the towering entry door was pulled open.

"Ah, Dower!" A figure I had last encountered in the darkness of the moonlit Cornish coast peered out at me. "You've arrived," the conspiratorial Stonebrake needlessly commented. He grasped my arm and pulled me toward Featherwhite House's unlit interior. "Get inside before anyone spies you—"

An Unsavory Attempt Is Made
upon Mr. Dower's Person

PIGEON droppings crusted the floors of Featherwhite House. Indeed, as Stonebrake drew me farther into the townhouse, slamming the door shut behind me with a thrust of his bootheel, I heard the soft fluttering of wings from somewhere over my head. Glancing above, I saw a startled flock of the creatures wheeling about, a few of their number escaping through the shattered oculi that studded the foyer's cathedral-like dome.

"It's good timing on your part, showing up like this." Stonebrake extracted the trunk from my arms and set it down on a *chaise longue* so ancient and sway-backed that its middle section rested upon the water-stained carpet beneath it. "Great things are already under way, and your involvement in them is urgently required."

"Indeed." My nose involuntarily wrinkled as I surveyed the room in which our conversation took place. The brackish pong of long abandonment hung heavy in the pent-up air, thin blade-like shafts of light slipping through the boards nailed over the high windows. Beasts other than the aviary with which I had been greeted, their winged forms now roosting amongst the rafters denuded of plaster, had evidently fed, mated, and defecated in the rooms' corners. Muslin-shrouded chandeliers dangled from the ceiling or, the links of their suspending chains having parted, lay in shards upon the floors, the fragments' glittering dulled by layers of dust.

Stonebrake himself appeared more presentable, without jacket at the moment, but a loosened cravat blossomed from beneath the buttons of an embroidered vest. Upon hearing his voice, while his figure had still been hidden behind the townhouse's entry door, I had almost expected him to be garbed in the wetly shining diving costume he had worn at our initial seaside encounter, as though such might have been his usual lounging habiliments, with or without the Atlantic at his elbow. To see him now as a respectably clad member of society required some mental adjustment on my part, in particular given the shabby grotesquerie of the building in which he and I stood, as if we had agreed to *rendezvous* in a haunted house for purposes of idle chat.

"I had some apprehension," he spoke, "that you might not have turned up at all. Given the gloomy situation in which I found you, and all. I'm gladdened to see that the expectation of wealth has outweighed your taste for self-destruction."

His smiling comment irked me. I found it to be in poor taste, to find amusement in others' despair.

"Let us not become overly familiar." I imparted to my words as much formal stiffness as I could summon. "You made a business proposition to me. I have come here for no other reason."

"That's what I find so admirable about you." Stonebrake clapped me heartily on the shoulder. "You never disappoint me. You, sir, are a rock of dependability."

"Be that as it may. I confess that I feel some sense of disappointment, however. My journey has wearied me, and I was anticipating more congenial and restorative quarters than these." I gazed around at the dank, decaying spaces, then back to my interlocutor. "Where, pray, is our host?"

Stonebrake frowned in puzzlement. "Host?"

"The Honourable Marston Dredgecock. The master of Featherwhite House—and more besides. I had expected to be greeted by him, or if not, by some senior chamberlain in his employ."

"Ah. A moment, if you please." He turned toward one of the dark hallways beyond the foyer in which we stood. "Oy!" His shout loosened plaster dust from the ceiling. "Where's old Dredgecock to be found?"

"What?" An answering cry echoed from whatever rooms lay beyond. "What's that you're after?"

"Dredgecock! Where's that fool Dredgecock?"

"How the flamin' hell should I know?" A clanging noise reverberated from the unseen distance, as though of a two-handed spanner being dropped upon some iron surface. A moment later, a short-statured figure appeared in the hallway, a fearsomely mustachioed and cloth-capped mechanical, wiping his grease-stained hands upon the leather apron extending to the tops of his boots. "Wouldn't surprise me if the old bastard's bleedin' dead." He glared at Stonebrake, this interruption to his labours evidently a personal affront. "Man was scarcely alive as it were, last I saw of him."

"There; you see?" Stonebrake turned to me for sympathy. "Such are the conditions I endure. When riches are in my hands—pardon; *our* hands—it will have been effort and forbearance that put them within reach. The upshot being, at this moment, that if you desired to be greeted by the Honourable under discussion, you've come to the wrong place."

"I fail to understand." My hand rose to gesture at the dilapidated walls. "I had been given to believe that this was his residence, at least while in town rather than his country estates."

"It might very well have been," replied Stonebrake, "at least at one time. But it has been, shall we say, *converted* to other uses."

As though to echo this sentiment, a chorus of industrial noises sounded from beyond the hallway by which the workman had appeared. Unpleasant memories were roused in my head and breast by the shriek and clatter of great engines firing up, the grind of sharp-edged gears meshing with each other, counterweights whirling about, all while the shrill whistle and hiss of escaping steam, the unseen machinery's propulsive force, filled in the mechanical choir's top octave.

"So it would seem." I raised my own voice above the cacophonous discord that trembled the once elegant house's musty air. Feathers drifted down from the agitated pigeons. "But what of Dredgecock himself? Has all this been accomplished with his permission? Or even his awareness?"

"It hardly matters." Stonebrake's amusement was apparent. "Even if the man is still alive, he's so far advanced in his dotage that his *awareness* of much at all is a debatable quality."

"But what of his various enterprises? His investments? The commanding position he grasps at the helm of those industries which draw this seething power from the bowels of the earth and convey it to Britain's homes and factories?"

"Your rhapsodizing about the fellow is indeed eloquent, my dear Dower, but hardly warranted by reality. Dredgecock possesses none of those things you ascribe to him. As a specimen of impoverished gentility—the like of which rather overpopulates the land, particularly after the advent of these wondrous technologies—the old codger's only usefulness was that of a front, a propped-up bit of pasteboard with his face and name painted on, behind which the actual masters of this new economy may go about their affairs at more convenience to themselves. As you might well imagine, certain grumbling types are not at all happy about certain changes that have come upon them; better that their incendiary—and sometimes even explosive—wrath be directed toward a dottering old fool of a figurehead, rather than the prosperous pillars upon which our society depends."

I knew whereof he spoke—the example of the darkly muttering carriage driver was still fresh in my mind—but his pious sanctimony nettled me. "Better for you," I noted. "And your various schemes. Given the desire for material gain, which you have already admitted is the only thing that animates you, I wouldn't be at all surprised if the poor old man is buried out in the garden."

"Actually," said Stonebrake, "I believe he's in Brighton. The monthly remittance sent to him, in compensation for the commercial use of his *persona,* is adequate for him to subsist in modest comfort at a boarding house close to the Pier. Or if he has indeed passed on, it's been enough for an anonymous burial service, the disposal of his meager effects, and a continuing discreet silence about the matter. Either way, it's money well spent."

Whatever small concern I might have had for the gentleman was dispelled by the mounting clang and screech from the townhouse's farther rooms. "For God's sake, what is going on back there?"

"Now we come to matters of more pertinent interest. Royston—" He turned and addressed the leather-aproned workman standing at the hallway's opening. "I'm sure Mr. Dower here would appreciate a bit of a tour."

"If he must." It was apparent by the man's sullen expression that he regarded me more as an inconvenience than a guest. "Come on, then, and make of it what you will."

Stonebrake followed as the workman led me toward the source of the increasingly louder mechanical clamour. Though the corridor remained as dark as the rest of the house behind its boarded windows, I felt as though I were walking from winter and into a summer day, the blazing sun evaporating what remained of a brief morning downpour, so warm and humid was the air about me. All that betrayed the vernal impression was the acrid scent of lubricating oils, of the sort injected with long nozzles into the workings of overheated machinery.

"Mind your step," advised Royston, aiming his ill-tempered glare over his shoulder at me. "The footing's a mite precarious from here forward."

Rounding a corner and entering to the wavering illumination of lamps inelegantly fastened overhead, I quickly perceived what he meant. The townhouse's floors had been ripped up, with vast openings created to accommodate the steam pipes that had been introduced throughout the structure. I might very well have stepped into a nest of the serpentine forms, so thickly clustered about were they, with hissing knots and loops constructed of their interpenetrating shapes. My clothes hung clammy upon my body, as though I were some tropic explorer, ill-clad for the frond-bedecked environs in which he had arrived.

The pipes plunged through what little remnants were left of the walls that had formerly divided up the space. From the evidence of the plaster scraps strewn about, the bulk of the partitions and their doors had been crudely demolished with axes and sledge-hammers, leaving one vast enclosure. Even the ornately corniced ceiling had been sacrificed to the new enterprise to which Featherwhite House was now dedicated; a quick glance upward revealed an aspect continuing vertically to what seemed the townhouse's roof.

These alterations had been accomplished for the sake of the mechanical constructions which dominated what had once been an abode of grace and charm, but which now seemed more like a seat of those industries so bleakly intimidating that a civilized society generally housed them amongst the lower classes who sweated at their forges.

"Tell me, Dower—" Stonebrake's sly voice spoke at my ear. "What do you see, that amazes you so?"

I had no hesitation in telling him. "These are my father's devices." I gazed about at the fiercely animated scene before me. "Created by him." This revelation seemed obvious, being indicated by the characteristically precise linkage of the interconnected parts, the sleek fury of the pistons' reciprocal motions, regulated by the whirl of the spherical governor apparatuses, so like an astronomer's model of our heliocentric universe, the planets reduced to hollow brass representations. Gears meshed with the inherent violence of unfeeling metal, their sharply machined teeth eager to rend the flesh of anyone so foolish as to lay a fingertip upon them. "No-one else," I spoke quietly, "could have invented them."

Stonebrake remained silent behind, leaving me to my filial meditations. For a moment, I seemed to have been hurled backward in time, to that long-past day when, standing upon a street in the district of Clerkenwell, I had shaken a key from a solicitor's envelope and unlocked the door of my inheritance, my deceased father's workshop. Marvels I had beheld then, upon the cobwebbed shelves and inside the dusty cabinets: devices such as these in their intricacy and mysterious purpose, their uncoiled mainsprings no longer set to life by their buried creator's hand . . .

What set apart those remembered machines was the far greater dimensions of the ones I now saw before me. At one time, when I had but first entered into adulthood and the clicking, whirring domain that my father had left to me, I had been so ignorant of the extent, while living, of his skills and ambition, that I had considered him to be no more than a watchmaker, exceedingly adept at bestowing his custom pieces with those features known in the trade as *Grand Complications*. Such creations, with their thousand-year calendars and astronomical displays and miniature larks springing from the cases to chirp out their minute repeater functions, are considered the pinnacle of *haute horlogerie*. Given the high prices they commanded amongst connoisseurs of fine timekeeping, I had been perplexed that my father had left no monetary estate to me. I had so little acquaintance with him during my childhood, that the most dreadful surmises had entered my imagination when the exact accounts of my penurious legacy had been revealed to me. Perhaps his mode of life had encompassed those unfortunate extravagances which beggared the most productive of men; I had had no way of knowing. Whatever the truth might have been, I had similarly assumed, upon the evidence of what I initially found in his workshop, that his creations had all been of such scale as to be easily encompassed in one's hand or conveniently mounted on the wall for the marking of the passing hours. It had been only later, with bitter experience, that I had been made familiar with the larger and more intricate of his devices, culminating with that monstrous equipage with which the crack-brained Lord Bendray had intended to reduce the very Earth to gravel and dust floating in cold, infinite space. That creation had been impressive enough when I had first laid eyes upon it—but the ones encased here at Featherwhite House were even larger.

Indeed, I saw now that there were sources of illumination other than the haphazardly arranged lamps. A section of the townhouse's exterior wall had been ripped away, from the ground to several floors above, in order to accommodate the massive devices that had been brought inside. Sections of canvas had been stitched together and hung from the eaves, affording a barely adequate protection against rain and other inclement weather; fluttering shafts of the late afternoon daylight slipped through, bringing random aspects of the machinery into brighter relief.

The conveyance of the devices had apparently not been without event. Beneath one such, the floor had given way, casting the machine partway into the basement, the heavy iron beams of its construction tilted at a severe angle. Evidently, there had been no means of hoisting the device and setting it on a level footing elsewhere; instead, the appropriate steam pipes had been attached to its receptacle mountings and the machinery urged into motion. Every stroke of its pistons set the ground trembling, the vibrations traveling up through the soles of my own boots.

"But what are these things?" I turned my head to enquire of Stonebrake. "That they were created by my father is indisputable—but what is their function?"

"Ah; there you have me at a loss." He stepped forward and to my side. "Those of your father's devices that are in the hands of the Royal Society, that were previously in your possession—those have been exhaustively studied by the finest scientific minds in Britain. Some have yielded a few of their technical secrets, yet others remain completely mysterious. These—" He gestured toward the clanking, hissing machines before us. "My backers and I have but recently acquired them, and it took some doing, I might tell you. We scoured the countryside for them, searched through rural estates and abandoned vicarages, followed every clew no matter how faint, spent untold sums—that is, I didn't personally, but my associates had their cash at the ready. But while our efforts met with considerable success in regard to acquisition, I cannot say we have been equally fortunate when it comes to the understanding of our prizes."

"My understanding is amiss as well," I said. "I had been led to believe that the Royal Society had already procured for its own studies all the remaining examples of my father's creations. It scarcely seems credible that they could have overlooked instances as massive as these."

"There are limits to even the Royal Society's resources," noted Stonebrake. "If not financial, then in regard to the space in which its acquisitions can be housed, and the time that its learned members can devote to them. The result being that the Society, in fact, took to its collective bosom certain of the devices created by your father, and spurned others, leaving those to moulder and rust out in the wild, as it were." He pointed again to the clanking and hammering machines. "Your father, it would seem, was even more prescient than anyone had conceived before of him. The clever devices by which his reputation was established, amongst those privileged to know anything of him at all, were contrived to operate by that which we term *clockwork,* the unwinding of coiled mainsprings providing the motive force required for the mechanisms to go through their various functions. To be sure, some of those mainsprings were of intimidating dimensions, requiring several men with levers, or even teams of drayhorses, to wind to their tightest constrictions. And of course, little imagination is required to envision the dangers involved with workings built to such scale. When the mainspring of a pocket watch snaps, the broken end of metal might be sharp enough to draw blood from one's fingertip; the same event, involving a coil of steel vaster than many of this great house's drawing-rooms, is fully capable of slaying a dozen workmen, the unleashed metal bifurcating them in the blink of an eye. This is not an hypothetical occurrence; indeed, some of the labourers employed here still shudder at the recollection of the deaths of their colleagues."

Following the direction of his hand, I now observed in the space's shadows those others, of similar garb to the ill-natured one to whom Stonebrake had addressed his previous requests and orders. The fellow Royston was apparently the foreman of a team of subordinate workers, all busily engaged in maintaining the operations of the devices towering beyond their cloth-capped heads. So intent were they upon their labours that they barely allowed themselves a glance in our direction.

"Such a fate," I spoke, "would hardly seem to weigh upon their minds now. For these machines are all apparently driven by steam."

"Exactly so." Stonebrake nodded in concurrence. "And therein lies the proof of your father's astonishing prescience. For when he built such devices as these, a source of power adequate for their operations did not yet exist. But build them he did, as though he knew that at some future date that power would come to exist, and in such abundance as to set whirring the entire arsenal of his imagination. In that regard, your father was a greater and more far-seeing intellect than all the members of the Royal Society. For when they went scavenging about the nation, snapping up your father's creations and freighting them to their headquarters here in London, they did not anticipate, as your father had, how our world was about to be transformed. Any devices they found, large or small, that did not in some manner operate on the clockwork principles of mainsprings and escapement, was considered by them to be merely so much useless ironwork, follies on their creator's part, inert and incapable of motion—and thus were left behind by them, to moulder and rust away, in sheds and warehouses and lumber-rooms."

"How many were there?"

Another voice answered. "A damned lot of the bastards; that's for certain." The foreman Royston's glaring visage had come up alongside us. "These're just the ones the lads call the big 'uns; there're any number of others, scattered all 'bout this place."

I turned toward him. "And you've restored all of them to operating condition?"

"Most." He shrugged. "Some of the lot were so rubbished, there were naught to do but scrap 'em for parts."

"Indeed." I directed a raised eyebrow at Stonebrake. "And have you and your workmen found amongst all these that great *Vox Universalis,* upon which your schemes depend?"

"No—" A frown replaced the man's usual and casual smile. "Not yet."

"Perhaps it no longer exists. If it ever did."

"We'll unearth it." Stonebrake's face set hard with determination. "Even as we speak, agents hired by my backers are turning over every stone, rummaging through every cupboard, in pursuit of the device. There are some quite promising leads that we are following up, I can assure you."

Before I could comment upon this resolve of his, a commotion broke out in the farther reaches of Featherwhite House. I could hear voices shouting in alarm, and the rapidly multiplying impact of running feet.

"It's broken loose!" A workman, out of breath and face flushed with panic, bolted through an adjacent doorway and grasped Royston by the arm. "It's headed this way!"

"You dolt!" The foreman's anger was apparent in his starkly widened eyes. "Didn't I tell the lot of you to keep the thing strapped down? What happened to its chains?"

"Snapped them, it did! As though they were bloody bits o' string! We did our best, but—"

As though they were a crested tide, bearing down upon us where we stood, the noises increased in volume and implied threat.

"We'd best remove to safer ground." Stonebrake appeared to know the exact import of the clamour and the frightened workman's statement. He tugged me by one arm toward the doorway through which we had first entered. "This way—"

His attempted retreat came too late, at least for myself. I needed little encouragement to vacate the spot—I was in actuality already moving toward a prudent exit—but my resulting efforts were of no avail to me. Between one accelerating heartbeat and the next, I found myself rising in the air, a constricting encumbrance circling my chest, pinning my arms to the side. I vainly kicked and writhed in an attempt to free myself, but managed only to twist about in the grasp of whatever had seized upon me, sufficiently to catch a glimpse of its exact nature.

Equal quantities of fear and bafflement surged within me, as I viewed a hideously grinning visage, symmetrical rows of teeth leaking steam through the equidistant gaps between them, and fiery sparks emitted from the perfectly circular eye-sockets. Jointed iron arms, swathed in matted and tangled orange fur, pressed me close to the barrel chest of the animate device. For a machine it appeared to be: caught between partial disassembly and re-assembly, enough of its exterior was absent to reveal the furious reciprocating pistons and meshing cogwheels typical of my father's design, all encased in a bolted rib cage surmounting a gimbaled base. The contracting and flexing armatures of a pair of mechanical legs, curved and bandied as an elderly sailor's in form but possessing the exorbitant strength necessary to lurch the entire construction through one spring-loaded pace after another, showed through more rents in the same tatty fur that brushed against my own face.

My apprehension of being crushed to death by the bear-like squeeze of the device's arms was only partially abated by a relaxing of its grasp about me. Before I could fathom what intent, if any, the mechanism harboured toward me, I was thrown forward, landing upon my chest. Scarcely had I managed to gain a position upon my hands and knees, when I felt the pincer grip of the hand-like extrusion at the end of one of the device's arms, seizing upon the back of my neck and thrusting with force sufficient to bounce my forehead against the floor. Confounded by the blow, I was scarcely able to direct my swimming gaze back upon the nightmarish vision of the device, red sparks yet flying from the sockets above its fixed ivory grimace.

On many occasions before, I had dolefully thought to myself, *This is the worst day of my life, come at last.* But at no point did that observation seem more appropriate than now, as I felt the device's other hand at the small of my back, gripping the waistband of my trousers and pulling them downward. In the same moment, I glimpsed through its tangled orange fur, another aspect of its construction that I had not ascertained before. At the juncture of the mechanism's legs, a third iron appendage thrust forward, of lesser dimension than the others, but still possessed of a dismaying length and girth. A scalding jet of steam hissed from the nozzle-like aperture at its prow . . .

"The pipe, man; the pipe!" From somewhere beyond my dizzied comprehension, I heard Royston's voice gruffly shouting. "Take an axe to the bloody pipe!"

To my ear came the sound of the prescribed blow, but I did not witness it. I was set free as the articulated metal hands went limp, their motivating force extinguished. Hurriedly scrambling from the spot at which I had been pinned, I halted only when my shoulder struck the farthest wall. Pressing my spine against the crumbling

plaster, I saw one of the narrower steam pipes clanking and thrashing about as though it were a beheaded serpent, white vapours gust-
ing forth from its parted end. A similar pipe, wetly dripping, dangled
from the back of the now lifeless device that had seized upon me. As
though it were a creation of flesh and blood rather than brass and
iron, it slumped upon its haunches, befurred head lolling forward,
its sparking eye-sockets now dead and hollow. Behind it, slowly regaining his own breath, one of the workmen leaned upon the handle
of the axe with which he had deprived the device of its ability to
carry out its wicked intents.

"I trust you're all right?" Stonebrake reached a hand down toward me. "Bit shaken, I suppose."

"Do you? Do you indeed?" I brushed away his offer of help and
shakily managed to stand, balancing myself against the wall behind
me. I could not restrain my shouting: "Why should you assume
that? I would have assumed that in this new, wondrous steam-
powered London of yours, being sodomized by something out of an
ironmonger's shed is an everyday occurrence, enjoyed by all."

"Calm yourself," advised Stonebrake. "I can understand your
degree of agitation—"

"I'm sure you're able to." I stalked away from him and stood glaring at the machine which had assaulted me. "What *is* this damnable
thing? And that fur in which it is wrapped—was that supposed to
serve some decorative purpose?"

From across the space, Royston barked out a laugh. "Makes it all
the uglier, you ask me."

"You need to remember," said Stonebrake, "that your father
served a clientele possessed of both wealth and those jaded enthusiasms that wealth engenders. The device whose embrace you have
just endured is in fact a mechanical simulacrum of that beast known
as an *Orang-Utan,* the so-called Wild Man of far-off Borneo. Thus
the distinctive orange pelt, by which such a creature is distinguished
in its native habitat. One of your father's clients apparently had the
fancy of setting up a hunting preserve in Yorkshire, in which he and
his titled friends might amuse themselves by bagging one or two, out

on the moors. In pursuit of that objective, they had a number of the animals captured and shipped to some point north of Brimley."

"You must excuse my disbelief." I set about dusting off and straightening the clothes that had become disarranged during the machine's attack upon my person. "This seems a daft notion."

"Actually . . . it rather *was*. Two impediments arose rather quickly: First, the northern climate disagreed severely with the apes, despite their shaggy coats, with croup and consumption eliminating most before anyone could take so much as a shot at them. And secondly, those that did survive the perpetual drizzle were not as impressively threatening as your father's client had conceived them to be. In fact, they seemed to be by nature on the shy and retiring side, with not much more sport in killing them than would be gotten by putting a rifle's muzzle to the head of an elderly lapdog. Consequently, your father was engaged to devise a more satisfying trophy, an Orang-Utan with a sufficiently violent demeanour, so that the pride of a British nobleman might be sufficiently engaged by firing off both barrels of a Purdey over-and-under into its mechanical chest."

"*Violent*, you say?" I pointed to the silent device, still huddled where it had come to rest. "It seemed to have something else on its mind just now."

"Yes, well, your father was an accommodating craftsman—that much is undeniable. No request was beyond him, it would seem. In this instance, his client was the product of one of those schools, to which the nobility have sent their children for generations, at which the affections between the young scholars and their instructors is expressed in the manner of the ancient Grecians. Nothing remarkable about that, of course; however, a simultaneous enthusiasm for exotic beasts had somehow become muddled up in the gentleman's thoughts with his other carnal interests. Sadly for him, the timorous Orang-Utans brought over from their tropic home were apparently even less given to the seductive arts than they had been suited for bounding over the moors with a pack of hounds baying after them. Thus the device you see here, effectively filling two desperate needs with the same contrivance."

"How fortunate for the parties involved."

"Perhaps." Stonebrake nodded musingly. "At least for a time. Alas, human flesh is not as sturdy as your father's creations. From the hushed reports I've heard, his client apparently succumbed to his passions, his heart giving out while he was preoccupied, so to speak, with this very machine. His heirs kept a wise discretion about the matter, storing your father's handiwork in the stonewalled outbuilding where our agents located it."

"Piece o' shite, it is." The sullen Royston gave the device a kick. "Deprived me of one of my best workmen."

"Surely you jest." I stared aghast at him. "It murdered the poor fellow? Or worse?"

"Put your mind at ease," said Stonebrake. "The man was not of such a robust mentality as you have displayed. He is presently a resident of the asylum at Colney Hatch, his reason having been unhinged by an ordeal that, admittedly, went a bit further than the one which you endured."

"Jackie's perfectly fine," insisted Royston. "Bleeding doctors won't let him go, is all."

"Of course they won't." The foreman's comment appeared to exasperate Stonebrake. "You're not likely to be discharged from a lunatic asylum, are you, if you keep insisting you've been buggered by a steam engine with flaming eyes and shaggy orange hair. For most people, this is simply not a credible account."

Perhaps because of its humid atmosphere, the room seemed to swim about me for a moment. "Is there a place where I might lie down for a moment? I confess myself a bit wearied by all that's happened."

"Buck up, man." Stonebrake clapped me on the shoulder. "Time is hurtling past us, and we must make haste if we are to catch up with the fortunes we seek."

"Haste? To do what?"

"There are personages of note awaiting us. Royston, have the carriage brought about. Come along, Dower." He headed toward the townhouse's door. "We have a party to go to."

CHAPTER

8

An Elegant Soirée,
with Revelations

AT the best of times, a man of my nature finds sociability to be a trial. Humanity is a commodity I have enjoyed, to the degree that I can at all, in the abstract; if personal circumstances did not dictate a desperate pursuit of my own interest, I could easily have been one of those early notables of the Christian faith, who found living alone in a cave and subsisting on a diet of locusts and wild honey more congenial than the yammering, ceaseless chatter of their own unenlightened kind.

Even so, there is something to be said for loitering about in an elegant drawing-room with a glass of a fine vintage in one's hand and the expectation of a dinner of equal quality in the offing. The singular advantage of being in as wearied a condition as had been produced by my long traveling was that it required but a little alcohol to set me in an elevated frame of mind.

"Ah, Dower!" Lord Fusible, in his portly and similarly inebriated exuberance—for it was to his fashionable townhouse that my co-conspirator, Stonebrake, had transported me—wrapped an arm around me and exhaled brandy fumes into my face. "So good to see you again. Stonebrake here had promised your reappearance upon the scene, and he has performed admirably in that regard."

"I'm glad your lordship thinks so." Stonebrake lowered his own half-drained glass. "It is a pleasure to accommodate your wishes."

That sort of obsequious truckling to the upper classes always nettled me, but on this occasion I said nothing about it. Instead, I gave a single nod and told Fusible, "Nothing could have kept me away, I assure you."

A few feet away from where we stood, the drawing-room was crowded with various sycophants and well-dressed dignitaries; Lady Fusible held court at the space's farthest reach, surrounded by the wives of Phototrope Limited's executive officers, most of whom I recognized from the recent launch of their company's latest perambulating lighthouse.

"I expect not." Fusible leered at me with a *crêpe*-lidded wink and an elbow to my ribs. "About to do some grand business together, aren't we? The keepers of the Sea and Light Book will soon rue the day they accepted our wagers!"

I became aware of an encircling constellation of knowing glances and self-satisfied smiles, all turned in my direction from the others listening to our conversation. It became clear to me that the bulk of my affairs was an open secret to the dinner party's attendees. A certain degree of discomfiture was attached to that realization, given my own doubts as to the legality of the enterprise to which I had become a central figure. The other doubts I found myself entertaining revolved around the eagerness to defend or rescue my person, that any of the assorted toffs might display were our collective plans to go amiss. The sly signs of greed and calculation marked their features; it seemed hardly likely to me that any of them had reached their current state of wealth by being overly concerned of their fellow creatures' well-being.

Liquor and fatigue had loosened my tongue, though. I offered a few words of advice, unmindful of their impertinence: "Perhaps your lordship might consider it wise to display a bit more discretion, concerning these matters."

My admonition scarcely seemed to bother him. "Don't worry yourself about it, old man. You're amongst friends here. There's no need to keep confidences from each other—indeed, you would be hard-pressed to accomplish that, given the manner in which this lot relishes gossiping about one another. There's not the slightest amusing gaffe or scrape that doesn't get circulated amongst them, as quickly as their tongues can wag of it."

I raised an eyebrow. "Is that so?"

"You'll know the truth of it soon enough," insisted Lord Fusible. "I was just back in the house's kitchen a moment or so ago, securing a morsel to tide me over until the dinner gong is struck, and I overheard the footmen and maids having a fine old laugh with that sourly amusing devil Royston, as to some wicked goings-on of which you yourself were the center. Who knew that a mechanical ape could be driven by such amorous longings? The fellow made it sound as if its interests were rather reciprocated on your part as well. To each his own, eh?" Fusible bestowed another wink and nudge upon me. "If the gentlefolk you see assembled in the room are not already aware of the incident, they will be by the time they head to home, and they exchange a few words with their servants as the bedcovers are turned down."

Such information filled me with a degree of dismay, though not surprise. Years before this, scurrilous rumours had circulated through every stratum of London society, concerning other carnal indulgences to which I was supposedly given. At that time, the stories had been in regard to the ill-famed procuress Mollie Maud's stable of *green girls,* the piscine jades servicing the city's most debauched appetites. Reputation is a fragile commodity, determined by others' whims more than by one's own behaviour. My attempts to lead a discreet if not spotless life had not met with great success before; why should they now? Particularly in light of the fact that I had embarked upon enterprises of dubious morality, let alone legality. Upon further reflection, any subsequent besmirchment of my public character might be no more than my due.

"Don't fret about it, my dear fellow." Seeing the play of emotions across my face, Lord Fusible proffered further advice. "It's not really the sort of thing that people will hold against you. At least not in London's fashionable society."

"That's good news," I said. "I have had enough unpleasant things held against me, as it is. Literally."

As it had at the lighthouse launch party, alcohol made Fusible expansive and voluble. "Indeed," he said, gesturing with his empty glass, "an eccentricity such as that only serves to render you more interesting, to people of gentility and education. As word gets out, I can assure you, a great many invitations to elegant functions will be offered to you."

"If they involve either apes or buggery, or both, I'm afraid I will have to decline them."

"Suit yourself." Lord Fusible's shoulders lifted in a shrug. "*De gustibus non est disputandum,* as those waggish Greeks would have put it—"

"The Romans, actually. And not the more respectable ones."

"Regardless. But consider this. Our mutual friend Stonebrake informs me that you are desirous of becoming wealthy. A laudable ambition, indeed, and so much so that the means necessary to achieve that state are of little consequence, as long as they are successful. Such has been the guiding principle of my own endeavours, and I rather fancy that it would be the same for most of the people here tonight. A fortune in one's purse has its advantages, I can tell you that." Fusible's barrel chest swelled to even greater dimensions, as though inflated by his lofty thoughts. "The common morality? The binding confines of those notions that others, those without money to jingle in their pockets, consider so important? All those become as trifles, without weight or mass, as easily blown away by a puff of one's breath as though they were but dust wafting in the air. A man may cut his morals as he pleases, provided he is a rich man."

"I am certain it facilitates the process," was my observation, "but you must admit that there have been at least a few who have managed to become similarly depraved, without the benefit of ample finances."

"Pooh." Fusible's plump hand waved my words away. "Petty criminals and lunatics, or so they are regarded by both the rabble and the authorities, and each as likely to wind up incarcerated behind stone walls. What is illegal for those without funds, becomes merely eccentric or even somewhat charming when it is practiced by the wealthy. Do you doubt me?"

"Of course not." As yet unsure of what importance the other man might be to my gamey future prospects, I considered it best to not insult him. "If I'm a bit of the agnostic persuasion on the matter, I am certain you can forgive me. Coming from a lesser economic sphere, I don't have as much experience along these lines as you do."

"Soon you shall!" The perpetual enthusiasm resident in Fusible's breast flushed a roseate hue across his wide, wattled face. "And immediately—come, let me introduce you to the exact exemplar of which I speak."

The dregs slopped from my glass as Fusible tugged me by the arm across the crowded drawing-room. Within moments, I found myself gazing into a fiercely bearded visage, surmounting a muscular, sun-bronzed figure clad only in rudely knotted animal skins. I might well have been face-to-face with one of our primitive ancestors, a cave-dweller from the epochs when great tusked beasts ponderously steered their shaggy bulks around a verdantly primeval landscape, daring lesser creatures armed with sticks and rocks to fall upon them for the sake of a raw cutlet torn from their flanks.

"Viscount Carnomere . . ." A casual and chummy hand was laid upon the gentleman's bared shoulder, as Fusible directed his attention toward me. "Here's an interesting fellow, whose acquaintance you should make. May I introduce our renowned friend, Mr. George Dower?"

"Dower, eh?" A disordered, ursine eyebrow rose as Carnomere regarded me with no less mistrust than he seemed to bestow upon the world at large. "You're the fellow, I take it, who's supposed to make this whole ungodly lot wealthier than it already is?"

"So I have been led to believe." By now, I was no longer surprised by every person I met seeming to be well-versed in those allegedly secretive conspiracies into which Stonebrake had recruited me. "Time will tell, if such is to be the case."

"Not worth fretting about, as far as I'm bloody concerned." Tangled, unkempt hair framed either side of the dyspeptic Carnomere's face, the unshorn locks mingling with a beard so similarly primeval as to have actual bits of twigs and other earthen debris embedded in it. "All this grubbing about for money is but a footnote to the history of our dull-witted species' decline."

Fusible turned to me with an easy smile. "The viscount holds some amusing notions about modern society. Of which, he is more than capable of informing you."

"Let no man say I did not warn him." The scowl darkened behind the matted beard, as storm clouds might have blotted out the sun beyond hillsides fringed with wild brambles. "There'll be a reckoning soon enough, for the folly of our ways."

I edged away from the man. The resemblance between him and one of our harshly dispositioned forebears was heightened by the weapon he carried, a rude spear tipped with a stone blade that might have been fashioned by the efforts of his own teeth, so rough and jagged were its edges. Despite the implement's crudity, I had no desire to have its effectiveness tested upon my hide.

"Tell him, Carnomere." My host egged on the other. "It's grand stuff," he assured me. "Puts the *blood* back into *bloody-minded,* that's the truth."

" 'Tis the fault of agriculture; there's the truth for you." Viscount Carnomere appeared to require little coaxing for him to launch upon his familiar diatribe. "That is the turning point in the road of Time, at which we went wrong. Educated folk might grumble all they wish, about the ravages that this new-fangled allegiance to Steam and its attendant workings is bestowing upon both English countryside and society—"

"And if they did," Fusible drily interjected, "they would be criticizing exactly that which has feathered your own nest so handsomely."

The glare that Carnomere shot him was so ill-tempered, I believed for a moment that it might be accompanied with a thrust of the spear sufficient to skewer his lordship *en brochette.*

"You needn't remind me of those sins which already weigh upon my conscience." Carnomere's growl was so deeply chthonic, it might well have presaged the ground splitting open beneath his bare, blackened feet. "You would be better off searching the grimy pit of your own soul, while there is yet time."

It struck me that the viscount's rugged semblance might be due to his being a *soi-disant* biblical prophet, of the variety that eked out a subsistence on locusts and wild honey, when at home in their bleak desert caves, rather than expounding upon coming dooms to bemused townspeople. In this supposition I proved to be not far wrong, as he expounded further upon his all-encompassing theories.

"What you must see, Dower—" As with many freethinkers, he evidently regarded even the slightest honorifics of address as unseemly affectations. "What all men *will* see someday—is that all the evils of our present mode of life arise from those fundamental errors made upon the Sumerian river deltas by our deluded ancestors, millennia ago. *There* was Adam's fall, when first he ground between his teeth that which would enslave him to the sweating ways of modern husbandry. Foolish bastards, the lot of 'em!"

"Pardon me?" It seemed as if he were inveighing against an army of Adams, munching *en masse* upon orchards of damning apples. "I'm not quite sure that I see the connection between original sin and steam power—"

"Bother your steam power, man. Hardly worth speaking of, if one is tallying the errors of the human race. This! *This* is what I'm referring to." An equally fur-bearing pouch, fashioned from the hide of some smaller animal, hung from a tendon-like strap knotted about Carnomere's waist; he rummaged in it and extracted an object the size of his fist, which he thrust under my nose. "From this is where all the evils stem, which afflict befuddled Mankind!"

I drew back in order to focus upon the item displayed upon his palm. For a moment, I thought it might be some variety of bath sponge; then I realized that it was a hunk of common bread, stiffened with age and spotted with blue and green mould.

"Really, Carnomere—" From beside me, a note of disgust sounded in Lord Fusible's voice. "Isn't it about time you acquired a new prop for your speechifying? That one's seen better days."

An odour of powdery decay rose from the bread, such that it might be considered edible only by the most desperate of London's poor.

"You must forgive me," I apologized even as the distaste with which I regarded the crumbling hunk was no doubt evident in my gaze. "But I'm not quite following the import of your words—"

"Open your eyes!" The bearded figure thrust the substance in question closer to my face. "It's bread!"

"Yes, I see that—"

"Wheat! Grain! *Agriculture!*" His imprecations became even more forceful. "That is the curse laid upon our brow." Crumbs dispersed in the drawing-room's scented air as his grasp tightened upon the spotted lump. "Before the introduction of this poisonous concoction, human beings roamed free upon the face of the Earth. They ate their fill of Nature's bounty, and lived in tranquil equality, with no man the master of another." A fervent tone heightened Carnomere's voice; his eyes misted, as though contemplating that vanished realm of communitarian bliss. "Now a polished boot stands upon the throat of the masses, their hollow-eyed children starving for exactly that which enslaves them."

"Bravo! Go to it!" Fusible clapped his pudgy hands together in delight. "I must confess, I greatly admire the passion with which some of my fellow oligarchs inveigh against those social arrangements that keep them comfortably elevated above the rabble. Seems deucedly sporting of them."

"You mock me, sir." The viscount turned his fierce and shag-browed scowl upon the other. "A day will come when we are all cast down to the level we deserve."

"Perhaps." A passing butler had renewed the wineglass in Fusible's hand. "I await the event with little if any trepidation."

"But those primitive lives of which you speak—" I attempted to steer the conversation back to safer and less personal territory. "Were they not, as the philosophers state, rather on the nasty, brutish, and short side?"

"Stuff and nonsense, man." Small creatures seemed to be evicted from Viscount Carnomere's tangled locks as he decisively shook his head. "Rhetoric from those who would keep our species shackled to the processes of the farming combines and their masters. Who are, I would have you know, mere *parvenus* in the course of human history, recently arrived to work their iniquities. Even the most learned biblical scholars concede that post-lapsarian Mankind existed in the Earth's nourishing plains and gardens for millennia before the Mesopotamian basin was bound up and given over to the planting and harvesting of these wicked grains." He returned the mouldy lump of bread to his pouch, the better to focus my attention by laying a prophetic hand upon my shirtfront. "Even as we speak, men of the greatest learning are examining the bones that have been dug up from our ancestors' stone-laden graves. And what do they find?"

"I have no idea."

"Exactly this, Dower: that our forebears were of sturdier frame and longer lives, free of the debilitating infirmities that have reduced the representatives of our modern civilization to such a rank and puny condition. Go to the streets, man, and observe your fellow creatures!" One bare, dirt-streaked hand pointed to the townhouse's night-filled windows. "Witness their degenerate state! Can you really credit that these bantam cockneys and their pale, fragile offspring are the zenith of human evolution? Tenacious and feisty they might very well be—and given the harsh, scrabbling conditions they endure, 'tis little wonder that they are so—but their matchstick bones can be snapped between one's thumb and forefinger, as though they were but kindling. And of course, this febrile phenomenon is not limited to the British Empire; one might find our natives' scrawny cousins in every land in which the demon *Agriculture* has taken root."

I entertained no desire to debate the contention with him. "Am I correct in assuming that there is some remedy that you propose?"

"*Remedy,* you say? Rather more than that, you may rest assured. What is needed is more than some slight and ultimately ineffectual remediation."

"You'll love this," noted Fusible as he plucked another glass from the silver tray passing near him.

Viscount Carnomere pressed forward, in the full vigour of those primeval virtues he embodied in himself. "It's *Revolution* that is required." His crusted hand thrust with greater firmness against my chest, staggering me backward a step. "Nothing less than a complete

renovation and restoration of those dietary practices which once en-
nobled our species."

"No more than that?" I confess to have felt a little disappointment at his pronouncement. Despite the ferocity of his primitive
appearance, he seemed suddenly diminished in my regard. Were
all his shouts and seething, teeth-clenched condemnations nothing
more than an over-enthused variation on the fastidious sermons of
those cranks pushing forward their brothy cures for Mankind's ills?
"I take it that you would have us eat no more bread. Please refrain
from bringing out that example you showed before. What would you
have us consume in its place?"

"I would forbid you not just bread—that filthy stuff!—but all
grains of any sort; in truth, any product of human cultivation." To
my concern, Carnomere reached again into the crudely fashioned
pouch and extracted a darker and seemingly more fibrous object.
He raised it to his mouth, his impressively white and sturdy teeth
sinking into its mass, and I recognized it as some sort of dried animal flesh, such as the tribes of distant lands render for their sustenance. Chewing with evident relish, he offered the gobbet to me. I
declined with a politely raised hand. "You do yourself a disservice,"
he said as he took another bite for himself. "This is what you need,
to restore yourself to the full flush of radiant health. Meat! That's the
prescription for all Mankind—meat, I say!"

"Very well—"

"It is what our forefathers ate, and upon which they flourished!"
His eyes widened with fervour. "Even now, there are tribes in far-
flung corners of the globe, who have not fallen under those delusions
that compel their civilized brethren to grub rows and trenches in the
hard, stubborn soil, all for compelling grasses to spring up and be
ground between our molars, as though we were cows rather than
free and heroic human beings. And we are informed by our own adventurers and travelers, when they come upon such peoples, either
in the frozen north or the more temperate lands about the Equator,
that they are not only possessed of more robust health than ourselves, but of more innate happiness as well. For the economic stric-

tures required by agricultural practices have not forced them to
divide into masters and peasants—pharaohs with whips and flails in
their hands, sneering at the masses toiling in the riparian muck, all
to fill the granaries upon which so much self-glorifying magnifi-
cence is based. Rather, our so-called primitive cousins have no call
to lord it over one another, being content as they are to catch one of
the running beasts of the wild, rend its flesh from the bones, and
share it amongst themselves."

He stopped for breath, creating a hiatus enduring long enough
for me to hazard an enquiry. "And these wild tribespeople of which
you speak—are they entirely carnivorous, by nature or inclining
habit?"

"For the most part." Carnomere shrugged. "They might throw in
the odd bit of fruit on occasion, and whatever other vegetation is
capable of being consumed in its raw state, with no necessity of cook-
ing or otherwise moderating the toxins that make so many other
plants unfit for the human digestion. But the blood that courses
through the veins of such fortunate people is infused with the
strength that comes from animate creatures. Of all forms and sizes,
you must bear in mind; a wren is hardly the smallest fluttering bit to
make its way into their grateful stomachs. There is a good deal of
nutrition to be found in insects and those other creatures that we ig-
norantly describe as worthless vermin."

"I will try to remember that."

"You should." Carnomere's temper had ebbed to a more affable
state. "For if you do, you will be in excellent company. The enthusiasm for a healthily primitive mode of existence is sweeping through
all levels of society; it is hardly limited to those such as myself, with
the financial wherewithal to indulge in practices that the unenlightened might regard as dangerously perverse, rather than merely eccentric."

A singular vision appeared in my mind's eye. "Do they all . . ."
I searched for a polite manner of framing my enquiry. "Garb themselves as you do? That is . . . the furs and such-like."

"Much depends upon the weather," allowed Carnomere. "Our

ancestors were a sturdier breed, and could turn their faces toward degrees of inclement weather at which we, their weaker progeny, would quail. I confess that as comfortable as these rugged furs might be while standing in a well-heated drawing-room, during the winter months I have been known to supplement them with a full overcoat and a pair of waterproof Indian rubber boots, at least when out of doors."

"Very wise, I'm sure."

"Yes, given my age," conceded the viscount, "and the late stage in life in which I discovered the manifest virtues of primitive manners and a carnivorous diet. But I have hopes for the generations to come. Especially those of the lower classes, as we characterize their position in the social order. Accustomed as they are, both male and female, to hardships of which we the elite generally know little, the return to ancestral ways is more easily accomplished by them, and with a deal less grumbling and whining every time the sky clouds over. I am greatly heartened by the advent of these *meatpunks,* as they are sometimes described."

"Pardon me? 'Meatpunks'—did I hear that aright?"

"Amusing, isn't it?" From behind his effulgent beard, Carnomere bestowed upon me a smile more suited to an Afric savage. "The coinage might be ill-educated—I would have preferred something derived from one of the classical tongues—but evidences a certain rude cleverness. As did the person from whom I first heard it, who assured me similar formulations will soon be an essential element of the Queen's English—combining as they do an obvious prefix with the syllable I have been given to understand connotes a somewhat raucous enthusiasm for that upon which the greater society still looks askance."

"Perhaps," I said, "there are reasons for such a negative regard."

"Mere prejudice; that is all." Carnomere thumped the less lethal end of his spear upon the floor. "And an unthinking faith in the over-vaunted Future, which continually entices us with its promises, then cruelly disappoints as it shambles into reality as the dull, threadbare Present we must endure. The meatpunks, by contrast, hurl themselves headlong into a glorious, blood-reddened Past. If, in their ragged fancies, they get a few details wrong . . ." He shrugged. "Such seems an error easily overlooked."

Another vision rolled through my inward perception, as though the curve of bone behind my brow were the fluttering panel upon which a magic lantern show was displayed. For a moment, I did not see the glittering, affable assemblage in a fashionable room all about me, but instead the dark London streets, the night barely interrupted by feebly guttering lamps. The shadows that wavered across the locked and boarded storefronts were cast by the flaring torches held aloft by a gleeful laughing mob, all clad as Carnomere was, in ragged furs and tribal paraphernalia, their tangled, matted locks streaming behind them as they ran; their faces shone with the bright grease of recent feasting, the bloodied heads of the aristocracy's lap-dogs and housecats swaying as pendants, gnawed rib bones strung and clattering upon these new savages' bared chests. The shrieks and cries of the resurgent ages swept over me, ocean-like, until I could hear nothing else . . .

"Come along, Dower." A familiar voice succeeded in piercing the deep fog by which my thoughts had been engulfed. "Let's leave Carnomere to bend some other poor bastard's ear."

I blinked my vision clear and found myself being dragged by the arm toward some other part of the townhouse, away from the drawing-room and the guests assembled there.

"He's a harmless enough old duffer," continued Lord Fusible, "but of course, completely mad, with all that carnivorous chatter of his." Gesturing with a redolent cigar, Fusible drew me on through a dimly lit hallway, more functional than decorative in appearance. "I trust you found him amusing."

"Not in the slightest—" Keeping up with the other's vigorous pace rendered me somewhat breathless. "I wasn't certain whether to judge him pathetic or terrifying."

"Eh? Is that a fact?" Fusible exhaled a great plume of grey smoke from his cigar. "No matter, then. I am sure that you will find that which I am about to display to you to be far more diverting.

But of course, anything to do with making great piles of money is *always* so."

He pushed open a door festooned with iron rivets and shoved me through before him. For a moment, I gazed about in utter darkness, then Fusible ignited a glass-chimneyed lantern and carried it farther into the space.

"There!" The lantern's glow was sufficient to reveal an object somewhat taller than the man himself. "What do you think of *that*! Bloody marvelous, isn't it?"

A moment longer was required for me to discern the exact lineaments of the thing, whatever it might be. At last I realized that it had all the appearances of a lighthouse—the tapering cylindrical form, the windows circling about the top level—though in greatly miniaturized stature. Specifically, it represented one of the so-called *walking light* variety, complete to the articulated crab-like legs extending from its base.

"That one we just launched out there in Cornwall—rubbish!" Fusible's disdain was evident in the manner in which he flicked the cigar's ashes away from himself. "This is the ruddy great bastard with which we'll absolutely make our fortunes."

"I'm afraid I don't follow you." The object, though of an impressive size and detail for a model, did not seem much different from all the other lighthouses I had glimpsed in my lifetime. "It's very . . . *nice* and all, but—"

"By God, you're slow in the uptake." Fusible pityingly shook his head. "This will completely revolutionize our business' operations."

I was still somewhat baffled by his assertions. The possibility arose in my mind that I had misunderstood his presentation of the object before us, and what I had taken to be a model was in reality the thing itself. Conceivably, a human being of adult stature might have fitted himself inside it, though the structure would have fitted tight about a man's shoulders. Perhaps this was some essential alteration in Phototrope Limited's future inventory of devices, and henceforth all its lighthouses would be of such relatively abbreviated dimensions. A vision came to me of swarms of such little towers clambering over the sea-coast's wave-dashed rocks, very like the crustaceans they resembled, each holding its cramped operative and setting up *en masse* to blink their tiny lights toward the mercantile ships sailing past.

"But is there not some resulting loss of elevation?" I pointed toward the object. "That is, from making the lighthouses so much smaller?"

"Smaller?" Fusible frowned at me. "What are you going on about, you twit? We're not making them smaller—we're making them bloody *bigger*. Look there—" He pointed at the object's base, near its jointed legs. "That's the size of the one we just launched out in Cornwall."

I saw then a second object, of similar appearance but much subordinate in dimension. This scarcely reached a foot in height, coming up but a fraction of the vertical expanse of the larger one beside it. All of which meant that my initial perception of gazing upon some detailed model had been correct—but also that the actual thing which it represented would be of an intimidatingly enormous construction.

"*Now* you see, don't you?" Lord Fusible smiled gloatingly at me. "Magnificent, isn't it? We call it the *Colossus of Blackpool*."

"But certainly . . ." I felt dizzied, as though the apprehension of such a monstrous device, dwarfing all its predecessors, had sent swirling the thoughts within my head. "Certainly such a thing could never actually exist—"

"The bloody hell it can't." Ash drifted from the ember of Fusible's grandly outflung cigar. "It's under construction at this very moment, in our land docks up in North London. Damn near finished, too. We've managed to keep it a secret from the world—but soon everybody and his brother will gaze upon it and marvel. That'll be a fine day, won't it?"

I could make no reply to him. Something about this impending monstrosity appalled my soul. An unbidden image came within me, of this Colossus towering above the landscape, the searing light of its beam sweeping across both city and ocean. Great billows of steam wreathed the vision, as though some cyclopean giant were peering down through the clouds, inventorying his possessions.

"A fine day, indeed." Another voice spoke up, neither Fusible's nor mine. "I look forward to it . . ."

Turning, I saw that Captain Crowcroft had followed us into this chamber, far from the other guests and his betrothed. As I watched, he stepped forward into the circled glow cast by the lantern. A dismayingly fervent gleam sparked in his eyes as he laid his hands atop the Colossus model, as might a practitioner of some primitive religion approach a sacred idol.

"So you should." Fusible nodded in evident appreciation of the other man's enthusiasm. "When you're at the helm of this bloody great blighter, there'll not be much that won't look up to you!"

The air in the chamber felt suddenly oppressive, my lungs futilely labouring as though I were trapped within the windowless cells of some charitable lodging for the insane. The others' voices faded from my perception as the space grew infinitely larger, the better to accommodate the Colossus swelling and towering above me . . .

⸎

"**FOR** God's sake, man, pull yourself together." A single voice now barked close to my ear. "You're embarrassing me."

I opened my eyes, discovering thereby that I was no longer standing up, but rather partly reclining upon the sort of *chaise longue* favoured by ladies of taste, when gripped by an event of the vapours. The noises of the gathering, the mingled voices and discreetly purring laughter, still came to my ear, but from a distance. My unconscious person, as well as Stonebrake—for it was he who was energetically jostling my shoulder—had evidently been removed to an otherwise empty chamber, away from that chamber slowly and mistily resolving itself in my recent memory.

"What happened?" I lifted my head, which was a mistake, that small motion evoking a dizzied constellation to sparkle across my tenuous vision.

"Went down like a bloody tentpole, you did." A distinct lack of sympathy was evident in Stonebrake's voice. He frowned as he leaned over me, dabbing at the corner of my brow with a folded handkerchief; when he pulled it away, the cloth was only slightly reddened. "Right in front of Lord Fusible—and all because he showed you that model of Phototrope Limited's Colossus of Blackpool construction." He shook his head. "If such is your notion of conveying a favourable impression on our backers, it's rather a failure, in my estimation."

"I was not aware I was required to make an impression of any kind, upon anyone." My boots found the room's floor as I managed to sit upright. "You might have warned me."

"The matter seemed so obvious to me, that no comment was considered necessary." Stonebrake tucked the stained handkerchief inside his jacket. "The enterprise upon which we have launched ourselves is of a nature that relies upon both extensive financial support as well as discretion." He gestured toward the distant drawing-room. "These are the people upon whom we depend; important people, figures of the highest social standing—and wealth."

"So?" My fingers tentatively prodded my throbbing forehead. "You had led me to believe that they were already committed to the success of our plans."

"They might very well be—for the present moment. But they are more than capable of altering their minds. As they would have every right to do, upon seeing a crucial element such as yourself, swooning to the ground like a maiden just out of finishing school. Be assured, you are not yet cutting an impressive figure."

"I suppose not." A bitter, metallic taste crept over my tongue, as though I had been administered some medicinal tincture. "Feel free to give my apologies to our hosts. Generally, I am composed of at least slightly stronger stuff than I have exhibited so far. I must be more wearied from traveling than I had realized."

"Excuses have been taken care of, already." Stonebrake turned toward the doorway. "Allow me to see if Royston has brought around our carriage. Do not move from this spot—understood?"

I assured him that I had no intent otherwise. The room about me still seemed a bit vague at its edges; I lay back down on the *chaise,* with no expectation of further adventures, at least not for this night.

The event proved me wrong. Scarcely had I closed my eyes again than a woman's urgent whisper sounded at my ear.

"You must come with me, Mr. Dower." A note of fearful desperation tautened the words, as a twist upon a violin's tuning peg would draw the note of its string higher. "Immediately—for the sake of your life and mine—"

Such an alarming message snapped my eyes wide open. I saw above me a fair and anxious face. The same as that, which the last time it had gazed upon me, not too many days past, had been marked with the utmost contempt and hatred.

CHAPTER
9

*Of the Capacities
of Women's Hearts*

I HAD not previously been aware that poisoning random individuals was a practice much engaged in by young Englishwomen of quality." Disdain was evident in my voice, as was my intent. "I appear to have been misinformed on the subject."

"Pray accept my apologies, Mr. Dower. I meant you no harm." Lord Fusible's daughter, Evangeline, whom I had last glimpsed at the lighthouse launch party on the Cornish coast, wrung a silk kerchief in her hands. The depth of her distress was apparent in her well-favoured features. "I wouldn't have done it if there had been any alternative available to me."

As I prepared my retort, I preoccupied myself with straightening the cuffs of my jacket. My thoughts were somewhat disordered by the communication I had received from the young lady, immediately upon my fellow conspirator Stonebrake's exit from the room, that she had been responsible for my loss of consciousness, in the midst of the drawing-room's gathering.

"It was but a medicinal tincture," Evangeline had informed me. "That my mother's uncle had brought back from his merchant days with the firm of Jardine Matheson in Shanghai. Reputedly popular for feminine complaints, but my experience has been that, combined with spirits, it invokes slumber rather than mere analgesia."

Some filthy opiate, I decided; the sort of thing one would imagine being concocted by devious Chinese chemists. Upon her instructions, it had been conveyed to my lips in the wineglass forced upon me by one of the household's servants.

"You might," I noted, "have killed me. I took a hard fall."

"It was a chance worth taking."

My eyebrow raised in mute response to her comment. Though she was not gazing upon me with the same annihilating hatred that she had displayed upon our first encounter, it was still possible that she might hold some murderous ambitions toward me.

"You see," continued Fusible's daughter, "I had to speak to you. In private. And I could see no other way of bringing that about."

"Has the British post ceased operations?" The aftertaste of the drug crept across my tongue, as though it were some small fur-bearing animal. "You could just as well have sent me an invitation to tea, care of my hosts at Featherwhite House. I would have been happy to oblige you."

"There is no time for that!" Her agitation became even more apparent. "Events are hurtling past us at a breakneck speed!"

A wearied sigh escaped from my own breast. I had heard nearly this exact sentiment on so many occasions, that it might as well have been emblazoned on the fluttering banner which I was condemned to carry through life. Perhaps it was a curse that had been laid against me, for having once embarked, however unsuccessfully, upon commerce in those ticking devices that chivvy submissive Mankind through its dwindling hours, as though the hands of every watch and clock held little whips to lash against our backs. Perhaps the meat-eating viscount, with whom I had so recently made acquaintance, was correct in his assessment of our fallen state, and the unhurried glories of those primitive days when men reckoned Time only by the position of the sun above their unshod passage across the Earth.

"My assumption is that you speak of those enterprises upon which your father and his business associates have newly launched themselves." I sat back against the corner of the *chaise*. "They seek to multiply their fortunes by wagering with the Sea and Light Book— though *wager* is perhaps not an apt term in these circumstances, as they propose to remove all doubt as to the outcome of the under-lying events. Very well; I admit having allowed myself to be re-cruited into their schemes. If you have become party to them as well, perhaps by entrusting your father with whatever finances are under your control, so that he might place them at the betting counter on your behalf—then we are moral equals, if not social ones."

Evangeline hurriedly sat next to me, leaning close so as to place her trembling hand against the front of my shirt. Somewhere be-neath her touch, my heart trembled in response, and rather more so; my experience with the fairer sex had not been so great that a young woman bringing her face close to mine ranked as an everyday hap-penstance.

"This is not about money." Her whisper drew me into her confi-dence. "May I rely upon you, Mr. Dower?"

"As much . . . as anyone can." The request evoked my own in-ward fears. "I possess no reputation for being a pillar of strength."

"But you will have my gratitude," she said, "for whatever aid you might supply to me. There is no-one else to whom I can turn."

If such were the case, the young lady's situation was indeed des-perate. "Ask of me what you will. But there is little I can promise you."

"To begin, your discretion will suffice; do I have that? For those I fear most are close at hand."

I hazarded a guess. "You speak of Stonebrake?"

"Yes—" She gave a rapid nod. "Him, amongst others. Including my father."

"Indeed?" The latter accusation took me by surprise. "He doesn't seem like such a bad sort. A bit on the overbearing side, but not altogether—"

"You mistake my meaning. I have all the appropriate affections for him, but the conspiracies with which he has allowed himself to become entangled—they weigh heavily and darkly upon all chances of my future happiness, and that of those whom I love."

"The reference is, I take it, to the esteemed Captain Crowcroft?" Bit by bit, a picture was assembling in my mind, though I had some concern as to whether all its details would be painted in by the time

Stonebrake returned to fetch me. "He evidenced himself as a capable enough man when I was introduced to him. And his position with Phototrope Limited seems honourable and straightforward; to steer a lighthouse from crag to crag, and cast its helpful beam across the ocean—surely that renders him of such value as to be past the reach of all these conniving schemes?" I attempted to cast my voice in as comforting a manner as possible, as the girl seemed but a quivering eyelash's length away from shedding tears. "If I were to place a wager, it would be that a gentleman such as your betrothed is more than capable of guarding your prospects in this world."

"Oh, Mr. Dower—would that it were so!" Her bosom rose and fell with one of those overly dramatic sighs to which creatures of her youth and gender were given. "And not long ago, I would have believed you had the truth of the matter. The good captain has more than won my trust, in addition to my desire." Her expression turned reflective. "Which serves to illustrate how mysterious are the ways of the heart, seeing how great was my initial loathing of him."

I took some comfort in the perception that the lethal regard she had bestowed, in our previous encounter, was not a personal and specific matter relating to me, but evidently something that she directed in general toward the male species. Or at least until she got to know one of them to a better degree.

"Many successful marriages," I advised her now, "have commenced in exactly such a fashion."

"Of that, I have no doubt; my mother has told me as much. But you must understand, Mr. Dower, that the circumstances of my engagement to Captain Crowcroft might have been expressly designed to raise the emotions of contempt and loathing within me."

"Oh?" My sympathies lay more with her *fiancé;* she seemed capable of anything, if provoked. Having seemingly escaped her wrath, I endeavoured to remain on her congenial side. "I'm sure you wish to keep all that private—"

"No, no; I *must* tell you!"

My own heart sank within me. There seemed no end to these revelations.

"You see," Evangeline continued with even greater earnestness, "my engagement to Captain Crowcroft was none of my doing, or in fact, anything I wished for. It was all my father's idea, in pursuance of those schemes of which you yourself are now a part. He believed— and I imagine still does—that having the most celebrated lighthouse commander as his son-in-law would in some way further the plans that he had laid."

"So it might," I said. "Through you, his daughter, there would be another channel of information as to the operations and maneuvers upon which the Sea and Light Book accepts its clients' wagers. Or possibly, your father and his associates might be able to induce your husband to steer his various light-bearing craft in such a manner as they had predetermined, and upon which they had appropriately made their bets."

"No doubt," conceded Evangeline, "my father's reasoning was something along those lines. Though I little cared at the time, when the engagement between myself and Captain Crowcroft was announced—the shame and chagrin I felt, at being affianced to a man with whom I was barely acquainted, let alone loved, was more than I could bear. However, as I came to know him, my feelings altered."

"Very likely." I gave a shrug. "He doesn't seem such a bad sort."

"Oh, more than that, Mr. Dower; he is a very fine man, indeed. He has more than won my heart, though the first tenderness of my regard for him was motivated more by pity than affection."

Her words puzzled me. "Why pity? He seems almost literally on top of the world he inhabits."

"If you but knew! I am sure that many things seem benign and straightforward to an honest man such as yourself—"

I said nothing.

"But if you obtained any sense of the deviousness of those in whose schemes my poor Captain Crowcroft has become ensnared, I am sure you would fear for his prospects, as well as mine." She slowly shook her head, gaze drifting beyond me to some horrid vision of disaster. "How cruelly ironic it seems, that my own father's machinations should have brought about both my greatest happiness and my direst forebodings."

"Well . . . I am not sure *irony* is the correct term to use in this case." I was at a loss for anything else to say, though I felt compelled to make an utterance of some kind. "It might just be simpler to call it a dastardly thing to do to one's own child."

"If I believed that destroying all my hopes had been my father's intent," said Evangeline, "I might agree with you. But his wickedness is more of the unthinking kind, that lays waste without prior consideration, rather than the premeditated variety. He and his associates construct their schemes, then wind them up as though they were but clockwork toys, setting them into motion with no care as to what ultimate damage they might wreak. And as my father bears no actual malice toward me, I am certain that if he were aware of the blighted desert he were about to make of my life as well as Captain Crowcroft's, he would be greatly chagrined."

"Perhaps you should mention it to him."

"I would as profitably speak to a wall!" Her inclination to the higher sort of personal drama manifested itself again. "You've spoken with my father, Mr. Dower; you know what he is like when he is caught up in one of his various enthusiasms. Nothing else matters; others' voices are as the buzzing of gnats to him. Ruin might lie straight, and even his own flesh and blood could no more speak warning of it than alter the course of the sun in the sky."

Stonebrake was taking an inconveniently long time in arranging for my transportation from this place. If Fusible's daughter spent much more time unburdening her maidenly heart, I feared I might collapse under the weight.

"Your apprehension, then, is that your father's current scheme might fail, and disastrously so?"

"Worse, Mr. Dower! It will succeed! And then all my felicitous hopes are dashed."

Now I was confused. "I fear I am not quite following you in this regard . . ."

She regarded me with dismay. "Do you not see?"

"Quite frankly, no."

"It is my betrothed's very soul for which I am so concerned!"

"Oh." I nodded my head. "That's very good of you, I am sure. And the captain undoubtedly has a care for yours."

"Mine is not in the same peril," said Evangeline. "You apparently do not understand—"

I held my tongue, feeling it redundant to agree with her once more on that point.

"Perhaps no man is capable of doing so." Her head drooped mournfully. "Perhaps it is only a woman's tender senses, so easily bruised by this world's hard, unyielding realities, that can apprehend such a dolorous future as the one that awaits us now."

"I am sure that is the case." Perhaps it would be better if I concocted some pretext for making my excuses and going off in search of Stonebrake and the carriage. "These do seem like unnerving times, to even one as dull as myself."

"You have little idea, Mr. Dower. Situated as I am here, in the midst of all these schemes and plots, I find myself close to the center of events, the unfolding of which will horrify you."

"I have been sufficiently horrified already." The automated Orang-Utan still ticked and leered at the back of my thoughts. "It has been a long day, and a disagreeable one."

"Worse will come," predicted the young lady in somber tones. "You men have been so clever, with all your tinkering about and devising, setting great hissing pipes across the countryside and through the urban streets, the better that machines might serve you—"

"I wouldn't exactly call it *serve*—"

"Just so!" She seized my arm, her features alighting, as though suddenly recognizing a fellow disciple in some deeply held faith. "For now, we are their masters—but soon they shall be ours."

"Indeed." As my arm was numbing with the fervour of her grip, I thought it best to concur. "I have heard similar premonitions expressed before. Though if such is to be our species' fate, I am not exactly sure what I can do about it."

"Do you really think I care about our species, as you call it?" She let go of me, so as to lay the back of her hand against her own brow. "A woman's heart is not so capacious as that, Mr. Dower! We love the individual, the fleshly creatures who hold us in their embrace, not these huge, gaseous abstractions spoken of by bearded philosophers. And I have already witnessed the horrible process commenced, in the one who has captured my heart. When you look upon my *fiancé,* you see a man admired by every level of our society, a hero to all— but I discern more deeply than that. I know the price he pays, the burden that his commanding rank imposes upon him. These 'walking lights'—the intricacy of their construction, the minute adjustments necessary for their mobility, the fearsome explosive forces at their core, the scalding deaths that might be inflicted upon every man inside, the result of the slightest miscalculation at the helm—it is more than any man can bear, no matter his strength and resolve."

"It does seem," I allowed, "to be a demanding job—"

"More than demands, Mr. Dower; it *consumes.* This truth is known to me, as all that impinges upon my good captain is known. I have watched it happen to him. Little by little, a bit at a time; a bit more today than yesterday, and a bit more to come tomorrow. The intricacies and complications of operating such a device have taken over his soul; he is at risk of becoming no more than a sort of flesh-and-blood appendage to whichever lighthouse he commands." Evangeline's voice softened for a moment. "This is why I hope that you might pardon me, for I blush to recall with what venomous regard I looked upon you, when first I apprehended that you were the son of that genius-possessed inventor who created the essential elements upon which the walking lights depend."

"Think nothing of it," I assured her. In fact, a degree of relief was evoked by her confession; it was but another instance of someone's opinion of me being based more upon my lineage than any personal failing. "I'm sure you are aware of what is so often said, regarding the sins of the fathers being visited upon their sons."

"No, Mr. Dower; it is kind of you not to condemn, but it was still wicked to hate someone I did not even know, if only for a moment. Though it was a dark moment indeed; the sight of you at the launch party, there in Cornwall, overwhelmed all my better instincts—you seemed to represent to me all the evils of such cleverness, which values intricately working machinery more than human beings."

"Whatever cleverness I possess, as it were, has been greatly overestimated."

"So I have discovered," said Evangeline. "The resolution I had already vowed, to forgive you upon our next encounter, was made considerably easier by the reports I received just this evening, as to the degree of not just ineptitude but sheer terror that you appear to display when confronted by your father's creations."

My own resolution, vowed at this immediate moment, was to dismantle that accursed Orang-Utan at the earliest opportunity.

"Ineptitude, perhaps." I attempted not to bristle at her comments. "Though I believe *terror* to be putting it a trifle harshly."

"Please don't be angry with me, Mr. Dower." She laid her hand upon my arm, lightly enough to allow the blood to continue to circulate. "For if you had been terrified, it would only cause me to regard you even more highly. For such is my reaction, when I contemplate all these so-called technological wonders that have marched and hissed their way into our world." To my paralyzed surprise, she leaned forward and kissed me on one side of my face, then drew back as though to assess the effect this momentary tenderness had upon me. "Though Captain Crowcroft owns all my heart," she spoke softly, "I have some gentle feeling for you as well. For I have now come to see that you are as much a victim as he is, of all this unrelenting machinery."

I remained silent, oddly touched as I was by Evangeline's confession. I had not led so bleak a life as would render a young woman's kiss, however slight and momentary, completely unknown to me. Yet arriving as that intimacy had now, upon the eve of my advancing years and their concomitant personal decline, the impact was substantial. Another resolution formed inside me, which I also left unspoken to her. I might be a confirmed and aging bachelor, for whom the love of a beautiful young woman such as her could never be realized, but nevertheless: I did not know how I would accomplish it at the moment, I was unsure of how I would accomplish much of anything—but whatever was required to save her *fiancé*, Captain Crowcroft, from the sharp-edged gears of the trap into which the young man had fallen, that I would do.

"Take some comfort from my words." Her evident distress enabled my speech; she had turned from me, attempting to conceal the tear that had coursed from her eye. "However well-founded your apprehensions of the Future, we at least know that nothing more dangerous threatens us, than these clattering, hissing instances of my father's handiwork."

Evangeline turned again toward me, her eyes now wide with astonishment. "How is it possible that you could believe such a thing?"

"Mere logic is the proof," I said calmly. "Of all matters mechanical, my father stood at the pinnacle of human ingenuity. As appalling as his creations are—and I have seen more of them than any other person has—they nevertheless represent the limits of what can be accomplished along these lines. It's obvious that any subsequent technician could do better—or worse, as the case might be."

"Oh! Mr. Dower!" She looked upon me with pity. "There is clearly so much of which you are not yet aware. Has no-one spoken to you of the *Iron Lady*?"

"Such a terms seems familiar," I allowed, "but rather more as an historical reference, than in a context of technological advance."

Evangeline sprang from the seat beside me, her hand shielding her mouth as though to stifle a cry of dismay. I awaited any explanation as to the cause of such high emotion; instead, she turned and fled from the room, abandoning me to my now multiplied perplexity.

CHAPTER

10

Greater Pressure Is Placed
upon Mr. Dower

A YOUNG lady's fretting should not concern you." Stone-brake gazed out the carriage's window as he spoke. "We have matters of more consequence with which to concern ourselves."

"You heard of which she spoke?" To a large degree, I was not surprised. Back at the townhouse from which we had just departed, he had manifested himself immediately upon Evangeline's departure from me, indicating a strong possibility that he had been eavesdropping upon our conversation.

"All of it. And not for the first time." Outside the carriage, the dark city shapes rolled by, swathed in the vapours emitted by the swarming steam pipes. To one with his eyes closed, it might have seemed that we were traveling through some tropical rainforest, so warm and moist was the moonlit air. "Lord Fusible's daughter, despite her many charms, is one of those tiresome individuals who view the Future as some dark pit to which Humanity is madly rushing, in order to throw ourselves upon whatever razor-sharp crags lie below. Attitudes such as that are basically gloomy and unhealthy; you would think that one as young and full of vitality as herself would know better. I ascribe it as the result of reading too many popular and sensational novels, which is a pastime that afflicts many of the coming generation."

As the attitudes derisively attributed to the young woman were in their essence shared by me, I made no comment on them. Instead,

I hazarded a more factual enquiry: "She spoke of some things, of which I confess I am still ignorant—"

"Imagine that."

I let that comment slide by as well. "Specifically," I continued, "there was mention of some entity she named as the *Iron Lady*. It seemed to arouse considerable trepidation in her. Are you familiar whereof she referred?"

"Of course," allowed Stonebrake. He folded his arms across his chest, letting his chin sink toward them. "As would be the raggedest urchin scurrying barefoot through London's gutters."

The surliness of his response caught me unprepared. In our so far brief acquaintance, I had become used to a certain level of enthusiastic spirits on his part, bordering on the maniacal. Before this moment, his mood had seemed as perennially elevated as though he had already laid hands upon those fortunes whose imminent arrival he anticipated. Now he seemed immersed in sullen reflection, the shadows of which clustered about him as though they were personally appointed storm clouds.

"Is there a chance that you might elucidate upon them to me?"

"For God's sake, man." He turned his wrath-filled scowl upon me. "Do you believe it is my responsibility to instruct you in every slight detail of the world? You ask about things which are common knowledge; so common as to be near the province of infants in their cradles." He shook his head, indicating the dismay produced by his contemplation of me. "If you are ignorant of these matters—as well be unaware of the ground beneath your feet!—it is the damnable fault of no-one other than yourself. While you were sequestered in your mouldering little village, you might have raised your head from your slumbers now and again, and surveyed the aspect beyond your window." He sank back into the carriage's seat. "You exhaust me, Dower."

"Very well," I said stiffly. "It had been my belief that we were embarked upon an endeavour that was to be of mutual benefit. Such remarks as you have just made indicate that you have thought better of that effort, and that you regard my continued association with you as being more burdensome than beneficial. So be it. I can easily say farewell to London, and make my own return to those rural haunts I previously frequented."

"Do so, and you are a dead man." Stonebrake's sullen torpor was quickly dispelled, with sufficient force as to allow him to seize the front of my shirt and pull me toward his fierce expression. His eyes narrowed as he spoke through gritted teeth. "We are not engaged upon an enterprise designed for your amusement. Our futures have become tangled with the interests of serious men, who expect a return upon their investment. People such as Fusible and his associates did not become as wealthy as they already are by letting the odd farthing slip through their fingers. It's not a game with them."

"It had not been my assumption that it was." I drew back as far as possible from him. "What makes you believe that I'm not as committed to the enterprise as yourself?"

"Indeed; exactly so." He loosed his choking grasp upon my garments and dropped himself heavily into his portion of the carriage's seat, his anger seeming to have evaporated as quickly as it had come upon him. "You'll have to forgive me, Dower; while you were engaged in conversation with that ridiculous Viscount Carnomere, with his tatty furs and silly notions, I was having a less pleasant conversation upstairs, with Fusible and his friends."

"I gather that it somehow did not go well for you."

"To put it mildly," said Stonebrake. "While his lordship might have displayed an affable *façade* in public, I can assure you that he is considerably less so when encountered in private. It would seem that he and his associates were not as amused by their reception of the various accounts of your dalliances back at Featherwhite House as they had previously portrayed themselves as being."

"My *dalliances*? I'm not quite certain that I know to what you're referring."

"Do I have to spell it out for you? I was trying to be discreet in this regard, in order to spare your feelings. But if everything needs to be rendered explicitly for you, so be it: The subject of their remarks was your recent unfortunate involvement with your father's creation, the steam-powered Orang-Utan."

Again, that miserable beast—or contraption, to be more precise. My mood darkened as I envisioned the device once more.

"Excuse me," I said. "But the damnable thing pressed its attentions upon me, rather than the other way around. I hardly see how I can be held to blame for those events, however sordid they might appear to others."

"Nevertheless," continued Stonebrake, "I was given to understand by Fusible and the others—rather strenuously, I might add—that the accounts, at least in the versions that reached their ears, indicated a paucity of serious intent as far as you are concerned. They have invested a great deal of money into investigating your father's creations, in particular those that have come to be lodged at Featherwhite House; your larking about and making a fool of yourself with one of the machines reflects poorly upon a man of your tenuous position."

"I will endeavour to maintain as much ever present in my mind." My bitterly formed thoughts turned to that which so many poets and sages have remarked upon, as to the fleeting, bubble-like nature of one's reputation in this wicked world. "You keep that hissing ape away from me, and I assure you I will not go seeking it out."

"As you wish." Stonebrake's shrug indicated no great concern over this point. "I would have thought that this was a personal matter between you and the ape, but I'm more than happy to do whatever I can to assist."

"You mock me, sir." I made no effort to conceal my irritation. "Such attempts at levity are distasteful in the extreme."

"You should be glad that I maintain such a level disposition, Dower. All the more so, as our situation is—as I have tried to impart the sense to you—imbued with much greater urgency than before. Not only do our future comforts and pleasures depend upon the successful completion of the enterprise upon which we have launched, but our very lives as well."

"Dear Christ." This latest statement appalled me.

"You might very well say so, but it would be doubtful if we will receive much aid from that ethereal quarter; we are on our own, I am afraid, and we will live or die only by our own efforts."

"How did our situation reach such an extreme condition?"

"As I have already sought to impress upon you," said Stonebrake, "our backers require a return upon their investment—which they impressed upon me, at the *soirée* from which we have just departed, they regard as having already amounted to a considerable sum."

"That would seem to be rather more your doing than mine. I have only recently enlisted in this scheme, the overseeing of which has been your responsibility."

"You draw a finer distinction between ourselves than Fusible and his associates are willing to entertain." Stonebrake pointed a gloved finger toward me. "As far as they are concerned, their expenses have gone into a single pocket, shared jointly by us. That is why your unfortunate antics reflect so poorly upon myself. Like it or not, we will be considered equally to blame for the loss of whatever money they have expended so far. I very likely have had greater experience with the wealthy and powerful than you have had in your life, so you will perhaps have to take it on faith when I inform you that, from what I have witnessed in this fallen world, the more money an individual possesses, the more viciously he holds on to every ha'penny of it. These are people with enormous fortunes, and they are virtually demented on the subject. *And* ready to inflict their wrath upon anyone they come to believe has lightened their wallets to any degree. Vindictive murder is not beyond them, and would be considered merely as an unfortunate but necessary business expense, to forewarn anyone else who might have designs upon the contents of their pocketbooks."

For the moment, I was at a loss to speak. I turned from my unfortunate companion and gazed bleakly at the view of the London streets disclosed through the opposite window. I could see a few hunched-over figures shambling upon their nocturnal errands, the very embodiments of poverty and regret, passing like slow, grimy wraiths through the leaking clouds of steam. As any reasonable persons would, upon finding themselves in my position, I pitied myself more than I did those wretches passing by. They at least were not tormented by the cruel irony I suffered, of having fled the prospect of my own self-destruction, only to greeted by persons willing and capable of putting me in my grave with even greater dispatch. If I were to die, I would just as soon have achieved the state with less inconvenience and embarrassment than I had suffered recently. Much of the sinister glamour of one's own death, and the cessation of the world's continually nagging problems, is abated and the attractive force lessened when it is someone else's finger on the initiating trigger and not one's own.

Was it too late to flee from the city and return to the sheltering obscurity of my foolishly abandoned rural village? The dark streets faded from my thoughts as I pondered the matter. The irrevocable loss of my anonymity, and the dependent nest of my private affairs, seemed to have been accomplished now, with Stonebrake's latest pronouncements merely the epitaph on its headstone. If he were the only person who wished to do me evil, in pursuit of his own mercenary designs, there might have been the possibility of some evading avenue open to me; however, his having brought me to the attention of Lord Fusible and his associates, with their vastly greater resources and vindictiveness, put paid to that notion. For which, of course, there was no-one to blame other than myself. My own cupidity had been the motivator for setting my foot upon this narrowing path; having done so, I had no apparent choice for the moment, except to take the next few steps along it, however dire the likely destination now seemed.

"Very well," I addressed my co-conspirator, having come to my own bleak determination of my circumstances. "It would appear that as a matter of practicality, we are little worse off than we were before. The concerns that Fusible so strenuously expressed to you centered upon the diligence of our pursuing those schemes upon which we are already engaged—did they not?"

"Exactly so," concurred Stonebrake. "It wasn't pleasant."

"There is no doubt in my mind about that," I continued. "You were chastised upon this occasion; likely it will be my turn next, to which I am not looking forward with any great anticipation. The less I have to do with Fusible and that crowd, the happier I will be. Therefore, it would seem the wisest course to ameliorate their fears of financial loss, by applying ourselves with greater determination to that scheme upon which we have already launched ourselves."

"Oh, yes; a bloody marvelous idea, that is." His sullen voice was of a match with his darkened expression. "More easily said than accomplished, I fear."

"How so? You and your associates have already scoured the length of Britain for those previously unearthed creations of my father, amongst which should be found that great *Vox Universalis* device, upon which depend the next stages of your plans. From what I've seen, Featherwhite House is stuffed with the contraptions. As to why you believed that one covered in ratty orange fur and bearing a simian grimace might be the machine for which you search—that is beyond me. But it seems that you merely need to complete your inventory of the devices, rigging them up to the steam pipes and activating them as necessary, and thereby determine which is the *Vox Universalis*. To do so would greatly dispel Fusible's concerns as to where his and the others' money is going, and propel us all toward that wealth which is our goal."

"There's the rub," Stonebrake spoke moodily. "I didn't have Royston and his subordinates work upon that bloody Orang-Utan because I believed its gears and pistons constituted the device we are actually seeking; I had them do so because there are no other of your father's creations left to bring into operation."

"Pardon me?" I blinked at him in befuddlement. "Are you saying—"

"You heard me aright. The ape was the final one of the lot. We have activated all of the other devices, and none of them were any closer to being the *Vox Universalis* than was the Orang-Utan."

"Good Christ." The implications of his statement appalled me. "Did you inform Lord Fusible of this?"

"Of course not. Do you think me an idiot?" Stonebrake shook his head with a scowl. "He and the others voiced their concerns strenuously enough, without me causing them to doubt the eventual outcome of our quest. Their present impatience with the speed at which matters are proceeding would turn to something rather angrier—perhaps fatally so—if they were to determine that their money had been wasted on some wild goose chase, now concluded with no apparent results worth mentioning."

"This is terrible news." Bleaker and bleaker consequences unfolded to my inward vision. "If this is true, then all—" I broke off my words, another realization forming in my thoughts. "Wait; I believe I see now." My companion in the carriage took on a more sinister aspect as I regarded him. "This was known to you before; before you recruited me into your schemes. All that you related to me, in order to induce me to join up with you—all that was based upon a heinous deception."

"You speak harshly." The man apparently had some remaining capacity for shame; he slumped down in the carriage's seat. "I did no more than was necessary."

"Necessary to inveigle me into what I now realize are hopeless complications." My voice grew louder, my heated words expelled with growing force. "That was low of you; I was led to believe that your discovery of the *Vox Universalis* device was imminent, and that as soon as it was in your hands, my involvement in its operation was all that was required to deposit vast fortunes in our hands."

"Your involvement *is* required," Stonebrake maintained steadfastly. "Just not for the purpose I had previously described to you."

"Indeed?" I raised a skeptical eyebrow. "And what other purpose would there be?"

"As I have indicated to you—but certainly not to Fusible and that well-heeled crew—my associates and I have not been able to find that device, created by your late father, which is essential to our plans. I very much doubt that there is a garden shed or lumber-room in all of England into which we have not poked our noses—alas, with no success."

"Have you ever considered that this device, as with many others supposedly issuing from my late father's workshop, no longer exists, if it ever did? I am hardly the first person to have been inconvenienced— indeed, bodily threatened—by one of his dreadful machines. It seems entirely reasonable to me that a number of them were dismantled to their separate parts with the judicious use of a sledge-hammer."

"Such might be the case." Stonebrake's face set grim. "And if that were so, then we are both, to use a term I've overheard from Royston's uneducated mechanics, royally screwed."

I had not heard the precise phrase before, but could divine its ill-omened meaning easily enough. "More so yourself, than I. You were the one who made all those grand assurances to Lord Fusible. The responsibility for their failure would seem to lie upon your shoulders."

"If we were dealing with reasonable men, true; but we are not. Their wrath would extend to anyone who they believed was to the slightest degree involved with their personal embarrassment. You fall within that number."

"That hardly seems fair. I was inveigled into this scheme, as duplicitously as anyone. I am the victim of your base chicanery."

"Perhaps so," said Stonebrake, "but I doubt if you will be allowed to plead your case anywhere short of the afterlife. Whatever the justice of the matter, we are allied in this as in so much else."

Rankled by the man's thorough exposition, I brooded for several moments before speaking again. "As the author of the predicament in which we find ourselves, what then are your thoughts on how we should next proceed?"

"Much as they were when I first enlisted your coöperation." Stonebrake resumed the confident, energetic manner that seemed usual for him, whenever he was expounding his schemes. "As you have reasoned out for yourself, when first I spoke to you there on the Cornish coast, the extremity of my situation was already known to me. While I assured you that my possession of the *Vox Universalis* device was speedily imminent, I was aware that my agents had already come a cropper in that regard. Indeed, that was my motivation in enlisting your aid: not to bring whatever resources you possess as your father's son to the operation of the device, but to find it for us."

"Find it?" I gaped at the other in amazement. "You and your agents have not been able to do so. What makes you believe that such a task is within my abilities?"

"If I were to tell you," said Stonebrake, "that nothing formed this notion beyond sheer desperation, and the lack of any other hope, however small, I would be only halfway honest with you."

"That would be rather more than you had previously been. We are making progress."

"Speak as waspishly as you wish, my dear Dower. Our situation is not altered thereby." He gestured with one wearily upraised hand. "We still have need of your father's *Vox Universalis* machine; therefore I have need of your locating it."

"And how do you propose I should accomplish that?" I pointed beyond the carriage's window to the city's blackened shapes, shrouded in night and clouds of steam. A few human-seeming figures slunk past, intent on their own mysterious errands, or merely wandering in the inward deserts of remorse and inebriation. "Searching about, as though I were some rifle-toting expeditionary on the dark continent, would have been difficult enough for me in the London of my memory. This city has been completely transformed from the one I remember."

"Much of it remains unaltered," said Stonebrake. "The changes you observe are mere surface phenomena."

"Rather more than that, I believe. What seems minor and ephemeral to you are things to which you have become accustomed, all the more so because they came about one little piece at a time. Men can grow used to the greatest abominations, when they are introduced on such a sneaky and incremental basis. I, however, am at a disadvantage regarding the modish world, all hissing and clanking; sequestered as I had been in my rural retreat, I see the changes composing one great mass, almost literally thundering down upon my poor head—as one might view with justifiable apprehension a tidal wave hurling itself upon what had been only a moment before a placid seaside strand, upon which one strolled as upon many previous occasions without such newly arisen dangers."

"You wax philosophical." Stonebrake dismissed my observations with a wave of his hand. "If our present situation was less urgent, I might derive some amusement by passing the hours with such trivial debate. Its relevance seems a little strained at the moment, though."

"Not at all," I protested. "My assessment, of both my own nature and that of today's London, is completely *a propos*. Things being as they are—and you seem to concur by default in my description of them—I fail to see how you could entertain much faith in the notion of my brazenly sailing out into the city's maze of boulevards and alleys, bold adventurer I, and succeed where your more skillful minions failed. Do you propose I should knock on every door in London and enquire, *Dear sir or madam, do you happen to have an enormous talking device on the premises? Might I borrow it for a day or two?* I can well imagine the reception I would receive."

"Perhaps not just London's doors." A corner of Stonebrake's mouth lifted in an unpleasant smile. "The scope of your investigations could be considerably enlarged. Have you considered the possibility that the machine might be anywhere in England?"

"Might have been shipped to the bloody Raj, for all we know." I was nettled by his evident amusement. "If this *Vox Universalis* is capable of conversing with whales, as you believe, it could just as well jabber away in the tongues of the Indian subcontinent. Perhaps you could put the touch on Lord Fusible for funds sufficient to ship me over on the P and O line, and I could wander about wearing a pith helmet, and poking a walking stick into every rude hut while making my enquiries."

"I hope not to put you to such an inconvenience. Due to their mass and delicate complications, evidently few of your father's creations were shipped abroad. And if it is any comfort, I do believe that the one we require is here in London. What references to the machine we have come across in your father's invoices and other documents all indicate that upon its completion it was delivered to somewhere in this city. So the necessity of your traipsing about the wilds of York or Lincolnshire would seem to be slight."

"A pity you don't have the exact street number to which it was conveyed."

"Yes, isn't it?" Stonebrake gave a judicious nod. "The absence of that information raises the suspicion that your father's client, for whom the device was originally designed and constructed, desired some obfuscating secrecy about the matter."

"Given the unseemly nature of so many of my father's creations, such seems reasonable enough."

"Either that," mused my companion, "or the revealing details were destroyed at a later date—perhaps recently—so as to avoid some potential embarrassment to those in whose hands the device has now fallen."

If the continuance or termination of my life at the hands of Lord Fusible and his associates had not become predicated upon finding the *Vox Universalis,* I would have been tempted to regard the device as being best left in the possession of those mysterious personages who might have acquired it.

"Very well," I said. "You are apparently unable to provide me with the slightest clew as to where I would be able to find your precious machine—"

"If I had such a clew, I would have brought it into my grasp already."

"Exactly so. Yet you display a childlike faith in my ability to accomplish that in which you have failed. A conviction so strong that you went to the considerable bother of traveling to the Cornish coast and rousting me from my hiding-place there—"

"And convincing you to take the pistol away from your brow, with which you intended to do away with yourself. Don't forget that."

"I am beginning to think that you did me no favour thereby. Nevertheless, here I am. And you still have not explicated the reasons for your faith in me."

Stonebrake gave a shrug. "I would hardly have thought it necessary to do so. Your past dealings with your father's creations, the history of which I am fully acquainted with, demonstrate the degree to which many of their operations are invisibly connected to the rather softer and subtler machinery you carry up here." He reached over and tapped a forefinger upon my brow. "It is not merely the occultists, with their charts and chanted devotions to hypothesized celestial forces, who believe that the human brain emits ethereal vibrations which can not only be detected, as a precisely adjusted violin string might reverberate to a tuning fork when struck, but also employed for various purposes. Your father knew this to be the case, and mastered the application of this principle in the devices he created."

"A few of them—"

"Perhaps in more than you previously thought. How are you to know the exact number? You were but a babe when he ascertained the exact frequency trembling in your skull, which has remained at the same pitch your entire life, as other men's apparently do as well, from the cradle to the grave."

He raised a sore point with me, upon which I had grudgingly meditated many times before. Whatever filial piety I bore toward the senior Dower was considerably eroded by the knowledge that he used a mere child such as myself, the progeny of his own loins, as a useful implement in his endless mechanical tinkerings. Given the inconvenience it had caused me in my later life, his having done so did not seem an act of paternal fondness.

"I fail to see the application to our present concerns."

"Is it not obvious?" His hand described another rhetorical arc in the carriage's pent air. "The machines respond to you, a vibration to which they are precisely calibrated—as was evidenced by the mechanical Orang-Utan so passionately hurling itself upon you."

"The beast did not do so upon any urging from me, I can assure you. The conjugation it desired was entirely its own idea."

"Give yourself some credit, man. It never responded to anyone else so forcefully."

The tender mercies of Lord Fusible and his associates began to seem less onerous to me. "Leave the steam-powered monkey out of the discussion."

"I am more than happy to. I was merely referring to it by way of illustration. All that I was attempting to impress upon you is the clearly evident fact that your father's creations were designed by him to respond to you. Simple reciprocity would indicate that you respond to them in turn."

The intent of his argument began to dawn upon me. "Am I to understand that you desire to use me as some sort of dowsing stick, similar to those employed by rural witches to locate sources of underground water?"

"Rather so." He nodded. "The principle would be the same, at least."

"If you believe for a moment that I will coöperate with being carried about hand and foot by a crew of your workmen, and prodded toward every door and window in London as though I were some sort of battering ram—"

"That would hardly be necessary," said Stonebrake. "And in fact, ill-advised. Even in London, such a performance would draw comment from bystanders in the street. We still have need for secrecy, if our schemes are to reach fruition."

"Then how is all this to be accomplished?"

"You agitate yourself for no cause. You are perfectly capable of ambulation; a solitary man might stroll about any quarter of London without notice. All that is required is that you locate the *Vox Universalis* device by means of those subtle vibrations to which both you and it are tuned, then report back to Featherwhite House with the information. I wasn't anticipating that you would haul it back to us upon your own shoulders."

"This sounds perilous," I darkly muttered. "Who knows in what seedy district the thing is housed?"

"For God's sake, Dower, steel yourself. Wherever it is, you hardly will be in greater danger there than that in which you already find yourself."

I was reluctant to allow the validity of this point, but did so at last, just as the carriage slowed in its progress, having reached the rusting gates of that dilapidated townhouse to which we had returned.

"You'll see—" Stonebrake's manner was abominably cheerful—easy enough for him!—as he pushed upon the carriage's door. "The entire matter will be simply achieved, and thus we will sail away from the rock-strewn shoals, and toward a calmer and more profitable harbour."

No rejoinder came from me. I followed him toward the unlit doorway, my heart already possessed with an appropriate dread of the morning to come and what it would require from me.

CHAPTER

11

Of Matters Fexual

W E have so been looking forward to making your acquaintance, Mr. Dower."

Sentiments such as these, accompanied by overly widened eyes
and a general manner of rapacious sociability, have often preceded
the most unpleasant moments in my life. While my preference for
a hermit's life, far from the vexing encounters of everyday society,
might be an innate component of my nature, the tendency has been
reinforced over the years by my fellow man's unexcelled ability to
annoy me.

"Indeed?" I found it difficult to form a cogent response. "I can't
imagine why such would be the case."

"*Must* you?" Stonebrake grasped me by the arm and drew me a
few paces away, his whisper seething at my ear. "For God's sake,
man, we are engaged on serious business here. Try not to make the
task any more difficult than it needs to be. These people can assist
us; a trifling amount of courtesy wouldn't go amiss."

I refrained from pointing out that by my personal standards, I
was being courteous. Nothing in my normal inclinations would have
ever brought me into a commercial establishment such as the one in
which we now stood, somewhere upon the more mercantile stretches
of London's Kings Road. When I had been a shopkeeper years before, upon my inheritance of my father's legacy of watches and other
timepieces, I had maintained the premises in the Clerkenwell district

in a subdued and tasteful fashion, befitting the elegant and well-to-do clientele which I had hoped to attract. By contrast, the emporium to which my fellow conspirator, Stonebrake, had bodily dragged me—the first morning after his revelation to me of how desperate were our actual circumstances—seemed to have been modeled upon one of those infamously lurid Parisian *bordellos,* rumoured to be the haunts of those whose wealth enabled them to achieve depths of sensuous debauchery undreamt of by the safely penurious. Great swathes of darkly red velvet, of the oppressive weight from which theatre curtains were ordinarily made, hung from the ceiling's unillumined recesses and obscured every nook and corner. The effect achieved thereby rendered so perceptibly close the space about oneself, that one might as well have been magically inserted into the ruder coloured plates of a physician's gynecological atlas. No daylight penetrated the similarly shrouded windows; my eyes strained to adjust to the murky glow cast by guttering candelabra, placed with ineffectual artfulness about the furniture as though readying the set for the final scene of an amateur dramatic society's Gothic melodrama; all that was required to complete the effect would have been a fetchingly poisoned young woman languishing on top of the eight-foot-long Bechstein grand piano as though it were some accommodating catafalque. The air trapped between the draperies smelt of camphor and old iniquities, depleted of so much of its original oxygen that it might well have been the canary-annihilating atmosphere of an abandoned mine shaft.

Not that the seemingly ancient *accoutrements* appeared to have any depressive effect upon the spirits of Miss Stromneth, our hostess. As Stonebrake conveyed me back to her proximity, her powder-whitened face lit up with even more seemingly inappropriate enthusiasm. I had encountered her sentimental type before, when waiting upon certain eccentric gentry in my watchmaker's shop. In what others, of less crepuscular outlook, found sinister, she took delight; if she could have made her bed in some suitably familial tomb, furnished with the yellowing bones and gap-toothed skulls of ancestors enumerated in *Debrett's Peerage,* she would doubtless have shivered with delight inside her mildew-spotted nightgown. At the moment of my encountering her, however, she was dressed in the somber black of expensive widow's weeds, complete to the faceted jet of the mourning jewelry draped about her pallid neck—I rather doubted that she had been bereaved any time recently, or at all, at least to the degree that she wished to convey.

She picked up the thread of our conversation, just as though the censorious Stonebrake had not whisked me out of her hearing for a moment.

"As to *why*, Mr. Dower—" Miss Stromneth twinkled at me, in a girlish manner appalling in one who was at least a pair of decades removed from her finishing school days. "Surely it's obvious?"

"Not to me." The point of Stonebrake's elbow lodged itself in my ribs. "That is," I corrected myself, "your hospitality exceeds anything to which I, a stranger, thought myself entitled."

"You are too modest. Your fame precedes you; to be known by one's reputation is the surest guaranty of others' friendship and regard, wouldn't you agree?"

"I am sure you are correct." I gave the woman a courteous nod. "Even if my own experience has been somewhat to the contrary."

"That is where you fall into error," said Miss Stromneth. "All your travails—of which I am greatly aware, I may assure you—are merely the result of keeping company with the wrong sort of person. You are made of finer stuff, as are the entirety of the . . . shall we say, 'social circles' which I am fortunate to frequent. And into which, I hasten to assure, you are now most welcome."

I had been afraid of exactly that, though I made no comment that might have indicated my trepidation. Which was based not merely upon the fact that virtually everyone I had met recently seemed to have some sinister designs upon my person, but also upon Stonebrake's assurances to me, upon our morning's departure from Featherwhite House, that the parties to whom he intended to introduce me—he had named Miss Stromneth in particular, but had indicated that there would be others as well—would be of the utmost assistance in the quest upon which we had launched ourselves. To my current set of mind, such knowledge on anyone's part seemed more regrettable than strictly helpful.

"Very kind of you, indeed." I warily eyed the cup of tea that she had poured and set before me. If a comparative innocent such as Lord Fusible's daughter was capable of poisoning someone, however temporarily, God alone knew what might happen in an establishment such as this. "I hope you will not take it amiss if I inform you that I am rather more of a private creature, than a sociable one."

"We can work on that." Eyes half-lidded, Miss Stromneth turned a dismayingly roguish smile in my direction. "In fact, that is rather our speciality here at Fex. Bringing the shy and less . . . shall we say, *experienced* of English society out of the turtle-like shells they so fervently, in their heart of hearts, wish to discard."

"Pardon me—but what was that you said?"

"Turtles," elaborated the woman before me. "They are very much like turtles, don't you feel? Reclusive and guarded, as it were, their innate defenses preventing the embrace of their desires—"

"No, not that." I had heard as much before; the discretion which maddened reformers such as Miss Stromneth lamented— continuously and tiresomely—had always struck me as one of the more admirable features of our species. "That word—what did you call this place?"

"Oh!" She brightened, features illuminated as though lit by a sudden combustion of animal spirits. "*Fex,* of course."

"What the devil does that mean?" A spark of irritation flashed inside me. "I have never heard the term."

"Why, Mr. Dower, it is the name of this establishment. We endeavour to present all that we do in as comfortable and even homey a manner as possible—and I like to believe that we succeed in that to a considerable degree—but at its heart this is a commercial enterprise. However high-minded, we all must make a living. You've been a member of the trade; surely you understand."

"But not of *this* trade." I glanced about at the lurid, over-stuffed furnishings, suggestive as they were of blushing flesh and carnal vices. "I sold the occasional watch—and not many of them, I confess. My suspicion is that your customers have needs other than the mere ascertaining of the time of day."

"Indeed they do," said Miss Stromneth. "And in that, may a bountiful God bless and keep them. And not just for putting a few coppers in the till. Here at Fex, we amuse ourselves with the pretension that our work is not just mercenary, but *missionary* in purpose. Our clientele is bettered by having engaged our services—in a spiritual manner, we like to think."

This comment evoked a raised eyebrow even from Stonebrake, who had been idly diverting himself with the examination of a mechanical songbird, kept under a glass dome on the chamber's mantelpiece. He had found the minuscule key required and had wound the device's mainspring thereby, but no amount of prodding with a fingertip stirred the feathered creature sitting on its cast-iron branch. Disappointed, he returned his attention to the conversation unfolding nearby.

"Didn't you see the sign, Dower?" He gestured toward one of the windows, hidden behind heavy layers of damask and brocade. "As we came up the street—I wouldn't have thought that it could be any more obvious."

In fact, I had. Above the brougham, an ominous green radiance had penetrated the rising clouds of steam. Peering out, I had perceived the outlines of three enormous capital letters, illuminated from within by the same arrangements of flaring gas jets and faceted mirrors employed in Phototrope Limited's ambulating lighthouses. The word, if such it was, had been erected higher than any of the surrounding rooftops, as the cupola of an Arabian mosque might overlook all in the vicinity, the better to command the attention of its devotees. Not yet aware of its meaning, I had dismissed the phenomenon as just one more mysterious feature of the transformed London to which I had returned.

"We *do* like our clients to be well directed," simpered Miss Stromneth. "Not all of them have the advantage of a knowledgeable escort upon their first visit to us. Despite our reputation—which seems more bandied about with the passing of every day; for which we are grateful, of course—there are still those who pretend to be unaware of our very existence. Which hampers them, when the day comes in which they wish to avail themselves of our services, and they are the victims of their prior reluctance to learn our address."

The repetition of the term *services* aroused the direst presentiments within me. Visions were evoked, of procedures more clinical than sensual—or even enjoyable—in nature.

"My apologies, Dower." At the mantelpiece, Stonebrake replaced the glass dome over the uncoöperative thrush. "I have again underestimated the degree of your ignorance about the modern world. Somehow I had been of the impression that even in your muddy little village, the details of an enterprise as salacious as this one would have penetrated. Were the engines of rumour, pushed along by your local gossip-mongers, as inert as all that? It seems scarcely credible."

"Believe whatever you wish." I felt compelled to defend my rural outpost. "Not everybody in the world is as obsessed with their procreational appendages as are city-dwellers. You lot seem positively obsessed with these matters."

"Procreational?" Miss Stromneth frowned in puzzlement, then regained her characteristic good humour when simple understanding manifested itself. "Oh, you mean *genitalia*."

"If you must." I could feel every bone of my spine lock into place, knit by instinctive revulsion. Would there be no end to this new world's rudeness? The woman had spoken as easily as one might have regarding the blossoming of the flowers in spring. "I had hoped to avoid such unpleasantries."

"No need for that!" Stonebrake interjected with oppressive heartiness. "We are all adults here. And of course, nowadays even the smallest prattling children are familiar with subjects that might dismay one of your innocence."

"Of that, I have no doubt." I had noted the conspiratorial wink passing between him and Miss Stromneth. "You obviously feel compelled to acquaint me with exactly that of which I would have preferred to remain ignorant. As I apparently have no choice in the matter, so be it. Proceed as you will." I spoke as one might when lying upon a surgeon's table, with a well-honed knife posed above one's abdomen. Though in my case, the operation was designed to place a loathsome matter within me, rather than pluck it from my malfunctioning bowels. "The only consideration I would ask of you is that you do so with as much abbreviation as possible; not only is the span of my attention limited, but the degree of my tolerance as well."

"As you wish." The other man spoke with lofty disdain for the feelings I had expressed. "You are not so dull of wit, Dower, that you have failed to discern the essential nature of this business establishment—"

"Shall I freshen your cup?" Miss Stromneth leaned toward me, a flowered Limoges pot in her hands. "You've hardly touched it."

"That's kind of you—" My initial suspicions had still not abated. "But I'd rather you didn't."

"As I was saying," continued Stonebrake, "the needs and desires of the customers who are catered to here, as a matter of commerce, are familiar in some degree to you. I would like to believe that I am correct in assuming as much."

"Assume as you please." I raised my shoulders in a dismissive shrug. "I wish I could say that I wasn't aware of what goes on in places such as this, and the low vices that are indulged for the exchange of money—"

"Oh, come, Mr. Dower." The twinkling smile from Miss Stromneth indicated that she was no more nettled by my comments than if I had pointed out the dust beneath the settee on which she perched. "It's not as bad as all *that*."

"You profit thereby." I spoke sternly, and perhaps even a little ungentlemanly. "You are hardly a disinterested party to the goings-on."

"Yes, but it all seems so *jolly* in the moment." She blithely disregarded my sermonizing. "Everyone seems to be having such a good time—it would seem rather a shame not to let them do it. And they don't appear to mind paying for their pleasures—but then again, the particular clientele here at Fex all have absolute *scads* of loot. I am sure they don't miss any of it a bit."

"That is hardly the issue." Something in the easy *bonhomie* permeating the room had ignited a reformer's fire in my breast; I might as well have been ranting from atop a wooden box at Speaker's Corner in Hyde Park. "These people are degraded enough as it is; you are facilitating them in the process of becoming even more so."

"Well, they do seem rather *intent* in that regard." The woman struck a thoughtful pose with a fingertip placed prettily to her chin. "I mean, even before they arrive on our doorstep here. That rather indicates to me that if we didn't accommodate them in their desires, they'd likely find someone else who would. And perhaps that other one would not possess the same high ethical standards as we do."

"I doubt if the word *ethics* is one that many people would employ in this regard." I shook my head in dismay. "You may eulogize your business however you wish—and likely there are others who would agree with you, or at least pretend to, for reasons of their own—but if there were still high-minded organizations such as the Society for the Prevention of Carnal Vice going about their work, this newly energized London might not seem quite so demonic."

"Ah, yes, the fine Mrs. Trabble and her do-gooders. I rather miss them." She spoke with more evident nostalgia than rancour. "That was *such* a long time ago! Though of course, I tend to remember her by the other name she went by then: Mollie Maud."

"As I'm sure Dower recalls her as well," Stonebrake drily added. "He had his own encounters with the woman, in both her guises."

"Yes, I do believe I heard something about all that." Miss Stromneth gazed upon me with a refreshed avidity. "It was one of the reasons I was so looking forward to making your acquaintance, in a rather more sedate manner. You'll have to forgive me, if I cannot yet place you amongst my treasured reminiscences. I was but a mere slip of a girl back then."

"You worked for her?" I instinctively recoiled.

"Which? Mrs. Trabble the reformer, or Mollie Maud the procuress?"

"Either."

"The latter, actually. Though not as I'm sure you're imagining, you *dog*." Her manner grew even more effusively cheerful, as a lamp might increase its glow by lengthening its wick. "I was a timid, scholarly little creature then—wouldn't have said *Boo!* to a goose, as the saying goes—but cast adrift on the currents of an unsolicitous world by the inconvenient deaths of my parents. Good with numbers, though—and still am—so I considered myself fortunate to wind up keeping the accounts for Mrs. Trabble's various enterprises, both respectable and otherwise. At the beginning, I thought it rather notable as to how many of the same persons of good society I encountered in both spheres—in one ledger book I would inscribe the amount of a worthy gentleman's donations paid to virtuously combat the identical practices that in another ledger I marked as services received by the same individual!" She shook her head in a display of mock exasperation. "At one time, I made the suggestion to Mrs. Trabble—or Mollie; we had become such dear friends by then—that the accounts would be greatly simplified if we merely had patrons make payment for both suppression and enjoyment at the same time, with just one cheque drawn upon their banks. To her credit, as a businesswoman she saw the logic in my proposal—but she clung to the old ways, sentimentalist that she was. Working both sides of the street, one might say. It must have made some sense to her, to at least pretend that her right hand didn't know much if any of what her left hand was up to."

I confess I experienced some fleeting relief at Miss Stromneth's biographical exposition, learning thereby that she had not been an actual member of the piscine stable of harlots that the notorious Mollie Maud had set combing through the streets of East London, in search of degenerates both moneyed and jaded of normal pleasures. Her mercenary attitude might have been similar to that of the "green girls," but the absence of those ichthyic details in her features had caused me to doubt the integrity of what I remembered concerning them.

"But all that is neither here nor there," continued Miss Stromneth, "when we address ourselves to the present day's concerns." With a slighter smile, of the sort that she herself would likely have acknowledged as foolish, she wiped the tear of fond remembrance from her eye with a silken handkerchief. "Why speak of the past, when it is the present world of which you seek knowledge?" She brought herself up straighter, leaning above the tea things and toward me. "Your good friend Mr. Stonebrake—"

"He is my business associate."

"No need to quibble; we are *all* friends here. When he spoke but a moment ago, he said that you were of course aware of the nature of this establishment—*to some degree.* One would have to be rather a dunce not to have deduced as much, as soon as one had walked through the door. But you remain ignorant of its *entirety.*" Tilting her head, Miss Stromneth gazed up through her eyelashes at me, her smile once again wickedly confiding. "That is where you have a few surprises as yet unrevealed. Give me your hand, Mr. Dower—oh, *do.* There is no need to be shy; I won't hurt you."

"For God's sake, don't be all day about it." Stonebrake's voice prodded me from his station at the mantelpiece. "Time advances, even if we do not."

Against my better judgement, I allowed my upraised hand to be captured between both of Miss Stromneth's. Her smile broadened as she laid my palm against the embroidered bodice of her gown.

"There," she said. "How does that feel to you, Mr. Dower?"

"Good God—" My immediate reaction was to snatch my hand away from this unexpected proximity, as though I had come into contact with a roaring stove. Literally—the heat radiating from her bosom would have been enough to set a kettle boiling. With a surprisingly forceful grasp upon my wrist, she prevented me from escaping the fiery sensation. "What is the meaning of—"

"Oh, *bother* meaning." Perceptible through the heightened temperature, the pulse of her heart accelerated. "We are in the realm of the sensations now; how pointless to chase after mere logic!"

"You very likely believe that to be the case—" I struggled to free myself, at risk of capsizing the table at my knees and the tea service upon it. "But I am of a differing opinion."

Miss Stromneth unexpectedly let go, allowing me to fall backward; I scarcely managed to retain my balance. Regarding her with increasing dismay, I watched as she reached behind herself to undo some tiny fastening at the back of her gown.

"Ah! That is ever more comfortable!"

I had closed my eyes, expecting the worst.

"Pay attention—" With a flattened hand, Stonebrake clopped me in the back of the head. "This is why we are here."

"Don't be afraid, Mr. Dower." The woman's voice was all solicitous and kind. "There's always a first time."

"I would rather it were the last." What remained of my discernment now lay in shards about my equally fragmented power of will. "But that doesn't seem to be up to me—"

"Indeed not." The cunning amusement was audible in her voice. "Which is precisely that for which our customers pay."

Opening my eyes, I beheld first her smile and now wildly licentious gaze, fastened upon me as some predator of the African plains might survey a trembling gazelle. From there, my perception expanded to include the bared flesh of her arms and shoulders, revealed by the discarding of the gown that now lay puddled about her feet. She stepped backward, a kick from one of her equally disinhibited legs launching the garment across the teapot and into my lap.

"You see?" If anything, the woman was even more relentlessly cheerful. "Nothing is ever so bad as one fears."

It seemed less than chivalrous to argue the matter, given Miss Stromneth's state of *déshabillé*. In addition, I was distracted by what seemed to be the sound of a nest of snakes that had been subtly introduced to the room in which I sat. Previously, I had thought the sibilant noise to be nothing more than that emitted by some iron apparatus employed to bring the chamber to a pleasant temperature. My dismay over the situation in which I found myself vaulted to a crisis as I realized that the hissing sounds came from the constricting undergarment in which Miss Stromneth's torso was encased.

"Don't fret yourself," she cooed. Having stepped around to my side of the low table, she fondly stroked my hair. This close to the combined radiance of her skin and the steam-powered corset cinched about it, I felt as though I were positioned beside a blacksmith's forge, newly enflamed by a hearty application of the bellows. "Consider the economy of the matter."

"Pardon me?" I had no earthly idea whereof she spoke.

"Others have paid, for that which you enjoy *gratis*." She performed the gesture of a theatrical impresario, her outspread hands raising her snowy bosom to greater prominence. "Count yourself fortunate, Mr. Dower."

"Small chance of that." From behind me, Stonebrake spoke with a sour intonation. "Given how little interest he displays in the, ahem, *finer* things this world affords, I've begun to wonder upon exactly what he will spend the riches he is engaged in securing."

The exchange between the two provided me with an uninterrupted moment, which I employed in scrutiny of Miss Stromneth's abbreviated garment, my interest being more technical than lustful in nature. If the darkly glistening corset were one of my father's inventions, it was of a variety previously unknown to me. I could see now that much of its elaborate construction comprised thin India rubber tubes, interconnected with small brass fittings, a few studded with pressure gauges complete with trembling black needles upon their glass-covered dials, the whole laced tightly about her ribs and abdomen. With each breath she managed to take—requiring some deliberate effort on her part, given the unrelenting compression forced upon her—small jets of steam vapour shot from various apertures. A braided hose of slightly greater diameter trailed from a mechanical juncture at the small of her back, tethering her to a motive source in a farther room of the house. Alerted to its existence, I could now detect the sighing and hissing noises emitted by the entire assemblage.

"Have a pity for the innocent," chided Miss Stromneth. By her easy manner, she seemed accustomed to engaging in conversations while less than fully clad. "It's hardly poor Mr. Dower's fault if he's unacquainted with such things. It's not as if Fex has set up branch operations in every English village. Though upon further reflection . . ." She gazed up at the room's ornately plastered ceiling, then nodded slowly. "It's not such a bad idea. Given that we expect an influx of capital from our participation in the matters under discussion. I will have to suggest it to senior management."

The woman's last comment took me by surprise. "It had been my impression," I said, "that you were the proprietor of this establishment."

"Heavens, no." An uplifted hand airily dismissed the notion. "Merely a trusted employee. It is the entrepreneur Duncan MacDuff— such a visionary!—in whose business concerns I am engaged. It is he and his distaff companion who have created all this you see about us."

I frowned, my thoughts piqued by the memory of having heard that name before. At last I recalled that it had been spoken to me by Stonebrake himself, in reference to the financing of the Mission to the Cetaceans' sea-going ministry.

"The enterprise has grown to such fiscal dimensions over the last few years," continued Miss Stromneth, "that those who commenced its operations must now bend their efforts to ever higher levels of society—some of whom might surprise you, were I to reveal their names and positions."

"Nothing," I vouchsafed, "surprises me anymore."

"I am sure we could put that to the test." She spoke with a renewed mischievous delight. "Do you believe I didn't notice your reaction to my own *ensemble*?" The fingertips of one hand traced delicately across the hissing tubes of her corset. "Of course, I would wish to flatter myself that the degree to which your eyes widened was due to a normal man's salacious interest in a woman's bared and bound flesh, but alas, it is only too well-known to me that I am no longer as young and fair as the latest to be hired by our business."

"Don't be too hard on yourself." Stonebrake offered a chivalrous protest. "You're still an extremely attractive specimen of your gender."

"How kind of you to say so." A sweetly tender smile was bestowed upon her defender, before she turned back to me. "Whether your friend's assessment is true or not, what remains incontestable, Mr. Dower, is that your discomfiture was occasioned by that which in fexual terms would be considered rather mild and modest—"

"Pardon me?" The one word had snared my attention, if not comprehension. "What is meant by *fexual*—I'm afraid that's one more item with which I'm unacquainted."

"You have my apologies. I forget that one of your apparent education and polished manners might not be as familiar as I am—or virtually any other modern-day Londoner—with what has become our common currency of discourse. Though I do suppose that there are likely a few elderly and shut-in residents who have not kept up on the latest developments in human desires. After all, it wasn't *that* many years ago, when the Fex establishment had not yet even come into commercial existence, and the word and its derivatives introduced to our English language. So rapidly has our vocabulary increased, it would be difficult for even the most assiduous of lexicographers to keep up, just with our contributions. Who could have foreseen that even the simple word *fex* would come to denote not just our humble little endeavour, but a whole new world of carnal delight?"

"Who, indeed."

Miss Stromneth's smile continued, but her eyes narrowed with the perception of my dry sarcasm. "Jest if you wish, Mr. Dower, but the facts are unassailable."

"If you say so, I'm sure it is true." I raised my hands to indicate my helplessness before the rhetorical onslaught. "Why would I cavil as to a word's meaning, when I am ignorant of even its etymology?"

"Oh, that's simple enough. I hope you haven't been tormented by as simple a question as that."

"Likely not," came Stonebrake's interjection. "Given how many other things Dower finds to worry about."

"Allow me to provide it to you in a nutshell." Miss Stromneth bent down, bringing her darkly constricted bosom to the level of my sight, in order to pat me comfortingly upon the hand. "As our world changes—as it must!—so too does our language, which is the tool used by our minds to grasp hold of that transmogrified world, to turn it about and examine it, to make sense of it. Does that seem too abstract a notion for you?"

"Perfectly understandable." Indeed, I thought reflections such as these all more or less twaddle, but refrained from saying so. "Pray, proceed."

"So with this word which intrigues you, and its derivatives . . ." she continued in her schoolmistress fashion, the effect rendered somewhat more captivating by her lack of outer garments. "As I am sure you have already noted, the present day's inhabitants are possessed and obsessed, as it were, with the advent of *Steam*." She spoke with exactly such emphasis as might the devotee of some outlandish foreign cult, waving a gold-bangled arm in the direction of its vaporous idol. "There was the world before—a poor, trudging sort of place, unaided muscles straining against every weight placed upon them—and now this one that has been revealed to us. In which every effort is multiplied and enhanced with this new force, and accomplishment is only limited by imagination and desire, and the degree to which one dares to incorporate this hissing spirit into the essence of one's being!"

"Yes . . . of course. Fascinating." I attempted to shrink back into the sofa as far as I could, not from any aversion to her naked skin, glistening with either ladylike perspiring or condensation from the various heated emissions from her elaborate corsetry, but rather from aversion to her maniacal gaze. Her eyes had widened even further, the coy cheerfulness exhibited before by her now replaced by something rather more intimidating. "As you say, this has come to my attention."

"You see only the surface phenomena." Miss Stromneth brought her dampish hand to my brow and rested it there. "As one might, who watches the waves ripple across a sheltered cove, and believes thereby that he knows the ocean entire. But—" She locked her fervent gaze with my rather more appalled one. "There are depths yet unknown to you. No doubt you regard my present state as somewhat extreme." Having drawn her hand away, she traced her fingertips down the trembling elements of her exposed undergarment. "Do you not?"

"It's not," I allowed, "the sort of thing that I have encountered before."

"I rather expected such to be the case. Which is, of course, half the amusement to be derived." She rested her hands upon her glistening hips. "But this—I assure you, my dear Mr. Dower—is nothing. Compared to those others, of whose existence I had intimated to you. My allegiance to *Steam*—" Once more, that oddly inflected emphasis. "Is, I confess, less apostle-like than that maintained by its more faithful adherents. I derive my living from an aspect of it; surely that convicts me of . . . which sin is it?" She frowned, briefly musing. "Simony, I believe it is."

"You would be better off enquiring of Mr. Stonebrake." I pointed to my companion beside the mantelpiece. "He has more of an ecclesiastical background than I do."

"The benefits of this world," he observed, "are of more interest to me than the punishments of the next."

"Then we have nothing to fear, do we?" Miss Stromneth resumed her previous cheerful manner. "Our wickedness is but a trifle now, thanks to the modern world. For if we have become enthusiasts for that which emerges from the steam mines in the north of England, we are hardly likely to be discomfited by finding ourselves in a deeper and hotter place, after we have been laid in our graves."

Once more, the conversation had veered onto what I judged to be a demented course. I wondered if perhaps the hissing and seething corset had produced a deleterious effect upon the balance of the woman's mind, as though the heat had transferred to her blood and been sufficient to poach the contents of her skull.

"You said there were others? Of a nature that I would somehow find even more impressive?" I attempted to steer her attention back to the matters from which she had digressed. "I find that difficult to believe."

"Oh, you have no *idea*, Mr. Dower. But you will! Given the elite circles into which you have just begun to set your feet. The wealthy are different from you and me—and the fabulously wealthy are fabulously so. The whole world, or at least the British species, adores *Steam*. They would eat and drink it if they could—and why not?—

and sleep upon billowing clouds of its vapours, if they could but knot their bedsheets around them. Would that not be Heaven?"

"A charming notion, indeed." The woman's enthusiasms continued to frighten me. "You must think about it a great deal."

"Not so much. If there were a way to generate a profit thereby, I might—but otherwise my interest is markedly less than that expressed by other people. *They* are the real enthusiasts! But, alas, for so many the world is not constructed as kindly as it is for the rich and powerful. The abilities of most people to indulge their fancies is confined by the meagerness of their pocketbooks. A few ill-manufactured contraptions, boilers and compressors and copper tubes, clanking pistons, snag-toothed gears grinding against one another—" She shook her head in dismay. "Scarcely a day goes by here in London, in which some tenement or other shabby hovel is not exploded to flinders by a malfunctioning steam-powered device, the mere possession of which had served as some scribbling law-clerk's or seamstress's testament and shrine to this, their new faith, supplanting the puny prayer-books and flickering votary candles of former beliefs. Indeed, these incendiary events happen so frequently that they go virtually uncommented upon by either the mundane press or the city's appointed keepers of public order. But if you take the time to listen carefully—" She cupped a hand to one ear and inclined herself toward the nearest of the shrouded windows. "You can hear them, off in the distance or as close as the neighbouring building, one after another . . . all through the day and the night . . ."

So evocative was her description of this auditory phenomenon, I imagined that I heard—or did in fact—a muffled, repeated boom traveling through the unseen streets, as though from the cannons of a besieging army that had managed to set itself up in Londoners' drawing-rooms, or what was left of them after Miss Stromneth's adored *Steam* had finished its destructive work.

"Poor sods," observed Stonebrake. "Rather gone off the deep end, one might say. Victims of their own enthusiasms."

"Well, I'm hardly one to be censorious in that regard." Miss Stromneth took her teacup from the table and daintily sipped from it. "If people weren't so ridden by their fancies, I and the rest of the staff here at Fex would be out on the streets instead. We pay our rent from others' follies."

"I would think you have more at stake than mere finances." Her comment had evoked another raised eyebrow from me. "Your mode of dress—or undress, as the case might be—indicates some degree of enthusiasm on your own part."

"Oh, Mr. Dower, there is—as I said before—*so* much of which you are unaware. This—" She laid both hands upon her corseted midriff. "This is but mere surface phenomena, as your scientific friends in the Royal Society might describe it. Something which can be discarded at a moment's whim—"

"Please; don't—"

"Have no fear. I perceive your discomfiture. That, too, is something which can be addressed when your own finances are at that higher tide you anticipate. All good things come in time. At this moment, however, all I wished to impart to your understanding was that my participation in this, as you have termed it, 'enthusiasm' is very minor indeed, compared to those who have both greater passion for it—*and* the monetary resources to indulge what can be a rather expensive taste."

"Which is, I presume, the custom you serve here. At Fex."

"Exactly so! To everyone's satisfaction, I have been assured."

"I rather hope," spoke Stonebrake, "to ascertain such facts for myself."

"Rest assured, you would be most welcome." Miss Stromneth tilted her head to direct her roguish smile at him. "Along with your ample bank account."

"Please . . ." I attempted by main force to drag the conversation back to a more productive channel. "You indicated but a moment ago that there was some hidden—or at least hidden to *me*—significance to the monosyllabic name of this enterprise. At this point, I would be satisfied myself, to know that much."

"That? Simple enough, Mr. Dower—though I estimate that it

would require a deal more to *satisfy* a manly specimen such as yourself."

I held my silence. The woman seemed fixated on unseemly things.

"Consider the surgeon, if you will."

"Pardon?" That comment's approach had not been foreseen by me. "I'm not quite sure what is meant . . ."

"A *surgeon*," Miss Stromneth. "A man of medicine, who employs a scalpel in the performance of his craft. You are aware, I'm sure, that are some such, who cut and trim not because their patients' lives might be endangered by some awkward growth lodged in their tissues, but rather on behalf of some vanity conceived in their thoughts?"

"Certainly—though why scars and stitches, however minor or well-concealed, would be considered attractive is a matter beyond my comprehension."

"*De gustibus non est disputandem,* Mr. Dower—an observation from the ancients, the truth of which I know better than most."

"It seems," I observed, "to have been adopted as the exculpatory motto of this new, ever-accommodating society."

"Regardless," she continued, "there is no disputing that if a person desired such services, and had the means to pay for them, it would have been to just such a skilled doctor the person would have turned. Now consider a pipe-fitter."

"Why?" The discourse had again veered onto an unexpected tangent. "What does that—"

"Just do," chided Miss Stromneth. "Indulge me for a moment. Surely it would seem equally obvious to you that individuals skilled in the juncturing of pipes, the securing of one to another so that their contents, however forceful, are channeled to the desired point—such individuals would be uniquely prized and rewarded in this, our world transformed by *Steam*?"

"Now that you mention it . . ." The possibility seemed logical enough. "I am sure they are."

"Thus we progress. Now imagine, as I expect you are capable, that certain wealthy individuals, who in previous duller times might have indulged their vanity by employing a scalpel-wielding surgeon, now wish to incorporate their enthusiasm for all things Steamy into their very bodies, their flesh and blood."

"What a ghastly notion."

"Please refrain from judgement, Mr. Dower. Money buys one a great deal of indulgence in this world; that is why people, including yourself, seek its possession. That which is considered rashly mad, even criminal, when practiced by the impecunious—acquires an ample if perhaps somewhat eccentric nobility when indulged in by the rich. Continue with your imagining, based on that principle. Which would such a wealthy, impassioned individual require for the fulfillment of his desires—a surgeon skilled in slicing through the soft and spongy tissues of the human body, or a fitter with the knowledge sufficient for coupling pipes and junction boxes so that the desired *Steam* would be steered to its appropriate destination?"

"I suppose such desires would call upon the services of both specialists."

"Yes! Exactly so." Miss Stromneth clasped her hands before the swell of her partially revealed bosom. "And thus our enterprise here at Fex has thrived. As in earlier days, when the proprietors of certain discreet establishments—such as my dear, now departed mentor, Mollie Maud—brought a grateful clientele into contact with those who could provide satisfaction to their desire, so do I and my staff, at the direction of our senior management, achieve the same result for a new but just as fortunate set of customers. In rather an augmented fashion, of course; such are the blessings of these new forces and contrivances that men as clever as your father have unleashed upon a submissive world. As in this case, with the establishment of the entire concept and dependent institution of *ferric sex.*"

Of all the things of which the woman had spoken, this sounded the worst.

"It only seems distasteful," continued Miss Stromneth, "upon first encounter." She had perceived my poorly disguised revulsion.

"But as I am sure your own experience has been with fleshly plea-sures, further acquaintance leads to not just acceptance, but even enthusiasm, of exactly those things from which one had first shrunk in horror."

"That might be the course of events," I allowed, "with those ac-tivities that are necessary for the continuation of the species. But such is Nature's cruel wisdom; our kind would have died out long ago if we had no innate, brutish capacity for those private activities which our higher selves regard as indecorous."

"Thanks be to a merciful Providence for *that*." She spoke with renewed cheer. "Otherwise I would be out of business, and Fex's senior management would be hard-pressed to eke out a living from an ironmonger's shop."

"Which would have seemed to be their appropriate calling in this world, or at least in what it used to be." Belatedly, I had man-aged to form a strategy for remaining abreast of her continuous string of revelations: I merely had to envision the least likely and most repellent possibility, and it would very likely be the next thing imparted to me. "Propagating the species is one matter, and if the means of doing so are on the unseemly side, it becomes more duty than pleasure. So be it—but I rather doubt that this notion of ferric sex qualifies in that regard. No doubt you and your customers have found some way of indulging your mania for *Steam*—" Her odd man-ner of emphasizing the word had crept into my own speech. "With those biological proclivities with which they were born. 'Ferric' be-ing the descriptor for metals such as iron, I can only assume that this is the well-spring of all your talk of surgeons and pipe-fitters en-abling the wishes of your esteemed clientele."

"Clever lad," muttered Stonebrake from behind me. "How can we fail, with one such as you on our side?"

"You have seized upon it in a trice, Mr. Dower!" Upon setting her cup down, Miss Stromneth clapped her hands together in delight. "Exactly so! Thank *God* for rich people, who have already jaded themselves through the satiation of those tastes they share with the less enabled rabble, so that it requires virtually no inducements at all to convince them to fling off the restraints of *Nature,* and not just embrace *Science,* but incorporate its seductions into their very being!"

"These are people with more money than brains, of which you speak."

"Thus we progress," she answered primly. "Common sense is but an anchor which keeps us mired in the shoals of existence. Our clientele has hoisted sail for those shores of experience which lie beyond the farthest horizons of possibility."

To myself, I thought it rather likely that the woman's clients would dash themselves to pieces upon those shores, as misguided ships did upon the rocks of that Cornish coast from which I had recently fled. But I kept silent upon that point.

"And thus this . . . whatever it is . . ." I gestured about the room and its opulent fixtures, as though they somehow signified all upon which we had discoursed. "This thing called *Fex*—both concept and commercial establishment."

"Well, yes—though it's rather difficult to say which came first." Miss Stromneth waxed philosophical, as was her occasional wont. "It's my recollection, however, that our senior management—bless their hearts! *and* their business acumen—desired a name for the enterprise, the alluring brevity of which would encompass all the power of that to which it pointed. In retrospect, it seems rather an obvious coinage, from 'ferric sex' to 'fex'—but are not all such strokes of genius marked by a seemingly inevitable simplicity?"

"Very clever, I am sure. Little wonder that you've done so well."

"As I indicated before, Mr. Dower—you have no idea. Those wealthy personages with whom you've recently consorted—the Fusibles and their lot, and no doubt others—they are but negligible in this grand transformative scheme. Oh, they know what they're about, all right—but their plots and maneuvers are on a smaller scale. Not that I'm belittling your own involvement with them, of course."

"Of course," I politely echoed.

"But there are others, of greater wealth, greater power, whose headlong leap into the fexual world has wrought such changes upon them, that one might scarcely regard them as human now."

"Hm." I shifted uncomfortably upon the settee. "Is being less than human actually a desirable state?"

"I did not say *less*, Mr. Dower. This is perhaps why the great spiritual leaders have commanded us to *Judge not*—so that we might see things as they are, and have become, rather than with our otherwise clouded perceptions."

"Perhaps." Another point over which I felt it was not worth arguing. Such was my general tendency toward matters religious. "If you say it is so, I am perfectly willing to take it on faith."

"You needn't." The woman stepped closer to me, so that I needed to tilt back my head to its farthest extreme in order to view her face. "There is nothing of which I speak, that I cannot prove to you."

This near to her, the heat radiated from the steam-powered corset commanded my senses, the hissing vapours seeming as portentous as storm clouds massing in the distance, lit sharply by flickering lightning. My own breath laboured in my throat, just above my accelerating heart.

"Would you like me to do that, Mr. Dower?" She reached down and stroked my hair. "Do you desire proof? Or more?"

I could not answer her. Suddenly, the room seemed vastly larger, and I lost within it.

My empty teacup shattered on the low table as though it were an egg-shell, as she brushed it from my compliant hand—the better to seize that hand in her own soft one and pull me will-less to my feet.

"We shall return," she assured Stonebrake, "in but a moment. This won't take long."

As a captive linnet tethered to a street vendor's thread, I allowed her to lead me to the chambers that lay deeper in the house of Fex.

CHAPTER
12

*A Dreadful Consummation
Is Achieved*

I THOUGHT it remarkable that someone would have a train station in their house.

"It's only a *small* one," Miss Stromneth replied to my observation. Anticipating the cooler temperature of the high-ceilinged space to which I had been escorted, she had acquired a Japanese *kimono* along the way, to serve as an exotic dressing gown. Beneath its sash and silken cherry-blossom pattern, the steam-powered corset continued to hiss. "And actually, for us here at Fex, it is more of a business expense than an amenity."

"Nevertheless—" Standing at the entrance to the platform, I gazed up at the spanning ironwork, oddly reminiscent of Victoria Station's dark, cathedral-like spaces. "I would not have anticipated that you have such a volume of clientele, that a dedicated rail spur was necessary to receive them all."

"Scarcely the reason, Dower." From the parlour, Stonebrake had sauntered along behind us, stepping over the pliant steam-hose trailing from beneath the hem of Miss Stromneth's Oriental gown. "The customers arrive here however they wish; their wealth affords transportation we can scarcely imagine. And for some of them, their requirements are . . . *unusual*." With a gesture of his hand, he directed my attention to the iron tracks and other industrial details. "But this has all been installed here for their enjoyment, as it were, while partaking of those specific services provided by the establishment."

"Once more," I spoke, "you have exceeded my imagination. I have no idea of what is meant by that."

"Oh, but you shall." Miss Stromneth took my arm. "Let us retire to a more . . . shall we say, *discreet* location, from which our regard will discomfit no-one."

A rackety spiral staircase, its iron treads clanking beneath our feet, brought us to an elevated chamber, scarcely large enough to accommodate the three of us. From its unlit windows, concealed behind a bolted lattice, we could vertiginously look down upon the platform we had left below and the tracks paralleling it. A few disoriented pigeons flapped about, marking the girders laced beneath the ceiling. The rain that the morning threatened had at last commenced, drizzling its soft percussion above our heads and adding to the general melancholia of the otherwise empty scene. The effect upon my spirits was similar to that experienced by a solitary traveler, who, having disembarked from a train shared by no other passengers, finds himself equally alone at a destination abandoned due to the lateness of the hour.

"What are we expecting to see?" I wrapped my arms across my chest in a vain attempt to fend off the surrounding chill. "Or is this the entirety of your exposition?"

"Patience, my dear Mr. Dower." It was rather more easily accomplished for Miss Stromneth to retain her smiling equanimity, given the comforting warmth of the undergarment now concealed. "All shall be revealed—perhaps more than you, in your impatience, wish to have."

"I fully expect as much."

"Ah!" She perceived the sour apprehension in my voice. "Let me attempt to soothe your mind in this regard—forewarned is forearmed, as the customary wisdom maintains. What you must realize is the essentially erotic nature of the technology of *Steam*."

"Surely you jest." I spoke my objection as forcefully as possible. "These are machines, not flesh and blood."

"Ah, yes—but consider the elements, both of construction and motion. All those furious pistons, pumping within cylinders so tight as to require constant lubrication; the mounting boil of the fiery chambers; the explosive release of the summoned energies—surely all these remind you somewhat of the more primitive animal passions?"

"Please." I heaved a sigh. "I find the comparison both obvious and strained. Not to mention distasteful."

"Perhaps so. Others, with the pecuniary means to follow such interests to their logical conclusions, find not just *satisfaction,* but *exaltation* beyond your experiences, in that connection." The transcendence achieved by Miss Stromneth's clientele seemed to radiate from her as well; her visage flushed with something other than the warmth from her softly hissing corset. "Given such a happy result, is it any great wonder that they hurl themselves upon the skilled attentions of those who can literally incorporate the steely lineaments of this new world into the soft and less impressive bodies they were given at birth?"

"These days, I wonder at nothing that people do."

"You might, Mr. Dower, if you were to see them! If nothing else, you would marvel at the sheer size, the immensity, that they encompass. As a wealthy man lives in a palace rather than a hut little wider than the miserable occupant's outstretched arms, so have certain individuals, blessed with both extravagant funds and the correspondingly unleashed imagination, magnified their forms. Why limit oneself to puny flesh and bone, when so much can be achieved with iron and steel?"

"Why indeed," I spoke aloud, keeping the words that followed—*If one has nothing better to do*—to myself. "What else is money for?"

"Precisely; I *knew* you could be brought about to see the light! When your great good fortune arrives—as surely it must!—perhaps we shall see you here again at Fex, as a customer rather than a conspirator."

"There are a few other things I would need to take care of first."

"All in good time, I'm sure—" She suddenly turned away from me, elevating her gaze and intently listening. "Do you hear that?"

A low rumble animated the cavernous space, at a pitch more perceptible in the gut than audible. "What is it?" I asked.

"I was *hoping* to have such good luck!" She laid hold of my arm and drew me a step closer, as though to better impart confidences. "The wealthy *do* have such irregular habits, don't they? They come and go as they please, the dears—of course, I don't mind any inconvenience, as I'm well enough recompensed for being at their beck and call, but it does make a trifle difficult the anticipation of their comings and goings."

The sound increased in both volume and ominousness, as though the earth below us were about to quake apart, rather than just the clouds above gathering to a storm. I could feel the vibrations traveling up my legs and into the base of the spine, an altogether unnerving sensation.

"It is this gentleman's usual time, at least on Tuesdays and Thursdays, but one can hardly count on such events, can one?" Miss Stromneth continued her chatter, though I now realized that her grasp upon my arm was less companionable than pragmatic, the anchor afforded thereby preventing her slighter form from being knocked off her feet. "Driven as they are by men's appetites—which, while impressively constant in their youth, do tend to become somewhat variable with advancing age."

Dust and pigeon droppings had begun to sift down from the exposed iron girders above us. From the corner of my eye, I saw Stonebrake swatting at the drifting particles with an expression of annoyance on his face. The bolts holding the structure together, wider than a man's doubled hands, creaked and strained in their sockets.

"There!" As her grip upon my arm tightened, Miss Stromneth directed my attention with her other hand. "You see? A thing of wonder, is it not?"

I had anticipated the appearance of some appalling thing, and in this regard my expectations were more than exceeded. Reader, recall if you will a sunlit stroll in a public garden, the pleasure multiplied by the absence of any thought other than the appreciation of the sunshine upon one's upturned face, the caroling of the songbirds in the trees' leafy canopy, the smiling whispers of parasoled maidens leaning close together to share their sweetly insubstantial confidences. Just such a memory, seemingly incongruous in the *faux* railway station's shadowed, high-ceilinged cavern, arose in my thoughts as I gazed at the apparition upon the tracks below. More so in London than elsewhere, I expect, a promenade as I have attempted to evoke will be interrupted by the appearance of one of those *grandees,* noble or otherwise, whose wealth and power seem literally to magnify their ponderous bulk. The effect transmitted to the onlooker is rendered even more overwhelming by the swarm of attendants— valets, amanuenses, footmen, and others—accompanying their progress, as a great ocean-going vessel is tethered by a small fleet of boats piloting it to port. One is often forced off the margin of the path by such a crowd, as rural peasants might prudently retreat before an approaching army.

Rather than some titled baron, engorged with wealth and honours, the entity upon the station tracks appeared first to my eye as a steam engine, billowing white clouds of vapour from its vents in sufficient amount to partially conceal its iron flanks and the horizontal pistons that drove its wheels forward. It was only upon further scrutiny, as I leaned forward in the elevated perch to which I had been led, that I was able to discern the disturbingly *human* elements of the creature I beheld. If the ancients had envisioned their mythical centaurs as, rather than a merging of the equine species with their own, instead a combination of man with *machine,* some notion of what I presently saw, fantastic as was its appearance, would have already been encompassed in our mental vocabulary. In this immediate instance, the individual's bearded face—in his original incarnation, he might have been a prosperous gentleman in his sixth decade, gaze narrowed and expression hardened with the self-satisfied contemplation of his estate in life—was the only part left revealed by the encroaching metal. His shoulders and upper torso, rearing from the front of the steam engine, were bulkily sheathed in what might have been a suit of armour, if such had been fabricated for industrial rather than military purpose. I could see no arms or hands, or indeed any apertures from which they might have protruded from the torso's iron-plated casing. What need the transmogrified individual might have had for such was served instead by the smaller, still entirely human figures who waited upon him, either clambering about the various mechanisms of the steam engine behind their master's upraised form or on foot beside it. Their uniform livery denoted employment in a household of not just great wealth, but social prestige as well.

"This is monstrous," I pronounced to my companions. I shook my head in dismay. "The clientele you serve, the patrons of Fex— they come here, seeking to be transformed into some unholy conglomeration of flesh and iron? All your talk of surgeons and pipe-fitters—and *this* is the result? For God's sake, what is achieved thereby?"

"Oh, dear." A frown appeared on Miss Stromneth's face. "I had hoped we were making headway in dispelling this unfortunately judgemental attitude of yours. How do you expect to get on in the modern world, Mr. Dower, if every novelty is greeted by you with such disdain?"

"*Novelty?* You must be joking." I drew back from the edge of our elevated perch and turned the full force of my gaze upon her. "If this is mere novelty, then what, pray tell, is *blasphemy?*"

"An outmoded concept," spoke Stonebrake drily. "And one ill-suited for our times. That's why I left the ministry."

"Really?" I encompassed him as well in my scorn. "I have come to doubt that you had ever been *in* it. Cozening gullible widows out of the funds necessary to go floating around on the ocean and proselytize whales—somehow, I am unable to believe that puts you anywhere in the line of apostolic succession. Our Lord and Savior told His disciples that He would make them fishers of men, not bloody whalers with breviaries stuck on the blades of their harpoons."

"Quiet!" Miss Stromneth interrupted before Stonebrake could assemble a retort. "You'll alert them to our presence here. This is supposed to be a *private* assignation."

"Good God." Her words appalled me to an even greater degree. "You imply that there is more than one."

"But of course," she replied. "We could hardly keep the business running with but a single customer. And you might regard me as an incurable romantic, but I like to believe that a *rendezvous* such as this does require a partner—"

No further explanation was required; the brute facts of what I now observed spoke with more crushing eloquence.

Upon a parallel set of tracks, another fearsome creation came into sight, of similar form if slightly smaller dimension than the first I had observed. It also was accompanied by a phalanx of liveried servants, only partly visible through the obscuring clouds as they attended to its various mechanical functions from aboard its bulk or pacing alongside its massive iron wheels. To my increasing dismay, the face visible atop the armoured torso at the front was distinctly feminine in appearance. This observation evoked a frisson of horror along my spine greater than that produced by the grey-bearded male face surmounting the other machine. The effect was little lessened by the fact that it was not a young woman's face, but rather the overly rouged and powdered visage of one of that foolish elderly tribe who fancy that the lines and crevices of Time can be filled and rendered dewy smooth from the pots and jars ranked like an apothecary's stock before their dressing-table's mirror. What it possessed in common with its male counterpart was the same narrow-eyed gaze and thin, self-satisfied smile, redolent of savouring wealth and prestige. As this dreadful creation advanced, I was able to perceive the marginally more decorative aspect of the armoured torso below the woman's face, gender suggested by the doubly rounded prow and the waist-like incurving that had been fashioned into the riveted metal.

"I've seen enough." Ghastly apprehensions filled my imagination, of the scenes that were about to ensue on the tracks below. "There's no need to remain here—"

"But there *is*, Dower." Stonebrake's animal spirits had been cruelly invigorated by the events trembling the structure about us. He pulled me away from Miss Stromneth and forced me to the edge of our elevated perch, directing my vision downward. "We're depending upon you for a great deal; all our plans will run aground without your unflagging devotion to them—"

"I can . . . assure you," I gasped as he brought my captured arm up behind my back, "that this is not . . . helping in that regard."

"It will." He continued relentless. "The more you know of this world and what it has become, and what it holds that it did not before, the less trepidation you will feel as you investigate its darker byways."

The futility of arguing further had already been proven to me. Indeed, I found myself incapable of even closing my eyes to ward off the hideous spectacle. My companions' previously expressed concerns about alerting others to our surreptitious presence were obviated by the deafening volume of the combined noises, the creaking and groaning of the structure's bolts and girders now combined with the blasts of train-like steam whistles, the masculine creation's basso groans answered by the higher-pitched shrieks issuing from its female counterpart. Stonebrake shouted something else into my ear, but I could no longer perceive his words.

But what appalled me more was my sudden realization that it was not the overwhelming volume of sound that shielded us from accidental detection, but rather the degree of absorption in their activities that was displayed by the creations below us. Just as dogs mating in the street cannot be interrupted by anything short of a bucket of cold water, so it was with the participants in this obscene, mechanized endeavour. And similarly to canine procreation, when breeders must at times assist with specimens too awkward and ungainly to accomplish the deed on their own, so now did the liveried attendants wait upon their master and mistress. The necessity for such numbers was explained by the sheer muscular force required to elevate the appropriate segment of the masculine creation, somewhat to the rear of its form, by the use of hinged levers swung out from its flanks. Footmen strained at their hand-holds, with others clasping them about their waists and struggling to draw them downward. At the same time, the transmogrified female's immense form was urged backward by its attendants, beneath the ponderously rearing *inamorata* upon which its favours were being bestowed.

The scene entire summoned secondhand memories to me, of

copperplate engravings in popular journals, adorning the writers' descriptions of the aftermath of tragic collisions upon the railways, resulting in engines and carriages stacked in wild disarray, one atop another. But here there were no travelers' corpses strewn about the bloodied fields on either side, but rather still more of the living throwing themselves into the struggle, their every effort directed toward facilitating this gargantuan conjugation.

I had not thought it possible, but the combined noise grew even louder, its invisible impacts reverberating through my chest as iron thrashed against iron. What I had initially judged to be one of the enormous pistons by which the masculine creation propelled its spoked wheels along the tracks, was now revealed to have an altogether different purpose, ruder in design than mere transportation. Wider than a brace of horses, the cylindrical apparatus drove itself into a reciprocally fashioned portal in the female's latter bulk, revealed by a pair of her attendants drawing aside curved plates large enough to have roofed the nave of a village church. Other servants, relieved of the task of hoisting one machine above another, busied themselves with frantic haste, wielding mops dipped in barrels and slathering glistening oil upon the polished metal surfaces sliding back and forth. As the piston's motion increased in both length and speed, the lubricating attendants found themselves outpaced; tendrils of dark smoke, thicker than men's arms, insinuated through the roiling clouds of steam as friction heated the metal to a red-hot glow . . .

Reader, let me reassure you that George Dower, originally of London's Clerkenwell district, is not unacquainted with the more unseemly aspects of matters biological. Though I possess an Englishman's proper reticence toward activities best done with the lantern extinguished and without an audience attending, I have nevertheless on occasion summoned the courage to *do my duty,* so to speak—once even sparing the world from total destruction thereby. I take more pride in having summoned the resolve to perform the untidy function, than in the salutary consequences achieved by having done so. Please bear in mind that I recount all this, however briefly, not in order to boast of my prowess, but merely to give evidence that I am not a blushing innocent when confronted with the carnal realm. And my knowledge is not confined to our own species; having resided for some time in a rural abode, surrounded by farms and all the beastly procreation committed on their premises, I frequently had my senses assaulted while on a meandering stroll, by the remarkably vigorous performances of various stallions and bulls in their fields, with their mates hardly less enthusiastic about the whole process.

I inform you of all this in order to allay any suspicion on the reader's part that my reaction to the thundering consummation of steam-augmented lust upon the tracks was due more to ignorance than by the essentially horrific nature of the deed itself. The mingled shriek and groan of the partially human creations rose in a dizzying *crescendo,* sufficient to have drawn blood from our ears if it had continued for more than a minute. There was no mercy in the noise's termination, however, as it was replaced by the seeming apocalypse of the ironclad forms reaching the percussive climax of their joint exertions. The female of the pair, with an idiot stare transfixed upon its open-mouthed face, somehow managed to heave itself upward from the rails beneath, sufficiently so as to throw its spent, gasping partner to one side, its weighty bulk toppling against the iron pillars. The impact shuddered the platform with force greater than any previous event; bolts and rivets sprang from their mountings, the small bits raining about our heads like a metallic hailstorm. I was flung backward against Miss Stromneth as the elevated perch on which we had been standing and watching, like voyeurs in some ghastly combination of steel foundry and *bordello,* was wrenched free of its supports. The riveted floor tilted precipitously; we both would have been cast to our deaths if I had not managed, through sheer desperate instinct, to encircle one arm around her *kimono*-clad waist and grasp with my other hand the curved rail of the spiraling staircase by which we had previously mounted to this height.

With that proverbial strength evoked by sudden terror, I drew both myself and Miss Stromneth onto the treads of the staircase, just as the platform we had abandoned fell with an echoing clatter onto the station platform below. Whether the rest of the surrounding structure would continue to disassemble itself and bury us beneath the wrack and clutter of its pieces, I had no idea at the moment.

The panicky course of my thoughts settled only a fraction as I found myself on top of Miss Stromneth, our position contorted by the rails and treads of the swaying staircase. Eyes widened, she gazed up at me—

And smiled.

"God in Heaven," she said. "I *love* this business."

PART THREE

❧ TO THE DEPTHS ❧

Into the Corridors of Power

AS they are," mused Stonebrake aloud, "so shall we become." He brought his gaze around from the brougham's window and toward me. "Don't you agree?"

His play on the venerable gravestone motto struck me as disagreeable. I shifted in the seat opposite him, arms folded across my chest to indicate the defensive mode of my thoughts.

"If by that," I replied, "you mean to assert that the day is coming when I will consent to have great slabs of iron bolted all about me, and a monstrous steam engine replacing the fleshly aspects with which I was born, then I can state with the utmost confidence that it will never happen. Do as you wish, of course, but I fail to see the attraction. Particularly after what we have just witnessed."

We continued our return journey through London's nocturnal streets, moonlight silvering the clouds of steam that were ceaselessly emitted by the pipes winding amongst the buildings. Enough time had passed since our departure from Fex's commercial premises, Miss Stromneth still clad in her silken *kimono,* somewhat dampened by the emissions of steam from beneath, and waving a cheery farewell to us from the building's opulent doorway, that I had managed to regain the majority of my composure. A sufficiency of irritation still resided in my breast, the emotion directed toward my co-conspirator. Scarcely had I managed to rescue both myself and Miss Stromneth from the collapse of the elevated perch in her establishment's *faux*

rail station than I had discovered that the coward Stonebrake had
fled before us and had already safely ensconced himself farther down
the spiral staircase.

"Ah, yes . . ." He nodded slowly, still deep within his doubt-
lessly mercantile ruminations. *"What we have witnessed*—exactly
so. Surely you must applaud the Stromneth woman's employers, the
genius MacDuff and his companion, for their perspicacity in found-
ing such a business as Fex. They have seized upon an opportunity
for great profits, well before others discerned the faintest outlines of
so much that is to come. One could almost suspect that they possessed some preternatural capacity for envisioning the Future."

"If so, whoever they might be, they are a burden upon Humanity.
I have known others who could see the world that lies ahead, and
you may trust me, nothing good came of their ability to do so. A
merciful Providence blinds us to all but the present Time." I unfolded my arms and pointed a single admonishing finger toward the
other man's chest. "Your enthusiasm for the Future, and its besieging horde of devices, is the indicator of a diseased mind."

"Perhaps so." His shrug indicated no great concern on his part.
"But it is a disease that will soon infect all Mankind, and fortunately
so. We shall be transformed in the twinkling of an eye, as is promised to us in Scripture, but without the necessity of waiting about for
an insufferably tardy deity to take care of the job for us. Surely you
were impressed with the *size,* the *force*—the every aspect!—of those
beings we spied upon, back at Fex."

"Impressed is scarcely the word," I replied stiffly. *"Revolted*
would be more like it. Such activities are unseemly enough when
performed at a human scale—by which I mean that which we used
to consider as human. When magnified in this way, wrapped about
in iron and steam providing the motive impulse rather than the excited pulse of the participants—I find it even less endearing."

"Yours is a minority opinion." He gestured to the brougham's
window and beyond, to the darkened windows of the buildings we
passed. "Vast numbers of your countrymen dream as they sleep, of
just such transformation being wrought upon themselves. And why

shouldn't they? Here in London, at least, they possess an advantage over you, of having become accustomed to a continual advent of wonders, one after another, and hastened by that power of Steam about which our hostess at Fex became so rhapsodic. In this, they anticipate the very near Future of Britain entire, in which virtually everyone will be a complete feckhead—"

"I beg your pardon?" My interruption was prompted by the obvious vulgarity of the term just pronounced by Stonebrake, though I merely suspected its meaning. "What was that you said?"

"The near Future of Britain?"

"No, the other. The very last."

"Feckhead?" He further irritated me with a patronizing smile. "I forget, that your innocence colours your language—or rather, drains the colour from it. Surely the etymology of our modern cant is obvious. Once you admit the existence of something such as *fex*—not the business establishment, but the absorbing activity itself—the replacement of previous rude language follows as a matter of course. Thus the verb *to feck,* the process of *getting fecked,* the insult *Feck you!*—even the revised meaning of the word *feckless,* which now more specifically refers to the condition of not getting any fex at all. Which would seem, Dower, to describe your own status."

"May a merciful deity grant that it remain such."

"I'm in a slightly better position," said Stonebrake, "to judge whether prayers are ever answered. In my previous employment, I heard enough of them—usually from Jacktars achieving a painful sobriety after a roistering night in port. They generally asked for divine Providence to keep the bottle far from their lips in the future— and that never happened, either. If wiser persons take it upon themselves to achieve their desires, I can only concur with a rationalist's *Bravo; well done.* And if that fulfillment here on Earth runs toward the large and intimidating, to the degree that can be afforded, such is merely human nature. Granted, there might be some advantage to making a timepiece as small as possible—and certainly your crafty father excelled in that pursuit—so that one can slip it into one's pocket rather than upon one's shoulder, or in a cart following behind. But when it comes to base anatomy, no man seeking transformation wishes to be *smaller* upon the other side of the division from his former self. On the contrary; he wishes to be greater."

"The one we witnessed was certainly that."

"Rightly so." Stonebrake's shoulders lifted in a shrug. "That particular gentleman—discretion forbids my revealing his name— inherited an ancestral fortune, of such immensity that he possesses no thought other than how to spend some portion of it. With the impressive results that you saw."

"It must make participating in the social calendar difficult." Legions of difficulties presented themselves in my thoughts. "I find it hard to imagine him making an appearance at a fashionable ball, without his ironclad aspect being the subject of waspish commentary."

"Scarcely an issue for them: these people travel in circles of which we have little if any comprehension."

"And to which," I observed, "you aspire."

"If it should come to that. These recent sights which you evidently found so appalling, I found to be rather . . . *stimulating.*"

"Indeed." This was not the first occasion on which I found myself speculating on the sanity of someone with whom my own fate had become entwined. "Perhaps it would be better if we concluded this topic of conversation, and moved on to more practical matters."

"Such as?"

"The search for my father's *Vox Universalis* device. Isn't that the reason you have gone to such lengths to drag me about this modern London?"

He nodded. "To a large degree, such was my motivation."

"I would have thought it was your entire motivation for doing so."

"Well . . . there has been a certain . . . shall we say, *amusement* to be derived from observing your reaction to these things. However rapidly these changes have come about in our society, it nevertheless has been a gradual process, so the urbane population has had the opportunity to become accustomed to the new steam-driven world in which they find themselves. It's a rare opportunity to come across someone such as yourself, possessed of both intelligence and innocence on such matters. It doesn't speak well for rural life, that it allowed you to become so out of touch with Progress."

"Speak of it as you will," I replied with as much *hauteur* as I could summon. "But for myself, my feeling is that the sooner we achieve our ambitions and are enriched thereby, the sooner I will be able to return to that sanctuary. London and the rest of the world can then continue its plunge into the steam-filled abyss without any involvement on my part."

"How sad for you. There is so much on which you will be missing out."

"Of that, I am already bleakly convinced. Thus my renewed sense of urgency. Now that you've derived whatever merriment could be gained from my discomfiture at that loathsome establishment Fex, and inured me against whatever shock I might have sustained from witnessing other such spectacles, I'm interested in knowing just how we proceed from here. I can't see how any of this has brought us closer to laying hands on the *Vox Universalis*—if it exists at all."

"Alas," said Stonebrake, "exactly so. I am a bit chastened thereby as well. Even though I was diverted just now by the company of the charming Miss Stromneth, the stoic maxim *Duty before pleasure* still came to mind."

"A fool's errand, then."

"Perhaps. But in my defense, our visit to the establishment which she oversees was initially prompted by other productive intentions. I had hoped that we would encounter not just her, but that couple by which she is employed."

"What manner of people are they? This MacDuff and his no doubt equally depraved consort?" I instinctively drew back, as if there were some chance they might suddenly appear inside the carriage, summoned by mere reference to them. "I found their chief employee alarming enough. Perhaps it was a stroke of good fortune that they were not present."

"I'm certain you will find them merely eccentric rather than frightening, when the time comes. Many of their distinguished patrons are quite smitten with them."

I kept a discreet silence. To myself, I imagined that the fondness displayed toward this mysterious pair by its clientele was due rather more to the accommodation provided to base desires than to engaging personalities.

"But as I indicated," Stonebrake continued, "your acquaintance with them waits upon another occasion. At this moment, we must press forward without the assistance they might have provided to us."

"What aid could they have possibly been?"

"Simple, my dear Dower." He gestured in a manner both magnanimous and dismissive. "The establishment known as Fex is more important—and more vital to our concerns—than would be encompassed by that judgement you have so prudishly bestowed upon it. Past its doors, and beyond the spaces revealed by them, its proprietors would be able to grant us access to strata of society otherwise unavailable."

"God in Heaven—" This time, I was unable to refrain from speaking up. "What good would it do for us to encounter even more such creatures, maddened by both sex and steam? If there are in fact, as you have said, great walled-off estates full of such transformed beings, surely they are but distractions from our pursuit. And as such, better left alone by us."

"This also is where you are in error. And if I have misled you in this regard, you have my utmost apologies. For it is not just *carnal* desires that are accommodated through the services of Fex and its proprietors. There are other lusts that Mankind possesses, beyond those of the senses. Power, ambition, the thrill of dominion over one's fellow human beings—indeed, one could assemble a veritable catalogue of such impulses, both from the pages of history and from the simple observance of everyday life."

"Doubtless," I replied. "But I fail to see how Fex and its legions of surgeons and pipe-fitters could aid in the fulfillment of those desires. Unless, of course, the iron rails at its business establishment

were to be used not just for such monstrous assignations as the one
which you forced me to witness, but also for tying sacrificial victims
to the tracks and then allowing those transformed customers to run
over them. And while I am sure that Miss Stromneth and her employers could find suitably hapless individuals amongst the city's
poor and kidnap them for such a purpose, nevertheless the legality
of such a pursuit seems questionable, even in the wretched circumstances to which this world has fallen of late."

"Ah, Dower; how I wish . . ." Stonebrake sadly shook his head.
"How I wish I could speak with *her* kindly tones. I must seem like a
cruel schoolmaster, dragging a reluctant pupil from one arduous les-
son to another. Your education continues, even this night."

I realized the import of his words: we were not returning to
Featherwhite House and its hissing, clattering assembly of my father's devices. Upon looking out the brougham's window at my side,
I saw that we had traveled elsewhere in the city, somewhat more
central but closer to the Thames. The larger shapes of the buildings
seemed familiar to me, but in the night's darkness I was unable to
establish immediate recognition of them.

"Is this absolutely necessary?" My voice rose in protest. "You
might relish one enormous novelty piled on top of another, but the
ordeal I have recently endured has brought me close to exhaustion."

"Be a man," Stonebrake curtly replied, "or at least make the attempt. But a moment ago, you were complaining of some dilatori-
ness in pursuing our aims. Very well, then. Let us seize this moment
and push forward."

"My suggestion was to persevere after appropriate—and much-
needed—rest."

"No time like the present." His dismaying cheerfulness had
surged to another high point. "Besides, we have already arrived at
our destination. So you might as well summon whatever resources
you have remaining, and bear up a while longer."

I perceived that the brougham had left the street and, after passing through a tightly constricted gate, entered upon an even darker
courtyard. The structures about us towered high enough to block

out all but the vision of the stars directly above, as though we had found ourselves at the bottom of a well. I could hear iron creaking through rust as a stiff-hinged gate was dragged shut behind us.

"Ye're late." A grizzled face scowled in at the carriage's window. "Been waitin' a right fair bit, I have."

"You have my apologies." Stonebrake further mollified the individual with a bright coin laid in one grime-blackened hand. "But unforeseen circumstances delayed us."

"*Sorghum stanzas* be buggered." The other gummed the coin, lacking sufficient teeth to test its authenticity. Frustrated, he pocketed it and yanked open the brougham's door. "Diff'cult enow to smuggle the two of you in, 'fore all the cursed yammering begins. Place be fookin' empty back then; could've fired a fookin' cannon down the halls, not hit a blessed soul." The sooty crevices of his face deepened with an even sourer expression. "Now'll be packed with fookin' bleeders, goin' 'bout their 'fernal pre-*ock*-upations."

"All the better for us, it would seem." Stonebrake had already dismounted from the carriage; he gestured for me to follow him. "We shall lose ourselves amongst the crowd."

"Aye, ye're a devious sort. Simple type such as meself would ne'er thought o' these wily stratagems."

Once outside the carriage, I was better able to look around, attempting to place myself on the perhaps outdated map of London that existed inside my head. The first thing I spotted—and difficult not to, given its size—was the four-sided tower rearing above my head, bearing massive clock faces at its highest elevation. A certain disorientation afflicted me, despite the landmark's familiarity, even to one absent from the city as long as I had been. As many occasions as I previously had seen the grand clock tower at the north end of Westminster Palace and set my pocket watch to coincide with its observance of the passing hours, it struck me that I had never glimpsed it from the precise angle at which I viewed it now. The secretive gate through which I had been conveyed, and the narrowly winding route leading to it, had placed me on some spot not otherwise accessible to the casual pedestrian.

"What is this place?" I turned toward Stonebrake, seeking the answer. "It must be of extreme importance to the nation, given that it exists where the Houses of Parliament formerly stood."

"Hargh!" The gatekeeper emitted a phlegmy laugh. "Ye're not so clever then as yer mate. Bluidy *is* Parliament, ye great booby."

"You'll have to forgive him." Stonebrake spoke with a condescending smile. "My companion has been out of town for a while. He has experienced so many changes upon his return, that he has evidently assumed *everything* must have been altered during his absence."

"Feh—we're not bluidy likely to prise up the centers o' guv'mint and plunk 'em down in the middle o' Swindon, just to 'commodate his fookin' self." He directed his glaring squint toward me. "They be fine where they are."

"Come along, Dower." Stonebrake seized my arm and drew me away from the carriage. "You've made enough of a fool of yourself for the time being, expert as you are at that."

A guttural shout followed after us: "Go 'bout yer business, ye daft prat!"

"It seemed a reasonable enough observation—" I shook myself free as our footsteps brought us through a low stone arch and into a dankly odorous corridor. A trickling sheen of water outlined the rough bricks by which we passed. "The fellow spoke of masses of people who would soon be thronging the corridors. What was I supposed to deduce from a comment such as that? Surely the Houses are not in session at this late hour, unless there is some great governmental crisis under way. Though if we were at the precipice of war with another land, I'm sure I would be the last to be informed of that as well."

"Calm yourself." He strode purposefully toward the flickering glow of gas lamps farther ahead. "The affairs of state are in no calamitous predicament. These are but the normal hours of business for the nation's leaders. Or rather, to be precise, those leaders when they are engaged in matters of actual consequence, rather than mere sunlit playacting."

"Pardon me?" I hurried to keep pace with him, taking care to avoid contact with the mouldering walls on either side. My surmise was that if we were entering upon the Houses of Parliament, we were doing so *via* some conduit for the disposal of whatever effluvia was generated by their inhabitants. "You seem to imply some subterfuge on the part of the government—"

"Imagine that." He spoke with evident sarcasm. "Is there no limit to human perfidy?"

"I suspect there isn't," I replied, "but this is the first I've heard of a nocturnal aspect to the regulation of state affairs, opposed to how they might be conducted during the day."

"As with so many things that come as a revelation to you, Dower, it is a recent development; that Steam, of which our friend Miss Stromneth spoke so reverently, has not only transformed the higher aspects of human sexuality, but the baser category of politics as well. But then—perhaps it's all really the same thing underneath the surface appearances."

"The connection, frankly, is completely occluded to me."

"Are you sure?" Stonebrake came to a sudden halt and turned upon me, the somberness of his altered expression once again indicative of his rapidly shifting temperament. "I see it quite clearly now." He leaned in closer to me, as though imparting some confidence made even more ominous by the grim tunnel in which we stood. "Is it not all about *Power,* however conveyed? When you think about it, what essential difference is there between the ability to express one's will in matters carnal—or in the case of that which you witnessed for the first time back at Fex, such an ability as augmented by steam and iron—and the capacity for making others heed one's will in matters political?"

"The ones whose attentions are fixated on the carnal realm—or carnal and ferric, in the case of Miss Stromneth's clientele—at least have the decency to pursue their obsessions in private." This was about the only virtue I could imagine them possessing. "Or at least they do so for the time being—God only knows how public they might make their activities in the future." A vision entered my thoughts, no less appalling by being sunlit, of the debauched and transmogrified creatures I had witnessed at Fex, continuing their monstrous *coitus* on tracks running through some previously idyllic English countryside, to the discomfiture of fleeing dairy herds and horrified rural onlookers. "Whereas politicians are by necessity in the public eye."

"Yes and no," mused Stonebrake, obviously deep into one of his occasional reflective moods. "We would often like to think so, until we discover more about them and their doings, and then we would prefer to have been left unencumbered by such dismal knowledge."

"Agreed." I stepped away from the man. "So let us leave now, before you have the opportunity to show me something else I would rather have not seen."

"For God's sake, Dower." The meditative state was just as easily transformed to irritation. "If you're this fearful now, what will you be like when something truly horrendous is placed before you?"

"I see no need to discover that, either. I'll meet you back at the carriage."

"Come along," snapped Stonebrake, his irascibility renewed. He took my arm firmly in his grasp, preventing me from turning and heading back toward my preferred destination. By main force, he dragged me toward the rough-hewn wooden door that terminated the passageway through which we had traveled. "Whatever courage you lack, it is more than made up for by the excess of my own."

Voices and the hubbub of churning human interactions swept over me, as we emerged into a high-ceilinged chamber with more of the appearance of civilization about it. The crowds of which the ill-favoured gatekeeper had spoken, enough to fill the building, seemed to have arrived as he had anticipated. And as Stonebrake had foreseen, their preoccupied state, as they rushed about their business, precluded any observation they might have made of us and our sudden appearance amongst them. They no more directed a gaze toward us than the fish thronging a mountain stream would have glanced through the surrounding waters at a figure who might have wandered, staff in hand, to the sandy bank beyond them. So oblivious were they of our presence, that Stonebrake took the caution of drawing me back against the darkly paneled wall, so that I might not be trampled by any of the chamber's hurrying denizens.

As my vision adjusted from the passageway's dimness to the more ample illumination in which we now stood, I discerned various aspects of the crowd. The sable robes of bewigged barristers fluttered behind them as they ran past us, great portfolios of pleadings and testaments and other legal documents tightly clasped under their arms. Other, less impressive minions trailed in their wake, towing wheeled file cabinets, presumably less important papers spilling from the oaken drawers. Wheedling supplicants, in every mode of garb from starched and brushed prosperity to utter tattered destitution, sprinted to keep pace with the great officials of the law, even more heedless of the others with whom they collided shoulder-first, as they breathlessly recited their petitions and protests into the jowled faces from which they hoped to derive some indication of mercy or concern.

"Why are there barristers here?" The mingled racket was of such deafening proportions that I was forced to shout into Stonebrake's ear to make myself heard. "Shouldn't they be at the inns of court?"

"Different times, Dower—" He cupped his hand to the side of my head, the better to amplify his own words. "Your memories of how legal procedures were conducted, and where, are but a thing of the past. There have been other changes in your absence, resulting in a great concentration of all elements of authority in one place, advantageously beneath the oversight of those in charge."

His explanation seemed to account for the breathless chaos I witnessed. Whatever inconvenience might have been associated with the former, archaic ways in which such matters were administered, the arrangement had at least resulted in some stately if somewhat ponderous grace in the slow, methodical dispensing of justice. It had been a situation much remarked upon, that one might grow old and die before one's case was adjudicated, allowing one to proceed to a greater reward or a more fitting punishment in the next world than one might ever have expected in this life. That dusty, creaking realm of the law was apparently no more, as evidenced by what I saw and my companion's explanation of it. Now all was a breathless fury of expectations and results, conducted at a sprinter's pace. Everyone engaged in the intermingling processes hurled themselves toward unseen destinations, as though pursued by demons wielding sulphurous pitchforks, brooking no delay from their harried victims. Indeed, as I watched, judgements were rendered on the fly, with pronouncements from judges so old and grey that they required assistance from ranks of bailiffs, holding the dignitaries upright and carrying them forward, slippered feet ineffectually paddling an inch above the once polished floor. Their words were hastily scribbled by the court-clerks, the worn iron nibs of their pens spattering ink across the vellum pages of massive leather-bound ledgers. In rippling circles about them, the plaintiffs, defendants, petitioners, the odd *amicus curiae* or two, morbid-minded spectators, and other interested parties either boisterously applauded the judges' verdicts or bewailed their fates, wringing hands, rending garments, or tearing hair, all depending upon what understanding they had been able to derive in the chamber's din. The officers of the court appeared to possess no greater comprehension, seizing upon various individuals as though at random and dragging them off through the encumbering crowd, either to some squalid dungeon or the gallows, judging from the flailing, panicked reaction of their elderly, mild-aspected captives. Such events took place concurrent with swarthy brigands, obvious criminal types from their appearance, delightedly receiving the misdirected proceeds, everything from antiquated jewelry to deeds of title, rummaged from brass-bound caskets that had been held by the court in escrow.

"This is madness," I sternly informed Stonebrake beside me. "How could anyone call this a *rationalization* of the legal process? It's worse than before!"

"Only in terms of outcome," he shouted back. The swirling, yammering chaos seemed to have a salutary effect on his mood. "The courts' pronouncements might be somewhat more variable than they had been, as far as the propagation of justice is concerned, but they are now rendered with astonishing, commendable speed. Think of it! A man might be accused, tried, convicted, and hung, all between midnight and the following hour. Surely that is a great relief to his mind, not to have to ponder over his fate for weeks or months, or even years."

"Truth be told, I would prefer to elongate the pondering as much as possible, if there were to be a rope at the end of it."

The unrelenting din had made Stonebrake's words difficult if not impossible to make out, but I felt confident that I had gleaned the essential gist of them, and that his general approval of all things modern was just as continuous as before. I had expected as much from him, a member of that happy tribe who throw themselves ecstatically headfirst into the abyss of the Future, resembling those more primitive types who cast themselves into tropical volcanoes to propitiate their rude deities.

"Very well, then." My own voice I raised as loudly as possible. "I have seen this latest hideous display—to what effect I am uncertain, unless you merely intended to oppress my spirits even further. Might we leave now?"

Now that I had become accustomed, however unhappily, to the chamber's tumult, further details had made themselves apparent to my senses. The perfuse flush on the faces of those madly rushing past was due not alone to the stress of their exertions, but to the humid atmosphere contained within the walls. Indeed, the air was so heated and damp that finger-thick rivulets of water trickled down the dark wooden panels like shimmering, translucent snakes. That degree of moisture had produced deleterious effects on the building's aged fixtures. I saw now that virtually every scrap of wood, some no doubt hewn centuries ago from the nation's ancient forests, had bent and warped; some of the larger panels were cracked and split from having been bent nearly double in this suffocating environment.

The source of the humidity was clearly evident, once I managed to peer beyond the hurriedly rushing human forms. Just as the coiling, hissing pipes transformed the London streets outside to environs more suitable to loinclothed Africans than England's woolen-garbed citizens, so had similar constructions made their way into the Houses of Parliament, emitting their scalding vapours to the same extent. The effect was, however, multiplied by the steam clouds remaining pent up in the building, rather than eventually being dispersed into the surrounding open air. Looking up, I saw the lofty heights of the chamber's ceiling obscured by opaque nimbuses, as mountain peaks are often hid by roiling storms. I would not have been surprised if at any moment, great flashes of lightning had shot out amidst rumbling peals of thunder, lashes of rain falling upon the scurrying figures below.

And in actuality, such an event might have afforded a degree of succour to those ensnared in the various and simultaneous legal proceedings. The dispersal of the steam pipes' radiated heat being stifled by the relatively close quarters through which they threaded, some lengths of them reddened with the fiery temperatures heightening within them—enough so as to endanger any who came into inadvertent contact with them. Indeed, as I watched, at least one white-wigged barrister's robes burst into flames as their black hems brushed over a particularly flagrant steam pipe. As though he were an astronomical meteor set upon a horizontal path, he rushed shrieking through the crowd, his portfolio tossed aside, its scattered papers drifting across the heads of those others who were so intent upon their private concerns that they could scarcely be bothered to note what must have been a fairly frequent occurrence within these confines.

Stonebrake seemed equally heedless of these incendiary happenings, as though the general dampness, however sultry, precluded the possibility of any general conflagration engulfing us.

"In short order," he replied to my enquiry on making our departure from the premises. "I rather expect that that which I have made arrangements for you to witness, and which I am confident you will find edifying, will soon take place. There is a great advantage to Steam having taken over so many aspects of human life; so many things which previously happened in a random, lackadaisical manner, just as people felt motivated or not, happen now with a commendable regularity. Surely one such as yourself, whose own existence has been so much given over to clockwork and its attendant properties, will admit that it is a considerable improvement to have placed Mankind's comings and goings along the lines of a railway timetable."

"Not in the least." I would have none of his sophistry, no matter what mood or state of exhaustion in which I found myself. "This strikes me rather as human beings serving clocks, rather than the other way around."

"As I said." He sailed in typical manner past my objection. "A considerable improvement. Come along. Having praised the punctuality that Steam makes it possible for us to achieve, it would be somewhat embarrassing to be late."

He laid hold of my arm again and pulled me away from the relative security of the wall against which I had placed my spine. As might a mariner who is tossed overboard into the swirling depths of Norway's dread *Maelstrom,* I involuntarily held my breath, perhaps wordlessly hoping thereby to survive the buffeting I was about to endure.

Without Stonebrake's aid, I would have not reached the other side of the chamber, nor would I have attempted the crossing. Such maritime language is apt in this case, as I quickly discovered that great pools of tepid water had formed, some more than a foot in depth, as the floorboards had been warped by their constant presence. Thus the process of going from one point to the opposite was rendered more like fording a marsh than making one's way through what had been at a previous time one of the grandest structures in all of Britain. The effort was made even more difficult by the press and rush of so many other human bodies around oneself, precluding any choice of the route one might take and forcing our steps toward whatever foothold we might achieve.

At last, my grudgingly followed companion achieved the destination he had fixed upon; with a strenuous effort, he pulled me out of the teeming, soggy crowd and alongside him, our backs placed near a high, vaulting doorway.

"It will be a trifle easier from here on, Dower." He spoke as though he were one of those sturdy adventurers who guide less experienced visitors through African forests. "Much less crowded, if nothing else. We are passing from the realm of the courts, into which anyone can venture, from the highest to the lowest." With a nod of his head, Stonebrake indicated the door close to us, in which a scowling guardsman stood, one bulky hand clutching the staff of an axe-bladed halberd, which seemed more ominously useful than merely ceremonial. "Beyond lies rather more privileged territory."

The guardsman's aspect was so threatening, that despite the press of the litigious crowd an empty space a yard or so in radius extended before him. I watched with some trepidation as Stonebrake stepped into this sanctum and engaged the guardsman in a discussion that initially resulted in the other's expression turning even grimmer and more threatening, his fists tightening upon his weapon as though he were about to raise it and strike my companion's head from his shoulders. I regarded this possibility with some apprehension. Admittedly, Stonebrake's company was not entirely congenial to me, and I would have reckoned his death as small loss in that regard—but I had not yet profited from my association with him in the manner that I wished. To that degree, I hoped he might survive this hushed conference.

A few more words passed between them, before the guardsman's heavy face indicated some success on the part of Stonebrake, at least to the point of not murdering him on the spot. A nod as a small packet passed to his hand from Stonebrake's outstretched fingers, then a signal to me as the guardsman pushed open the door behind him.

"Everything is in order," said Stonebrake. "You needn't look so nerve-afflicted. All we need to do is nip along smartly. I imagine that certain . . . *events,* shall we say . . . have already commenced."

"This is reprehensible," I said as I kept pace with him, through the door and into the next chamber beyond. "I don't know why, but even now I expected somewhat better of you."

"Really?" He sighed and shook his head. "Now what is it that you're agitated about?"

"You simply bribed that man for us to gain admittance."

"Surely you jest, Dower. Does as small a sin as that merit your disdain?"

"Not in the slightest." The din of the court's chaos faded behind us as the guardsman pulled the door shut. "I am a man of the world—"

"Oh, yes; very worldly, indeed. A person of vast sophistication."

"You're in no position to mock. I was not referring to your purchase of our entry here—wherever it is that you have brought me to now, and for what purpose. I have done as much, on more than one occasion, when I had previously made my residence in London. Such monetary considerations, a few coins deposited in an expectant upturned palm, are but the common price of passing through one doorway or another."

"Then what is it that you are complaining about?"

"A simple enough indictment," I replied. "You had previously boasted that there was some element of exclusivity to our eventual destination. If this be it, I fear that I see no hindrance to anyone from the street outside making their way here, with no more expense or effort than that which you have displayed just now. It seems no more exclusive than any grogshop with a bully at the door, demanding a ha'penny before one can stumble down in some wretched den smelling of spilled beer slops."

"You mistake the circumstances," said Stonebrake, "by which we gained admittance to these premises. The money I gave to that single-headed *Cerebrus* would not have been sufficient by itself to have caused him to step aside for us. You did not hear what words I spoke to him in addition, what name I dropped into his ear, in order to gain his favour."

"Lord Fusible's name, I would expect."

"Rubbish!" He gave an emphatic shake of his head. "You overvalue our connection with the merely wealthy. Fusible's income from Phototrope Limited and his other entrepreneurial ventures does indeed amount to an enviably tidy sum, but on a plutocratic scale he and his fellow investors are at a very low level indeed, compared to others. Believe me on this score, Dower, that there are figures abroad in this land whose financial holdings and attendant power dwarf anything that Fusible has at his command."

"Such as that formerly human dignitary, and now only partly so, whose lecherous activities I was forced to witness at Fex?"

"He would be one of them, yes. As both Miss Stromneth and I indicated to you there, those types of transformations are not cheaply acquired."

"That is understood by me." I continued walking at a brisk pace alongside Stonebrake. The space through which we passed was but dimly lit, barely enough so that I could make out the ornate details of its lofty ceiling. "And of course, the gentleman can squander his money however he pleases; it makes no difference to me how he does so."

"Very broad-minded of you, I'm sure. I doubt if he and the others like him are greatly concerned about your opinion, but if you enjoy dispensing it, then all the better for you." Stonebrake strode on. "But in point of fact, the name I uttered to gain access here was that of *MacDuff*."

"Be that as it may—you persist in evading the point that I am attempting to make." I was not about to let him off the hook, as the popular usage has it. "It is *your* constant over-valuation that makes this parade of squalid curiosities so irksome to me. According to you, I am being initiated at every turn into mysteries of such august nature that only comparison to the primal forces of nature is merited. And of course, it is only yourself who possesses the ability to bring these appalling scenes before me—or so you contend. Whereas in truth, as has just been evidenced, anyone with a few spare shillings in his pocket might have as easily gained entry here."

"That does it." My observation appeared to have irked him— which had to some degree been my vindictive intent, though not to the wrathful degree the man now exhibited. "You have no idea how burdensome I find all your continual whinging and complaining. Especially given the lengths to which I have gone, the things I have done for your benefit—"

"Please; spare me—"

"I warned you." Those last few words, in addition to the ones gone before, pushed Stonebrake over some emotional precipice. He halted in his stride, turned toward me, and violently grasped the lapels of my jacket, lifting me up from my own heels. "Yet you go on, heedless." He spoke through clenched teeth, nostrils flared and eyes glaring wide, as though suddenly possessed of a madman's demonic spirit. "Your incomprehension of the predicament into which you have been brought, the forces that encircle about your head—it is more than a reasonable person can endure!"

The extent of his reasonableness I found questionable, as a sudden thrust of his arm sent me sprawling backward. A great clattering of metal ensued as my spine and shoulders struck an empty suit of armour that had been decoratively positioned along the darkened chamber's wall.

This was, of course, not the first time I had suffered violence at the hands of some ill-chosen associate. Such events happened with so constant a frequency that I was more often than not surprised when they did not occur.

I straightened my coat, tugging upon its lapels, with as much dignity as I could summon. The resolve further hardened within me to be quit of this fractious mountebank, at the earliest opportunity in which I could profitably do so. At this point, only my self-admitted greed kept my fate linked with his.

"Let us not quarrel," I said. "Or at least no more than absolutely necessary. And certainly not here—however much the world has changed, I am certain that these chambers—housing as they do the august deliberations of Empire—yet retain some semblance of a decent propriety."

As quickly as it had been aroused, Stonebrake's wrathful temper dissipated. Eyes slyly half-lidded, he regarded me with a smile that was even less reassuring.

"Yes . . ." His nod was slow and measured. "Propriety, indeed. At times, Dower, you speak more truly than you might imagine. Proper is as proper does, eh?"

"Your meaning eludes me."

"It still might," said Stonebrake, "even after you become further acquainted with what is now considered normal and acceptable, as the lexicographers define the word."

He turned and led onward. With a heart laden with misgivings, I followed after.

CHAPTER 14

*An Intimidating Apparition
Is Revealed*

ONCE more, I found myself as an observer of disturbing events, stationed as I was at an elevated vantage point.

Stonebrake led me up a narrow, dilapidated stairway, the rotted wooden treads of which sagged and splintered beneath our every step. However rudely constructed, the iron stairs I had been forced to mount back at the Fex establishment had been a model of security compared to this upward passage.

The ruinous state of these stairs seemed entirely a result of the continuous billows of steam hissing through every crevice. Within seconds of initiating my ascent—to whatever destination Stonebrake, in his usual fashion, refused to divulge—every stitch of clothing on my body was as sodden as though our single-file trek were through sultry tropical climes rather than a location to be found anywhere in the more comfortably sub-tepid Britain to which I was accustomed. Finger-thick rivulets of sweat streamed down my face and under my wilting collar as I progressed higher. However deleterious the steam's effect upon the human frame, it was obvious to my misty scrutiny that its cumulative damage to the structure's fittings was even greater. My shoulder brushed against planks hewn from ancient oaks, now warped and split, each separating in wobbly fashion from the next, producing gaps as pronounced and ill-smelling as those in some elderly vagrant's dentition. Patches of mould and mildew, as large and elaborate as embroidered antimacassars, adorned the walls. All of Nature's obnoxious fecundity was on display, due in part to the soft glow of luminous fungi sprouting in every corner.

We escaped at last from the confining stairway, exiting into an only seemingly larger observation gallery of some sort. The empty benches were so deformed by the constant heat and moisture as to have corkscrewed themselves loose from their moorings. Their rotting cushions had tumbled to the slanting floor, there to be subsumed into the concaved boards' moist rot. I feared for my own safety as each of my steps set the structure flexing in a dismaying fashion. The general neglect and decay made it a facile matter to imagine my foot plunging through the spongy wood, to be followed in short order by my entire body.

"Here's a good spot." Stonebrake crouched down by the front of the gallery. "We should be afforded a decent enough view."

At first, I had thought his kneeling, hunched-over posture had been assumed merely to keep his head beneath the ceiling timbers, which were precipitously bowing toward us. However, the admonitory fingertip he held to his lips as I approached, cautiously as possible, signaled a different motive on his part. To wit, his desire to keep our presence here unobserved, presumably from whatever persons might already be in the larger chamber which our station overlooked. Accustomed by now to my companion's stealthy tendencies, I hunkered down beside him, all the better to gaze over the gallery's edge without alerting anyone who might have glanced up in our direction.

"What is this place?" I spoke as I gripped a handrail as moist as though it had been boiled in a soup kettle.

"For God's sake, man, keep your voice down." Stonebrake laid a hand on top of my head, pressing it level with his own. "These are people who prefer to keep their activities free of scrutiny."

"Indeed?" I acquiesced in keeping my comments to a whisper. "That's been the way it is with everyone you've carted me around to spy upon. We seem to be making a habit of intruding upon those who most value their privacy."

"*Habit* implies some unseemly predilection on my behalf. When in fact it is but a requirement of those business enterprises upon which we have launched ourselves."

"If you say so." I peered over the gallery rail with as much stealth as I could muster.

"I do indeed." He brought his own hushed voice close to my ear. "For as I am sure you will soon perceive, those here are engaged upon momentous matters of state. Of exactly that sort which the common rabble have no need to be aware. It's better for all concerned if some things remain shrouded in secrecy."

The exact meaning of his words did in fact become apparent to me. I had initially assumed that he had brought me, by way of his varied circuitous paths and attendant bribery, to gaze upon some obscure meeting-place, perhaps an adjunct to some department of Her Majesty's government—that institution being as fully populated with ministers and their staff, many of whose existence no one outside these premises was aware, as a dog had fleas. The cynical if accurate comment upon their numbers was that the true purpose of government was to increase the number of those governing, and anything else that was accomplished thereby was a mere accident. This was a view to which I had resignedly subscribed in my earlier days as an overly taxed and regulated shopkeeper.

A full measure of alarm thus entered my thoughts when I finally perceived the exact place to which Stonebrake had led me. The upper regions of the ill-kept chamber were so wrapped in shadow that our precautions were sufficient to mask our presence. Once confident that no one below had noticed our scrutiny of them, my companion voiced no objection to my raising my head sufficiently to gain a clear view of the area below.

However great the depredations of encroaching Steam had been upon the close stairway and other passages through which we had traveled, its damage was even more pronounced upon this larger chamber. The damp rot that had seeped into the floor's timbers was so advanced that great sections of it, befurred with grey mould, had buckled bowl-like toward the cavernous stone cellars beneath. A musty exhalation of long-pent, ancient vapours visibly clotted the air, like transparent green snakes spiraling on a slowly vertical course. Their stench came so sulphurous to one's nostrils that the sodden nature of the wood fittings now seemed like a fortuitous condition, preventing as it did the conflagration that might have been kindled by a single spark into the chamber's mingled gases.

Through the cloying fumes, I discerned at last the human figures confined within the chamber. At first apprehension of them, I failed to see aspects sufficient to have evoked the extraordinary caution displayed by Stonebrake at having come anywhere near their presence. Indeed, the men I spied below me appeared to have dwindled and shrunk in form, as though the heat of the all-encompassing Steam had rendered not just the flesh from their rickety bones, but the pluck and spirit from their hearts as well. Though garbed in respectable black, they seemed grey of cast, frail and timorous creatures scuttling about on obscure errands, with sheaves of trembling parchment trembling in their withered hands. Others huddled together with the permanently bent spines of domesticated animals inured to beatings so frequent that they dumbly considered them to be no more than their customary lot in life. A few glanced over their shoulders with fear-widened eyes, not directed upward to my and Stonebrake's hiding-place, but rather toward the massive iron doors that had been crudely forced into the far end of the chamber, much as the timbers of a centuries-old tithe-barn might have been sawn through to allow conversion to a grimly modern manufactory.

As I both watched and attempted to surmise exactly what it was that I beheld, a rumbling noise sounded from beyond those iron doors, not only loud enough to drown out the other wheezing and gasping mechanical emissions that were the constant audible backdrop of the building into which we had entered, but also of sufficient force to set the precarious overhang shuddering about us where we perched. I involuntarily looked behind myself, more than expecting to see the rear of this empty observation gallery wrenching free from whatever decayed anchor had secured it thus far to the highest point of the chamber walls. My fists tightened upon the sagging rail, as one apprehensively grips the rope of that variety of simple sledge upon which heedless children hurtle themselves down snow-covered inclines in winter. At any moment, I expected to make more intimate acquaintance with those others milling about the floor of the chamber, as the overhang tore free of its mooring and crashed upon their heads.

If a similar anxiety filled their thoughts, none of them exhibited it by turning their sight up toward us. The palpable fear that flooded the space, pervasive as the gaseous fumes and clouds of vapour, was instead entirely directed toward the iron doors as they began to ponderously swing open. The unadorned cylinders of their hinges groaned with the tonnage of the bolted metal. From the space revealed beyond, a more forceful gout of steam rolled outward, churning as those great thunderheads in a darkening sky which promise storms so violent and cataclysmic as to wrench oaks from the stony ground and transform placidly meandering rivers into torrents tumbling ancient bridges into their foaming waters.

The timid figures scrambled toward the sides of the chamber. Their doing so made a crucial revelation to me, by which I was at last able to hazard a guess as to the exact designation of the place to which I had been so dangerously guided.

"Why, this is Parliament—" I could hear the notes of both wonder and dismay in my own voice. "The House of Commons, to be precise—"

"How astute of you." Stonebrake's rejoinder was the only thing that retained a measure of dryness in my environs. "My confidence regarding your inductive abilities appears to have been well-founded."

My observation had been triggered by the sight of the black-clad creatures taking a trembling refuge amongst the damp-warped benches at the chamber's opposite walls. The resulting arrangement seemed guided less by what might have once been a desire to exhibit party allegiance than by the evident fear on the part of the members of Parliament toward whatever intimidating shape was even now lumbering past the iron doors, flung fully open with an echoing impact upon the splintering wood panels framing them. Whatever pride of position such men might have exuded in earlier, more properly historical days, had now evaporated. Literally, it seemed, as though the draconian jets of Steam had been sufficient to scour their hands from those levers of government they had once been given to manipulate. My gazing upon them seemed less like a vision granted of the workings of Empire's deliberative machinery than it was upon a pack of terrified children, cowering away from the approach of the school bully—

Which seemed, when at last exposed to a full apprehension of its hideous construct and design, to be an elder and immensely larger sibling of that appalling human and mechanical conjunction I had witnessed at the Fex emporium. Both grinding, hissing creations might have emerged from the same monstrous womb, hammered together more upon forge and anvil than by the slow, tender knitting of merely maternal privacies.

The daunting impression upon my thoughts and spirits was inevitably magnified by this apparition's greater size. With those amorous behemoths, whose steam-wreathed coupling I had been forced to witness, there had been a roughly centaur-like ratio between the iron-bound locomotive component and what remained of softer flesh and bone. In the present case, however, the seemingly human lineaments were dwarfed by the engulfing mechanical parts, so that the face and upper torso appeared as no more than those figureheads adorning the prows of the Royal Navy's greatest warships. Underneath such a bulk, the timbers of the chamber's floors creaked and swayed, the parallel iron tracks kept from buckling and collapsing entirely only by the bridge-like girders which had been rigged in place beneath, visible through the broken gaps revealing the underlying cellars.

As appalling as the construction's size might have been, as though a railway engine had burst through the wall of some minuscule village shop, and the dismaying proportion of metal to the whole, the perceptible transformation of the human fragment was even more repellent. Through the enveloping clouds emitted by the valves and connectors riveted to the gargantuan boiler, at its front was a visage barely recognizable as what might once have been a woman's, its square-cut jaws rendered even more cruelly androgyne by the surrounding steely cast. The features seemed more chiseled into place by some diabolical ironmonger than by Nature's hand. Its eyes were but slits, the spark of feminine wiles visible through them as sharply focused as those of an infantry sniper taking aim from a fortified position.

"Take me from here—" I turned toward my companion and guide, my doubled grasp seizing upon his arm as though it afforded the only security from toppling into the abyss on the edge of which I trembled. "I can endure no more."

I would not previously have thought it possible, but my fears had vaulted past their previous boundaries, impelled by the apparition below. Even so, as that which terrifies us the most still forces our scrutiny, I found myself compelled to direct my stricken gaze toward the monstrosity. Legions of uniformed attendants swarmed across its flanks with swan-necked oil cans and grease-blackened rags, much as smaller fish are described by ichthyologists as grooming the toothily smiling bulk of a shark capable of devouring scores of such devotees with a single sweeping gulp.

And then it spoke.

It took a moment for me to realize that such was happening. At first, I believed that one of the intimidating construction's gleaming brass whistles had burst forth, emitting an ear-piercing shriek as well as a jetting plume of vapour. I snatched my hands away from Stonebrake's arms, clapping them futilely to my ears. Through my quivering palms, I was able to discern actual words, both grinding and scalding, as though a Moloch-like boiler at a factory's deepest core had been granted voice.

"For God's sake, man—" I brought my gaze again to my companion, unable as I was to bear the sight of the House's members cringing from the lash of the construction's steam-impelled taunts and imprecations. "If you cannot bear me away from this place, at least tell me this much: What is that thing below?"

Stonebrake smiled as he spoke his answer. It mattered little that I could barely hear him through the stifling din, as I had been told once before that name by which the appalling creature was known. Its designation had been spoken to me, mysteriously at that time, by the far more feminine daughter of Lord Fusible.

"You really do not know?" A relishing malice appeared in Stonebrake's expression. "I brought you here so you might see the nation's Prime Minister in action. That's the Iron Lady."

⋯⊷≡⊙⊜≡⊶⋯

"**OF** course, you should not address her as such to her face." My companion gazed thoughtfully out the brougham window, then turned to me once more. "By all reliable reports, it is a matter of some sensitivity for Mrs. Fletcher. As current as might be her admittedly transmogrified appearance, in matters of propriety she evidently subscribes to the old forms."

"I will make certain that I never have occasion to address her in any matter." A cold grey dawn seeped through the vaporous streets, its light as feeble and ineffectual as a guttering candle in a smoke-filled room. "That there is some significant remainder of my life left for me to enjoy, or at least muddle through, is as much my hope as it is other men's. But even if it were a sum to be measured in years rather than days, and decades rather than years, it would still be too brief for me to encompass such a ghastly apparition into its mental furnishings."

"Furnish your mind as you see fit," retorted Stonebrake. "You will still need to deal with Mrs. Agatha Fletcher on some level, whether in person or at the same remove as the great majority of your fellow citizens. There is no escape, whether in the meanest, most ignominious hovel or the most exalted townhouse—so great is the Iron Lady's influence upon even the minutest aspects of our lives. The threads of this life in which we find ourselves may be spun from Steam, but it is *her* hand that tugs them into place upon the great loom."

The dire poetry of his description indicated to me that Stonebrake was at least partly enraptured by the fearsome woman—if enough tender parts of her former incarnation remained to qualify her of that gender. He seemed to admire as much as I loathed the mere thought of her, without my having made any greater acquaintance than having observed her from my perch in the crumbling observation gallery. I rather suspected that he suffered from that tendency which afflicts so many of the ambitious: to wit, however vaunted his estimation of his own worth and powers, he was ready at a moment's notice to grovel as a perfect acolyte at the feet of those he ranked above himself.

Of course, it was a matter of conjecture as to whether the formidable Mrs. Fletcher still actually possessed any flesh-and-bone feet, or whether, in a similar fashion to that fabled Queen of Spain who officially had no such appendages, she had dispossessed herself of those as well. Perhaps they still existed but were hidden, tucked away in some cabinet inside that fearsome mechanical Juggernaut which I had seen make its ritual entry to the intimidated House of Commons. If such were the case, no doubt they sat upon some neglected shelf, next to the shriveled remnant of her now superfluous heart.

For such was the import of Stonebrake's further revelations, spoken to me as the brougham conveyed us back to the more familiar, if only slightly hazardous, confines of Featherwhite House.

"What you must understand," my companion instructed me, "is that Mrs. Fletcher has embraced the transformative power of Steam, to a greater degree than any other public figure—"

"Embraced it?" His words sent one of my eyebrows arching upward. "It would seem rather more accurate to say that she *embodies* it."

"Precisely so—and nicely put," said Stonebrake approvingly. "Yes, you might indeed say that she represents in her self a rigid distillation of these wonders that have been bestowed upon us. And in doing so, she has brought them to their greatest fruition. What for other people are merely amusements, expensive diversions for their idle hours and lives, for her has become the perfect instrument for achieving political domination. From such, it is a given that even greater sources of wealth and power will flow."

"From what little I saw, it might have seemed that she had already achieved a surfeit of those things."

"As do most men, Dower, you underestimate the reach of a woman's desires. And in this case, a woman no longer hobbled by a mawkish sentimentality, having abandoned both surgically and in the processes of her spirit those feminine elements that might have impaired her climb to the pinnacle from which she now surveys those aspects of life which she has not yet brought under her command. In place of those weaker personal aspects, she has brought both Steel and Steam. Thus her rebirth into the form in which you beheld her. Indeed, without those puissant forces, she would have realized nothing at all of those longings which she had previously concealed behind the usual decorous modesty. But Mrs. Fletcher was born for these times and has grasped their full potentialities. The lecherous beings you witnessed at Fex, thrashing about in their steam-powered consummations, were but the precursors for that evolution which she alone has realized."

"To have undertaken all this," I observed, "would seem to have required an impressive personality, even while it had been housed in mere flesh."

"In that you are correct. Those who remember her from before— and there are at least a few that she lets continue to walk abroad— have described well how her bounding ambitions chafed against the limitations that tradition-bound society places upon women whose creative tendencies would be better expressed in the battlefield of politics rather than endless needlework and ecclesiastical charities. I have yet to come across any record of how she was first introduced to those surgeons and engineers who cater to that wealth-obscured *demimonde* which forms the clientele of Miss Stromneth and her establishment's backers. Given the sternly British stolidity of her personality in that regard, it hardly seems likely that she drifted into those circles while motivated for a taste in otherwise illicit excitements. Perhaps it was the smell of money that drew her on—those who long for dominance over others readily see the advantages that wealth can provide in such matters. However it came about, though, it is entirely a tribute to her innate genius that she was able to seize upon the possibilities presented by *such* transformation. The first few alterations must have been dearly bought, almost surely with commitments to bend the currents of government to those who might otherwise have come under the onerous scrutiny of the authorities."

"Such indentures are often the genesis of great political careers."

"An astute observation, Dower. And in this case, it was a transaction well worth whatever price she paid, both physical and financial. The redoubtable Mrs. Fletcher's ironclad transformation, complete with hissing boilers and shrieking valves, have made her into an indomitable force, almost literally crushing her political rivals—just as you witnessed now at the House of Commons. Not only has she vanquished any possible opposition, she has also neatly solved that slight technical impediment to her full participation in the processes of government. Some of the more intellectual members of the weaker sex might bewail their exclusion from that suffrage by which their fathers and husbands are allowed to cast their increasingly nominal votes, but the sternly altered Mrs. Fletcher has circumvented the matter entire. Since she's been so completely transformed, no-one can be exactly sure whether she is female any longer, or male or whatever. Since there's no prohibition against androgynes voting or holding office, one might say that the Iron Lady is home free on that count."

"How convenient for her." Without having made the acquaintance of the woman in her previous, less iron-bound incarnation, I nevertheless felt confident that, as Stonebrake had indicated, any loss suffered in this legal attainment was considered negligible by Mrs. Fletcher. "The consequences for everyone else do seem to be a bit dire, however."

"Do you really believe so?" Stonebrake seemed perplexed by my comment. "In what manner?"

"You jest." Either that, or he was blind. "The members of Parliament seemed rather overawed by the woman—I thought that much was apparent."

"True, true—but that is not necessarily a bad thing." As with all devotees of a new religion, any of its resulting excesses were but motes to his eye. "In their present intimidated condition, they offer no resistance to her plans for reformation of British society. Indeed, they are utterly convinced that their only hopes for survival—not just politically, but personally as well—are to aid her in those monumental schemes, to the utmost their strength will allow. Thus, we plunge forward into an exciting Future at even greater speed. The world to come rushes toward us with its all-consuming embrace."

"I had rather it didn't."

"You have no choice in the matter. Best to become accustomed to the notion."

"Scarcely the first time I have been so advised." I grumpily settled myself back into the brougham's upholstered seat. "But surely, man, you could hardly believe the wrack visited upon the actual structure of the Houses of Parliament to be so wonderful? The place looked a sodden ruin, as though some great industrial enterprise had been relocated to a tropical swamp."

"Such alterations are inevitable." Stonebrake waved their consideration away with a nonchalant hand. "Her transformation is such, encompassing masses of iron, that she can hardly be expected to move from place to place as we do—thus the railway tracks that have been laid throughout the appropriate government buildings. And of course, great resources of power are necessary for her to rumble about, imposing her will upon ministers and members alike. The steam conduits that have been engineered throughout the structure, as well as those churning smokestacks above, might seem a depredation to one as fixated upon the well-vanished Past as you are, Dower—but I prefer to view them as the emblems and heralds of our little island having been placed at last upon a sound scientific basis."

I endeavoured to remove the whole oppressing memory from my mind. With little success: those once imposing chambers through which I had been dragged weighed uncomfortably upon my soul, as though they had been a hissing and clanking combination of the poet Milton's satanic mills and a railway terminal larger and louder than Victoria Station.

Closing my eyes, I attempted to find some comfort in a partial, dreamless slumber before we reached our destination. In this, I was a failure as well. As on so many occasions before, I was riven with doubts concerning not the world's Future, but merely my own. I might have recklessly summoned up enough moral fortitude to have become involved with Stonebrake and his fellow conspirators—who I now had reason to believe encompassed far worse than Lord Fusible and the other gambling-obsessed Steam Barons—but my spirit still quailed at the further prospects I dimly beheld.

For it now seemed everything around me had been transmogrified into a nightmare vision of my father's creations. Rather than escaping from his overarching influence, I felt as though I—and everyone else—has been engulfed by it.

I turned my feverish-hot face against the leather cushion, damp with London's seemingly constant exudations, as I sought some impossible refuge from this world's sharp-edged gears and the scalding forces that set them into such furious motion . . .

In this small, pathetic quest, as with so many other things I had desired to achieve in my life, I was soon disappointed. For no sooner had I closed my eyes than the brougham lurched to a sudden stop, violent enough to nearly throw me from my seat. From outside our conveyance came the whickering neighs and sharper clops of the horses rearing backward in their tracks, the driver pulling on the reins doubled in his tightened grasp.

The shouts of men engaged upon some furious, self-righteous errand assaulted my ears. They spoke not with the high-pitched tones of the rural highwaymen of a long-past day, but with the deeper *basso profundo* of those secure in their command, acting with the full authority of those empowered to detain ordinary citizens and brigands alike.

I turned toward Stonebrake beside me. "What is going on?"

"No need to fret." He seemed oddly unconcerned about this latest occurrence. "You shall see soon enough."

At the brougham's window appeared a fiercely mustachioed face, surmounted by a bowler hat, its brim pulled low toward beetling eyebrows. He scowled past Stonebrake and directly toward me. "Mister George Dower, I take it?"

"Possibly . . ." At one time, I would have replied with less caution. "What is the reason for your enquiry?"

"Don't muck about with me, lad." The man yanked open the brougham's door. "You're in a parcel of trouble already." He reached in and grabbed me by my shirtfront, his black-bristled hands coming close to strangling me with their sudden force. "Come along, then—"

No more than a second passed, before I found myself stumbling to keep my balance upon the wet cobblestones. I briefly speculated that I had been struck upon the head by the truncheon in my attacker's other hand—for I saw not just him, but a half dozen more, similarly behatted and garbed in officious black overcoats. They closely surrounded me, scowling with an intimidating mien.

"This is more for your security than ours—" The one who had rudely hauled me from the brougham appeared to be in charge of the general group. At his signal, a subordinate pulled my hands behind me and clapped on a set of manacles. "Otherwise, seeing as how anarchists such as yourself are given to desperate attempts to evade justice, we'd have no choice but to beat you bloody senseless."

"Actually, sir . . ." The youngest of the group spoke up. "I'd rather fancy having a go at that."

"Time enough," growled his superior, "when we've got this bastard stowed away in a cell." He nodded in anticipated satisfaction. "Then we can do it at our leisure."

"But—" The shock of this unforeseen arrest dissipated—barely so, but enough to allow me to produce an utterance of my own. "Who are you? What is the meaning of this?"

"As if you didn't know." My captor thrust the handle of his truncheon into my stomach, hard enough to double me over. "You're in the custody of the Metropolitan Police—as well you should be."

Clutching a forearm to my belly, I gasped for breath. "On . . ." The words came out in an asphyxiated wheeze. "On what charge?"

"You'll have a stack of those to read over. It'll give you something to do, to pass the hours where you're going. As for now, being a bloody menace to society should be sufficient."

I was shoved toward another, much grimmer-looking carriage, with bars upon its tiny windows. Glancing back over my shoulder, I saw that Stonebrake had dismounted from the brougham, seemingly of his own volition. He stood with a casual, unsurprised air with the constables, as though he might have been one of their number.

"Stonebrake," I called out to him as I was forced upon the steps leading to the carriage's dark interior. "Help me—"

My outburst was not looked upon with favour by those into whose hands I had fallen. This time, the truncheon did indeed land upon my skull, the blow directed from behind. If not of sufficient force to render me completely unconscious, it nevertheless sent the world spinning about me, constituent elements flying in all directions.

Which left me in utter, toppling darkness when the carriage's iron doors were slammed shut at my feet. Lying upon its narrow floor, I was distantly aware of the vehicle lurching forward, carrying me to some unknown but still dreaded destination.

CHAPTER
15

*A Prisoner Speaks
Dismissively of Plans
and Schemes*

THE attentive reader might well recall the distaste I have expressed on previous pages, regarding the unease I had experienced upon being forced to survey various events while ensconced in locations made even more precarious by their elevation. Those judgements now seemed a cause for chagrin, as I discovered that low, secluded places could be even less comfortable.

I speak of the cell to which I had been conveyed by those agents of the Metropolitan Police that I had but lately encountered on the streets of London. "Encountered" being, of course, a euphemism for having been rendered unconscious through the obviously well-practiced application of a constable's truncheon upon my skull. A dim memory of transport in a carriage locked from the exterior, with blurred glimpses of the city's clouds roiling past the barred windows, ebbed from my awareness as I painfully raised myself to a sitting position on a cold stone floor.

With one hand rubbing the bruised knot at the back of my head, I wincingly examined my confines. The cell was of such limited dimensions that I would scarcely have been able to stand upright or stretch out my arms to their full extent. The only illumination came from a flickering lamp somewhere in the corridor outside, the feeble glow barely able to make its passage through the bars of the minute window in the riveted iron door. More by the sense of smell than sight, I perceived a rusting bucket underneath the chain-swung bunk at one side, that being the cell's only furnishing. The filth-crusted pail had presumably been placed there for hygienic purposes—or if not, it certainly seemed to have been so used by legions of the cell's previous unhappy occupants.

Seating myself on the bunk, as far from the odorous receptacle as possible, I bleakly contemplated my situation. This seemed a new low point in my progress through the world. If I had previously not considered that such was possible, then the blinders had certainly been lifted from my eyes. How much wisdom Mankind attains, when its individual specimens remind themselves that things can always get worse.

Such was my philosophical conclusion, quickly reached. But its broad strokes did little to limn the exact details of my predicament. The literal aspect of my conveyance hence—being dragged from the brougham *en route* back to Featherwhite House, then menaced by policemen who had subsequently made good on their threats, and at last the jouncing, semi-conscious ride in the locked carriage—was all more or less retained in my thoughts, jumbled as they still might have been. As was also the image of the traitorous Stonebrake, so obviously in league with the police, poised in chummy familiarity with them.

Or perhaps he *was* one of them—that dark suspicion entered my mind now. In some lesser or greater capacity—perhaps as a paid informant, one of those loathsome individuals who make a shabby living by selling out their unsuspecting confederates, or even an actual member of the Metropolitan force. By now, given the unsettling things I had witnessed, no possibility remained which I was willing to rule out of bounds. The one element they had in common was the degree to which I had been hoodwinked by the artful Stonebrake, whoever and whatever he might be in reality. As to what motive he might have had in so deluding me—that was even further beyond conjecture.

Leaning forward on the bunk, I agitatedly chewed upon a knuckle, castigating myself for the folly of having ever trusted the man. It seemed a fundamental injustice in the Universe's composition that an Englishman could not simply go about his plans for suicide, as I had been doing, without being interrupted therein and inveigled into less productive endeavours. If I had but the opportunity to confront the villain . . .

"Dower . . ." A whisper touched lightly upon my senses. "Over here—"

Either my recent misadventures, compounded by the truncheon's impact, had completely disarranged my reason—or I had arrived in some more fortuitous mode of existence, in which to mercly wish something was the same as having it delivered upon the proverbial silver platter. For upon looking up toward the apparent source of what I had first believed to be an auditory hallucination, I beheld the very face of my tormentor, peering in at me through the cell door's iron-barred window.

"Stonebrake . . ."

"Keep it down, man." In the dim light afforded by the corridor's lantern, I saw him turn his face away, then look back toward me. "We don't want them to overhear us."

Of whom he spoke was but one more mystery laid upon the others in towering proportion. I squinted in his direction, attempting to ascertain beyond doubt that he was of actual substance and not a figure conjured from my disordered imagination.

"That being the case . . ." I decided to accept the man's existence on a provisional basis. "Perhaps it would be better if we did not speak at all. What with there being few pleasantries we could exchange at the moment, which would be worth whatever risk it is you speak of."

"Are you feeling quite all right?" Stonebrake pressed his face closer to the bars, studying me with some apparent perplexity. "You seem unnaturally calm. I confess that I had anticipated some ill temper on your part—given the circumstances."

"Why should I be angry?" I rose from the bunk and stepped to the door, bringing my face as close as possible to his. "I'm sure it's all some sort of misunderstanding. And yes, you're right: we do need to keep our voices down."

"I'm glad you feel that way toward me . . ."

So relieved was Stonebrake, he did not notice my reaching through the bars at the side of the aperture.

"And yes, it is a misunderstanding. Of a sort—"

His words were cut off by the simple fact of my suddenly grasping the back of his head and, with as much violence as I was capable, slamming his face against the bars.

"Miscreant!" To the best of my recall, I spoke not that word but one of a cruder variety, albeit of approximately the same meaning. "Do you really imagine me so foolish as to listen once more to you? Whatever further scheme you might be hatching, the chances of my being inveigled into it are nil." Having taken him by surprise, I was able to bring his face sharply against the bars again. A satisfying blossom of red burst from one nostril. "It's not as if your previous ones have worked out so wonderfully, is it?"

"For God's sake, leave off—" He managed to extricate himself from my grasp. "Of what do you imagine that *you* have to complain?"

"Complain? I'll give you *complain*." Reaching through the bars to the full extent of my arm, I futilely attempted to once more ensnare his head. "I'm in *prison*—or hadn't you noticed?"

"Technically, not so." Stonebrake stanched his bleeding nose with a pocket handkerchief. "One can only be imprisoned upon a successful prosecution by the state—and so far, you haven't even had formal charges laid against you."

"So this is not prison?" I glanced around my bleak confines, then back to him. "I must confess, then, that whatever it is, I find the difference between it and actual prison to be vanishingly small."

"A mere matter of perception." Stonebrake examined the bloodied cloth in his hand, then applied it to his nose again. "It only seems to be that way to you. In fact, you are housed several levels below the Houses of Parliament, in the ancient cellars of Westminster Palace. That's not so bad, is it?"

"I'd be freer to see it so congenially, if I were standing where you are. Rather than in here."

"Soon enough," he replied, "you won't be where you currently are. That is why we need to talk, while there is time."

"Upon further reflection, perhaps I would prefer to remain where I am." Our brief altercation, while initially gratifying, had left me both physically exhausted and emotionally enervated. "I can only imagine that whatever place to which I might be spirited would somehow be even worse than this. It's not exactly as if you possess a shining history in this regard."

"I assure you, Dower, there *are* worse places—"

"You would know."

"*And* I am endeavouring to save you from them."

"By handing me over to the police?" I gazed at him in astonishment. "On whatever trumped-up pretext you related to them? Please—spare me any further kindnesses on your part."

"You fret yourself needlessly," said Stonebrake. "Your arrest was nothing."

"A statement easily made by you." I rubbed the back of my own head, feeling the tender knot that the constable's truncheon had raised there. "I assure you, it felt substantial at the moment."

"Do move on, Dower. It was no more than was necessary. All part of a greater plan."

"*Everything* is, according to you. Plans within plans, within schemes, all without apparent end."

"Yes, yes; whatever you say." He spoke with even more apparent haste. "This is hardly the occasion for such petty bickering. If you'd but listen to me, you'd realize that you are in nearly as grave a danger as I am."

"As *you* are?" An involuntary laugh escaped from me. "You might recall that I'm the one in prison—or whatever this is, that my mind is supposed to be so much more at ease about."

"Try to keep some perspective on the matter, Dower. You are at risk, at the most, of being summarily executed."

"Good God." I felt the blood drain from my face, as tepid water rushes downward when a bathtub plug is removed. "Is that likely?"

"There's a good possibility," Stonebrake allowed. "For our schemes to advance, we needed to set forth on admittedly treacherous ground. But do bear in mind, that if such were to happen—and I imagine that a hastily convened military firing squad would be the probable arrangement along those lines—all you would endure would be that demise, and by virtually the same means, that not too long ago you were attempting to engineer for yourself. Whereas if our joint endeavours were indeed to run aground, I would have all my hopes and dreams of wealth dashed to pieces."

"Yes, of course. How selfish of me not to regard the state of your bank account as the greatest good to be achieved in this world. Obviously, my life pales in comparison."

My sarcasm had no apparent effect on him; he might not even have perceived it. For myself, I was increasingly annoyed by having my earlier attempts at self-destruction constantly thrown in my face as a debating point. Having once engaged in that sort of activity, it would seem that one is henceforth at a disadvantage in negotiation with others. If Stonebrake were typical in this regard—and I had no reason to believe he wasn't—the assumption is made that one has little or no interest in avoiding a volley of bullets into one's vital organs. This, I believe, is essentially a self-serving position on the part of not just someone such as Stonebrake, but the population in general.

"I'm glad you see it that way." Something unseen rattled inside the door as Stonebrake spoke. "A helpful attitude will facilitate what we so urgently need to do."

To my further amazement, the cell door swung inward, creaking on its ancient hinges as it did so. Revealed through the opened doorway was the great iron key that Stonebrake held in his grasp.

"Thank God!" I sprang to my feet. "Disregard whichever of my previous comments you choose. Let us make haste—"

"Not so quickly." Stonebrake halted my forward progress with a hand against my chest. "You must remain here a while longer."

"Pardon me?" I blinked in confusion. "But—you said a moment

ago—that there were others on their way here." I had assumed he meant my gaolers or others I had no wish to encounter. "Surely you came to rescue me from them."

"Actually, not." With greater force, he pushed me back from the cell's doorway. "That's not part of the plan—"

"Bugger your plan." My emotions had been heightened by the prospect of fleeing from the spot; to have that prospect seemingly snatched away was more than I could endure. "I'm entirely comfortable with the notion of your staying here, if you so choose. I'm for taking to my heels—"

"Don't be a fool." His restraining hand remained where it was. "Highly unlikely that you'd be able to find your way out of these facilities."

"I'm willing to take the chance. Let me go—"

"And destroy our chances of achieving our goal and its attendant wealth? I think not. Everything now depends upon your utter coöperation, Dower."

"More's the pity, then." I frantically attempted to get around the man, but he successfully blocked all access to the cell's exit. "This might be a good time to dissolve our partnership—"

"Too late for that." Stonebrake clapped his hands to my shoulders and roughly shoved me back down upon the narrow bunk. "Are you unconvinced as to the severity of the attentions you might soon be forced to endure? Think well; consider your situation here."

My companion—for so he still seemed to be, whether I wished it or not—had made a valid point. But it was one that was already uppermost in my thoughts. Even before the steam-powered transformation of British society, dire rumours of what some would term *enhanced interrogation techniques* had circulated through the general populace. Dreadful accounts were whispered of the zeal expressed by certain police specialists in getting information, confessions, whatever they desired, from those who wound up in cells exactly like the one in which I had found myself. A repeated application of a truncheon was the least I had to worry about.

"I alone," continued Stonebrake, "can save you from that fate."

"Save me?" His words made no sense. "You were the one who put me here."

"Merely part of the—"

"Yes, yes, I know." I raised a hand to prevent him from uttering further along those lines. "These diabolically unending plans of yours." I wearily shook my head. "Would that I had never heard the slightest fragment of them."

"Bear with me but a while longer, Dower, and you will be grateful that you did."

"I rather doubt it. But at the moment, I again seem to have little choice about it."

"Exactly so. Such is the beginning of wisdom on your part." Stonebrake turned his attention away from me and toward the cell door. We both heard some ominously clanging noises, metal upon metal, echoing distantly through the corridor beyond. Upon darting there, he quickly glanced about in either direction outside the cell, then returned and sat down beside me on the bunk. "We have but a few moments. Listen carefully—"

"To you? That was how I got into these troubles, to begin with."

"Quiet. I am about to impart to you a full elucidation of your current predicament."

"Pardon my skepticism. But I've heard similar preambles from you before now."

"First attend to my words, then judge." Stonebrake leaned close toward me in order to impart his confidences. "It might have indeed been this city's Metropolitan Police who arrested you. And yes, before you make some self-pitying comment, it was indeed upon my information that they did so. But that was all—"

"Yes, of course. The plan. Pray continue."

"If you will refrain from interruption." Stonebrake grasped my arm, tightly squeezing it. "As I say, the Metropolitan Police were the agents who brought about your confinement here. But you are not in their hands. These premises are not controlled by them, but by another organization. One of which you have in all likelihood been ignorant until this moment, but of which you should be much more concerned."

"Who would that be?"

He brought his whisper close to my ear, as though imparting the name of something so dreadful as to be scarce spoken aloud. "Her Majesty's Department," he said, "of Technography and Statistics."

"Never heard of them."

"Exactly. I told you that the chances of your having done so were slight. Indeed, in this respect, you are aligned with the majority of the population. For while they are an official organ of the British government, the existence is a secret closely kept. Those aware of this agency are either affiliated with it in some manner, thus keeping their silence as a way of facilitating its operations—or they are opposed to it. And seek to keep themselves from being brought to its scrutiny."

"I expect I would have done the same," I said, "whether or not I had known who they were. Not that I would have had reason to be afraid of such an innocuously designated institution, but just as a matter of general principles."

"And that's exactly where you would've gone wrong, Dower. For while you might evince little knowledge or interest in the Department, you may be assured that its officials have a considerable dossier of information concerning yourself. Which they have of course acquired as a result of their keen curiosity about your affairs."

"Why so? I would have thought I had outlived any possible notoriety."

"Again, you go wrong. And you do so by ignoring the most obvious reasons for your being a subject of official interest."

A familiar realization returned to my mind. "I suspect this has much to do with my father. And his less respectable activities."

"Exactly so," said Stonebrake. "As it has been in many situations in your life. But in this particular instance, your familial predecessor connects precisely with the official portfolio of the Department of Technography and Statistics. Indeed, one might say that the Department and its agents exist in their present configuration solely as a result of your father and his inventions."

"Present configuration? What were they before?"

"Originally, the Department was much less intimidating in its functions. Then it was known as the Department of *Topography* and Statistics. As such, it was merely the intelligence-gathering section of the British army during the late Crimean War. More dull than sinister, but worthily so. The Department mainly produced the various maps by which Lord Cardigan and his officers directed their troops in one direction or another, chasing various Russian military forces about that grim territory."

"Without notable success, of course." Even in my isolated rural village, I had heard tell of the disastrous results of the Light Brigade's suicidal charge, as well as other incidents indicating vast befuddlement at the army's senior levels.

"Hardly the Department's fault," noted Stonebrake. "Its maps were punctiliously correct to the slightest detail. As was also the various statistical information it gathered—number of enemy troops, composition of armaments, all that sort of thing. What Cardigan and the rest of those well-born idiots did with the data is none of our concern."

"What does all that have to do with my father? Or me, for that matter?"

"Exactly this," said Stonebrake. "The general disappointment in the army's conduct in the Crimean Peninsula, and the unhappy results thereof, extended to such agencies as the Department of Topography and Statistics as well, however suitably they might have accomplished their own particular missions. Such being the case, there was little opposition when our new Prime Minister, Mrs. Fletcher, and her scurrying subordinates saw fit to alter both the Department's name and the uses to which the Department is put. Out goes inoffensive and moderately useful Topography, in comes Technography, much more secretive—and for Mrs. Fletcher's purposes, much more useful. An individual as powerful and understandably given to endless suspicions as she is, naturally feels compelled to keep an eye upon anything that presents a threat to the maintenance of her position. And of course, your father's devices fall under that purview."

"I scarcely see the cause for her worries." I gave a dismissive shrug, as well as I could given Stonebrake's grasp upon my arm. "She already has most of them under her control, doesn't she? Surely the Prime Minister, and especially one as intimidating as her, has access to all the warehouses of the British Museum and wherever else all those devices are presently stored."

"It's the ones she *doesn't* have under her thumb—the ones still out in the wild, as it were—that concern Mrs. Fletcher. They have concerned her for a great deal of time, and well before the initiation of those schemes into which I have brought you. And it's not just the devices conceived and created by your father that weigh upon her mind. He was of that generation of scientist and artisan almost supernaturally capable in everything they undertook. Who knows what other inventions and devices they might have left behind, of unknown but threatening potential? Even if your father's creations were the most powerful in their effects, the others are still worrisome to one such as Mrs. Fletcher. Her enemies—of which she still has a considerable number, despite having eliminated many of them—might turn anything against her. Or so she believes."

"Ah." The etymology of the previously unfamiliar word became clear to me. "Thus *Technography*—the description and evaluation of that landscape of scientific creation, rather than the Earth's cloddish terrain."

"Exactly so, Dower. From a cobweb-shrouded gaggle of dronesome mapmakers, the Department has been transformed and enlarged into a network of spies, all answering directly to Mrs. Fletcher as they comb all of England's cities and countryside. They keep track of and report on every past remnant of invention, or current scientific and technological activity in Britain—official or amateur, public or secretive, large or small. As you might well imagine, such is a considerable enterprise, and only succeeds in its operations by the most daunting ruthlessness."

"And of course . . ." Another realization formed inside my thoughts. "Your concern is that this so-called Department of Topography and Statistics might already have found and secreted away that device which you and associates have been so eager to locate. To wit, my father's *Vox Universalis*."

There was no need for Stonebrake to reply—I could discern that I had laid my finger upon the precise motivator of his increasing agitation. He let go of my arm and leaned convulsively forward from the edge of the cell's bunk, his hands seized into trembling, white-knuckled fists. As I observed this response on his part, I heard the clanging sounds from the corridor outside increase in volume. The noises seemed to be coming steadily closer, the banging of metal upon metal now accompanied by what might have been cascades of brick and stone, as heard at the collapse of earthquake-stricken buildings.

"Yes!" Wild-eyed, Stonebrake whirled about, the monosyllabic cry issuing from his lips. "They might have! The bastards . . . the skulking thieves . . ."

"They are only doing," I mildly pointed out, "what we ourselves have been engaged upon."

The comment seemed to enrage him. He seized the front of my shirt, drawing me close to his maddened gaze. For a moment, I anticipated renewed violence from the man—then he visibly gained control of himself once more. He let go again and drew back from me.

"Yes . . ." He gave a slow nod. "Of course. And we must turn that to our advantage."

"Why not just let them have it? My father's invention, that is—if this Department of Whatever has indeed found it. If it's as important to Mrs. Fletcher as you've indicated, then perhaps it would not be a brilliant idea to attempt to take it away from her—even if we could, of course. From the little bit I saw, she doesn't seem like the sort of person who lightly takes being crossed."

"I have two points in rejoinder." Stonebrake spoke in a rigid and controlled manner, as though keeping his fiery emotions under tight control. "The first is that I will see you and Mrs. Fletcher in Hell before I allow that to happen. I have not come this far to let the prize slip out of my grasp. The second point is that we do *not* yet know whether her Department has obtained the *Vox Universalis*. This is what we must find out."

"Somehow . . . I am gaining the impression that this is where I make my entrance upon the scene."

"You surmise correctly. I have gone to great pains—and much subterfuge—to establish within the Department of Technography and Statistics that you represent a grave danger to Mrs. Fletcher."

"Pardon me?"

"And indeed to the entirety of the British nation."

"*What?*" I had thought myself beyond further surprise by the man. In the event, I was proven wrong—again. "You told them . . . that I am . . ."

"A falsehood, but a modest one. And all in service of our plan."

"How relieved I am to know that it wasn't done for frivolous purposes. I'm sure I will take that comfort to my grave—likely any day now."

"Not quite that soon." Stonebrake shook his head. "First there is the necessity of your interrogation."

"That sounds less than cordial."

"A mere formality. I am confident that you will endure it . . . tolerably well. Some of their methods might be a bit harsh, but you have considerable value to them. This is, of course, despite their belief that you are in league with bloodthirsty anarchists, bent on overthrow of the established order—for which your father's creations are their chief means of destruction."

"I confess that you have me at a loss here." This was the occasion for my shaken head. "Why in God's name would you tell them something such as that? And do not say, *The plan*."

"It's exceedingly simple, Dower." He spoke over the advancing noises from the corridor. "We need to establish what the Department of Technography and Statistics knows regarding the locations of your father's *Vox Universalis* device. What better way than to foster in their minds the desire to establish what *you* know about it?"

"A moment. You told these people I am specifically eager to locate the *Vox Universalis?* What would they believe I want with such a thing, if they are unfamiliar with all the rest of your scheming? The negotiating with whales about the movements of lighthouses and all of that?"

"They hardly need to know your exact purpose. All that is required is that they believe it somehow essential to you and your associates' fiendish schemes. And I have convinced them of that."

How that served his purposes, I could well envision. But I failed to see how it accomplished much, if anything, for myself.

I indicated as much to Stonebrake: "What happens when it is ascertained that I do not, in fact, know anything about the location of the *Vox Universalis* device? If this Department of Technography and Statistics does not already possess it, I rather suspect they wish to do so as speedily as possible, to prevent it from falling into the hands of these imagined seditious associates of mine. If I cannot assist the Department in this regard, I would also believe that my value to them is greatly lessened."

"Yes . . ." He nodded, mulling over my words. "And so . . . ?"

"So they would make speedy dispatch of me. And in a permanent manner."

"Ah. So that is what you are concerned about, rather than the success or failure of—"

"Don't say it. And yes, I *am* concerned about my own survival. It is my life to dispose of, and I shall do so when I choose. Or not. Before that moment, I would prefer that the decision not be taken from me."

"As you wish. And to be certain, as I've assured you before, you have considerable value to me as well."

"And what am I to take as proof of that?"

"You will have all the proof you require, Dower—if anything should go amiss. For in a similar fashion to that in which I inveigled myself into the confidences of the Department of Technography and Statistics, so have others. I speak of *our* associates, naturally. So great are the fortunes we pursue, that there are more than you can imagine who are aligned with us, seeking to become as wealthy as we shall be. A significant number have penetrated the ranks of the Department, in which they pass completely free of suspicion. If that moment should come—and it might—when your person is in actual danger, these persons will spring into action, all for the purpose of rescuing you therefrom."

The last of his words were delivered in a veritable shout, so loud had the surrounding noises become. It seemed as though the building above us were in the process of complete demolishment. Indeed, clouds of white dust began to float through the cell in which I had been incarcerated, the stones beneath our feet shivering with unseen impacts.

I was unable to order my thoughts in such clamour. Whether I had any option other than to assume my role within Stonebrake's intertwining subterfuges, I could not determine.

"Very well!" I shouted back at him. "I will, as criminal types put it, play along with what you have contrived. But if the Department's interrogators should lay a hand upon me—"

"Interrogators?" Actual bits of stone and crumbling brick began to rain down upon our heads. "I don't believe you realize how personally important this matter is to the Prime Minister—"

I soon did. The walls on either side of the cell's doorway crumbled into pieces, the door itself falling with a thud at our feet. Through the dust clouds, I was able to perceive hastening workmen hoisting mallets above their heads, then hammering the spikes of iron railway tracks into the corridor's stone floor. They worked at frantic speed, seemingly unaware of the arched ceiling above their heads splitting open.

With an ear-piercing shriek, billows of steam rolled into the cell. The mechanical noises reached a deafening pitch. For a moment, my hindered vision could just perceive great spoked wheels turning and thrusting pistons more enormous than imperial cannons—

The wall behind me sundered to dust, pitching the unchained bunk to the cell's floor. The clouds of steam parted and I found myself gazing up into the unsmiling visage of Mrs. Fletcher.

CHAPTER
16

Mr. Dower Receives the Brunt of a Scalding Wrath

S O *you* . . . are the person who has caused such an uproar."
Given the great rumbling and shattering of the building's firmament that had accompanied Mrs. Fletcher's arrival, I had expected a deeper, more profound pitch to her voice. In this, I was disappointed. On the sole occasion I had opportunity to overhear some utterances from her, when Stonebrake had been secretively ensconced in the gallery overlooking the Commons' erstwhile deliberations, I had thought that the noises I had perceived as emanating from the monstrous iron construction were but a malfunction, perhaps one of the alarm whistles bolted to the cylindrical boiler's flank shrieking out of turn. But now that I was face-to-face with the transmogrified Prime Minister, I more correctly perceived that the sound was her actual voice—not the impressive bass that would seemingly have been more suited to both her immense form and position of power, but instead a nagging, wheedling verbal semblance, more suited to a schoolmistress than a despot.

"You must excuse me—" After having been upended by the general collapse of the cell around me, I had regained my feet with as much dignity as I could muster, given the circumstances. "But I was not aware that I had caused any such disturbance. And if I have, it was not my intent."

"Perhaps not." The square-jawed face surmounting the partial torso shifted in its squinting appraisal of me. Again, I was reminded of the manner in which a nominally female figurehead might be mounted to the prow of a large ocean-going vessel—though in this case, certainly not a fetching, bare-breasted mermaid with streaming tresses, but rather the more formidable shape of one of those termagant-like creatures whose masculinizing tendencies have rendered them as stevedores working the East London docks. "Now that I see you directly," continued Mrs. Fletcher, "rather than merely listening to secondhand reports of your doings, I suspect that I might have been somewhat misled as to the threat you represent to Her Majesty's government."

Despite its dismissive tone, I was heartened by this appraisal. With any luck, the Prime Minister might determine that I was not worthy of any further attention, not even to the point of being eliminated from the face of the Earth, and I would be set free to go about my inconsequential ways.

"Appearances can be deceiving . . ."

This voice came from close behind me. I glanced over my shoulder and saw Stonebrake brushing the powdery dust from his lapels. Straightening his garments, he gave a respectful nod of the head to Mrs. Fletcher.

"It might be worth the Prime Minister's time to undertake a thorough questioning of this man." Stonebrake's intent was obviously to raise the issue of the location of my father's *Vox Universalis* device, rather than to acquire my freedom. "Just to definitively ascertain that he possesses no useful information."

"Indeed." From above, Mrs. Fletcher squinted down at me. Behind the human component of her form, a corps of attendants—different from the sweating navvies who had lain down the railway tracks by which she traveled from place to place—swarmed over the greater mechanical bulk. Their busy hands made minute but essential adjustments to the various valves and other appurtenances that extended from the larger machinery. "Such is my intent."

My heart sank again within me, as the prospect of my release faded once more. This close to the Iron Lady's intimidating construction, more steam engine than woman, it became apparent to me that any appeal to what arguably might have remained of her more tender feminine nature was doomed to failure. Only sheer bravado on my part, evoked by the desperate situation in which I was encumbered, kept me from flinging myself bodily to the cracked cell floor in despair.

"My sources tell me," continued the ever-helpful Stonebrake, "that this person and his heinous associates are endeavouring to locate a certain device capable of simulating not just human voices, but communications made by other species as well."

"Yes . . ." Mrs. Fletcher's steely head gave a slow nod as she studied me. "I am familiar with the nature of the device of which you speak. The question, of course, is that of *your* knowledge." Her narrow gaze fastened even harder upon me. "Tell us of your expertise, Mr. Dower."

"I make no claim to any." In this situation, I had decided that honesty might be the wisest course. If nothing else, it might be considered disarming, given how unusual it was in these various interlocking circles. "Other than that my father was the creator of the device being discussed. There are some who feel that such a filial status might give me a unique insight to its operations. Whether that is true or not remains to be seen, as I have yet to even see this all-purpose vocalizing apparatus."

From my position in the jumbled ruins of the cell, I kept close watch upon Mrs. Fletcher's reaction to my words. Even though her face seemed more composed of grey iron than pinkish skin, as though the sturdier atoms of her mechanical bulk had somehow insinuated themselves into her flesh, a few flashes of the human were still discernible, like muted lightning in overhanging storm clouds. To the degree I was capable upon such short notice, I had crafted my statement as much in pursuit of Stonebrake's goal as my own. If the Prime Minister and her associates at the Department of Technography and Statistics were indeed in possession of the *Vox Universalis,* there was a good chance that they were as stymied about its functions as were most people who came into contact with my father's devices. And if that were the case, the response I was hoping to evoke from her would establish not only the machine's location, but also some continued value to her, in regard to my remaining alive.

A scalding gout of steam jetted from one of the valves closest behind her torso, as though her darkly musing cogitations had triggered some expression of force from the immense cylindrical boiler. "You haven't seen it?" The expression on Mrs. Fletcher's stiffened face turned even grimmer. "I had been led to believe—indeed, on the assurances that the informant standing behind you had given to my Department of Technography and Statistics—that you had not just a connection through your father to the apparatus under discussion, but also extensive experience in its operation. Hands on, as it were."

"So he does—" Stonebrake hastened to interject his putative correction. "Disregard this comment he has just made. The man is a desperate and violent criminal, fully in league with the worst rampageous groups. Thus, it was necessary for the constables to apply a rigorous amount of physical force in order to make his apprehension. Very likely, his memory has been temporarily deranged by these events." With the sharp point of his elbow, he gave me an admonishing dig in the ribs. After a quick, scathing glance, he turned his gaze back toward the Prime Minister. "I'm sure it will all come back to him in short order, though."

"You seem to know a great deal about him. How is that?"

"Entirely done in your service." Stonebrake spread his hands wide. "I have kept this individual under the closest scrutiny. I can give you a complete account, if you were to be interested, of his various peregrinations about the city. As I have trailed behind him, he has led me through some of the most secretive locales possible, the very knowledge of which on his part indicates his association with those evildoers who skulk about at our world's nocturnal fringes. How else would he have gained secretive entry to not just the intimate chambers of that certain emporium catering to those transformed similarly to yourself, not to mention spying upon you at the House of Commons?"

"Yes, yes; that has all been reported to me. In great detail. His identity as a thorough felon is well established thereby."

I turned and looked at Stonebrake beside me, a new revelation dawning in my mind as to his recent actions. Previously, I been considerably doubtful as to why he was going to such great efforts to shuttle me about from place to place, all unbidden on my part. His protestations that this long travail had somehow been designed as a means of locating my father's *Vox Universalis* device, by way of the supposed ethereal vibrations emitted by my brain, I now saw as a hollow sham. My exhausting journey had been merely for the purpose of convincing those agents of the Prime Minister, all of whom must have been keeping us under their own observance, that I was engaged upon some nefarious errands—presumably at the bidding of these malignant anarchists with which I was presumed to be in sympathy. And thus it had been conveyed to the Prime Minister. To what ultimate effect, though, I was still not sure.

"I feel, however, that your confidence on this point is misplaced." As she spoke again, more geyser-like spouts of steam burst from various apertures arrayed on Mrs. Fletcher's mechanical bulk. "And more than any other failing that ordinary men are capable of, expressing deliberate falsehoods to me is the one that I find the most grievous."

Chastened—and deservedly so—by the Prime Minister's admonishment, Stonebrake shrank backward, as though to shelter himself as best he could behind me.

"Let me bluntly ask you this much." Her gaze, like gun slits in a military fortification, fastened with greater force upon me. "The Department of Technography and Statistics have established that your father devised a certain apparatus, designated as the *Vox Universalis*. Do you know of it? Pray keep your reply as brief as possible."

"As I attempted to indicate to you—I have been told about it."

"More briefly than that—to match my waning patience. Do you know if this device still exists?"

For my own sake, I knew I should have attempted prevarication on these points. If I wanted her to place even a slight value on my continued existence, it would have been better for her to believe that the *Vox Universalis,* if not yet in her possession, might still be ac-

quired by her agents. And when that at last happened, the result of
the Department of Technography and Statistics' diligent scouring of
every obscure hiding-place in which the device might reside, then I
would presumably be able to assist in determining its exact functions and mode of operation. If I sought to ensure my own survival,
such were the notions that I should have attempted to more firmly
embed in her thoughts. But the withering scorn she had just directed at Stonebrake, for his failed attempts along these lines, spoke
volumes about the possible fate I would endure for a similar effort, if
my statements were to be discerned as untruthful.

"No," I confessed. "I don't even know if such a device ever existed."

A great metallic clatter issued from deep within the Prime Minister's form, the reverberations so strong as to cause a new storm of
dust and debris to fall through the ruins about me. What few riven
walls had been left still standing along the corridor behind her, now
trembled with imminent collapse.

"Great God, man—" Through the mounting noise, I heard
Stonebrake's appalled whisper at my ear. "Now you've done it."

"So, in actuality . . ." Mrs. Fletcher persisted in her enquiries.
"There is no possible aid you can provide us, when it comes to locating the device?"

"None whatsoever—"

In retrospect, that was not the wisest answer I could have given.

For a moment, it seemed as if the great engine embodying the
Prime Minister would rear entirely free of the hastily laid tracks
upon which her sharp-circumferenced wheels rested, so violent was
the shock that visibly ran through her iron components. From the
trembling boiler, rivets sprang like bullets, embedding themselves
in the cell's stone fragments. The escaping gouts of steam were now
so enlarged in force and volume as to send flying the attendants
scrambling to bring the construction back under control.

"Down!" Stonebrake grasped my shoulders from behind, attempting to pull me to the floor. "Shield yourself—"

It was too late. The last image entering my consciousness was that of Mrs. Fletcher, infuriated beyond even the abilities of her transmogrified frame to contain, howling like a Fury in my direction. Through the unleashed clouds of steam, their billows roiling like an ocean tide through the cell's broken confines, I had a nightmarish glimpse of her face, eyes now fully widened, brow dark with murderous, all-encompassing rage.

Then the explosion, scalding and churning the very air with its force—I felt myself bodily lifted, all earthly components obliterated. I shot into space, blinded to all thought and trajectory.

PART FOUR

THE AFTERLIFE AND BEYOND

CHAPTER
17

Mr. Dower Is Saved,
Then Lost Again

I DREAMT.

Which was a great comfort to me, given my most recent experiences.

Shortly before awareness returned to my being, I had been engulfed in billows of steam, only marginally less scathing than the regard of that creature which reportedly had once been a woman, but her own vaulting ambition had transformed into a monster of force and brutality. All else had crumbled away, scoured by that great entity Steam which had been unleashed upon the world.

But the place in which I found myself now—in the soothing compass of my dreaming—was rather more pleasant. Without opening my eyes, or imagining myself to do so, I knew that I was drifting in a boat, lying at full length inside it. One of my hands was draped over the side, so that my scalded hand was lapped by the cooling water. A freshening wind touched lightly upon my face, like a remembered kiss. On its soft current came the sour, invigorating scent of a great city somewhere in the distance, its inhabitants' exudations mingling into a perfume both sweatily pungent and provocative.

The boat slowly moved in its placid course, rocking me from side to side, evoking recall of tendernesses placed even further away in Time. Distance softened the tumult of a great roaring as well, sounding to my sleep-enmired ear as gentle as some orchestral amusement full of drums and trumpets. Perhaps the earnest musicians were busily engaged in their craft in a leafy park somewhere on the river's bank . . .

I refrained from opening my eyes, fearful of the dispelling thereby of this unbidden idyll. To my slowing thoughts came just enough remembrance of all from which I had fled, to invoke my wish to avoid that other, less felicitous world a while longer.

Alas, it was not to be.

"Wake up there—" Someone else's hand roughly prodded my shoulder where I lay. "I want no dead bodies, of gennulmun or others, in my p'session. You hear me? Oop and aboot, kindly!"

Whether I wished them to or not, my eyes sprang open. I found myself gazing up into an unwashed, stubble-bearded visage, previously unknown to me. The features of the man, whoever he might be, were flickeringly lit orange and red, as though by the glow of a fire somewhere beyond.

I set my hands against the dampish boards beneath and raised myself to a sitting position, discovering thereby that at least this important component of my dreaming was based in reality. For I was indeed in a boat, a slight enough craft to be adequately rowed by one person manning the oars behind my interlocutor.

"Begging your pardon . . ." I shook my head, as if that motion would be enough to dispel the muddle clinging to its interior. "You'll have to excuse my disorientation, my good man. I've been through . . . rather a lot lately."

"Ye might avow as much," conceded the boatman sitting before me. "Getting fished out of the Thames is naught ye should make a reg'lar practice of."

"The Thames?" Bit by bit, further recollections assembled themselves in my thoughts. So abrupt had been my explosive transition from one mode of existence to another, I had scarcely been able to determine whether I was still alive and within London's urban limits, or that the boat's shadowily perceived crew were ferrying me across the Styx. "Indeed . . ." I ran my hands over my garments and found them to be as thoroughly sodden as the boatman's description of my latest adventure would have predicted. "But how?"

"How what, laddie?"

"How did I get here?" A spark of irritation flared inside me. What else did he think I'd care to know?

"Bluidy great blast flung ye here." He gestured toward the boat's gunwales, scarcely his arms' length apart from each other. "Not here lit'rally, I mean, like ye were some fookin' carp that'd flopped itself into our laps." One work-gnarled hand pointed across the dark water. "Rather sev'ral yards away, to be exact."

"Made a right impressive splash, ye did." The one at the oars spoke with eye-glittering enthusiasm. "Could've been a ver'table cannonball shot at us." What I could discern of his gap-toothed smile faded a bit. "Pity it weren't—that'd've been ever more int'resting."

"'F we hadn't been about here and paddled over to where ye landed, ye'd have like as drowned. Seeing as how ye weren't in full p'session of yer faculties, as it were."

"No . . . I don't imagine I was." My cogitation had reached that point where I could aid to some degree the reassembly of my memory. "I was in . . . a cell . . ."

"Ye see?" The first boatman gave a nod to the one at the oars. "I told ye it was likely a desperate criminal." He turned back to me. "There be a great plenty of you lot, bomb-throwing anarchists and such, around these days."

"Streets be full of 'em, what I hear." The other added this observation as he dipped the oars into the river. "Can scarce get from Bowditch to the Isle of Dogs, for the sheer number o' the breed."

"I'm actually not an anarchist. Bomb-throwing or otherwise—"

"Of course ye're not." The boatman winked at me. "Nobody ever *says* they are. It'd be better proof in yer favor if ye said ye were."

I let that logic pass without comment. I was still attempting to evoke the recollection of precisely where I had been before landing in the river.

A flaring light suddenly filled the sky, rendering the watery vista around me as brightly illuminated as though it had been mid-day. At the same time, the rumbling sound of a great explosion washed over the little boat.

"Ah!" The oarsman expressed keen appreciation. "That were a nice 'un!"

Looking over my shoulder, in the direction from which the deep report had emanated, I saw stately buildings in the distance, arrayed along the river's edge. Churning flames leapt past towers and chaotic smokestacks, still belching forth smoke and steam.

As soon as I recognized the Houses of Parliament, my memories flashed into place, restored by the sight of the architectural wreckage. At once, I recalled the tightly confining cell, the appearance of first Stonebrake there, then the much more appalling arrival of Mrs. Fletcher. The sound of her furiously squalling voice battered about inside my skull, to the extent that it was a comfort to remember what little I could of the explosive event that had evidently precipitated my aerial launch into the Thames.

"You see now, don't you?"

A voice, a different one, spoke behind me. A woman's . . . softer and more familiar . . .

I turned again and saw another figure in the boat, seated at the angle of the prow. Her face was hidden by the heavy shawl that she had wrapped about herself, to fend off the river's chill.

The woman spoke again: "That which you so narrowly escaped— you are fortunate to be alive, Mr. Dower!"

The light from the most recent explosion began to fade, but there was still enough from the remaining fires, by which I could recognize her face when she cast back the shawl from her shoulders.

"Evangeline—" Startled, I was able to but speak the single name.

"Yes, of course." Lord Fusible's daughter gave me a welcoming smile. "Surely you did not believe that you had been absent from my thoughts?"

⊷≔◉≕⊷

BEING present in a woman's thoughts at all, especially those of one as young and fair as this, was a relative novelty for me. On some other occasion, less stressful than that in which I currently found

myself, that might have been the most flattering aspect of this renewed acquaintance with the young lady. Given the circumstances,
though, what was even more welcome was her elucidation of all that
had just happened to me.

"Poor Mr. Dower! You're soaked through!" She had changed
places with the first boatman, the better to hold conversation with
me. "You will catch your death, I'm sure."

"So far, I haven't." As with most men in the company of attractive women, I attempted as much of a valiant *façade* as I could muster. "Though not for lack of attempts on the parts of others."

"You're quite correct about that; it's shameful the way you've
been treated. You must think this a hateful world, for it to be so cruel
toward you. And all without cause!"

"As a general rule, I do try to avoid provoking murderous
assaults."

"Here, take this." She wrapped her shawl about me, leaning
close to snug its folds tight at my throat. "You need to stay warm."

"That's quite all right. I'll be fine, I assure you—"

"I fear you do not understand—even now." Her hand kept the
shawl firmly in place. "You have more value to me than any of mere
sentiment."

The young woman's comment worried me a bit. The last person
to obscurely speak of my *value* had been Stonebrake. Even though I
was endeavouring, without great success, to refrain from thinking ill
of the man—for surely the chances of his escaping the explosion at
the Houses of Parliament, as I had, were slender—any words similar
to his inveigling verbiage still struck me amiss. I would rather have
been of *less* value to so many people, if such would have rendered me
both freer and safer.

"That is why," continued Evangeline, "I stationed myself here
upon the river, in the company of these loyal servants of my father."

"Don't know as much about *loyal,* miss." The one at the prow
spoke up. "Seemed more of a lark, to be abs'lutely truthful. More
enjoyable than mucking out the carriage house, as 'twere."

"There's no need to minimize your usefulness. If you hadn't come here with me, poor Mr. Dower here would be dead and drowned by now."

"Ye're right—that *would* be a great pity and all. 'Pears a pleasant enow fellow. Not one of them bleedin' Mission folk, is he, that ye're allus rattling on about?"

"Mission?" That sparked another remembrance inside me. I glanced over to Evangeline beside me. "Does he mean the Mission to the Cetaceans?"

"He does," said Evangeline. "Both these gentlemen are familiar—to a degree—with that organization, though of course they are not actual members of it."

"Not likely t'ever be, either." The boatman's scorn was evident. "Seem a right daft lot, ye ask me."

"Be that as it may." Evangeline took as sternly chastening a tone as one so young could manage. "The Mission to the Cetaceans certainly proved their merit in this case." She directed her attention back to me. "For it was through them that I was informed of this heinous plot against your person, Mr. Dower."

"Plot?" The boat rocked gently as we continued to drift along the night-dark river. "Against *me*? Why should anyone—"

"Well," the young lady allowed, "not so much against you specifically. You were but a prop, a necessary element in a larger scheme. The attempt was not directed upon your life, but that of the Prime Minister, Mrs. Fletcher."

"That seems more reasonable." I felt no need to further elaborate on my statement, as I felt sure that Evangeline was familiar with the horrifying nature of the other woman. "But who was it who wished to do her harm?"

"Ye don't know?" The boatman snorted in derision. "Why, that devious, scheming blaggard—yer friend Stonebrake!"

"Are you sure?" I was now completely mystified. "Why would he want to accomplish something such as that? I was of the conviction that he needed to ascertain from Mrs. Fletcher the exact location of a certain device created by my father."

"The *Vox Universalis*?" Evangeline nodded sagely. "Yes, I am sure he would have used that as a pretext to advance his lethal agenda. But that merely serves to demonstrate the cunning of the man. There's a very good chance that every word Stonebrake spoke to you was a lie of one kind or another."

"I'd hardly dispute that. I've suspected as much, for some time now."

"Not so much," said the boatman, "as to refrain from followin' along with the bastard, willy-nilly-like."

The comments stiffened my spine. "Were you acquainted with the man?"

"Me? Not bluidy likely!"

"Then let me assure you—he was *very* persuasive."

The boatman exchanged glances, complete to raised eyebrows, with his companion at the oars, but said no more.

"We needn't worry about Mr. Stonebrake any longer." Evangeline took command of the discussion once again. "Which will be a relief to those for whom he had been putatively working, but who had suspected him of duplicity for some time now. I speak, of course, of the leadership of the Mission to the Cetaceans, with whom I have been in contact."

"I doubt if your father would approve of that, if he were to find out. I had gained the impression that your betrothal to Captain Crowcroft was just about as much involvement with the business of walking lighthouses as he cared for you to have."

"That much you are correct about, Mr. Dower—but it was my concern for my *fiancé* that prompted my going behind my father's back in such a manner. As such, I would entreat you with all my heart, should the occasion arise, not to reveal to him what I have done—and what I now wish to impart to you."

"You have my word upon that." To make such an assurance to an attractive young woman was a small but genuine pleasure for me, as I assume it would be for most men. If we are not as noble in keeping such pledges as our courtly forebears were, it is merely an indication of our generally fallen state. "Pray continue with your revelations."

"Here is what you should know," said Evangeline. "As I have in-dicated already, the leadership of the Mission had suspected for some time that Stonebrake had been playing some kind of double game, as I believe such is called by those given to devious activities. In this case, it was not so much initiated by Stonebrake himself— rather, he was following an agenda directed by other sinister and mysterious forces."

"Aye, she's right about that, laddie." The boatman could not re-frain from commenting upon the exchange he overheard. "All of that tosh 'bout passing ye off as a dangerous sort, keen on 'quiring some 'laborate gadget needed for whatever deviltry ye and yer lot were up to—that was but a ruse to get ye face-to-face with that Fletcher woman. Or whate'er it might be, that she is these days. Or so 'twas 'splained to me."

"Exactly so." Lord Fusible's daughter leaned closer to me. "Take this as an indicator of the degree of hazard from which you have been so precipitously extracted. I am confident that such never would have been your intention, but you have unwittingly played a crucial part in what was an assassination attempt upon the Prime Minister. You were but the bait to lure the preternaturally suspicious Prime Minister from her fortified hiding place elsewhere in the Pal-ace of Westminster, to those subterranean cells which Stonebrake's associates had previously mined with explosives."

"You are, of course, correct—about me, that is." I was surprised but not hugely startled by what Evangeline had just told me. Given what I had just experienced of the fearsome Mrs. Fletcher, I would have more likely imagined that attempts to assassinate her were initi-ated on virtually a daily basis. "Stonebrake said nothing to me of such a motive."

"Aye, them anarchists are a tight-mouthed lot." The boatman spoke up again. "If ye were t'ask me, this here Stonebrake fellow might well have been 'un of that Walsall bunch—ye know all 'bout them, I 'magine."

"No . . . I can't say as I do."

"Ye should. Quite a menace they are—leastways, the author'ties say so. Much given to setting off incendiary devices in public places—not quite sure why, 'less it's for the sheer merriment of doing so."

"Don't be so daft," said the other manning the oars. "If ye'd but stir yerself as to read their man'festo, ye'd know why they do it."

"That *Anarchist Feast at the Opera* book?" The boatman shook his head in disgust. "Couldn't be bothered. Seemed a right load o' rubbish, when I took a glance at it."

"Bollocks. Quite high-minded, I thought it."

"Ye would, being the prat ye are."

"Gentlemen—please. Perhaps you could postpone your political discussion to another time. I have a bit more information to divulge to Mr. Dower."

"As ye wish, miss."

Evangeline turned back to me. "It gladdens me," she said, "that you have been so fortunate. Whatever Stonebrake and his actual associates might have been trying to achieve, your usefulness to them is now ended. And better: Even if there were some remaining value, they have no way of knowing that you are in fact alive. It is much more reasonable to assume that you died in that same explosion in which Stonebrake's life was ended."

"There ye be, laddie—ye're off the hook!"

"Just so," continued Evangeline. "You can now hide aboard the headquarters ship of the Mission to the Cetaceans, which is where you are being taken now. It will be a safe refuge until it is prudent for you to show your face again, having achieved the anonymity that accompanies being presumed dead."

"Indeed." I nodded, impressed with her reasoning. "That would be an advantageous situation."

"From which, Mr. Dower, you could then proceed to pick up the pieces of whatever is left of the life you had been leading before you got enmired in all these schemes. Or . . ." Evangeline pressed her hand to my arm. "You might choose to be of greater service to me."

That put me rather on the spot. The possibility of removing myself from this beastly, scorching London and returning to the sheltering obscurities of the countryside was extraordinarily attractive to my sensibilities. My being able to do so, with the rest of the world believing that my existence had come to an end, multiplied the benefits to be derived therefrom.

Thus, the reader might well imagine the wonderment I felt when I heard my reply to the young woman.

"Even if you had not saved my life . . ." I spoke as reassuringly as I was able to her. "Still, I would not abandon you in whatever hour of need in which you have found yourself."

"Thank you, Mr. Dower—I had hoped such would be your response." She clasped both her hands upon mine, still clutching the edges of the shawl she had wrapped about me. "For my initiative in making contact with the Mission to the Cetaceans was prompted by concern for another—my *fiancé*."

"In what danger would Captain Crowcroft be? He pilots the walking lights, and is therefore of value to your father and the other shareholders of Phototrope Limited—but surely their concern for him ends there. Why would they or anyone else, pursuing whatever conspiracies they wish, threaten him?"

"If this were a better world, Mr. Dower, your reasoning would prevail. But alas, it is not. My betrothed is in even greater peril than that from which you have so recently escaped. I feel obliged to tell you this, because you are in fact the only person I can count upon to rescue him from these dire circumstances."

"I?"

My fear had been that Evangeline would say something of this sort. As charitable as was the spirit I discerned within the young woman, it would hardly seem likely that she would have gone to the speculative effort of stationing herself upon the Thames with two accomplices recruited from amongst her father's servants, for the mere purpose of saving me from drowning. Indeed, she would have had little reason to believe that I would have landed in the river's waters, with my person more or less in one piece, rather than be smashed to items by the explosion directed toward the Prime Minister. Thus, it was reasonable to conclude that she had her own motive, one closer to her heart, for embarking upon a venture with seemingly so little chance of success. The situation in which Captain Crowcroft was trapped must be dire indeed, if a slender reed such as myself was her only hope of extricating him.

"Yes . . ." She confirmed my hasty speculations. "I would not attempt to prevail upon you otherwise, given our brief acquaintance— and the hostility I shamefully admit I displayed to you upon our initial encounters."

"That is nothing you need to concern yourself about. It happens so frequently to me, that I have become quite inured to bafflement at the responses from others, whom I've never met before—"

Without intending for them to do so, my eyes drifted shut for a moment as a wave of exhaustion swept over me. I had been fatigued before these most recent events, culminating in my unexpected immersion; their cumulative effects now caught up with me.

"Would it be at all possible," I spoke, "to postpone your exposition until such time as I have recovered a bit of my strength? Even a few hours' rest would greatly suffice in that regard. I am sure that time is pressing, as it always seems to be anymore, but I fear that I am close to the end of my personal resources."

"Yes, of course," the young lady hastened to reassure me. "Dear Mr. Dower, I had no intent to divest you of every scrap of your capabilities. Indeed, I anticipated that if we were at all able to effect your rescue, you would hardly be able to continue on without respite. Here—" She produced from about her person a small, folded piece of paper and pressed it into my grasp. "I have written down an address, to be found here in the city. That is to where you must—"

"Oy!" A sudden, panicked shout came from the boatman. "'Ave a care, you lot!"

I soon saw that which had triggered the man's alarm. Gripping the gunwales of the boat, he gazed with wide-eyed fright at the dark waters below us. With but the stars and a sliver of moon for illumination, I was also able to discern some huge shape coming up from the depths of the river, directly beneath the boat. With a considerable portion of my thoughts still agitated by my recent experiences, a horrific vision swam before my eyes. It was of Mrs. Fletcher in her steam-powered, ironclad transformation, but even larger and more intimidating than before. Her broad, sullen-aspected face grimaced with all of the malice she had previously directed toward me. Her massive form seemed to hurtle toward us, as though her intent were to capture and drag me under the water's inky surface.

The broad swell that capsized the boat might have been a tidal wave, so great was its force and capacity. For the second time in one night, I found myself thrown bodily in the air, landing moments later in the Thames' cold embrace.

This much was different, though—no-one was there to rescue me. Floundering with every limb, struggling to keep what breath I could in my lungs, I could see no trace of either Evangeline or her able companions. Given the violence of that which had just transpired, their situation was likely worse than my own—perhaps fatally so.

Which was likely my fate as well. The black waters closed over my head, all light and air slipping from me . . .

CHAPTER

18

Awakening in Disagreeable Circumstances

G IVEN that I considered myself more sinned against than sinner in my progress through earthly existence, my first impression of the afterlife was that an egregious injustice had been committed.

That I had awakened, after my watery transition from the realm of the living to whatever came next, in some place of eternal punishment seemed obvious to my perception. As though to mock me further, its essential elements all provided unappealing reminders of the world I had just left. If I had ever believed that by the mere act of dying I could leave behind all the clanking, hissing dismalness of Steam-transformed London, my illusions were now quickly dispelled. Far from fleeing that relentlessly mechanical world, I found that I had been translated to one even more given to gear and boiler, crankshaft and cog. The realization that I would be here for Eternity greatly disheartened me.

At the least, I could have been given a dry change of clothing by whatever meddlesome demons were in charge of the facilities. The same garments in which I had drowned still clung damply to my frame as I pushed my hands against the gritty, oily terrain on which I had been deposited. With what little strength had been allowed to me, I managed to bring myself into a roughly sitting position, from which I could survey my new abode. If there had been the roaring flames that the stern and terrifying preachers of my childhood had promised, I would have almost welcomed them as a means of rendering my jacket and trousers dry and my body somewhat less chilled from its final immersion.

Eternal night—that, at least, came as no surprise. My vision slowly adjusted to the darkness into which I had been cast, enough that I could discern the rude metal shapes surrounding me.

It might as well have been the afterlife of every defunct steam engine and other thundering device, rent asunder by the force that had once driven its functions. I could see enormous constructs on all sides, railway engines toppled onto their sides, spiraling copper tubes thick in diameter as a man's body, driving shafts that might have propelled the earth's own motion about its axis, industrial furnaces that might have sent a thousand looms spinning, carriages and cranes so vast as to blot out the dark sky against which they reared— all the gargantuan, hypertrophied machinery of a world bereft of any organic animation. Yet as massive as were the silent, unmoving devices, they seemed somehow pathetic, more to be pitied than feared due to their evident broken and discarded condition. The entire scene, extending in every direction from where I sat, might have been some giant toddler's playpen, all his playthings reduced to rubbish by a display of infantile spleen. Scattered across the ground were the smaller bits and pieces strewn by that hypothetical tantrum, gears and sharp-toothed cogwheels lying thick about as the flinty stones of one of Britain's more inhospitable ocean strands.

Oddly, an indication of mortal life came to hand as I gazed about the forlorn purview. I pricked my finger on the jagged end of a spring-coil close to me—my brow knit in puzzlement as I detected a drop of blood ooze from the tiny wound. Such seemed improbable to me—why would I require the circulation of vital fluids through my body, if I were no longer alive? Even more strangely, when I placed the flat of my hand against my soggy shirtfront, I unmistakably felt the pulse of my heart—seemingly wearied by all the exertions preceding my death, yet still staggering on relentlessly, one beat after another.

A glint of light struck my eye, unexpected as a flash of lightning.

I raised my head and watched as the same yellowish gleam moved across the brass and iron forms nearest to me.

"Over there, Cyril—that seems a likely lot."

The voice that sifted through the gloom did not seem demonic in tone; rather more like one's average Englishman, at least of the un-educated sort.

Wobbling a bit, I gained my feet and peered toward the source of the illumination. I perceived a lantern with a fluttering wick inside, held aloft in the hand of a silhouetted figure. Another cloth-capped figure, of slightly lesser stature, accompanied him.

The two men perceived me at the same time. The shorter of the pair brandished a pry-bar in my direction.

"If ye're lookin' for trouble, mate—" He lowered his voice to what was evidently meant to be a threatening growl. "We're more than ready for yez."

They both seemed rather coarser and given to violence than the two servants that Lord Fusible's daughter had recruited to man the boat by which I had been briefly rescued from drowning in the Thames. I felt a twinge of regret, knowing that the pair—and Evan-geline as well—had evidently suffered the fate from which they had sought to save me. Being of rather more respectable moral character than myself, no doubt the young woman had been translated to a more felicitous district of the afterlife; perhaps her companions had accompanied her there. I should have felt happy for their sakes, but I admit the thought actually rendered me somewhat sadder. I would have appreciated some familiar company in my new, even more doleful circumstances—especially given that I was slated to endure the situation for all Eternity.

"Let me assure you—" I addressed my words to the two shad-owed figures. "I am not looking for any more trouble than I have, possessing already a surfeit thereof."

"Ooh—he do speak well, Cyril." One turned to the other and nodded in appreciation. "Very fancy-like."

"Summat of a visitor, then." The second signaled his agreement with a matching nod. "Obv'usly not from 'round these parts." He

peered at me, scratching his own head with the point of his improvised cudgel. "Wonder how he got here?"

"I beg your pardon . . ." My sight had adjusted enough that I
could see the man's unshaven face and the greasy rag knotted around
his neck. "Did you say *visitor*? Perhaps I heard amiss, but it seems
that was what you said."

"Aye, I did. Surely that's what ye be, mate—unless ye're fixing to
take up residence here. Which, as a gen'ral rule, I'd scarce advise."

"I was under the impression that I didn't have a choice about
the matter. That in fact I had been consigned to stay here for all
Eternity."

"That sounds rather harsh," said the first of the pair. "What fracas has a respectable gennulmun such as yerself gotten into, that
ye'd need to hide out for as long as that, in a sty such as this 'un?"

"Well . . ." Much of what had been spoken puzzled me. "Not so
much of a fracas, as it were—more the result of a series of bad decisions, most of them admittedly my own. Resulting, of course, in
my death—"

"In yer what?"

"My death," I repeated. "There was a time when I actually
wished to be dead, and was even prepared to act upon that resolve.
However, upon initial acquaintance with the next world—this one,
that is—I'm starting to regret that rash impulse."

"Did you hear that, Cyril? Blighter thinks he's *dead*."

"Aren't I? It seemed a reasonable assumption."

"Can't say I know as how reason'ble it is." Another scratch of his
head. "I do know that it's not true, however."

"Indeed?" A bright thread of hope insinuated itself into my spirits. "And these are not the infernal regions?"

"The what?"

"Hell," I said. "I am not aware of how much time you might have
spent in church, but surely you are aware of that much of Christian
doctrine. You know—the place of eternal torment, to which sinners
are consigned beyond the grave."

"Oh, *that*. Well, there'd be many as would say it's not the most pleasant place to find oneself—and I'd be the first t'agree. I only come down here for purposes of commerce, as it were. But Hell?" The man gave a decisive shake of his head. "I wouldn't go so far as to describe it in sech a manner."

"He's a loony, Cyril." A note of alarm sounded in his companion's voice. "Ye need be careful around him, in case he snaps and throws hisself 'pon yez."

I made no comment regarding that observation, the man being perfectly justified in that assessment, based upon the evidence I had provided him. It hardly mattered to me, now that I had been gratefully disabused of my previous convictions as to my mode of existence. I was still alive—remarkably so—and not yet suffering for my sins. Wherever I was, it seemed at least a small improvement upon my initial conclusion.

My mind was still flooded with questions, though. Something had happened while I had been in that small boat, of which I had only the most fragmentary and confusing recollections. A hazy memory slipped into my thoughts, of some great shape coming up from below, the river swelling therefrom with sufficient force and volume to capsize the vessel. No doubt the others, including my rescuer, Evangeline, had been hurled into the dark water as I had been. That I had survived, and they evidently hadn't, oppressed my spirits to some degree.

Nevertheless, my safety was hardly assured, merely by having reached whatever place this was. And my options were greatly diminished—I might no longer be ensnared in the devious Stonebrake's various schemes, due to his death in the explosion at Westminster Palace, but I was also now devoid of what assistance he had given in navigating through London's treacherous, Steam-transformed streets.

The realization came upon me with even greater force, that I did not even currently know where I was. If not Hell, then where? That *lacuna* in my bearings seemed to be the first one I should rectify.

"Excuse me . . ." I addressed my two new acquaintances. "Would it be at all possible for you gentlemen to tell me where I am?"

"Ye don't know?"

"I said as much, Cyril—bugger's completely daft."

"Please . . . the matter is somewhat important to me."

"No doubt." The first of the pair took pity on me. "Ev'ryone needs to know where they're at, leastways some of the time. Ye're in the boneyard."

Though it was sincerely given, this information availed me little. "Precisely what and where is this . . . *boneyard?*"

"However ye got here, fellow, ye've made yer way to the east part of London. Not gen'rally considered the poshest part of the city by yer likes, but it's as much home as we working types will ever know—"

"Gent arrived here by the river, of course. That's why he's all soaked through."

"The Thames?" I searched across their faces. "Is it nearby?"

"Scarcely a dozen yards away from you. Ye could see it if it weren't for that great bluidy pile of junk directly behind yez." The lantern was lifted higher, illuminating the ground about me. "There be yer track, where ye likely crawled here from th'edge of the water."

"Very well." The information was sketchy, but afforded at least a vague idea of my location. "And what is this boneyard of which you spoke? What sort of place is it?"

"Ye'll hardly be flattered when ye know. Ye've wound up where all the various sorts of rubbish are discarded. Partic'larly of the industrial and mechanical type."

"Powerful lot of that sort of thing," his companion agreed. "As of recent times, ye know. All these steam-powered contraptions, one wild-eyed monstrous device after another—it do lead to reg'lar mountains o' junk and tosh. Seems like most every day, some contrivance is blowing up, somewhere in the city. Scalding puir innocent folks raw with their unleashed gouts of steam, beheading them with flying bits o' scrap—just terr'ble, it is."

"But, Cyril—" The other protested this judgement. "We wouldn't have all the modern conveniences we do, if it weren't for incinerating a few people now and then. 'Tis a hard lot for them, of course, but that's the price o' progress, innit?"

"Hm. Not so sure 'bout that—"

"Please. You were saying . . ."

"Aye, the boneyard here. I must say, ye seem profoundly unfamil'ar with matters that are common knowledge for most."

"Pray forgive me," I said. "I have but recently arrived in London."

"Do tell." The man rubbed his dark-stubbled chin, regarding me as if he had never seen such a wonder before—and which he probably hadn't. "Then as I were telling yez, this be where all manner of scrap metal and defunct machinery gets barged down the river to, then heaved out 'pon the banks. No doubt it 'pears to one of your cultured sensibilities as less than aesthetic and all, but it do provide some opportunities to resourceful types such as ourselves."

"You rummage about here for discarded items of value?"

"Exactly so. Some bits o' metal are more valuable than others, and are worth the labour o' breaking apart from the rest. Takes a keen eye, it does, to know the diff'rence. And a strong back for the prying and wrestling about o' the great lumps. Which is why I bring him along." He smiled and pointed to his companion.

"Yer arse, Cyril."

I decided that I had ascertained as much of specific value as I was likely to from the men. In addition, my garments had dried to a tolerable degree. This, plus the return of a small measure of my bodily strength, motivated a further resolve.

"You gentlemen are familiar with the streets and alleys of East London?"

"We'd bluidy well better be. Seeing as how we live here."

I dug inside my coat, then produced the folded scrap of paper that had been given to me by Evangeline, just prior to the capsizing of the boat.

"Then perhaps you would be so kind . . ." I unfolded the damp paper and held it before them. The words were still legible upon it. "To direct me to this address."

The lantern was brought lower, both men leaning into its glow to study the white square in my hand.

"Ye must be joking—" The first of the pair reared straight again, fixing an angry glare upon me. "Of all the . . ."

"I told ye to keep an eye on him!" His companion's expression was that of wide-eyed horror. "Let's away, Cyril—'fore summat worse happens!"

"I'm afraid I don't understand." I stepped closer to the men, the paper still extended before me. "I have money—I can pay you to take me to this address."

"Leave off—I'd no more take ye or anyone else there, for all the Chinee tea there is!"

"But why not?" Their responses had rendered me even more baffled than before. "Surely there is no danger to you, familiar as you are with these environs—"

"There's danger, then there's certain destruction! I'd just as soon not take that sort o' risk, thank ye very much!"

"Of what are you speaking?"

"As if ye didn't know!" The man's fury increased. "Quite a fine show ye give, with all yer mummery of *Where am I?* and *Be I alive or dead?* More fools we, for having fallen for it! But it's clear now that ye're up to some sinister purpose, else ye wouldn't be looking for a place such as that—" He pointed to the scrap of paper. "No doubt your diabol'cal confed'rates are waiting for ye there. Go and join them, then—and to hell with the lot o' yez!"

Both men turned and retreated from me. Left alone in the darkness, I plaintively cried after them.

"Just tell me—tell me in which direction I should go—"

I could just discern one of the men's outflung hand.

"That way!" He pointed opposite from where he and his companion were heading. "Ye'll soon enough find all the trouble and misery ye wish!"

Then they were gone, the lantern's glow vanished behind the mountainous piles of damaged metal.

For a moment, I stood gazing down at the piece of paper in my grasp. The temptation was strong to fling it away, the destination inscribed upon it left unsearched for. If the river was indeed close at hand, all I had to do was follow along its course until I reached some waterfront inn or village remote from London itself. From there, I would most likely be able to return to my rural haunts and that obscurity which now seemed more desirable than ever before.

And surely, I reasoned, Evangeline's death by drowning had absolved me of any commitment I might have rashly made to her. And even if by some stretch of the moral imagination I were not, no-one but me knew of any such promise. Thus, there was no chance of anyone reproaching me for a failure to carry it out.

I looked at the paper for several minutes longer. Then at last I folded it up again and returned it to my jacket pocket. I started walking, not toward the river—but toward the yet darker streets of East London.

CHAPTER
19

**Mr. Dower Arrives at a
Scene of Horror**

AS a general rule of life, I find that my regrets increase in proportion to my efforts. I have little doubt that this is true for most people: the more we exert ourselves to achieve aims and desires, the nature of which we but dimly comprehend, the more we end up wishing we hadn't bothered. Yet we try again and again, regardless.

Such was the nature of my foray into that district to which the pair of scavengers had directed me. In short order, my steps arrived at East London's ill-lit streets and narrow, shabby courtyards, reeking of over-ripe refuse and promising an unpleasant welcome to any so foolhardy as to venture therein. Even here, though, the predations of Steam and the all-transforming Future it promised were apparent—the same hissing pipes, albeit of smaller diameter and a sadder state of repair, snaked chaotically along the close-set thoroughfares and up the flanks of the shuttered, soot-stained buildings. The predominant effect was of some unhygienic slum to which a monstrous form of external plumbing had been introduced, without having had a noticeable effect on the waste and filth accumulated over slothful, alcohol-sodden decades.

To my greater dismay, as I wandered through those dark streets, I found memories of them stirring within my thoughts. I realized that I had been here before, a circumstance for which I can hardly be blamed if I had managed to expunge it from my cherished recollections. To be precise, this was the foreboding district that I had come to years previously, when I had attempted to penetrate to the bottom of those mysteries surrounding my father's creations in which I had first become enmeshed. At that time, I had found myself making an entirely unwanted acquaintance with the loathsome procuress named Mollie Maud, as well as her retinue of green girls, those revoltingly piscine jades who appealed to the lowest and most degenerate of carnal tastes. Or what had been so back then—I supposed it was a further indication of the progress that Mankind supposedly had made, that we seemed to have devised yet worse ones.

Such were the unbidden reflections that circulated within my brain. Once again, the notion rose within me that it would be better if I broke off this ill-advised expedition and fled posthaste from the scene. I had but little idea of what it was that I was attempting to accomplish by carrying out the tragically abbreviated instructions I had received from Lord Fusible's daughter. Even if I were to locate at last the address she had given me, what would I find there? And what was I supposed to do with it? The laudable efforts on the part of Evangeline might well have rescued my bodily form, but only at the price of casting me further into overlapping confusions.

My memories of my earlier progress through East London became more distinct and complete in detail, the farther I slunk into the unprepossessing district. I kept close to the various structures' dank and dirty walls, primarily as a method of reducing the chances of anyone spotting such a stranger and potential victim of brigandage. Similarly, I had no wish to engage in conversation with any of the proverbial ladies of easy virtue prowling about for trade. They might have been more normally visaged than those ghastly bauds that I had previously encountered here, but I doubted whether they would be of much more service in pointing my way to the address on the slip of paper contained in my jacket pocket. Indeed, given the manner in which the two boneyard scavengers had reacted to it, I was loath to ask directions from any honest citizen, were the highly unlikely circumstance of my stumbling upon one to come about.

At last, more by chance than design, I came upon what was

presumably the courtyard I sought. By the dim light seeping through the ash-curtained windows of a low gin den, I took out the paper and attempted confirmation. Evangeline's immaculate copperplate hand, the product no doubt of some finishing school far from these environs, oddly contrasted with the villainous surroundings to which I had made my way. As shrieks of inebriated laughter and the thumping collisions of furious blind combat seeped from the doorway of the drinking establishment, I established that I had indeed arrived at the street crossing described on the paper. There were of course no brass numbers mounted on the building's wall, as one might have expected in more decorous neighbourhoods, but the alley close by my elbow was the only one that matched the rest of the note's details.

Fearing imminent disaster, I cautiously proceeded into the narrow space, leaving what little illumination had been available beyond its entrance. A sleek bevy of rats scurried away from my steps, their red eyes glittering at me from atop mounds of unidentifiable rubbish, before they disappeared through the bars of the nearest sewer gratings.

A dilapidated wooden staircase terminated the alley. Standing at its foot, I gazed up toward the broken, treacherous-appearing landings above. Removed from the vicinity of the gin den, I perceived a troubling silence about the spot at which I had placed myself. From my prior excursions into East London, it had been my usual experience that such tenements were shockingly loud at all hours, one's ears assaulted with all the clamorous discord of households overrun with ragged, barefoot children, their education consisting almost entirely of clouts from the heavy-knuckled fists of whatever ruffian had been installed as lord of such a squalid home. In such environments, the truth was forcefully borne upon one that the chief benefit of even a modicum of wealth was the purchasing of as much peace and quiet as one could afford. To be in the company of other human beings was to be forced to endure their ceaseless racket—and the more such were crammed into a small space, the louder that which one was made to suffer.

But not here. That fact installed a suspicious apprehension within my breast. I heard none of the shouts and threats and despairing wails that usually shivered the thin walls of such ramshackle buildings. The resulting quiet was of a more sinister nature than the sharpest razor displayed before one's startled face.

With scant success, I argued with my own forebodings. I took the inward rhetorical position that I was frightening myself for no reason, that in fact there was nothing to be alarmed about in the darkened structure's perceptible aspects. All my fears were groundless; without doubt, there were other such buildings scattered throughout East London and elsewhere, that had decayed to such an inhospitable condition that even the most wretched of the poor disdained their shelter.

None of these reasonings along these lines prevailed over the anxiety I felt as I set my foot upon the first of the steps. Flagellating myself as both a fool and a coward, I began making my way upward, testing each tread before putting my full weight upon it, as though that precaution would be sufficient to keep me from crashing through the rotted boards and falling precipitously to the rubbish-strewn earth below.

I reached the first landing and peered inside the doorless aperture I discovered there. There was naught to indicate that any human specimens resided within the lightless space. Not wishing to hazard further investigation, I resumed my progress to the next floor—

At which I was rewarded with at least some small sign of recent habitation. At the terminus of a dank, low-ceilinged corridor, a glimmer of yellow lamplight seeped through the wavering gap between a closed door and the sill below its bottom edge.

Perhaps this was where Evangeline had wished me to enquire, though as to what ultimate purpose I was still unsure. Summoning the last scraps of my resolve, I stepped from the rickety landing and toward the door ahead.

It opened with but the slightest touch of my hand, swinging inward on creaking hinges. Ducking my head, I peered inside—

Then wished I hadn't.

My immediate impulse, prompted by that which was revealed to me in the room beyond, was to turn and run, clattering my way down the building's exterior staircase as quickly as possible, all the sooner to set myself at rapid liberty in the streets beyond. Such was not merely an emotional response, but the best-reasoned one as well, given what I now beheld.

Indeed, it was my emotions, in the form of utter shock, that kept me rooted to the spot, one hand still pressed to the roughened wood of the door. If my brain had been fully in command of my limbs, there would have been no question as to how quickly I would have vacated the scene.

But I could not even induce the comfort of closing my eyes as a means of escape, so horridly fixated was I by that upon which the flickering lamp cast its tremulous glow.

The room was every bit the squalid, ramshackle space that I had anticipated. But it was rendered vastly more repulsive by the quantities of blood splashed about on the walls and floor, the light glinting upon the congealing red fluid. I might as well have stood in the alley doorway of some knacker's enterprise, wherein whole carcasses were disjointed and stripped of their flesh, so inundating was the gore.

Two figures were there in the room, one lying face-down upon an equally blood-sodden bed, its thin, shabby mattress bowed with the woman's disrobed weight. Her skin, what could still be seen of it, was rendered even more pallid by the bright, wet wounds that had so obviously brought about her demise.

The other figure was that of a man, seated in a broken-slatted chair, the room's only other furnishing. His trousers and shirtfront were similarly emblazoned with red, as though he were either the initiator of whatever violent event had taken place here or had been close by enough to have been spattered during its commission. He was bent forward, face pressed tight to his cupped palms, as though he sought to expunge by sheer force the recollection of what had taken place.

Into the frozen muddle of my own stricken thoughts, a possibility lit up spark-like. I tentatively discerned the reason that Evangeline had directed me to this unsuspected *abbatoir*.

"Captain Crowcroft?" My voice was barely a whisper as I spoke the name. "Would that be you?"

The man raised his face and I saw that I had indeed been correct in my surmise. When I had seen him before, either at the helm of one of the awe-inspiring ambulatory lighthouses he commanded or as an honored guest at the fashionable *soirée* in Lord Fusible's townhouse, he had cut a dashing figure, secured at the pinnacle of a fawning world. Now he was a trembling wreck, his fear-widened eyes staring in immense confusion at me.

"I know you . . ." His voice a harsh croak, he peered even more intently toward the doorway in which I stood. "I've seen you before . . ."

"Yes—of course you have." I stepped cautiously into the room, attempting to avoid the largest of the pools of blood. "It's George Dower—"

"Dower! Ah!" He flung his head back, hands clenched into trembling, white-knuckled fists at his knees. "You are responsible for all this!"

"Actually—I think not." Even had he not made this remarkable statement, I would have been able to detect that Crowcroft was obviously maddened beyond endurance. "I'm reasonably sure that this is nothing that can be blamed upon me."

"If not you, then your cursed father! And all your abominable lineage!"

"I beg your pardon—but it might be prudent to keep one's voice down." I had not experienced many occasions on which I had found myself in a room with a hacked-up corpse, the blood from which was still dripping from the bedsheets to the floor, but it seemed a reasonable precaution to avoid drawing others' attention to the scene. "I'm aware that you are upset, but—"

"*Upset?*" He drew back in evident loathing. "Look about you! What kind of cold monster are you, that you are able to maintain your emotions in so placid a state, when surrounded by such atrocities as these?"

"Yes, well . . . I have been through rather a lot recently. So perhaps my responses are a bit blunted thereby. I assure you that I'll try to react more appropriately, when I have more time and opportunity than we presently do. But at the present moment, I think that flight from these premises would have a rather higher priority—"

"I have no desire to flee from either discovery or the appropriate punishment for my wickedness." Crowcroft wrung his hands in a perfect enactment of self-lacerating despair. "If the agents of the law were to burst upon us at this very moment, take one look around, then render summary judgement by throttling me with their bare hands, I would have little disagreement with such an end to what my wretched life has become."

"Be that as it may . . ." I refrained from informing him that while such a fate might have its attractions for him, I, however, had a few problems with it. "The authorities will, I am confident, be able to mete out all the appropriate punishment just as readily elsewhere as at the scene of the crime. That being the case, I see no need to enflame their passions by remaining any longer here."

"Depart if you wish," muttered Crowcroft. "My place is here or the Pit, in which I can sink no lower."

I had been concerned that I would receive this sort of response from the obviously addled man. No doubt Evangeline had sent me here, with some intent on her part for me to rescue her *fiancé*. Very likely, she'd had only a partial notion of exactly what sort of *contretemps* into which her betrothed had fallen—if she had known the full particulars, she wouldn't have enabled such a full and shameful discovery on my part or anyone else's. Who would have blamed her if she had broken off the engagement? As a lifelong bachelor, I had small knowledge of matrimonial etiquette, but I felt it would be only reasonable to consider murder as sufficient cause to transfer one's affections elsewhere.

However that might be, such considerations failed to assist me in my present circumstance. Even if I were to consider my promise to the late, drowned daughter of Lord Fusible to have been fulfilled by my simply having made my way to the address she had given me and extending an offer of aid, subsequently refused, to her beloved captain, I could foresee certain personal difficulties if I were to leave him at this dire scene. Witnesses already existed, in the form of the two scavengers I had encountered upon first regaining consciousness after my immersion in the river, who could testify as to my wishing to find this address; there were likely others who had observed my traversing the dark alley and heading up the rickety staircase to this floor. Even if they did not know my name, they might be able to give a description sufficient for the Metropolitan Police force to track me down elsewhere.

And of course, none of that would be necessary for the authorities' punitive purposes, with Captain Crowcroft sitting here waiting for their arrival. I could hardly rely upon him not to blurt out that a certain George Dower had visited him in his distress, then fled the premises in such a manner as to indicate some guilty association with these sanguinary events. Even if I were inclined to violate the late Evangeline's trust by going down to the street, hailing the first constable I might see, and reporting Crowcroft as a murderer, that would hardly dissipate the predicament in which I found myself. Two thoughts prompted this realization: first, that the authorities would have the keenest and most unwelcome curiosity as to exactly how I had stumbled upon this room otherwise occluded to respectable persons; and second, I was technically already a fugitive from justice, being implicated in the explosion at Parliament which had enabled my escape into the Thames. Considering all these things, I could deduce that the prospect of my continuing freedom would best be served by convincing the recalcitrant Crowcroft to accompany me in as hasty a removal from the premises as possible—

"Listen to me, Dower." His words broke in on my desperate musing. "I must make confession to some other human being, tempted as I am to take my own life as final payment for my sins."

"Is that really necessary?" I attempted to calculate whether leaving two corpses here, his and that of the unfortunate woman upon the blood-soaked bed, would be favourable to me or not. Perhaps the investigating authorities would conclude that he had been the author of the unfortunate woman's death, then his own, motivated by some sense of wretched remorse. But then, with the course in which my own fortunes had been unfolding, it would be just as likely that the police would conclude that I had done in both of them, to use the criminal parlance. Unable to reach a conclusion, I pleaded for him to reconsider this unfortunate desire. "I feel that we are a trifle pressed for time."

Selfishly concerned only for himself, Crowcroft ignored my protests.

"She who most loves me—I speak naturally of my *fiancée*, Evangeline—"

Out of consideration for his disordered feelings, I thought it only wise to continue my silence as regarding the poor girl's death. He obviously had enough on his mind as it was.

"She was entirely correct," he continued, "to be concerned about my welfare. I am aware that she spoke to you, amongst others, about such well-merited concerns on her part. In her womanly heart, she had perceived that my involvement with the walking lights, by which I had achieved such renown, had led to a similar overpowering interest in those innovative technologies by which they had come into this seafaring nation's service. In short, I had become—this I admit, wretch that I am!—a full-fledged devotee of all things steam-powered."

His confession failed to surprise me. It seemed no more than admitting that he was but one of many, all of whom had fallen into the widespread mania afflicting these sad times.

"My obsession soon spiraled out of control." Nothing, it seemed, would prevent Captain Crowcroft from making an exhausting display of his various failings. "This is why you have found me in this sordid district. Despite my being affianced to one whose every virtue and charm should have prevailed at keeping me chaste until the night of our wedding, I plummeted first into dalliance, then patronage, and at last a complete and heedless addiction to . . ."

He fell silent, as though his shame were too much for his tongue to relate.

"Please go on," I said. "We really don't have all day."

"To . . ." His stricken whisper reluctantly emerged from his lips. "To . . . the *valve girls*."

"Indeed." I confess that the designation was a novelty to me, though I fully anticipated that a complete exposition of its meaning would be something unseemly. "And what exactly are they?"

"You don't know?" His gaze swung up to my face. "Fortunate man!"

"I don't know how accurate is that assessment. A certain amount of troubles have been my lot in life, even if they haven't included an encounter with this particular distaff tribe."

"Maintain your innocence, Dower, if you value your soul—or even merely your ability to sleep at night, undisturbed by dreams both lustful and self-indicting."

"Well . . ." His warning irked me somewhat. "Not that it should be any of your concern, but I've never been greatly tempted along those lines—not from any great pretense to virtue, but just as general inclination."

"Do you . . ." An odd glint appeared in his narrowed eyes as he leaned forward in his chair. "Wish to know more?"

"Concerning what?"

"The valve girls, you fool. What else?"

"If I must." It seemed obvious to me that there would be no flight from the blood-soaked room until he had finished imparting every unsavory detail to me. "Proceed."

The man made a visible effort to pull himself together, so urgent was his self-imposed obligation to unburden his soul to me.

"There are," said Crowcroft, "some matters which I am sure I do not need to explicate in laborious detail . . ."

I could not refrain from thinking to myself, *Thank God for that.*

"Matters of a more . . . *delicate* nature," he continued. "I know that you are, as the saying goes, a man of the world."

"Perhaps not as much as you might think." A suspicion arose as to where Crowcroft might be heading with his comments. "My reputation along those lines has been greatly exaggerated in various circles."

"I can well understand your wish to minimize such things. Not everyone would look with as much tolerance as I do, upon your carnal interest in mechanical Orang-Utans."

"Now that is exactly the sort of thing I was talking about. I assure you that I never—"

He bulled right past, unmindful of my protests. "So I feel safe in assuming that you are familiar with that which is known as fex—not merely the business enterprise which goes by that name, but the larger and more encompassing topic as well."

"Much more so than I would ever have wanted to."

"The valve girls are, as you might already have surmised, part of that darkly alluring world. Women who, either at their own mercantile initiative or that of the swaggering bullies who subsist upon their illicit earnings, are fexually modified to suit their customers' degenerate tastes—which, alas, had become my own."

"Why *valve*, though?" I distracted myself with this etymological musing. "Seems an odd choice of words."

"If you were as familiar with the workings of modern machinery as I am, Dower, you would be aware of that component apparatus which is technically known as the *valve gear*, which is the mechanism in an engine that operates the inlet and exhaust valves to admit steam into the cylinder and allow exhaust steam to escape. While I am no lexicographer, it seems to me but a simple extension from the mechanical to the physiological—the essential part of these prostitutes' surgically altered anatomies is known to jaded connoisseurs such as myself, naturally enough, as the *valva*—"

"You really needn't have told me all that. I could have done without."

"And by equal logic, the purchased act of *coitus* with such a steam-powered female is known by us as a *valve job*."

"As I said." Once begun, there seemed no end of off-putting revelations from him. "To be frank, I find all this to be so thoroughly unpleasant, I can scarcely imagine how one of presumably normal appetites could become an enthusiast of such deviancies."

"MacDuff."

"I beg your pardon?" I thought that perhaps Crowcroft was making some manner of Shakespearean allusion.

"He is the one responsible—Duncan MacDuff. The secretive

owner of the Fex establishment. It was through his enticements, personally directed toward me, that I was lured into this depraved *milieu*."

Again I heard that name, which Ms. Stromneth had mentioned when explaining that she was but Fex's manageress and public face, operating at the behest of those others hidden by a concealing corporate veil.

"This MacDuff person must be greatly seductive—depending, of course, upon one's natural inclinations. I doubt if he would have been able to cozen me in a similar manner."

"Count yourself fortunate," said Crowcroft, "that you have never met the man. He has a forceful character, to say the least. And more—he has a compelling vision of the Future."

"Everybody seems to have as much, these days." I gave a shrug. "The late Stonebrake could hardly be silenced about the topic of those things he so greatly desired to come about in our world."

"You misunderstand me." The lighthouse captain gave me a look both dismissive and pitying. "I mean that MacDuff *sees* the Future— literally. And in elaborately convincing detail. He does not merely *wish* for certain things to come, he knows that they *will*."

"If you say so," I replied. "I have known similar Nostradamus-like prognosticators; they were all rogues. There must be something about knowing the Future—or at least claiming to—that attracts a certain devious mind. Perhaps honest people content themselves with merely facing the actual, knowable Present. Be that as it may, I'm hardly lording it over you by pointing out the unlikelihood of my falling for such a rhetorical devil. As I said, I have the advantage of prior experience along these lines."

"Ah—but you have not met his even more convincing partner."

"So I haven't." I recalled that there was more than one individual jointly pulling the strings behind the *façade* of the Fex enterprise. "And what is his name?"

"*Her* name, actually. MacDuff's business partner is a woman who goes by the *nom d'artiste* of Valvienne."

"Hm. Yes, I had heard tell of a female companion. I suppose this obvious pseudonym is somehow rudely appropriate, given her line of work—I mean, with these so-called valve girls of which you have informed me."

"Just so," said Crowcroft. "Valvienne styles herself as the designer of the various fexual modifications which are then purveyed to Fex's well-moneyed clients. Her malignant influence is then transmitted to the lower classes, including the unfortunate valve girls, who imitate their betters by inflicting similar disfigurements upon themselves, either by their own hands or those of various discredited surgeons who wield scalpel and chloroform in order to finance their own low tastes—chiefly gin and music hall performers, I've been given to understand."

"And *this* is the person under whose spell you have fallen?"

"Both persons," he amended. "It is the combination of them, acting in tandem, that renders them so persuasive. She enables, to a fierce degree, his verbal *legerdemain*—as I said, Valvienne is the designer, whereas her consort, MacDuff, would be more properly considered the promoter. Thus they do not operate as seedy procurers, but instead derive their ill-gotten profits by supplying the steam-powered apparatuses demanded by their jaded customers."

"It would have gone better for you if you had ceased all contact with the pair, as soon as you had discerned their true nature."

"Better if I had never made their acquaintance at all!" Face contorted with emotion, Crowcroft ran his hands through his equally disordered hair. "For my fall from grace was as precipitous as those original sinners cast from the Garden, an event also resulting from such serpentine blandishments. For as my newly inculcated obsessions advanced, I rapidly descended into the darker aspects of this appalling world. I confess that I began neglecting my duties as a lighthouse commander—as well as withdrawing my attentions from the one who is most deserving of them, my *fiancée,* Evangeline."

"Comfort yourself, man—she had not forgotten you. I am here at her urging, to offer what assistance I might to you in your hour of need."

"Too late! I fear that I am irrevocably lost to these lusts, both fleshly and vaporous. The hours and money that I spent on my fexual mania have yielded tragic results."

"Yes, I rather see that."

"More so," said Crowcroft, "than you perceive—or that I can even remember! I have no memory of what happened in this room. All that persists in my jumbled thoughts is the dim recollection of getting soddenly drunk at one of this district's low dens, as I have done so with increasing frequency, then picking up one of these loathsome valve girls from the street beyond and bringing her here—then it all goes blank!"

"Perhaps it is fortunate for you that it does. From the looks of things, it couldn't have been very pleasant."

"Pray do not mock me, Dower. Can you not imagine the horror I felt when I regained consciousness—and discovered the lifeless body of the poor woman there on the bed?"

"It would require a bit of an effort on my part. I have enough problems as it is."

"Would that you had been the constables instead, so that I might have been dragged away to a fitting punishment." Crowcroft covered his eyes with one trembling hand, while with the other he pointed to the sagging bed at the other side of the room. "The image of my crime is emblazoned in my vision, never to depart!"

So engrossed had I been in the lighthouse captain's exposition, despite my initial reluctance to hear it, that I had forgotten for the moment about the lifeless body that was the chamber's other occupant. The motion of Crowcroft's outflung hand directed my own involuntary gaze toward the grisly scene—

Which now seemed to complicate matters a great deal, and in a manner unanticipated by me.

For while the bed was still soaked in blood, no unclothed body lay upon it, fatally hacked or not. While Crowcroft and I had discussed these grim affairs, the chief evidence for them had somehow gotten up and walked away.

If it had ever been there at all . . .

CHAPTER
20

Old Acquaintances Are Met Again

A NUMBER of speculations rapidly coursed through my thoughts, in regard to this latest mysterious occurrence.

"I had been under the impression that the unfortunate woman was deceased." I pointed to the bed, its mattress still soaked with blood but now otherwise vacant. "Or so it appeared to me."

"So she was—I assure you of that." Captain Crowcroft stared at the aspect before us, his eyes widening with incomprehension. "This is terrible, Dower. All is now lost."

"Do you think so? I confess that I see it rather differently." However it had happened, the disappearance of such a dire piece of incriminating evidence as a murdered body struck me as a happy circumstance. Crowcroft and I had been so engrossed in our conversation, with all its references to valve girls and the malign influence of the enigmatic Duncan MacDuff and his partner, Valvienne, that if some degree of animation had remained in the prostitute, despite her apparent wounds, she might very well have been able to resurrect herself from the scene of whatever crime had taken place and exit from the room, all unnoticed by us. The room and the corridor beyond were so enshrouded in darkness that the door might well have been stealthily opened without either Crowcroft or myself being aware of it, the sound of its latch and hinges disguised by those creaking noises common to ancient, dilapidated buildings such as this. Nor might anyone else have taken notice, for that matter. In this district, a naked and bloodied woman emerging from one of the ramshackle buildings, then disappearing into the night, very likely happened so frequently that it caused relatively small comment amongst the locals.

Alternately, if the woman had indeed been as lifeless as both Crowcroft and I had surmised, some other party might have surreptitiously entered the room and carried the body from it. My understanding was that there was still a flourishing trade in providing fresh subjects for dissection to the less scrupulous medical schools in the city. Prowling about for additional commerce, any number of stealthy body-snatchers might have glanced inside the room, ascertained that the attention of both Crowcroft and myself had been absorbed elsewhere, entered, and then absconded with the poor woman's remains. To my mind, if they had in fact done so, they might very well have provided to us a favor—

Or not. As I reviewed these possibilities, a dismaying clamour arose from downstairs. I could hear the thudding of booted feet upon the rickety wooden steps and the shouting of various gruff voices, including that of one with the evident tone of command, directing the others.

"The police!" Crowcroft raised his head, having come to the same quick conclusion that I had. "We've been discovered—"

"Not yet." From the sounds below, it seemed as if the officers were intent upon searching the rooms of the floor beneath us, kicking open doors as they proceeded. "We must make haste, though."

I made no effort to determine what exact chain of events might have led the authorities to this location. Perhaps the nearest street constable had intercepted my hypothesized resurrectionists in the act of carrying away their cold, limp prize, who had then sought to absolve themselves of guilt in the woman's death by revealing from where they had acquired it. Whatever the sequence, it scarcely mattered. All that concerned me was to escape from the scene as quickly as possible—and to bring Captain Crowcroft along with me, not from a sentimental concern for his late *fiancée*'s wishes, but to preclude any witness to my presence at this dire scene from falling into the hands of the authorities.

"Let us throw ourselves upon their mercies." Crowcroft expressed a rather different wish. "Perhaps they will be so kind as to execute us upon the spot, thus sparing us the humiliation of a public trial."

"Perhaps," I said, "we should keep that as a last resort. In the meantime, there is the window."

I stepped hurriedly across the room. With a teeth-clenching concentration of effort, I managed to draw open the stubborn aperture in question. Peering out, I discerned the one feature of the building that would be of possible assistance to us: close to hand, a drainpipe extended from the roof's edge down to the alley. The plumbing appeared to be of dubious provenance and construction, as flimsy and ill-prepared to bear our weight as though it might have been a leafless vine clinging to the dark, wet bricks.

"Come along—" I already had one leg over the sill when I spoke again to Crowcroft. "This is our only chance."

"Save yourself, if you must." He turned his face toward the door, as though expecting a fiery salvation to burst through it at any moment. "I await judgement with as much equanimity as I can muster."

"That is all very well for you—but what about your beloved Evangeline?"

It was a despicable ruse on my part. Greater honesty would have been mine if I had simply abandoned the addlepated man to his chosen fate, rather than pretending that his *fiancée* might still be alive. But I could hardly expect that Crowcroft, once launched into full confession before a magistrate, would have the necessary discretion to omit any mention of me.

"If you do not come with me now," I continued, "you have scant chance of ever seeing her again."

This observation appeared to have some effect upon him. He swung his gaze from the door and over toward me, his brow furrowing.

Hearing footsteps clattering in the hallway beyond him, I determined that I could tarry no longer. I reached over and grasped the drainpipe, my hands locking tight upon it as I cast my bodily weight from off the windowsill.

As I awkwardly clambered down to the alley, I looked up and saw that my entreaties had succeeded in their intent. Crowcoft was directly above me, having reconsidered the extent of his previous remorse and now deciding to make his escape as well.

But only for a moment. As I had initially feared, the drainpipe proved inadequate for the purposes to which we had put it. Our combined weight tore it free from the building's exterior, then it disassembled itself entire, every component section separating from the others.

I was still so far above the ground when the pipe gave way that I landed upon my back with sufficient force to knock the breath from my lungs. Worse, the impact left me too dazed to evade the blow of Crowcroft's equally toppled mass coming down directly on top of me. For him, though, this proved fortunate: my prostrate form cushioned his fall sufficiently that he was able to scramble to his feet. With the world reeling about in my sight, I was just able to catch a glimpse of him running for the mouth of the alley, then vanishing into the unlit maze of the surrounding streets.

My fortunes deteriorated yet further. Scarcely had I managed to gather myself up onto my knees than rough official hands seized upon my upraised shoulders.

"Murderer!" A truncheon was applied with some obviously expert skill, rendering me nearly unconscious. "You'll bluidy well pay for what you've done—"

I could hardly protest this accusation, so enfeebled was I by the harsh manner of my apprehension. For the second time in a dismayingly short period, my wrists were bound behind me in iron shackles. Quickly, I was more flung than carried into the unlit compartment of what might well have been the same unwelcome carriage in which I had ridden before. Lying on its damp floor, a trickle of blood seeping down from the corner of my brow, I was dimly aware of its horses being urged into motion. The wheels jounced across the cobblestones as I was conveyed to yet another unpleasant destination.

--->≡⊚⊂≡<---

EVEN though the stone cell in which I had previously found myself had been explosively transformed to dust, I expected to find myself in one of similar dimension and discomfort. To my extreme surprise, when the shackles were removed from my wrists, my immediate environs were rather that of a properly upholstered drawing-room, the furnishings as lavish and expensive as that of Lord Fusible's townhouse. Recent memory supplanted my amazed condition, as I realized that I had been here before, with Stonebrake, in fact. This was the luxurious environs of the Fex establishment.

It was equally startling when I perceived that it was not a uniformed constable or dark-suited police agent who freed me, but rather a liveried servant, of the stiff and formal bearing that one might well have expected to encounter in such elegant surroundings.

"Pray have a seat." With a bow of his head, he directed me toward one of the handsome couches. "Mister MacDuff will be with you shortly."

My capacity for shock having been exhausted, I sat myself down as directed and awaited the arrival of that enigmatic person, of whose name only I had been previously apprised. As I did so, I spied a small sheet of deckle-edged notepaper on the low table before me. I picked it up and read the words inscribed upon it in a delicate ladylike hand:

> *I have received a better offer. Please forward my effects*
> *to the address I will shortly provide.*
> *With affectionate regard, Miss Stromneth.*

"George Dower!" a braying voice sounded from a doorway behind me. "Well, just look at *you*! How frickin' long's it been?"

Such had been the astonishing variety of events through which

I had just suffered that I had thought myself incapable of further surprise—the heavens might have opened up and rained pomegranates and I would have gazed upon the scene with perfect *sang-froid*. But in the actual event, it turned out that this world could yet startle me.

For I recognized those coarse, strange vocal tones. From long ago . . .

I dropped the notepaper and turned about on the couch, looking toward the one who had so addressed me. He seemed older—but not greatly so—and perhaps better and more expensively dressed than as I recalled him. But otherwise he was remarkably the same as when I had last seen him.

"Scape—" His name emerged unbidden from my lips. "Somehow . . . somehow . . . I should have known it would be you."

"Yeah, you should've." As he passed by the drawing-room's fireplace, he lifted a decanter of brandy from the heavy oaken mantel. "You know what they say: *Can't keep a good man down.* Hey, you're here, aren't you? I wouldn't have expected that, either."

Another figure, well remembered by me, had followed him into the drawing room. "Hello, Dower . . ." The consort and accomplice of my old nemesis bestowed upon me one of her wickedly knowing smiles. Miss McThane seemed even less touched by the greying hand of time than her partner, Scape. "Long time no see."

The perceptive reader will note the peculiarities of these persons' distinctive speech. When I had first encountered them, upon the occasion of my initial enmirement into the mysteries and conspiracies revolving around my father's creations, I had thought their vocal eccentricities to be both off-putting and bewildering. Never did I become accustomed to them. At some point, however, the explanation offered by Scape for them had gained, if not probability, then at least some measure of possibility in my estimation. This was, of course, due to my further acquaintance with the awesome capabilities of those devices invented and constructed by my immediate paternal ancestor. To one of these in particular, with which I had no direct experience, Scape attributed all of those effects which so distinguished both him and Miss McThane from myself and other living Englishmen. By his description, the device had consisted of a source of brilliant illumination, before which was suspended a rapidly spinning disk, the pattern of holes and slits in it producing a unique pattern and sequence of light flashing into the eyes of anyone so reckless as to gaze thereon. Which was, of course, exactly what the two of them had done, both being unexpectedly transformed as a result. For it was Scape's claim, made as he had been so busily instigating all those troubles that had befallen me then, that my father's device had somehow been able to summon *personae* from some distant point in the Future—complete with the knowledge and habits of what would be the progeny of current persons—and install them inside the receptive skulls of himself and Miss McThane. He had assured me that he had become, in not just speech and other manners, but in every other mental and spiritual aspect as well, what everybody would be someday. At the time, I had scoffed at such a prediction—but now, having seen that into which the world had been transfigured through the power of Steam, I was no longer so confident in my dismissal. All that which I had known and with which I had been familiar now seemed to be fleeing into the obscurity of a Past soon to be forgotten; the discouraging specter of the world to come, which the man so embodied, appeared to be dolefully inevitable. With any small stroke of fortune, I would be safely dead by then. Not for the first time, I reminded myself that all earthly things end in the grave—and that was the good news.

"It has indeed been a considerable time," I replied to Miss McThane. While she was as much a scoundrel—and perhaps more reprehensibly so, given her gender—I bore her somewhat less resentment than I did her companion. The previous association between the two of us had culminated in the thwarting of the demented Lord Bendray's attempt to shatter the Earth to pieces. That this had been achieved through a carnal act and the sacrifice of my innocence—hers had been disposed of quite some time before then—did to some degree make my feelings toward her a bit more on the tender side, though certainly not enough to allay my justified suspicions toward her every action and statement. "The last I had heard of you," I continued, "was that crofters in the remotest Highlands were being swindled of their meager savings by way of your various confidence schemes."

"Yeah, well—you know how it is," interjected Scape. He took a swig from the decanter, then offered it toward me. Upon my refusal, he took another pull before setting it down on the low table before him. "Gotta make a living, right? We had a pretty good thing going for a while, before it all blew up in our faces. For us it did, I mean— *you* came out of it nicely set up."

"Are you insane?" I stared back at his lean, vulpine face, still adorned with the lopsided, insinuating smile I recalled from before. "I was irrevocably scarred by those events."

"Really?" Miss McThane set herself down on the arm of the couch. "That's not a very flattering thing to say."

"Perhaps not *all* those events, then. But bear in mind that I was so disgraced in the eyes of polite society that I was obliged to flee from my native London."

"With a pile of loot, you lucky bastard." Scape laced his hands behind his head, leaning back and studying me. "And now you're back here again. That's wild, Dower. How exactly is that?"

I could feel my eyes narrowing to slits as I returned his gaze. "Somehow," I said, "I believe you already are familiar with those circumstances."

"Bingo." Scape's smile grew wider and even more disconcerting. "Though you'd probably still be surprised at finding out exactly how much we know. All *kinds* of stuff."

"On the contrary—I'm no more surprised than I am to discover that you are once more engaged in various disreputable schemes. It is entirely in your natures—"

"Duh."

"Nor am I shocked to learn that you conceal your identities behind these absurd pseudonyms. How long have you been passing yourself off as . . . what is it? Ah, yes—as *Duncan MacDuff.* Is that really the best you could come up with?"

"Does the job. Everybody here in the south thinks that Highlanders are all crazy wild men and stuff. And I like people thinking I'm crazy. Adds to the dangerous factor, you know?"

"As if you needed that." I looked over to Miss McThane. "And *Valvienne*? Please."

"What're you gonna do?" She pointed toward Scape. "It was his idea."

"About that, at least, I am not surprised. He had a great many ideas before; I am certain he has as many now, if not more."

"You got that right, Dower." Sitting forward on the couch, Scape pointed toward me. "And you're part of them. Cool, huh?"

"Let me assure you," I spoke stiffly, "that I have no wish to be."

"Too late for that. You already are."

"He's telling you the truth," said Miss McThane. "You were already in hip-deep with us, even before what happened with you and Crowcroft, back in that little room."

"Indeed?" I raised a quizzical eyebrow. "What exactly do you know about all of that?"

"Everything," she replied. "I was there. I listened in on every word that you and Crowcroft said to each other."

"I do not understand. Where would there have been for you to hide?"

"Hide? Who needed to hide?" There was a glint of triumph in her smile, the same that she expressed whenever she put something over on a fellow human being. "I was right there on the bed."

"That . . . was *you*?"

"Look, I know we only had the one time before and all, and there was kind of a lot going on back then, with the whole place falling down around us—but a girl's not exactly flattered when you don't recognize one of her best parts. I mean, it's not like you've seen a lot of others, have you?"

"Hardly the point that needs to be addressed." The rudeness of her observation served to nettle me into regaining a measure of my composure. "Why would I have expected someone of even brief acquaintance to masquerade as a bloodied corpse? I hope I am correct in assuming that all of your apparent wounds were but theatrical in nature."

"That much you got right." With no pretense at modesty, she lifted the hem of her gown sufficiently to expose much of the naked flesh I had glimpsed before, still daubed with the red greasepaint that I had previously mistaken for blood. "Got *you*, suckah!"

"Don't fret about it," interjected Scape. "We weren't doing it just to run a number on you. We were gaming ol' Crowcroft."

"Which you certainly seem to have succeeded at. The poor man was distraught to the point of self-destruction."

"What a moron," Scape sneered as he shook his head. "You know, if you can't roll with the punches, you're in a world of trouble."

"You display no more sympathy for your fellow man than I would have expected from you. What exactly could have been the purpose of making him believe that in a fit of drunken passion, he had somehow murdered some unfortunate prostitute? Or valve girl, as I've been informed they are called."

"Don't worry about that," said Scape. "Let's talk about *you*."

"Yeah . . ." A typically disconcerting smile appeared on Miss McThane's face. "Let's."

"Because this was totally cool that you showed up there." Scape nodded in satisfaction. "We weren't expecting that."

"But when I saw it was you," said Miss McThane, "I really flashed on how useful you could be."

"Useful? To whom?"

"To us, of course. Jeez." Scape glanced over at his partner. "Did he land on his head when he climbed out of that building?"

"I have absolutely no interest in becoming once more involved in your various schemes, whatever they might be."

"Too bad. Like I told you, you're already in them. You're too valuable for us to just let you slip away."

"That's why I snuck out of the room." Miss McThane continued her own exposition. "Good thing we already had some of our people waiting nearby. That made it a lot easier to organize getting you out of there. And over here, where we can talk."

"Your people?" These words invoked a frown from me. "Are you telling me that those were not actual agents of the Metropolitan Police force, who seized upon and conveyed me hither?"

"Of course they were." Scape made a show of being offended. "We're a quality operation. We don't go in for fakes."

"But then that would imply . . . that you are in league with the authorities."

"Sure—all the best criminals usually are." His oddly lunatical smile was even wider than before. "We've come up in the world, Dower."

"I had been led to believe that you were merely some sort of disreputable entrepreneurs." I struggled to make sense of all this new information. "I mean, that is, in your roles as the so-named Duncan MacDuff and Valvienne."

"Oh, you mean all that Fex stuff?" Scape nodded. "Yeah, that's been a pretty good little racket. Real decent money in that—but then there always is, when you're dealing with people with more cash than brains. Those people are so whacked out—the weirder you get, the easier it is to lift a wad off of 'em."

As before, the man's odd diction and vocabulary left me a trifle unsure as to his exact meaning, though the general intent was easily deduced.

"So you have formed some sort of mutually profitable alliance with important elements of the police." I saw things a bit more clearly now. "That explains a great deal, as to why you have been able to conduct such a business without interference."

"Oh, Dower—it's not just the cops." Miss McThane gazed pityingly at me. "Keeping the vice squad off your tits isn't that big a deal. What we're talking about is—we go all the way to the top. And by top, I mean the *top* top."

"What meaning is that supposed to convey to me?"

"Simple," she said. "We work for Mrs. Fletcher."

❧⸺◉⸺❧

PERHAPS I should have expected that latest revelation. But I confess that it caught me unprepared. Without being invited, I sat down

on the couch, Scape making room for me beside him, to prevent my
legs giving out from beneath me due to the shock.

"You poor thing." From her perch on the couch's arm, Miss Mc-
Thane ran a caressing hand through my hair. "I don't think you're
really cut out for all these conspiracies and stuff. You look a little
overwhelmed."

"If I appear so, it is because I am." I closed my eyes for a moment
as I leaned my head back against the cushions. "Forgive me if I point
out that I am more accustomed to thinking of the pair of you as little
better than felons, irrevocably opposed to the regular functioning of
society. To discover that you are now in alliance with the highest
levels of government—"

"Yeah." Scape nodded. "Disappointing, isn't it? Took me a while
to get my head around it, I can tell you. Kind of a new thing for us.
Like the people in these days would put it, we're a little more used to
running with the hares than the hounds. But, like the people from
up in the future would say: *Hard times will make a rat eat a red
onion.* Gotta hustle to make a buck, in other words."

To further revive and strengthen myself, I took a long gurgling
swallow from the decanter that Scape had set on the table before us.
As though its underpinnings had been loosened by the alcohol
fumes, the room swam and tilted about me for a moment, then settled back down. I felt emboldened enough to present a direct enquiry to the pair.

"What exactly is it," I said, "that you do for the Prime Minister?
Something to do with the walking lights, I imagine, and Phototrope
Limited, and all those various gamblers seeking to further enrich
themselves. They very likely require having a close watch kept upon
them."

"That bunch? Don't make me laugh." Scape shook his head as
he took the decanter from me. "They're not even players—at least
not at the level we're talking about."

"What about Stonebrake, then? He may be deceased, reduced to
his component atoms by the explosion at Parliament, but while alive he
gave the appearance of being complicit in all manner of conspiracies."

"Yeah, he would, the punk." With the back of his hand, Scape wiped his mouth after imbibing once more. "Guys like that give me a cramp. Always running around, making with the big talk—like the world revolves around their ass." His nose wrinkled in evident disdain. "Just as well you got rid of him—you were wasting your time with him."

"Which is, I am supposed to take it, more productively spent with you?"

"Hell, yeah. This stuff we're doing with that Fletcher woman—I mean, if you can still call her that—it's big. Super big. It'll change the whole frickin' world by the time we're done."

"Hasn't it been changed enough already? Perhaps it has earned something of a rest by now."

"Forget that noise, pal. Like a shark—always gotta keep movin' forward, or else you drown." The spirits produced a moment of brooding meditation on his part. "You'll see. This is our chance. Not just for a big score . . . but something else. Something even bigger."

"And this is Mrs. Fletcher's ambition as well? To change the world?"

"Ee-yep."

"In what way?"

"Get this, Dower." He leaned close toward me, bringing his face within an inch of mine. "You know all this Steam stuff?"

"More," I said, "than I would ever have cared to, had I the choice."

"She's gonna get rid of it." Scape lowered his voice, as though imparting the deepest confidence possible. "Ka-boom. All gone." He made a dismissive gesture with one hand. "Yesterday's news. Who the hell needs it?"

"Well . . . that sounds pleasant." I nodded slowly, inhaling the alcohol-laden fumes he breathed in my direction. "Such would indeed be a profound change, devoutly to be wished for. All of Britain would revert to its former pastoral state, a place of hearty yeomen and verdant fields crossed by no more than the hedges and farmers' stone fences. I can see it now—"

"Are you kidding?" Scape drew back from me, his brows knitted in disdain. "Why would anybody want that crap? Come on, Dower, get with the program. We're talking about getting rid of Steam so we can replace it with something else."

"It's okay," spoke Miss McThane in a soothing manner. "He tends to get a little over-excited when he talks about this stuff."

"Can't get too excited," said Scape, "far as I'm concerned. How often do you get a chance to blow up everything that the world depends on? *And* get rich while you're doing it."

In this aspect, he was no different from my former companion Stonebrake. With such rascals, the money is ever uppermost in their thoughts. The other ambitions of which he spoke, the overthrow of Steam and so forth, did strike me as something new, though.

"Very well." I endeavoured to speak in as measured a tone as possible, to keep from setting him off again. "Rid the world of Steam, if you wish—I will hardly attempt to stop you. But what is it that you seek to replace it with?"

Scape jabbed his forefinger into my chest.

"Coal."

I waited for him to say something more. But he remained silent as he leaned back to gaze at me in satisfaction, just as if no profounder statement could have been made.

"That's it?"

"Hell, yeah." Scape seemed to take offense at the question. "Isn't that enough?"

"Ah. I see." I gave a slow nod of my head. "Very droll. I am glad to see that your sense of humour has not been diminished by the passage of years."

"Wait a minute—you think I'm jerking you around? I'm serious, pal. It really is coal that Mrs. Fletcher is all hyped up about. You need to get up to speed on this, if you don't want to get left behind."

"I somehow suspect, given your sudden reappearance in my life, that I will not be given much of a choice as to whether I will be left behind, or swept up in whatever schemes you have been concocting.

So tell me, then—what exactly is it about this filthy, nasty stuff known as coal that our terrifying Prime Minister finds so fascinating?"

"Look, Dower, it's not that she's so cranked up about it just on its own. I mean—it burns, okay? So it makes heat—pretty nice heat, actually—"

"Yeah," agreed Miss McThane. "I love a coal fire. It's like . . . cozy. You know?"

"Whatever." Scape forged ahead with his elucidation for my benefit. "But here's the deal. The reason why Mrs. Fletcher is all fired up about the coal thing is—*it's not Steam.*"

"Why would she find that attractive? I had been given to understand that the woman is a great enthusiast of all things steampowered. Indeed, she has had herself transformed into a creature whose very essence—her lifeblood, as it were—is Steam. How could she bear the slightest animus toward it?"

"Okay, you got a good point there, Dower. I mean, the whole thing about coal as a power source is that you can get a boiler going with it, and then you get things moving around—like factory engines and trains—even prime ministers, as long as they've been all remodeled the way she's been. So Steam *per se* isn't the problem for her. The problem is the way that it's been set up, the whole delivery system and all, with the stuff being piped in from the steam mines up there in the Lake District. That's what ticks her off. As long as everything depends on those people, then there's a limit to what she can do. And she's not the kind of person who likes to have limits— that's why she had herself made over the way she did."

"We made a bundle off her," said Miss McThane, "over at Fex. Biggest job we ever did. We had our guys working for months on that one. Kind of customer we like."

"Yeah, and she was pretty happy with it all. You saw the way she's been able to shove her way around over there at Parliament. *Very* intimidating person, if you know what I mean. So everything was fine for her with the whole Steam business until she started to figure out she had made some real enemies in the process—her definition of enemies being anybody who gets in her way."

"And who would do that?" His explanation did not yet make sense to me. "As you have indicated, Mrs. Fletcher is somewhat of an overpowering personage."

"You know, Dower—you really need to start keeping up on politics. I mean, what's going on in the world around you."

"I have been somewhat preoccupied of late."

"That's how you wind up having stuff sneak up on you. Like this. I bet you probably haven't even heard of the SMU."

"I confess the acronym is unfamiliar to me. What does it represent?"

"What it stands for, Dower, is the Steam Miners' Union. It represents those poor bastards who have to go down in that great big hole and send all the steam through the pipes that run everywhere now, making stuff go. Believe me, it's a crappy job."

"I expect it would be."

"No, I mean a *really* crappy job." Scape spoke with exaggerated emphasis. "You're down there digging away or doing whatever else it is you have to do, you're in danger of getting scalded to death at any moment—they lose a bunch of miners that way every year—and on top of that, you don't get paid squat. So it's no wonder that even with all the thugs the government has sent up there to whack people over the head, the miners have still managed to get themselves organized. You gotta give 'em credit for that much, at least."

"They would seem to be very dedicated to their labours." I gave a slight shrug. "What would be the source of Mrs. Fletcher's contentious relationship with them?"

"Well, for one thing, they'd like to get paid a living wage. I mean, yeah, their standards are low, being all working class and stuff—but still, they'd probably like to be able to feed their kids."

"A laudable ambition."

"Yeah, but it's more than that," said Scape. "In general, the miners just don't *like* being ground under Mrs. Fletcher's wheels. Nobody does, actually, but these guys are the only ones with the guts to do anything about it. That makes 'em a problem. As long as everybody else depends on the steam miners providing the power everything runs on, then they can dictate their own terms."

"How utterly despicable of them." I shook my head. "Is there no limit to human perfidy?"

"Whatever that is—probably not." Scape took another swallow from the decanter. "There's a bunch of industrial re-organization schemes—that's what Mrs. Fletcher calls 'em—that she'd like to get going, but the miners' union has completely shut her down so far. As a matter of fact—and don't let on that I told you this—" Decanter in hand, Scape leaned close to me again, the better to impart another confidence. "The miners . . . have gone on *strike.*" He straightened himself, watching for my reaction. "Believe it."

"Actually, it is a little difficult to credit such an assertion." I gestured about myself and by inference to the greater world beyond the room's walls. "There appears to have been no great interference with the supply of steam and its attendant power."

"Yeah—*so far.*" Scape attempted to make his words sound as alarming as possible. "That's because there were already some reserves in the system. But when those run out, everything stops. And that's when things will get ugly. *Real* ugly. As in so ugly, it could bring down Mrs. Fletcher's government. Nothing's moving, people are freezing in the streets—that's riot time, pal. Complete anarchy. And there are plenty of anarchists around, I can tell you, who'll be more than willing to make it all happen. You heard about that Walsall bunch?"

"Only that I was accused of being one of their number, while I was in the custody of Mrs. Fletcher's henchmen."

"Well, they're not the only ones she's got to worry about. Like I said, she's got a lot of enemies. She could find herself dismantled and the pieces thrown out for scrap, in that boneyard down the river. That's how bad it is. The miners have already shut down a couple of the major steam pits. Fletcher knows that if they close down the whole operation, she's in big trouble."

"I'm not quite sure I understand." My brow creased as I attempted to make sense of all that I had just been told. "What does this have to do with *coal*?"

"Let me give it a shot," said Miss McThane. "Now listen to me real carefully. Mrs. Fletcher needs to break the Steam Miners' Union. She can't do what she wants with them having a gun pointed at her head. So to speak. But she can't get rid of them while everything still depends on steam power. Right?"

"I suppose . . ."

"So she needs to get everything, the whole society, *off* steam. So she's going to convert everything to running off coal. If people need steam, they won't get it from some pipe that runs all the way back to the steam pits, up there in the middle of nowhere. They'll just light up some coal and run a boiler with it, or whatever other kind of engine they've got. Simple, huh? No big steam delivery system running all over the country, people using coal instead for what they need—and the steam miners can go screw themselves. They're done with. They can go back to starving to death, or whatever else it was they were doing before all this steam stuff happened."

"You know . . ." Scape spoke in a deeply musing tone. "The weird thing is . . . when I think about the Future—the way I can see it inside my head, the way it's going to be—it's like Steam and the way everything is right now—it's like that's some kind of dream. Just a little blip. Like this wasn't supposed to happen at all. Like it's one of those *alternate history* things."

"I don't know what those are, either."

"Yeah, right—you wouldn't. Those are something else from the Future. Like a game people cook up, thinking about ways everything could've been, different from the way they really happened. Only the weird thing is that maybe *this* is one of those alternate histories." Scape gestured about himself. "And by getting rid of Steam, the way it is right now, Mrs. Fletcher's actually changing everything back to the way it was supposed to be. So we can get back to the Future I remember. Crazy, huh?"

I made no reply, but I did in fact agree with him about the insanity of what he had just spoken. As before, when he had first claimed to be able to foresee the Future, just as if he had somehow come from that distant time, I considered any discussion of being somehow able to recall that which supposedly had yet to happen—and might never happen, God willing—as an indicator of serious derangement on his part.

"So this is what Mrs. Fletcher wishes to accomplish." That much, I provisionally accepted as being true. "In what manner do the two of you become part of her schemes?"

"Oh," said Miss McThane, "that's even better. Fletcher's a smart cookie. She knows that it's easy to screw people over, when you can make 'em think that it's all their idea. If she just tries to shove it down everybody's throats, they might actually go over to the side of the steam miners. So she needs to create a popular movement in favor of coal over steam. That way, when everybody wants it, she just has to give it to them—and then she's done. Doesn't matter whether it's actually good for people or not."

"See, *that's* where we come in." Scape leaned back against the sofa's cushions, a smirk of self-satisfaction on his face. "We're basically marketing types. Making people want stuff is what we *do*. That's what Fex is all about. I mean, the stuff we do there—if we tried to force people into having that done to themselves, we'd get killed. And we sure as hell wouldn't make any money. But if you can convince people that's what they want, then you can do anything. *And* get paid for it."

To myself, I supposed it was ever thus, for those imbued with both a criminal nature and a contemptuous disdain for their fellow man.

"So we've been using the Fex business as a front, for what we're really doing." Miss McThane warmed to the subject. "That's where all those rich people come in, the ones that we've been servicing with all our fexual modifications. It's not as private as we've led them to believe it is. That's why we've got that observation platform in the back room—it's not just for those rich morons' amusement, you know."

"It helps us get the word out," said Scape. "To the coalpunks."

"To whom?" I wasn't sure I had heard him correctly.

"The *coalpunks.*" He gave the word a pronounced emphasis. "They're the latest thing. Or they will be."

"Just a moment." A previously unconnected thread secured an anchor in my thoughts. "Did you ever have conversations with a certain Viscount Carnomere?"

"Oh, yeah." Scape nodded. "Buncha times. He's a very forward-looking guy, if you know what I mean. Other than running around in those caveman furs, that is."

Thus one small, inconsequential puzzlement was dispelled. These strange, awkward formulations had been introduced into our formerly graceful language from that ghastly Future with which Scape claimed to somehow be in contact. It seemed but one more offense to be charged against him.

"You see, Dower—" Miss McThane picked up the interrupted exposition. "What we've done is associate steam power with all the wealthy and snobbish pricks in the world. The ones with all the money, the people you love to hate. I mean, you do if you're an ordinary person. Lord Fusible and his crowd—they're the target, right? Then you've got the poor people and the working people—and there's a *lot* more of them, believe me—and you tap into their natural rebellious attitude, especially the young ones. Bam, just like that, you got the coalpunk movement."

"They're a lot of fun." Scape smiled. "We've already had a bunch of riots, all over London. There's nothing like throwing a brick through a shop window to get the blood pumping. No wonder it's getting so popular. Who doesn't like to set stuff on fire? 'Long as it's somebody's else stuff, that is. And it's spreading—that's the cool part. It's spreading all across the country."

"And you know what else? That's really neat?" Running her soft hand across the back of my neck, Miss McThane leaned down to kiss me on the brow. "You get to be part of it."

CHAPTER
21

The Key to All the Schemes

"IF it would be all the same to you," I said, "my preference is to be left out of whatever plans you might be concocting."

"I told you." Miss McThane glanced over at her accomplice, Scape. "I knew he wouldn't want to help us."

"Good thing for us, then, that he doesn't have a choice about it." Scape leaned back, arms flung expansively across the back of the couch. "You see, Dower, you're already up to your eyeballs in it. Our plans, I mean. The only way you're going to get *out* of them is to ride along with us for a while."

"I think not." I gave him as cold a gaze as possible. "That hardly worked in my benefit before. I fail to see how it would now."

"You know, that lack of imagination is what holds you back." Scape sadly shook his head. "No wonder things don't work out for you."

"Oh, I see—just as if everything has gone so swimmingly for the two of you."

"Maybe not so much in the past," said Scape. "But we're definitely on top of it now. And whether you like it or not, so are you. Here's the deal—" He laid a hand on my shoulder, bringing his face close toward mine again. "Mrs. Fletcher didn't get to where she is by overlooking the small stuff. She makes sure every detail is covered. So it's not enough for her to have us running a campaign against Steam, with our little coalpunks running around in the streets and making trouble. I mean, they're cute and all, but you gotta have more than that going on. That's why Mrs. Fletcher's got a two-pronged attack."

"Of that, I am not surprised. What is the second prong?"

"Nothing too big," said Scape dismissively. "Just breaking some heads."

"I beg your pardon?"

"Oh, come on, Dower—don't act like you don't know about stuff like this. You want to get something done in this world, sometimes you gotta mess a few people up. Or a lot of them—like these steam miners, with their union and all. Mrs. Fletcher needs a legal excuse to crack down on them. That's why she set up that explosion at the Houses of Parliament—"

"She did *what*?"

"Yeah . . ." From the corner of my eye, I could see Miss Mc-Thane give a slow nod. "You probably still think those anarchists—that Walsall bunch or whatever they're called—that they did it."

I turned and looked toward her. "Didn't they?"

"'Course not," she replied. "They just got blamed for it, that's all. That's what anarchists are good for—you can blame 'em for anything. Then you can crack down on whoever you want, 'long as you say they're all hooked up together. Just standard operating procedure for the government. How they stay in business, if you know what I mean."

"And that's what Mrs. Fletcher is claiming? That the striking steam miners are in league with these anarchists—and together they set off the explosion at Parliament?"

"Sure," said Scape from beside me. "A little bang goes off—enough to throw you out in the river, that is—she makes certain ahead of time that she won't get hurt in it, then she can start bringing every police truncheon in Britain down on the heads of the steam miners. All works perfect. You get to play your part, too—since she and her bunch can also claim that it all went off while she was personally questioning some dangerous terrorist. That'd be *you*, Dower.

So she also gets a bunch of personal credit for being so brave, and so forth. Big sympathy factor there. It's all politics."

I fell silent, my bleak musing prompted by these revelations. That I had been made a credulous fool once again, led to believe one thing when its exact opposite was the truth, was no longer any great embarrassment to me. By now, I was rather used to it. What did vex me, though, was to see Scape and Miss McThane reduced to working as behind-the-scenes string-pullers and hacks for the repressive Mrs. Fletcher. It all seemed just one more reason to consider this world as a sad, degraded place.

"What happens now?" I spoke up after a few seconds had passed. "Presumably, the Prime Minister has a free hand to change the world all she wishes, for her own personal aggrandizement. Does this indicate that lesser beings—I speak of myself, of course—can now freely go about our affairs without being subject to governmental interference?"

"All depends, Dower." Leaning back against the couch once more, Scape folded his hands across his waistcoated stomach. "I mean, the changes never stop for somebody like Mrs. Fletcher. We've already heard from her about that. When I said she'd made sure she didn't get hurt in the explosion, I meant the parts of her that are still flesh and blood. Some of the ironworks, all that steam-powered stuff that makes her look like a railway engine—that apparently took a hard knock. Which is okay, actually—gives her the chance for a total retrofit."

"Meaning exactly what?"

"Well, if she's coming down on Steam, about how wicked and all it is, she can't very well go around hooked up to it, can she? So she's getting herself all tricked up—new outfit, sort of. That's the way women are, right?"

"Yeah," observed Miss McThane, "and you like it that way."

"So right now," continued Scape, "the Prime Minister's getting herself done over, based on coal furnace technology. Wild, huh? And that's just what's going on over at the Fex workshops. There are whole armies of workmen over at the Houses of Parliament, ripping out the steam pipes, then shoving in more furnaces and firing them up."

I was unable to prevent from entering into my thoughts a nightmarish vision of a smoke-belching factory upon the banks of the Thames. In short order, the skies over London would be cast even darker, with great, black clouds roiling perpetually over the populace's heads.

"Everything you have told me, I find to be thoroughly disagreeable." I spoke through the scowling expression fixed upon my face. "More to the point, I don't see what any of it now has to do with me. I've already been used as an unwitting pawn more than once in this devious game; why can't I simply be allowed to slink away into peaceful obscurity? Or at least as much peace as anyone can hope to have in what this world has been turned into."

"Love to let you do that," said Scape. "Because frankly, you're already getting on my nerves again. But you've still got some value, one way or another, in some of these schemes that are going on. At least, in *our* schemes you do."

"That's certainly accommodating of you, I'm sure. However, if you had enquired as to whether I wished to be so, I might have declined."

"Yeah, that's why we didn't ask."

"So what exactly is it that you are hoping I'll be able to do for you?"

"I'll tell you," said Scape. "It's all got to do with those devices that your father cooked up."

"I was afraid of that."

"Don't worry—" He dismissed my concerns with a wave of his hand. "It's just one that we've got to deal with. The one that he invented for simulating voices."

"The *Vox Universalis*? If you expect me to locate it for you, then you will be sadly disappointed. If the agents of Mrs. Fletcher's Department of Technography and Statistics, busily scouring the length and breadth of the British Isles for such a thing, have not been able to turn it up, I can scarcely see how you could expect me to."

"Why would I want you to find it? I've already got it."

"You do?" If true, that would present a new aspect to the situation. "Then why are Mrs. Fletcher and her agents searching for it?"

"Because I haven't told her I've got it. Jeez, Dower, just because we're working for the woman, and she trusts us and all—that doesn't mean I'm going to tell her something like that. Especially if I've got a better use for it than she does."

"Which would be?"

"*That* part," said Scape, "you don't need to concern yourself about. Just trust me on that one."

"Yes, of course. Just as Mrs. Fletcher trusts you."

"She doesn't know me as well as you do, Dower. If she falls for any line I've handed her, that's her lookout."

"I see. That being the case, where exactly is the device under discussion?"

"You don't need to know that, either. What is it with all the questions, all of a sudden?"

"That seems obvious to me." I laid one of my hands flat against my chest. "The presumption I am making is that you desire me to somehow assist you in the operation of the device. In doing so, you perpetuate the same error that others have made, that because I am the son of that man who created them, that lineage in some way gives me an insight into the machines' functions. Many is the time that I've protested otherwise, but nobody ever seems to listen. Very well; so be it. But if this is indeed what you seek of me, I would at the least wish to know whether I am to be conveyed to someplace here in London, or dragged off to some more remote locale where you might have hidden the device."

"Actually," interjected Miss McThane, "we're pretty sure we don't need you, just to make stuff happen with the thing. You're forgetting how much experience we had, a while back, with that Paganinicon contraption your father built—remember it? You know, the one that could play the violin and talk and . . . a bunch of other stuff besides."

There was no need for her to elaborate. I appreciated her delicacy, not often displayed, in not mentioning the horrid capacities for carnal activity which the device had possessed. The unleashing of the machine upon an unsuspecting world had been the most griev- ous reason for the disrepute into which I had been cast at that time.

"Anyway," she continued, "that thing worked on the same gen- eral priciples. Or at least some of it did. Other parts . . ." She smiled. "They were a little different. But the talking bit—since we pretty much had that figured out back then, we shouldn't have any problem getting that *Vox Universalis* thing going the way we want it to."

"That is indeed excellent news. I congratulate you." I straight- ened the lapels of my coat, preparing to stand. "It would appear that despite your earlier assertions, you would evidently not require my help in any of your schemes. That being the case, I'll say good eve- ning to you—and go about my own affairs."

"Sit down." Scape gripped my shoulder and prevented me from moving any further. "I told you that we've got the device—and that's true. And we know how to run it—that's true, also. But there's more to it than just that."

"What, in God's name? If possession of the device and the ability to administer its functions do not suffice for you, then what would?"

"The key."

He had spoken with such conviction as to indicate that I would know to what he was referring. I didn't.

"Key? What key?"

"There's something missing," Scape insisted urgently. "A piece of the apparatus. We're pretty sure it's what controls the whole *Vox Universalis* device. There's a socket that the piece should fit into, the way a key fits into a lock. Without that piece, we're screwed."

"Have you attempted to locate it?"

"Hell—why didn't I think of that?" He grimaced in angry dis- gust at me. "Of course we've tried to find it, you frickin' moron. If we'd found it, we wouldn't be talking to you right now."

"Ah. I see. You wish me to assist you in finding this . . . key. Is that it?"

"You're the last chance we have," said Miss McThane. "We've tried everything else."

"What makes you believe that I could be of any aid to you in this regard?"

"I don't know." Scape spoke again. "We're pretty much scraping the bottom of the barrel." He gripped my arm and squeezed it tight enough to cut off the circulation of blood within. "Maybe you've seen it. When you had that watchmaker's shop, with the back room crammed full of your father's stuff. Maybe you remember it from then . . ."

"How would I know?" My shoulders lifted in an involuntary shrug. "I don't even know what this thing looks like, which you are intent on finding."

"Here." He released me, so that he could rummage through the pockets of his own coat. "There were a bunch of papers with the *Vox Universalis,* when we found it. Diagrams, schematics . . . that sort of thing." Having extracted a yellowed sheet of parchment, he quickly unfolded it. "We're pretty sure this is the gizmo we need. Take a look."

Scape thrust the paper into my view. I looked down at the faded diagram inscribed upon it—

I had seen the device before—the key to the *Vox Universalis.* I had even held it in my hands.

And I knew exactly where it was.

"So . . ." I took the paper from his grasp. I nodded slowly as I gazed upon the image, feeling a remote but definite sense of possibilities unfolding within me. Of actual salvation, or at least escape from the situations in which I had become enmired. "This device, then—I am correct in assuming that it has considerable value for you?"

"What did I just tell you? Of course it does!"

"In what way?" I peered more closely at the man, attempting to discern whether he was lying—again—to me or not. "The schemes you have told me about hardly seem to rely upon some voice-simulating craft for their advancement. Your own fortunes are tied to those of Mrs. Fletcher, as she pries away the grip of Steam upon British society and substitutes coal in its stead—are they not? Those plans appear to be already well under way. Soon you will reap the benefits of the Prime Minister's gratitude. Such being the case, why do you perturb yourselves with setting my father's *Vox Universalis* device into operation?"

Unseen by Scape, his female companion tightly squeezed my shoulder, as though to warn me that I had managed to tread upon dangerous ground in the course of my enquiries.

"That's nothing you need to know about." Scape's previous affability evaporated as he pointed to the paper in my hand. "It's a no-questions-asked deal—I mean, no questions from *you*. Either you're able to help us find the key for the device, or you can't. But if you can dig it up, believe me, we'll make it worth your while."

"To what degree? Would you be willing, say, to have me spirited out of London, removed from all these entangling conspiracies?"

"You know . . ." His gaze narrowed as he studied me. "You actually do know where it is. Don't you?"

"Perhaps," I said. "But let us postulate that I do. If I were to transfer this desirable key device into your hands—by which you could activate the *Vox Universalis,* for whatever obscure purpose you contemplate—would your gratitude also be of a financial kind? That is to say, would you bestow upon me sufficient funds that I could comfortably turn my back upon the whole lot of you? I am not speaking of the sort of vast fortune with which you and the late Stonebrake continually enflame your imaginations. Just enough for a sufficiency of comforts—that's all I'm asking."

"Done," said Scape. "How soon can you get it here?"

"That all depends." I folded up the piece of yellowed paper and tucked it in my coat pocket. "Upon how soon you leave off with your endless haranguing, and allow me to proceed on what I assure you will be a simple quest."

"All right." He tilted his head to one side, as though newly assessing the person before him. "Then hit the bricks, pal."

CHAPTER
22

**Mr. Dower Converses with
Another He Had Never
Expected to See Again**

IN the event, it turned out that I had misspoken.

Within the comfortable environs of the Fex establishment, I had assured both Scape and his accomplice, Miss McThane, that it would be an enterprise of no great difficulty to lay my hands upon the key to the *Vox Universalis* device and bring it to them. Before my exit, as Scape had escorted me to the building's front door, he had offered to accompany me—not from any concern that I would fail to return with the desired article, motivated as I was by the promised reward for its delivery, but in order to facilitate my journey through the city. I had refused his assistance, relying upon the proverbial wisdom that a person travels fastest when he travels alone—and I had no wish to tarry further in the execution of these matters.

As I quickly realized, though, I should have taken him up on his offer.

While we had conversed in the drawing-room, I had been aware of distant shouts and clatter, the noises drifting to my ear as though from some remote battlefield. No sooner was I out upon Kings Road than it became apparent to me that the battle was closer to hand—in fact, was upon the city's doorsteps.

I shrank back against the nearest wall as a tumultuous mob roared past me, its assembled faces gleaming with fervid excitement, throats raw with the shouting of various coarse slogans. From what little I could understand of them, it was obvious that whatever their previous opinions might have been, they were all possessed of a passionate dislike for all things Steam-related. To hear the jostling people's cries and witness the brandishing of their various torches and improvised tools of destruction, one might have concluded that a sweltering Devil had descended upon London to impose some igneous tyranny, to the abolition of which these citizens had now dedicated themselves.

"Come on, mate!" One of the rioters spotted me and extended a laughing invitation as the crowd surged through the street. "Havin' a right smash-up, we are! Miss it and ye'll be sorry!"

The human tide moved past me in its chaotic yet single-minded fashion. I counted myself fortunate that the cumulative effect of my own recent adventures, while unenjoyable at the time of experiencing them, had rendered my own garments to a less respectable state, with various tears and stains, as well as general grime, evident on my coat and trousers. If not for such a disheveled appearance, I might have been mistaken for exactly the sort of well-mannered toff to which the mob was also directing its disdain. Various gentlemen, mistakenly believing they still possessed the liberty of moving about the city at will, were even as I watched being pummeled to the ground or, if less fortunate, hoisted onto lampposts by hempen ropes tightened about their necks. Either fate seemed to evoke even greater hilarity on the part of the rioters, shouting and brandishing their torches.

That the torches were not being used merely for illumination was soon made evident to me. The sharp, unmistakable noise of shattering glass reached my ear; beyond the close-pressed bodies of the mob, I saw flaring brands tossed inside a number of shops and residences. Soon, flames and sparks were swirling up into the night sky, a sight which served to further elevate the mood of the howling crowd.

At last, I glimpsed an opportunity to venture forth on my errand. Enough of the mob had passed by before me, that through the straggling remnant I could see the dark alleys across from me. From my long-ago upbringing in London, I was familiar enough with the

district that I could envision a circuitous route that would enable me
to bypass the rioting populace and safely reach my destination.
Summoning up my courage, I dashed into the street, shouldering
my way past the mob's stragglers, and succeeded at diving into the
unlit passageway beyond.

While I might have initially underestimated the difficulties involved in fetching the *Vox Universalis* key, I prudently ensured that
I would not similarly dismiss the mob's ability to do me harm. I was
familiar enough with the nature of human enthusiasms, so easily
stoked to the incendiary point, to know that while I might have once
escaped those attentions both mirthful and murderous, a second
encounter could not be guaranteed to go so well. Very likely, at a
certain point in their mingled inebriation and vandalism, they
would commence hanging one another just as readily as any perceived member of the genteel classes who fell into their hands.

Keeping a sharp ear out for the sounds of the mob's revelry, I
navigated a course as widely diverging from its course as possible.
My progress was made faster by the fact of the rioters having already
bestowed their efforts on the districts that lay before me. Once having reduced them to rubble and ash, they had quickly abandoned
them for fresher fields, with windows yet unsmashed and buildings
unrazed.

In short order, I found myself picking my way through Clerkenwell, in which my old watchmaker's shop had been located years
before. I saw no indication of it now having been converted to other
uses, so thoroughly had the area been transformed—first by the in-
vading advent of Steam, then by the mob's rampage. The great pipes
which coursed through the once familiar streets had been hammered asunder, their assailants apparently dismissive of their
chances of being scalded to death by the gouts of heated vapour
gushing forth. The resulting effect on the depopulated scene was of
some industrial disaster, perhaps a crashing wreck upon the railway
lines. I covered my ears against the mingled hisses and shrieks; I
would have been quickly deafened if I had not. Ducking beneath the
jets of steam and crawling on my stomach when necessary, and with

mist-sodden black ash clinging to my hands and face, I laboriously effected my passage to the district's perimeter and the marginally less hazardous streets beyond.

Continuing onward, I managed only through the greatest of prudence to avoid being scalded to death, mauled by various bands of rioters, or clubbed over the head by the constables futilely attempting to gain control of the London streets. At various moments in the course of my journey, I sought refuge behind various heaps of iron scrap, the detritus of the mob's increasingly frenzied vendetta against all things relative to Steam; at others, the great hissing clouds of vapour filling the passageways afforded me sufficient cover to elude any who might have sought to impede my progress.

At last, I spied my destination before me—Featherwhite House was but a few dozen paces or so away, with nothing blocking my path. I quickly broke into a run, anxious to reach the imposing structure before anything else could go amiss.

In that simple endeavour, I was thwarted—I should scarcely have been surprised by that, given all that had happened thus far. No sooner had I attained the gate opening onto the street than I heard the now familiar discord of shattering glass and mingled shouts indicating the presence of some contingent of rioters. Worse, a flaring light fell across my face as I halted in my tracks. As I watched, fire and smoke issued forth from the lower windows of Featherwhite House. Before I could seek a hiding-place, a giddily hilarious mob rushed past, knocking me to the ground beside the lane curving toward the building's ornate front door.

"You've come too late—" Dazed, I felt a hand grasp mine, pulling me again to my feet. "Likely, you should be thankful for that!"

By the light of the fire quickly engulfing the townhouse, I saw that I was being addressed by Royston, the foreman of those workers who had been engaged upon their various activities within Featherwhite House, chiefly to do with those devices created by my father which had been brought hither.

"What . . ." I was grateful to have avoided being trampled by the mob—in my previous haste, I might have been able to discern their presence if their torches had not all been used for purposes of arson. "What do you mean?"

"They've all fled!" Royston pointed to the burning structure with an outflung hand. "As they damn well should have!" Blood trickled down the man's brow, from a wound he had no doubt suffered in his own encounter with the mob. "As you should as well!"

Before I could elicit further information from the man, he had turned away and hurried from me, disappearing into the street's flickering shadows.

I was near enough to Featherwhite House that I could feel the heat from the flames quickly advancing through the ornate structure. There was no consideration of allowing that to deter me from approaching even more closely—not if I was to succeed in securing the object for which I had come all this way, under such dangerous circumstances.

The massive front door stood ajar, giving me full view of the townhouse's interior. It took but a second's scrutiny, one upraised hand protecting my face, to determine that it was primarily the outer walls that were engulfed in flame—the mob's fiery brands had not traveled more than a few feet through the smashed windows. I could see as well that the progress of the fire was to some degree retarded by the geysers of steam upwelling from the broken floorboards—at least some members of the mob, in their spiraling lust for destruction, had apparently turned their attentions to the detested machinery in the cellars. As I cringed back from the searing heat, a deafening explosion shook the building, an overheated boiler sending its sharp-edged fragments through the walls blackened by smoke.

Not for the first time, I realized the advantage that sheer desperation gives one, when confronted by circumstances at which more reasonable minds would quail. Though possessed of no great amount of physical courage, and certainly less of it than the majority of men, I found myself diving into the flame-engulfed premises, heading for the central staircase.

Blinded by the mingled smoke and steam, I availed myself of the carved wooden rail to pull myself upward. The structure had been so weakened by both the fire and the explosion from the cellars, that the rail swayed with every grasp of my hands, the steps beneath my feet yielding in a similarly precarious fashion. Looking above, I was able to discern the stairs' mounting creak away from the point at which it attached to the next story. Fearful of being plunged to the burning wreckage below, I made even greater haste, throwing myself headlong past the final steps and onto the floor of the upper hallway to which I had directed myself.

There having been only a relatively few occasions on which I had been inside Featherwhite House, it required some hurried investigation on my part, flinging open one door after another, to find the room which had been assigned as my temporary quarters. The diminished, smoke-filled air evoked fits of wracking coughs as I spotted my luggage still laid out on the narrow bench at the foot of the bed. Within moments I was inside the room, batting away a flurry of sparks with one hand as with the other I flung open the *portmanteau*'s battered lid.

Even in as unfortunate circumstances as these, I breathed a sigh of relief when I saw that the key to the *Vox Universalis* was where I had placed it, when I had first packed up my meager possessions and hied myself to London. So exact was its resemblance to the diagram I had obtained from Scape, there was no necessity for me to draw the paper from my coat for confirmation. Instead, I seized upon the device itself, lifting it and holding it in both hands, gazing upon the thing with new understanding—

For when I had grasped it before, it had been with the intention of employing it for my own self-destruction.

I had then thought it to be some manner of pistol, crafted by my father so that its intricate workings were somehow capable of hurling a projectile from what had seemed to be its muzzle. No wonder that I had been unable, despite all my poking and prying at the machine, to cause it to send a round crashing through my skull! Even those minutely detailed separate objects that I had previously discerned within it, which I had assumed to be bullets, my previous familiarity with my father's designs now informed me were but sub-mechanisms for altering the operations of the larger *Vox Univer-salis* device into which the key would be inserted. Their micro-scopic gears would interconnect with those larger than them, thereby producing the desired results, whatever those might be.

If there had been sufficient air to breathe in the increasingly sti-fling room, I might almost have laughed at the recall of my earlier frustrations. But now I was gratified to an even larger extent, to have been informed of the device's true purpose. The device trembled within my grasp, as though from its unlimited potentiality as well as the various mainsprings I had left wound before packing it away in my luggage. For it was not only the key by which my father's voice-simulating construction could be set into operation—it was as well the key to my own fortunes and security.

That was, of course, if I could find a way out of the fire-wracked building in which I presently stood.

As I brought my gaze up from the precious construction in my hands, an ominous noise reached my ear—a great clattering, as of timbers tearing apart from each other, then collapsing as rubble to somewhere below. Clutching the key device to my chest, I hurried from the room. Merely by my stepping into the hallway, my worst apprehensions were confirmed—Featherwhite House's central stair-case had separated into its component elements, leaving a smoke-filled vacancy where my route of escape had formerly stood.

"Mr. Dower! Is it you—"

While not completely startled by the collapse of the staircase—the event seemed in keeping with the general course of my fortunes—I was, however, taken by surprise at hearing a woman's voice calling out to me. And a familiar one—I turned about and peered through the billowing clouds of smoke and steam. To my further astonish-ment, Lord Fusible's daughter, Evangeline, stood but a few yards away from me.

"What is it you are doing here?" There was no time for formalities—or for explanations. I hastened to her side and laid hold of one arm to prevent her from collapsing. "We must find a way out—immediately—"

There was but little resistance on her part, so overcome was she by the thickening smoke. Her eyelids fluttered as she gasped for breath, her negligible weight pressed into the crook of my shoulder.

"Wait—we cannot—" She managed to raise one limp hand and point to a room at the end of the hallway. "There is another—we must save—"

There being no ready escape in the opposite direction, I bore her with me toward the door she had indicated. I had no idea of whom she spoke, but with any luck, it might be someone who could somehow assist us in making an exit from the burning townhouse.

The door was already ajar; I kicked it farther open and peered inside. The room, previously unvisited by me, seemed to be some sort of private parlour, of the sort employed when a small group of individuals seek to converse amongst themselves, separate from whatever larger gathering might have been taking place downstairs. A claw-footed oaken table was littered with gentlemanly paraphernalia, half-empty glasses of port, grey-ashed cigars stubbed out or still emitting tendrils of smoke combining with the suffocating haze that hung low from the ceiling. The disordered state of the furniture, with chairs scattered about or knocked backward to the floor, indicated the hasty flight of whoever had been there. No doubt they had taken to their heels when the rioters had first besieged Featherwhite House.

I spied the person of whom Evangeline had informed me. The possibility of aid from this source now seemed remote—the figure lay face downward before the room's fireplace, a widening pool of blood seeping around his head. The edge of the stone mantelpiece above him was similarly reddened, as though it had been in some manner the cause of the man's injury.

Leaving Evangeline for the moment at the room's doorway, I hurried into the room and knelt at the man's side. As I rolled him onto his back, I found myself gazing with astonishment into the face of none other than Stonebrake. How he had been transported here, rather than having been annihilated, as I had presumed, in the explosion at Westminster Palace—such, I could not conjecture.

However, it was quickly obvious to me that while he might have evaded death then, it had caught up with him now. The blow he had received to the corner of his brow had been sufficient to lay open his skull; no breath or other indicator of life was perceptible.

Leaving Stonebrake's corpse where it rested unmoving, I ran back toward the hallway and grasped Evangeline about the waist, before she could slip unconscious to the floor.

"The servants' access . . . there . . ." With a tilt of her head, she indicated a door, narrower than the rest, at the very end of the corridor. "That is how . . . I made my way up here . . ."

I carried her to the door and pushed it open with my shoulder. A pent-up billow of smoke escaped from it, driving me back, gasping and coughing. As the fumes partly dispersed, I managed to take a further look down the twisting stairway that had been revealed. No doubt it led to the kitchen and other service areas, from which the needs of the house's proprietors had once been met. Sparks flew up into my face as I futilely attempted to discern the stairs' terminus through the swiftly rising smoke.

There was no other way. Glancing behind myself, I saw a column of flame roar upward where the house's central staircase had been. It would be perhaps only a matter of minutes before the structure was completely engulfed, the hallway's floor collapsing out from beneath our feet. I held Evangeline closer to myself and pulled her into the narrowly winding passage. She pressed her face to my chest and struggled to breathe, as we fought to make our awkward course to whatever safety we could find . . .

My eyes, stinging with smoke and heat, caught a fragmentary glimpse of sinks and carving tables, the appurtenances of domestic labours, when we at last stumbled out of the stairwell. The smoke was even thicker here, rolling in like a choking tide from what had been the house's more elegant chambers. I spied an open exterior doorway, the night's dark revealed beyond, and dragged Evangeline's unresisting form through it.

Fresh, cold air was gratefully received into my lungs. Evangeline raised her own face from my chest, and I could see her reviving as well. With my remaining strength, I half carried, half dragged her to the farthest reach of the overgrown garden to which we had escaped. I lowered Evangeline onto a stone bench at the end of an ornamental pond, then collapsed beside her.

From here, we could both see the flames consuming Feather-white House. The widening column of smoke obscured the stars above our heads. Without doubt, Stonebrake's lifeless body was even now in the process of cremation within.

Then, for a moment, I believed myself wrong about this and that somehow the miscreant had retained some trembling thread of life, sufficient to escape the building. I pushed myself upright on the bench, witnessing in astonishment a figure wrapped in fire and smoke, crawling with grim determination from the blackened margin of Featherwhite House's walls. Within seconds, though, I realized that it was not Stonebrake I beheld, but the animated Orang-Utan of previous unpleasant encounters. Its tatty orange fur had been reduced to ashes, revealing the intricate mechanisms of its limbs and torso. Steam hissed from various apertures, as well as the hose trailing behind it. Damaged by the fire, the latter burst, ragged ends whipping about like beheaded snakes, then falling limp and inert to the ground. Deprived of motive force, the Orang-Utan seemingly died as well, its jointed metal paws curling into rigid fists. The entire device rolled onto its side, the now lidless spherical eyes casting one last glance toward me before its interlinked apparatuses shuddered to an agonized halt.

Another's voice came more graciously to my ear.

"I am indebted to you, Mr. Dower." Rendered somewhat hoarse, Lord Fusible's daughter reached over and squeezed my hand. "If not for you . . ." She left the remainder of the dire thought unspoken.

"Anything I did—" I broke off my words, seized by a spasm of coughing. I then managed to speak the rest. "Was but that which any would have done."

"Then the world is not such an entirely wicked place as I had believed." She gave me a wan smile, quickly extinguished by some more troubling consideration. "Though I fear that it is still sufficiently so, as to render all my chances of happiness beyond my reach! Better that you had left me where you had found me, or that my father's faithful servants had let me drown, rather than saving me from the capsizing of that little boat in which I last conversed with you. If they had not aided me so, I might have continued on to a more felicitous realm."

"You are speaking nonsense." To my own ear, my words sounded sterner and less sympathetic than I had intended—though perhaps they were better so. "You are young and with the greatest part of your life still before you. Time enough to think of the grave, and what lies beyond it, when you have reached my age. Though I must confess that I no longer contemplate those matters with as much enthusiasm as I formerly did."

"It gladdens my heart, to the degree that anything can, to hear you say as much, Mr. Dower. I had been somewhat grieved that in my unthinking self-concern, I had added to your cares. Please be as cheerful as is still within your power, as I cannot."

"For God's sake, why do you persist in speaking that way?" The urge was strong to seize her frail form by its shoulders and shake some sense into her. "Wait—make no attempt to answer that question. Merely tell me instead why you were here at all, in such precarious circumstances?"

"I thought . . ." Her grasp upon my hand tightened. "I thought I might be able to save my beloved, Captain Crowcroft."

"How so?" Her words perplexed me. "Was he here?"

"Indeed so—as was my father, in company with the rest of Phototrope Limited's owners and directors. Unbeknownst to my father and his fellow conspirators, I followed them here, in the hope of ascertaining at least some news of my *fiancé*'s whereabouts." She sadly shook her head. "As it turned out, I discovered much greater than I had bargained for. Horrible things, Mr. Dower—I can scarcely believe that which I eavesdropped upon, from outside the door of that room by which you found me."

"I would very likely be able to. I am not encumbered by your tender feelings toward either your father or humanity in general.

Such being the case, please do not hesitate to inform me of what you heard."

As the fire continued to wrap itself about the walls of Featherwhite House, Evangeline proceeded to relate all that she had so recently discovered.

"My father, Mr. Dower—would that there were no cause to tell you of such things!—he is involved in far darker conspiracies than those of which you have been led to believe. I know, for such things cannot be concealed from as attentive a daughter as myself, that you were told that all his efforts were turned toward some sordid gambling scheme, by which wagers upon the movements of various competing lighthouse corporations would be assured of pouring money into their pockets. Is this not so?"

"That is indeed what I was told—by your father, Lord Fusible, himself."

"Such a dishonorable charade! I blush to hear of such sins committed by one so closely related by blood to me. You should never have believed him in this regard—and for this simple reason. However such helpful information was to have been gained, by conversing with whales or any other equally fantastic method, there would have been no need for it. There are no competing lighthouse corporations—Phototrope Limited has secretly bought them all up, thus bringing them under its control. My father and his fellow directors know well ahead of time what decisions those other corporations will make—indeed, they are in fact the ones who decide! So they are aware in advance of what operations those puppet corporations will undertake, and to what remote craggy shores they will send their walking lights. If my father's intentions had been no more than to hoodwink the bookmakers and with his accomplices reap the rewards of such chicanery, he already possessed all the information that was required."

"I see." This revelation did indeed place a vastly different complexion upon the affairs in which I had become embroiled. "So if it were not to ensure the success of their wagers, then to what ends were your father and his associates intent?"

"Have you heard of a man named Duncan MacDuff? And his accomplice, a woman who goes by the unfortunate pseudonym of Valvienne?"

"They are well-known to me," I said. "Both by those names and by others, which might possibly be their true ones. You can never be certain with such types."

"I am not surprised by your knowledge," said Evangeline. "Though secretive in the conduct of their affairs, they are rightfully considered to be the worst of rogues by all who have had the misfortune of coming into contact with them."

"Yes." I gave an emphatic nod. "That has indeed been my experience."

"Then I hope that it will not cause you to think even more disparagingly of my father, for me to inform you that he is in league with this infamous pair."

By now, I was beyond all capacity for surprise. Merely to have discovered, as I so recently did, that Scape and Miss McThane were here in London—such a fact inevitably raised the possibility that they had inveigled themselves into what other unsavory dealings were under way.

"You have my sympathies," I told her. "I doubt if your father will have other than regret ensuing from his association with them. Am I correct in assuming that by extension, your father and his associates are also involved in the various schemes of the Prime Minister, Mrs. Fletcher?"

"Exactly so," said Evangeline. "And I fear that he will suffer more from her intrigues than he could ever have from the merely sordid and greedy ones concocted by MacDuff and his female companion. For Mrs. Fletcher's ambitions are of a vastly greater and more sinister variety."

"Well . . . they're not small," I allowed. "Seeing as she wishes to overturn everything upon which British society rests, one could hardly accuse her of a limited scope to her visions. I do not see, though, how the activities of your father and his associates have any bearing upon Mrs. Fletcher's schemes."

"This is astute of you, Mr. Dower, to make that observation. For in fact, Phototrope Limited and the illicit gambling operations connected to it, ostensibly pursued by my father and the other corporate directors, is a sham. It is nothing but a front, to employ the criminal jargon, for Mrs. Fletcher's larger conspiracy. Even the lighthouses they have constructed and set in motion, those technological wonders known as the 'walking lights,' are not what they seem. The reports of the assistance they have allegedly provided to the nation's various mercantile seafarers, preventing their valuable cargoes from being lost upon the coastline's forbidding rocks, are largely fictional, concocted by paid hacks in order to impress a favourable impression in the minds of the public."

"To what purpose?"

"To the obfuscation of the appalling use for which the lighthouses were actually designed and constructed, and to which use they will be shortly turned." Evangeline's voice was tinged with a righteous disdain. "You are aware, I take it, of the Prime Minister's desire to cast off whatever limitations she believes are imposed upon her by the strength of the Steam Miners' Union?"

"Yes." I gave a nod. "I have been informed of her desires in that regard, and how they motivate all of her tumultuous campaigns, including the fomenting of these riots sweeping the city."

"She seeks more than the lessening of their grasp upon the engines of power. Nothing will suffice for her designs but to turn the locale of the steam mines into one vast prison, in which those condemned to labour will have no chance of either escape or hope of struggling against that vision of the Future which she seeks to impose upon all of us. That is what the lighthouses were created for; they are an essential element of the oppressive regime being readied to be set in place. The lighthouses, mobile as they are, can easily be relocated for their new role in keeping the rebellious steam miners safely pent up. Not as lighthouses, but *guard towers*—their powerful beams will light up the ravaged landscape as though in perpetual daylight, harsh and revealing enough to prevent any from slipping past to freedom."

"And your father agreed to be a participant in this horrifying scheme? I would have thought better of him—or of almost any man!"

"Do not judge him too harshly, Mr. Dower. For he and his associates were duped by the Prime Minister. They had thought, for so they had been told by her, that the intent of all her schemes was to *maintain* that which we have as our *status quo,* which keeps all the elements of society functioning, rather than grinding to a halt. She had convinced the directors of Phototrope Limited that the grimly repressive measures she had devised against the Steam Miners' Union were necessary to ensure the continuing flow of vaporous energy through the pipes interlacing across the countryside. Without which, not only would their fortunes be lost, but all about them would fall into utter ruin—in that regard, they might well have considered themselves to be motivated not just from self-interest, but a general philanthropy toward their fellow citizens."

"So all men wish to view themselves," I observed. "Well, perhaps not Scape and those others like him. But certainly most."

"How loathsome, then, for Mrs. Fletcher to have turned an otherwise commendable altruism against them! For in pursuit of her own hidden agenda, she kept hidden from my father and his associates her larger plan, to not just cast aside and imprison the miners rendered superfluous by her actions, but to supplant Steam itself as the great motive force in our society. My father and the other Phototrope Limited directors would be reduced to beggary by this abrupt transition to coal—obviously they would never have consented to being cogs in the machinery of the Iron Lady's schemes, if they had been aware of her actual intentions."

"I imagine not." In consideration of the young woman's recent travails, I thought it prudent to keep unspoken my own assessment, that while her father and his associates might not have been the worst of men, at least in the scale of iniquity on which Mrs. Fletcher held so prominent a position, they were very likely not the best representatives of our kind, either.

"Consider my chagrin, Mr. Dower, to learn that another, the one closest to my heart, had been similarly deceived by this woman—or rather, to be precise, what had once been a member of my gender. For my beloved Captain Crowcroft was also a victim of her wiles, deluded into believing that there was some consummate virtue involved in his commanding the walking lights—only to have it revealed to him by Mrs. Fletcher herself that his position in her coming regime was to be of the brutal and degrading status of a common gaoler!"

Such must have been the information which Crowcroft had received, that had had such an unsettling effect upon him, and of which he had spoken to me in that horrid little room in East London. "Did he speak to you of this?"

"No." Evangeline shook her head. "I was forced to learn of it in secret. As the first reports of the riots spreading through the city reached my ear, I became aware as well of my father and his associates convening at this place." She pointed to what was left of Featherwhite House, its roof having collapsed in a flurry of sparks to the fire-engulfed structure below. "I overheard my father and his closest confidants speak of it—and that the captain would be here in attendance as well! Until that moment, I'd had no information as to his whereabouts, or what awful fate might have befallen him in his absence from me. From the tone of what I heard, I was convinced that he was in some grave danger, the nature of which it was incumbent upon me to discover. As my father and his associates took no more notice of me than they had ever been inclined to do, it was easy enough to surreptitiously follow them here and station myself where I could overhear every word they spoke."

"I rather suspect that you heard nothing that would allay your fears."

"Indeed so, Mr. Dower. I restrained my impulse to enter the room and clasp my beloved in my arms, the better to ascertain into what dreadful situation he had fallen. From what little I could glimpse of him, he seemed in a terrible state, more disheveled and overwrought than I had ever seen him. Some traumatic event had restored the balance of his reason—or so I heard him assert—which had been the immediate cause for his hastily summoning my father and the others to this conference, motivating them by threatening to make public their various illicit schemes."

One more item my silence concealed from her, that I had doubtless been present when Captain Crowcroft, previously adrift in his self-inflicted miseries, had been knocked back onto a truer and more virtuous course. Having escaped from the scene which to his mind had implicated him as a crazed murderer, he had apparently resolved to set as many matters aright as he was capable of doing.

"So he got them here," I said. "What was their response to his informing them of the degree to which they had been duped by Mrs. Fletcher?"

"There was a general angry outcry on their parts—and one who laughed in cruel mockery of their consternation."

"Who would that have been?"

"I had seen him but once before, in your company, Mr. Dower—when he brought you to a more celebratory gathering at my father's own house. That man Stonebrake."

"Rather, that had been his name." I took some ignoble satisfaction in telling her of his fate. "When I found him now, he lay dead upon the floor of the chamber."

"I feared as much," said Evangeline. "For it was a blow from Captain Crowcroft's hand that sent him hard upon the mantelpiece, with blood streaming from his brow. Though I can scarcely blame my beloved for his sudden rage, so bitterly received were the revelations that Stonebrake threw into the faces of the gathered company."

"What manner of thing did Stonebrake tell them, to evoke such a reaction?"

"No more than this, Mr. Dower—that virtually everything they had been led to believe was true, and upon which they had based so many of their own schemes and actions, was in fact a monstrous lie."

"I am not greatly startled to hear this." Such disclosures seemed to be coming thick and fast to me, varying only by their increasing degree of monumentality. "But what are the exact particulars of which he spoke?"

"They were such that I could scarcely credit them myself," said Evangeline. "The whole premise for which the walking lighthouses had been created and operated is a concocted fiction, according to what this man Stonebrake said. There are in fact no sentient oceans capable of shifting about from one section of the coastline to another. There never had been; that was all an elaborate ruse to justify Mrs. Fletcher's government pouring money into the pockets of the lighthouse corporations' owners, to build and operate the unneeded devices—unneeded, that is, until they could be employed for their true purpose as guard towers for the imprisoned steam miners. I heard Stonebrake make a similar claim about the nature of that supposedly worthy organization from which he had emerged, the so-called Mission to the Cetaceans—it is a vast concocted fraud as well. There might have been some humble members of the group who had naively believed that it was possible to deliver sermons to whales, but the actual purpose of the Mission had been no more than to use its floating headquarters ship to keep an eye on the various walking lighthouses stationed around the coastline, thus ascertaining their readiness to be used for the oppressive purpose which the Prime Minister intended them."

"I see." To tell the truth, I but partly did so, the multiplicity of these revelations overwhelming my ability to keep track and sort them out inside my head. The general tenor of them, however, was easily perceived: we had all been made fools of. More was discernible as well. "So—upon hearing all this, Captain Crowcroft flew into a rage and struck the mocking Stonebrake?"

"Yes." Evangeline sadly nodded. "I witnessed the blow, though I could not be sure of the severity of the effect upon its recipient. Things happened so quickly! There was no opportunity for any of the company to go to the aid of the fallen man, for just at that moment the first draughts of smoke wafted upward, and it became apparent that the rioters had cast their torches through the windows below. My father and the others hastened to make their escape."

"But you did not—"

"In the ensuing panic and chaos, I flew to the side of my betrothed, with no more intent in mind than to share in whatever fate would befall him."

"But then . . ." The young woman's assertion, believable as it was, left me more perplexed than before. "Why was he not there when I arrived upon the scene?"

"He thrust me aside," came Evangeline's mournful reply. "I could see that he was still possessed by a towering, vindictive rage, of a strength sufficient to overwhelm his concern for me. He said no more to me than that he had plans of his own, which he was now intent upon setting into motion. He vanished into the smoke filling the townhouse; that was the last I saw of him."

Whatever my own plans had been, to wrest some trifling advantage to myself, now seemed to have similarly vanished. If I succeeded in making my own escape from whatever remained of London, I would be as much of a pauper as I had been when conveyed here by that mendacious villain Stonebrake.

At the present moment, it seemed prudent to remain obscured in the overgrown garden to which Evangeline and I had fled, the grounds returning to darkness as the flames began to ebb inside the wreckage of Featherwhite House. We could both hear in the distance the mob's shouts and frenzied merriment, as it continued its destructive course through the city. I had no wish to encounter the rioters once more, or to be forced to hand over the distraught young woman to their mercies. Perhaps in the first light of morning, we might be able to discern some route to relative safety—

My timid musings were interrupted by a thundering roar, louder than any of the night's previous explosions. It transformed the air about us into an unseen hammer, battering with sufficient force to send us both toppling from the overturned garden bench.

Once more dazed and uncomprehending, I raised myself from the ground onto which I had been thrown. Looking up, I saw the sky turned to one vast sheet of churning orange and red, as though all the mingled clouds of steam and smoke had been ignited.

And worse, by that lurid illumination, I saw monstrous shapes, of dimensions beyond nightmare, rising up in the middle of the city.

The Colossus and the Iron Lady

WHATEVER event had transformed the mingled smoke and steam above into an inverted sea of fire, it was of a magnitude sufficient to be observed in every district of London. The rumbling clamour of the accompanying explosion, dwarfing all that I had previously experienced, rendered the air about us to a tangible entity, possessed of the same force that had bodily cast both myself and Lord Fusible's daughter from the garden bench and onto the wreckage-littered ground.

"We must away from here." Having regained my feet, I reached down and grasped Evangeline's hand, bringing her upright as well. "The farther we proceed from the midpoint of the city, the likelier we are to secure a degree of safety from such eruptions, whatever their cause might be."

"No!" She shook her head with a dismayingly fierce determination. "There is still too much at stake—if not for you, Mr. Dower, than surely for myself. Flee if you wish, but I must yet find a way to my beloved's side."

This struck me as an ambition unlikely to be achieved, no matter the strength of her devotion to Captain Crowcroft. I was at first greatly tempted to take the young woman up on her admonition to preserve my own skin—but found myself worrying but a moment later on the dangers she would certainly face in whatever course she rashly chose to follow. Beyond the already sufficiently hazardous fire, hissing gouts of steam, and crumbling buildings, there were also the dark hearts of the populace to be figured into one's calculations. Once the anarchic spirit has seized hold of men's minds, it casts aside all limits upon its attentions. The mob filling the streets had been urged on by the devious Scape's engines of whispered suspicion and shouted rumour. These rioters might have initially directed their wrath at all things related to what they now considered to be their great enemy Steam—but now, caught up in their spiraling fury, they were unlikely to cavil at any other target catching their eye. Were a young maiden of seemingly wealthy bearing be foolish enough to intrude upon their torch-lit revels, her murder would be the kindliest of the fates likely to befall her.

To which I felt unusually reluctant to abandon her, even if by doing so I might save myself from harm. Though never one given to inordinately chivalrous impulses, I nonetheless considered it incumbent upon myself to dissuade Evangeline from an undertaking as self-destructive as any I might have once considered.

"That rise—" Shouting to convey my meaning to her, I pointed to the highest point of the landscape beyond the perimeter of the demolished Featherwhite House's gardens. "We will be able to see what is happening from there."

Taking Evangeline by the hand once more, I led her up the hill's steep slope to its crest. Doubtless, she considered there would be some advantage in accompanying me there, so that she might conceive of a route into the midst of the turmoil, there to somehow locate her beloved Captain Crowcroft. My own calculation differed, in the hope that so terrifying a scene might be revealed to us, that she would yet be dissuaded from her announced intent.

In the event, as we stood gasping for breath in the smoke-filled air at the hill's summit, I was not disappointed—at least as far as terror was concerned. Certainly my senses were thrown from their normal channels of comprehension by what quickly ensued as we directed our gaze toward the burning distance.

No more than a heartbeat passed before an even more appalling sight greeted our eyes. Featherwhite House had been so closely situated to the centers of the nation's wealth and government, and the hill upon which we stood was of sufficient elevation, that Evangeline and I were afforded a clear perspective along the Thames toward the Houses of Parliament. Or what had been such—for even as we watched, the ornate *façade* of those ancient buildings sheared away, impelled in their collapse by the fiery surge upwelling from their center. Great quantities of brick and stone fell *en masse* to the river below; yet more clouds of steam billowed from the waters as the heated rubble struck their roiling surface.

If I had not already embraced a fervent desire to escape from this newly demonized London as quickly as possible, this would have been enough to plant such a sensible wish within my breast. But yet more ensued, to my mounting horror—

The fire-reddened smoke churning from the ruins obscured an entity of daunting proportions, rising upward as though awakened from chthonic slumber. I could discern only elements of its construction—hard-edged and rigid, propelled by inhuman strength—but enough to evoke the dread of witnessing some mechanical construction of more massive proportions and wicked intent than all I had previously seen.

In this, too, I was not disappointed, though I soon wished I had been. Grinding, clashing noises of deafening pitch and amplitude hammered the night air, as the apparition thrust itself up through the smoke, unfolding and revealing the greater portion of its bulk above the soot-weighted clouds.

"It's her—" Little chance that Evangeline was able to hear my stricken whisper through the accumulating din. "The Iron Lady—"

But not as she had been. A more thorough transformation had been wrought, in both size and substance. Intimidating as Mrs. Fletcher had appeared before, as though she were a railway engine bearing down upon oneself, there had still been some human, fleshly element remaining to her, incorporated into the prow of the assemblage of boilers, hissing valves, thrusting pistons, and spoked driving wheels. That relatively softer element had been discarded, as might some black-winged creature, unfurling itself to its full dimensions, spurn the lowly chrysalis that had incubated its swelling form. All was iron now, no mortal scrap retained. Even the planes and angles of her broad, overbearing face, expanded to vastly larger dimensions, were forged of that sullen metal, each segment riveted and hinged to another, fire flashing from the apertures of its eyes.

In truth, the transmogrified Prime Minister seemed to embody as much fire as metal. Furnace doors gaped open at numerous points about the appalling construction's torso, as flames and air-shimmering heat poured out from iron-doored apertures twice the height of the sweating, half-naked figures frantically shoveling coal into them. As this embodiment of Mrs. Fletcher, magnified and made yet more horrid by the total transformation from flesh to machine, reared itself higher into the smoke-occluded sky, more than one of her strenuously engaged attendants were toppled off balance, falling with shovels still at hand into the furnaces and consumed as quickly as moths fluttering about a lantern wick—all while their blackened comrades hastened at their toil.

A soul-crushing gaze swept across the city beneath the apparition. The searing flames visible behind the Iron Lady's eyes, like the fireholes in a blast furnace door, seemed to represent all the nation's power, swept up and embodied in but a single entity.

As appalled as I was by the genderless Titan rearing up from the ruins of Parliament, the effect upon those nearest to it was understandably even more fearful. The shrieks and cries of the mob changed tone, from the sheer enjoyment of setting torches to shop fronts and houses to the panicked haste of those perceiving the immensity of that which now stood towering above them. A great, concentric wave of Humanity, each desperate member tearing at the others surrounding it, fled through every available street and alley, seeking whatever implausible refuge they might be able to secure.

Which was a desire I shared as well, even at the distance from which I was able to observe these events. The sloping rise on which Evangeline and I stood trembled beneath our feet, as the pounding and grinding of the Iron Lady's component machinery was transmitted through the underlying rock to us. Those vibrations urged on the increasingly rapid beating within my own chest.

"Come along—" I pulled at the arm of the young woman beside me. "Before it is too late—"

It already was, though that which straitened our already dire circumstances came from a wholly unanticipated quarter. As we looked along the course of the Thames, unable to divert our joint gaze from the monstrosity unhindered before us, a shriek of steam mingled with the awesome industrial clamour of devices beyond all human scale and comprehension. The deafening sounds came from somewhere closer to us, and behind—

I turned about, thereby beholding what new and calamitous factor had entered upon our our precarious lives.

Or to be precise, I discerned some partial element of it. The sight of immense metal appendages, like those of a mechanical crab enlarged to daunting dimensions, evoked memories within me. For a moment, I seemed to be upon the Cornish shore once more, observing as that ambulatory lighthouse, the launch part of which I had attended, made its ponderous way to the wave-swept rocky crag of its destination.

As my gaze moved upward, along the tapering flank of the structure above the riveted iron legs, a more recent image swept the previous from my thoughts. It came from the *soirée* I had attended shortly after my arrival here in London, upon Lord Fusible's invitation. That had been when I had first laid eyes upon that culminating production of Phototrope Limited's ingenuity and finances, albeit in diminished form, the walking light to which Fusible had referred as the *Colossus of Blackpool.*

My first glimpse—but evidently not my final one. For what I beheld now, as I tilted my head farther back in order to fully encompass the form before me, was that very same Colossus, now in its vast and completed state, a monstrosity transported by its own locomotive systems from that grimly industrial facility in North London where it had been housed before. Even as I realized that this was the reality of that which I had seen but as a model on that previous occasion, one of its legs, jointed and clawed as some monstrous crustacean, swivelled about from the tower's base, its curved point thrusting

with tremendous force into the ground but a few yards from where
Evangeline stood, frozen with surprise.

Regaining some capacity to react, I grasped the young woman
about her shoulders and drew the two of us back to the relative safety
of the rounded boulders at the side of the hilltop. The ground shook
with even greater violence as the Colossus crawled its way past us,
heading toward some farther destination with unstoppable force.

As we gazed awe-struck at the towering machine in its passage,
I heard a voice cry out my name.

"Dower!" A man's voice, familiar to me, came from behind the
Colossus' clawing tread, as though the person had been following it
close behind. "The key! Do you have the key?"

I realized who it was even before my own arm was hurriedly
grasped by the individual. "For God's sake, Scape—" I gazed upon
him with a combination of scorn and amazement. "Have you no
capacity to set aside your paltry concerns?" With my outflung hand,
I indicated the immense form moving but a few paces away from us,
every synchronized movement of its clawed appendages shaking the
ground about us. "Surely there are more pressing matters than whatever daft scheme upon which you have fixed yourself."

"Actually, there isn't." He grabbed me by the front of my shirt,
pulling me away from Evangeline. "So just tell me—do you have it or
don't you?"

I was not greatly astonished at the man's sudden appearance in
this environment of mounting chaos. Both he and his companion,
Miss McThane, whom I glimpsed but a few paces farther away,
seemed to me like storm crows, inevitably in attendance upon whatever scenes of ruin fell upon the general body of Mankind. If I had
been of quicker apperception, I would have known from the beginning that they were somehow involved in all the various conspiracies that had flocked so densely about me.

There was scarcely a moment now in which I was able to reply to
his hurried enquiry. So desperate had been the escape of myself and
Lord Fusible's daughter from the burning Featherwhite House, that
I had paid little attention to the matter of that object which I had

come there to procure from my own luggage. Within an instant, Scape had pushed aside my coat and found what I had once assumed to be my father's clockwork pistol, where I had tucked it inside the waistband of my trousers. With a gleam of wild, avaricious triumph in his eyes, he snatched the device away from me, holding it up before himself with both fists clenched tightly about its handle.

Scape had but a split second in which to revel in his long-desired possession of that instrument, before we were both cast from our feet by the clawed tip of the last of the Colossus' jointed legs striking the ground immediately before us. Thrown once more upon my back, I managed to raise my head, just in time to perceive the iron claw rise from the hole it had dug in the ash-covered earth. As the Colossus shifted its balance, preparatory to taking another of its cumbersome steps forward, the claw swung about in the orbit of its range. Its riveted mass hurtled directly toward me with sufficient force to separate my head from the shoulders below.

There was not time to do aught but close my eyes, not wishing to see more of the instrument of my certain doom. I winced and braced myself, anticipating its impact—

Which either happened with such merciful swiftness as to be absolutely painless, or did not happen at all. I cautiously opened one eye, then the other, and saw that the claw had stopped in its horizontal arc a few inches from my face. Shifting my position upon the ground, I beheld that the immense tower had halted in its tracks. From deep within it still came the clanking sounds of its propulsive machinery, disengaged from those elements by which the construction made its way from place to place.

I could also see, some yards away, Evangeline still standing erect. Her eyes widened as she gazed upward to the crowning level of the Colossus, the back of one hand pressed against her mouth as though to stifle a cry of astonishment.

Turning about, I brought my own sight in line with hers and spied that upon which her vision had seized. Even at the lofty height above us, Captain Crowcroft's face was unmistakably apparent behind the curved glass windows of the walking light's bridge, his hands taut upon those controls which guided its progress. I could discern as well his gaze directed correspondingly downward—not to me, of course, but upon the visage of his beloved.

Even at this distance and inconvenient angle, the man appeared as distraught as when I had last seen him, in that small, supposedly blood-soaked room in East London. What change there was, consisted of a fierce, even maniacal, glint of determination in his eye, as though in his mind he had launched upon some great endeavour that would rectify all the world's injustices, or at least those immediately to hand.

"*Now* what?" Another had gained the same impression as I. Having scrambled to his knees, Scape looked upward at the tower and its commander with evident irritation. "What's he doing? He's going to screw the whole thing up!"

Miss McThane came to her companion's aid, grasping his arm and pulling him erect, with the *Vox Universalis* key still clutched to his chest. "Look—" She pointed to the curved flank of the Colossus. "He's shut down the pressure relief valves."

"Crap, you're right." Scape's expression shifted to one of alarm. "Crazy sonuvabitch—"

I could see that which she indicated, though I was yet ignorant of its significance. All along the length of the Colossus, various brass appendages protruded, appearing similar to barnacles encrusted upon the smooth hull of an ocean-going ship that had been tilted on end. I had some vague understanding of their function, that they facilitated the operation of the machine by expelling the surfeit of steam built up in the compressors within. I had witnessed much the same with the smaller lighthouse in Cornwall, in the form of continuous plumes of vapour escaping from the valves. On this occasion, however, no such emissions were visible. Indeed, the devices studding the exterior of the Colossus could actually be seen trembling and shivering, as though barely capable of restraining the swiftly mounting forces behind them.

Indeed, as I stood and gave greater scrutiny to the Colossus towering before us, its entire structure seemed to vibrate with an increasingly urgent tension. The conviction struck me that if I were to reach out and lay my hand against it, the sensation would resemble that of touching an animate creature, trembling with the destructive power contained inside.

"But does that not mean," I spoke as I looked toward Scape and Miss McThane, "that some terrible consequence is close upon us?"

"You got that right," a grim-faced Scape replied. "Not enough the guy has a walking lighthouse to stomp around in—he's gotta turn it into a bomb as well."

"Did I hear you correctly? A *bomb*?"

"Yeah—a steam bomb." Scape nodded toward the hissing construction. "You know how much pressure builds up in something like that, when you shut down the relief valves?"

"Not precisely," I said. "But I assume rather a lot."

"You're assuming right, pal. When that thing hits the overload point and it goes off, there's not going to be any of it left. Or anything around it, either."

"But—" I looked from him, up to the top of the Colossus, then back to Scape again. "What conceivable intent would Captain Crowcroft fulfill by initiating a cataclysm such as that?"

"If you'd been around when we were all talking—" Scape pointed to the smouldering ruins of Featherwhite House. "Then you'd know he's got a thing going on in his head, about the stuff that's been happening."

"You mean all these various conspiracies? Fusible and his companions' gambling, then Stonebrake and his mad scheming on top of that—"

"Gotta admit, that was pretty stupid of your buddy Stonebrake, to rub Crowcroft's face in the way he'd been jerked around." Scape shook his head. "No wonder he flipped and punched Stonebrake's lights out."

"This was something you witnessed?"

"The whole thing," said Scape. "Wouldn't have surprised me if Stonebrake had been dead even before he whanged his head on that mantelpiece in there. Crowcroft's a big guy, plus he was really worked up. Way not smart, to egg somebody on like that."

"But if Stonebrake is now dead—then why this?" I again indicated the enormous bulk of the Colossus, hissing and vibrating close to us. "Surely the captain, whether he intended the death of his tormentor or not, has had sufficient satisfaction thereby?"

"Sure, if that'd been all that Crowcroft was bugged about. But it wasn't just that he was going on about—"

"It was everything," chimed in Miss McThane. "The whole bit. Including Mrs. Fletcher—"

I wished to hear no more. Their joint dissertation on whatever motives prompted Captain Crowcroft's actions, rational or otherwise, had already continued at too great a length, given the perilous circumstances of a powerfully destructive device standing close to hand.

"Remain here if you wish," I said. "But whatever Crowcroft's ultimate intentions might be, I feel no desire to be in his proximity when he achieves his own self-destruction. I'm leaving—*now*."

In the event, my own efforts at escape were rendered superfluous. No sooner had I spoken than the Colossus' great crab-like legs stirred once again into motion. The enormous claws lifted each in turn from the jagged holes they had dug into the earth, propelling the lofty device to some further destination.

So ponderous and measured was the walking lighthouse's progress, that I nevertheless considered it well-advised to take to my own lighter heels, the better to increase the distance between myself and its inevitable explosion. I had little cause to doubt Scape's assurances along these lines, that the force of the blast would be immense, when it finally came. If its movement and my own were sufficient to put miles between myself and it, the undoubtedly safer I would be.

And not myself alone. I had formed a resolve to furnish what protection I could to Lord Fusible's daughter—what better time than the present to act upon that quixotic ambition? Turning about from Scape and Miss McThane, I looked to see where the young woman had gotten to, so that I might grasp her wrist and escort her—by force, if necessary—to some further, more secure location.

As I had anticipated, Evangeline had been rendered to a state of high emotion by having glimpsed her betrothed high above, at the controls of the Colossus. No doubt it had been an upsetting moment for both of them, all their possibilities of future happiness erased by whatever vengeful ambition Crowcroft had seized upon. The lighthouse passed lumberingly away from our midst, and I spotted the poor girl gazing after it, tears coursing down her face.

So extreme was her situation, that it was only my coming to her side that prevented her collapsing in a swoon to the ground.

"We must away." I bore her slight weight against my arm circling her shoulders. "There is likely scarce time left before—"

"No!" cried Evangeline. "There is no time left at all. Do you not see?"

"I see the necessity for removing ourselves from this place."

"Not that—" She pushed against my chest with both her hands, as she turned her tear-wet face toward the tower clumping away from us. "You do not know his mind as I do—you cannot! But even if I had not overheard all that he spoke to my father and the others, I would still have been able to discern his intentions. It is *Mrs. Fletcher* he wants! He seeks to *destroy* her!"

"But of course . . ." I nodded, perceiving that which she wished to convey to me. "And thereby redeem himself, for the wickedness of his sins . . ."

No opportunity provided itself for further exposition of the matter. For while we had spoken, another had spied the towering construction that had departed from us but a moment before. A great roaring, combined of cascading rubble and groaning machinery, assaulted our ears. Both Evangeline and I turned and saw, farther along the river's course, the Iron Lady revealing even vaster dimensions of her transmogrified self, as she reared higher from the ruins of the Houses of Parliament.

Flames leapt from every furnace-like aperture of the fleshless, mechanized body; Mrs. Fletcher's searing gaze swung about, fastening upon the slowly approaching Colossus. A bright avidity sprang up in that hideously magnified face, as though this encounter were one for which she somehow fiercely longed.

CHAPTER
24

*Mr. Dower Witnesses
the Fiery End of All Things*

So numerous have been reports of that cataclysmic encounter upon the Thames bank, that I further set pen to paper with little anticipation of relating much of which the reader has not already heard. And given that a circumspect silence in regard to my own affairs, on both my part and that of others, is something to which I have long aspired, I would hope for some indulgence were I to say no more of what transpired then.

Alas, the pen scribbles on, leaving its spidery ink trail across the page, as though even such as simple device as this were somehow possessed of that appalling animation by which my father's creations were characterized. So little do we know of ourselves and of what hidden mainsprings drive our actions! Were it to be unveiled tomorrow that all of Humanity, once flensed of skin and other softer bits, were nothing but ticking and hissing contrivances of clockwork and steam, I confess that I would not be greatly surprised. Not because the extraordinary nature of so much of my experience has rendered me incapable of astonishment, but simply because such a revelation would merely confirm my own belief, increasingly held, that we all move unheeding along iron rails and tracks not laid down by our own desires and cognition.

Which is to say no more than that much of what I did—and others as well—in those moments of fiery apocalypse, remains somewhat incomprehensible to me. Or at least unanticipated. If there is any value to my writing of them, and the reader musing over these inartful words, it would be in the explication of those actions around which so much error and rumour has circulated.

In the midst of that tumultuous night, seemingly composed of equal parts human riot and mechanical upheaval, Lord Fusible's daughter conveyed to me what she had surmised of Captain Crowcroft's intent. I had no reason to doubt her—only some overwhelming resolve on his part could have motivated his steering the Colossus of Blackpool toward its apparent destination. A more balanced composition of the mind might have inspired one still possessed of reasonableness to abandon the towering, ambulatory construction, the better to wrap his protecting arms around his beloved and convey her to some safer place. Leaving the latter to someone such as myself indicates a pronounced lack of consideration, particularly for one to whom he had previously avowed some degree of affection.

The inadequacy of my ability to protect Evangeline was soon made apparent. As the Colossus had rumbled away from us, with Captain Crowcroft at its elevated helm, both Evangeline and I had witnessed Mrs. Fletcher's white-hot gaze fasten upon the lighthouse. The malice incorporated in that regard was as quickly evident; no doubt the Iron Lady, now transformed to even more hideous dimensions and efficacy, perceived that the Colossus had been altered to an explosive device capable at least of severely harming, if not completely extinguishing, her. Granted, this would be suicidal as well on the lighthouse's commander, but we both felt certain that such was his grim state of mind.

"Prepare yourself—" I caught up Evangeline in my arms, pressing her tight against myself. My action was not so much a consequence of the above deliberations, which I might have formed into coherent words and thoughts if I had the time, but rather came from some instinctive presentiment of danger greater than that which already surrounded us. "She's about to do something—"

No sooner had I spoken than my foresight was confirmed. The immense form of the transmogrified Mrs. Fletcher, having reared higher into the smoke-heavy night sky from the ruins of the Houses of Parliament, now lunged forward, as might some smaller predatory creature from its rocky desert lair, in order to seize upon its prey. All along the Iron Lady's length, the open furnace doors flared with brighter and more consuming fires, as though her appetites were fuel greater than any amount of coal shoveled in by her sweat-glistening minions. Even from the distance at which we stood, we could feel the surge of heat radiating from her.

The vaulting horizontal arc of the Iron Lady fell short of its target, yet had devastating effect nonetheless. With Evangeline still in my arms, I braced for the impact of such a cumbersome mass striking the earth. Thus prepared, I managed to keep us both on our feet while the ground bucked and tilted, as might an ocean receiving an equivalent tonnage in its midst. Behind us, I could hear the last charred timbers of Featherwhite House shearing apart and toppling into the ashes at their center.

Another, larger object toppled as well, immediately before us. While in motion, transporting itself from one location to another, a walking light was self-evidently less secure in its mounting; the relatively slight elevation produced by the extension of the jointed claws beneath the tower's base rendered the entire structure out of balance. Given the exaggerated height of the Colossus of Blackpool, bringing a proportionately greater weight higher above the Earth's surface, the shock produced by Mrs. Fletcher's mass striking the Thames riverbank toppled the lighthouse. The towering construction began to fall forward as though it were one of those bare-chested wrestlers who amuse the crowds on market days, the more skillful opponent having swept the other's feet from beneath.

For a few moments, Evangeline and I watched aghast as the Colossus swayed back and forth, with Captain Crowcroft visible as he furiously manipulated the various levers and controls before him on the bridge, struggling to keep the tower aright. Taking no effort for his own safety, Crowcroft was unable to keep from being bodily flung toward the curved windows of the lighthouse's bridge. The glass shattered as he struck it, the glittering fragments sparkling as they fell through the churning smoke and steam. In their midst was the captain himself, tumbling end over end as he hurtled toward the ground.

To my own relief, I saw that Crowcroft's preceding exertions had had some effect, by which we all were spared immediate annihilation. I had anticipated, given the manner which the Colossus' exterior relief valves had been shut down, that the resulting steam bomb would explode as soon as the tower hammered itself to the earth. As close as we were, we would doubtless have been rendered into our component atoms. When I opened my eyes, I perceived that we had been spared this fate. The Colossus leaned forward at a precarious angle, but still sat trembling upon its clawlike legs, its awkward position due to whatever adjustments that Crowcroft had so quickly and deftly made.

Evangeline tore herself from my grasp and ran toward the figure of her beloved, lying motionless upon the ground. My attention was taken from the sight of her kneeling and raising Crowcroft into her arms—from above me came the deafening shriek of the lighthouse's relief valves as the escalating pressure within tore the brass fixtures from their mountings. The Colossus itself visibly shuddered, indicating that the cataclysm I feared was but moments away.

The temptation was strong to turn heel and flee, putting as much distance between myself and the lighthouse as was yet possible. As close as Evangeline and the fallen captain were to its base, they would likely be transported instantly and painlessly to the next world, a fate which no doubt would be the young woman's wish, so long as it could be accomplished together with him. I would like to believe it was not mere cowardice on my part, but some tender instinct, that prompted me to think that whatever avowal I had undertaken on the young woman's behalf was fulfilled by this much having been brought about, freeing me to preserve my own life as best I could.

In the event, however, there was not time to make a definitive ethical determination. For something even yet more extraordinary occurred.

I had been frozen to the spot by the combined horrific aspects of the Iron Lady some distance away, yet so close that my hair was singed by the heat belched forth from the furnace doors of her gargantuan body, and the hissing shrieks of the explosive tower close at hand. Finally, I stirred into motion—not *away* from the Colossus and the scalding forces building up inside, but rather *toward* it.

One part of my mind shouted at the other, accusing it of having abandoned all pretensions of rationality. That might well have been; insanity could alone explain my grasping the rail of the metal ladder dangling from the base of the Colossus and hoisting myself up toward the riveted door by which I could gain access to the construction's interior.

The sole comprehensible thought remaining to me, divorced from any consideration of my own security, was that once inside I would be able to mount the central spiraling staircase all the way to the bridge of the Colossus, from which Crowcroft had been so precipitously cast. Long before, on the coast of Cornwall, I had however briefly laid hands upon the controlling levers of such a walking light; now, a pitiable delusion had formed within me, that such brief experience would enable me to resume that operation commenced by that other man, guiding the lighthouse and its swiftly gathering explosive forces toward a desired consummation with the Iron Lady herself.

That such a self-destructive intent had now arisen, I attribute to the increasingly disordered state within my head, very likely the cumulative result of the various blows and buffeting I had received. I am not by nature greatly motivated by an altruistic love of my fellow man, so for me to undertake such an effort, seemingly for no other reason than to save Britain in general from the all-encompassing ambitions of its power-maddened Prime Minister, no doubt seems uncharacteristic on my part. Perhaps, at the end of the day, I was impelled by a worthier desire than to exact a final vengeance on that person who, most correctly perceived, had been the first instigator of all these schemes that had caused so much trouble for me. I derived some wry consolation, savoured in a flash as I laid my hand upon the heated metal of the ladder's rungs, that in doing so, I would lose no more than that life which I had already resolved to discard, back at that shabby room in Cornwall, in what now seemed ages ago.

If there were no longer any instinct of self-preservation to hinder me on this course, something else managed to intervene. No sooner had I progressed but a few hand-holds up the side of the Colossus toward its hatchway door than I was halted by the grip of a hand upon my ankle below.

Unable to move further, I looked down and saw that it was Scape who had seized hold of me. He stood upon the lowest of the ladder's rungs, having followed me there from the same spot on the ground from which I had proceeded.

"Hold up, Dower—" Face contorted with his sudden exertions, he called up to me. "You're not doing this—"

His presence in such immediate proximity took me by surprise. In truth, I had completely forgotten about both him and his companion, Miss McThane, no doubt due to the ferocity and alarming nature of the events that had swept across the scene. Beyond that, I had never had any reason to believe him as being impelled by other considerations than his own skin and fortunes—if my mind had turned to him at all, I would have reasonably concluded that he had long fled from the spot, as I should have done already, the better to save himself from the explosion that was now increasingly imminent.

"Leave off!" I kicked my leg, futilely attempting to free myself from the tightened clench of his grasp. "There is no way of preventing what is about to happen—so I might as well attempt to derive what good as I can from it."

"Don't be an idiot!" Scape struggled to keep me from escaping. "You can't—"

"What concern is it of yours?" The mingled jets of steam, escaping from all about us, were loud enough that I needed to shout in order to make myself heard. "Save yourself, if you wish. But this is what I have set my mind to accomplish."

"Yeah, well, that's the problem." Having hooked his arm around the rail of the ladder, he managed to set both hands upon my ankle, even more forcibly preventing me from climbing further. "You can do whatever the hell you want—I don't give a rat's ass—but not this, you moron."

"And why not, if I so choose?"

"Because you don't know the first thing about machines. Any kind of 'em, let alone this puppy." One of Scape's hands let go of me for a moment, so that it might grasp the next rung and pull him higher toward me. "You'd be a complete failure with a frickin' can opener, for Christ's sake. There's no way you could do anything with this."

Enough time had passed from my initial unthinking impulse—at least a few seconds—that some of its force had dissipated. The more rational part of my mind was reluctantly forced to agree that the man was very likely correct in what he had said. A clear memory arose in my thoughts, of standing on the bridge of that other lighthouse and being completely baffled by all the various levers and controls which Captain Crowcroft had wielded then.

Nevertheless, I persisted in my endeavour. Holding on to the ladder with one hand, I used the other to push against Scape's brow. "Be that as it may," I said. "If with myself resides the only possibility of setting this device in motion, thereby bringing it close enough to Mrs. Fletcher that she will be destroyed in the explosion which will soon take place, then I must take that chance. There is no other alternative but to admit failure, thereby allowing her to accelerate her reign of industrial terror."

"That's crap." Scape spoke through gritted teeth as he fought to evade my restraining hand. "Just because you're incapable of doing it, that doesn't mean I can't run this thing."

"You?" I peered down at him in bafflement. The roar and hiss of escaping steam, combined with the stifling smoke, caused me to wonder if I had heard him correctly. "But if you were to do so—that would mean—"

"Yeah, right. Whatever." Scape took advantage of my passing disorientation by reaching past my hand and seizing hold of my shirtfront. With that, he was able to pull himself up directly before me. For a moment, we looked into each other's eyes. "Let me worry about that, okay?"

The close juxtaposition of our bodies, and our precarious combined grasp upon the lighthouse's external ladder, forced an object from where it had been tucked into Scape's waistcoat. We both glanced down, watching the clockwork key to my father's *Vox Universalis* device—that article which Scape had taken such elaborate pains to acquire—as it fell to the ground below us. It struck a rock with sufficient force to burst it into component pieces, gears and cogs flying in all directions, impelled by the sudden uncoiling of the key's various tightly wound mainsprings. Within seconds, the coveted item was reduced to glittering debris, scattered across the ashen earth.

"Damn." A grimace slid over Scape's face as he regarded the wreckage, not merely physical but also embodying the demise of whatever of his ambitions had centered upon the device. "That sucks. That *really* sucks."

I was not quite sure of the exact meaning of such a comment, but the man's sharp disappointment was evident in the hard-set tightening of his mouth.

"I'm sorry." There seemed nothing else appropriate for me to say. "Its importance to you was something of which I was aware—"

"Shit happens."

His stoicism, however profane, impressed me. "If there were anything I could for you, to allay your feelings in this regard—"

"Actually . . ." Scape gave a slow nod. "Now that you mention it—there is."

Our bizarre colloquy proceeded, as we clung to the side of the ominously vibrating lighthouse tower.

"Yes?" I gazed with some small hope into his eyes. "And what is that?"

"Take a hike."

He raised one knee, high enough to press it against my abdomen, and pushed. His unanticipated action was sufficient to break my grasp upon the ladder's rungs. In the blink of an eye, I found myself toppling free, falling through space.

With the breath already expelled from my lungs, I landed upon my back. Dazed, I was but vaguely aware of the sharp-toothed fragments of the *Vox Universalis* key beneath me. My vision cleared enough that I was able to watch as Scape swarmed the rest of the way up the ladder, pulled open the riveted hatchway door, and vanished inside the lighthouse.

Gasping, I raised myself up onto my elbows. I ducked my head as one of the crab-like steel claws swung near, the lighthouse's propulsive mechanisms again stirring to life. With the sounds of intermingled mechanical groaning and clattering, the Colossus began moving once more toward the fiery shape of the Iron Lady in the distance, her withering, scornful gaze fastened upon the approaching machine.

In regaining my feet, I was assisted by Miss McThane, grasping my arm and drawing me upward. "Come on," she hurriedly spoke. "We gotta get away from here!"

"But—" I pointed to the Colossus lumbering away from us. Scape was but barely visible far above, yanking at the construction's various levers and controls, seemingly at random but with sufficient effect to guide it toward its destination. "What about—"

"There's no stopping him now." Miss McThane tugged again at my arm. "He's doing his thing, so let's do ours."

Swiftly glancing about, I spotted Evangeline and Captain Crowcroft, insensible to the world and all its calamitous doings, locked in a desperate embrace. I shook myself free of Miss McThane's attentions and ran toward the couple.

"There's no time for that—" I succeeded in raising the captain's vision from where he had lowered his face close to that of his beloved. "That monstrosity will go off any second now."

The man was not so far gone in his adoring reconciliation with the young woman that he was unable to perceive the imminent threat to her person as well as his. Still tightly holding her, he turned his gaze and beheld, as I did, the Colossus picking up speed as Scape piloted it toward the fiercely anticipatory Mrs. Fletcher. Clouds of churning steam trailed behind it, in vivid presentiment of the eruptive force that would soon transform the world around us.

"Yes—" With an arm wrapped around Evangeline's shoulders, he urged her forward. "Let us hurry."

Our small group swept up Miss McThane with us, quickly heading for whatever safety could be achieved with distance. As we passed by the smouldering ruins of Featherwhite House, I hesitated for a moment, allowing the others to continue their rapid pace as I glanced back over my shoulder. Thus I viewed the climactic event of the Iron Lady lunging forward once more, the flames bursting from her various furnace doors with such fierce heat as to cast aside the last of the attendants shovelling coal within. Her searing visage seemed possessed of such madness as would consume all before it, all that stood between her and whatever apotheosis had seized upon the engines of her desires.

That was the last I saw. One does not witness such a cataclysm as the one that followed . . .

One awakens from it.

I found myself face-down in the cobbled street beyond the grounds of the incinerated townhouse. A vague memory faded within my head, of waves of smoke and steam rolling above me. When before I had been explosively transported, unheedingly propelled from one spot to another, I had had the sensation of flying upon snow-white clouds, as might angels in a vaporous sky. On this occasion, I dreamt—however briefly—that I lay upon the ocean floor, all the universe's tumultuous events passing fathoms above my head.

The impression faded as I raised my muddied shirtfront from the cobblestones, over which the departed rioters had stormed, waving their rude torches. I could see no-one else, living or deceased, anywhere near me—my hope was that the others, unencumbered by my delay, had managed to reach some point safely beyond the worst of the explosion's effects.

A great quiet seemed to fill the empty spaces about me. For a moment, I thought I might have been deafened by the blast, my eardrums torn to tiny rags within my skull. But then I heard the soft patter of tiny metal fragments raining upon the ground, and realized that what I perceived was the comforting silence that ensues when fearsome machines are at last shut down.

Scarcely able to place one faltering foot before the other, I staggered back to that sloping rise from which I had previously been able to gaze along the length of the river, out toward where the Houses of Parliament had once stood. In the distance, I could see neither Mrs. Fletcher nor the Colossus. As the smoke dispersed above the city's smouldering ruins, nothing remained below of their fiery consummation.

EPILOGUE

I APPEND these final words from that locale where I commenced, in what seems centuries past. Adventures such as those befallen to me have the inevitable consequence of aging one; it is not our years that make us old, but our experiences.

Through the window of the inn—that same from which I had fled in both desperate penury and greed—comes to my ear the slow, ponderous roll of the waves heaving themselves upon the rocky Cornish coast. In that time before, I had considered the sound somewhat dreary and oppressive. Such reflects the disordered state of my mind then; now it seems rather peaceful to me.

As the pen scratches upon the paper, adding sheet after ink-marred sheet to the stack mounting beside the wobbly little table at which I sit, more tranquil thoughts—or at least resigned—slide past me as well.

Of those monstrous events which I have described, perhaps at tedious length, none were at last sufficient to place me in the quiet of that grave which I once sought. I am confident this seems obvious to the reader. There might still be some curiosity on others' parts as to the further details of my fate, and the fates of those entwined, however briefly, with mine. It is of those that I now write.

Concerning London itself, so grievously wounded in both structure and populace by the various explosions, fires, riots, and whatever else through which I had passed relatively unharmed, there is little need to speak. The city's reconstruction, complete to raising once more the ancient walls and chambers of the Palace of Westminster, is a matter of public knowledge. Perhaps the organs of government housed there, both chastened by fiery events and freed of the overbearing dominance of the late Mrs. Fletcher, will go about the affairs of state with greater wisdom than before. Experience shows that one always hopes as much, but is invariably disappointed. In this instance, however, an exception might prevail. Accounts have reached even this distant locale, of more debris than the smouldering, inanimate wreckage of the once Iron Lady being carted away from the city's heart, to be discarded upon those rubbish-laden riverbanks where I had once woken. Many of the steam-bearing pipes that had snaked through the busy streets and up the sides of buildings, having been irremediably damaged or become the object of general loathing by the citizenry, have been torn up and removed as well. Smaller, less intimidating sources of heat and power—coal-burning hearths, straining human and animal muscle, and the like, as existed before— have seemingly replaced those great, grim enterprises that had laced the countryside like a shining spider's web. The steam miners, released from the scalding dangers of their previous employment, are free to return to gentler, more agrarian pursuits. Whether these kinder arrangements will persist—who can foresee? Humanity possesses an infinite capacity to—as my late acquaintance Scape might have put it in his distasteful futuristic *patois*—screw up a good deal.

More of that odd figure in a bit. I first consider it necessary to assure those with an interest in the affairs of young romantics—as who is not?—that Lord Fusible's daughter, Evangeline, did indeed become the bride of a greatly reformed Captain Crowcroft. Her father's wealth had been greatly diminished in the wreckage of his own gambling schemes, the fraudulent wagers put forth by himself and his associates being confiscated by the Sea & Light Book upon exposure of their manifest chicaneries. Those gentlemen had all been unwitting pawns in the larger conspiracies swirling about them—as had been as well Evangeline's husband, Crowcroft's remunerative fame erased by the revelation of the walking lights as a vast concocted fiction. These lovers scarce considered that much of a loss, however, sustaining themselves on their renewed affection for each other and the honest labour that Crowcroft expends helming a fishing trawler out in the North Sea. Whatever dangers he faces there, they must seem light in comparison with those hideous vices to which he had once been addicted, and of which Evangeline has graciously forgiven him. I doubt that either has occasion to remark openly upon the conniving Stonebrake's death caused by that maddened blow from Crowcroft's fist, all evidence of what the world might ordinarily consider a crime having been consumed in the fiery destruction of Featherwhite House. They are wise in letting such an incident fade from memory. Join with me in wishing that once storm-tossed couple well, in whatever more tranquil harbor they have found.

My occasional nemesis Scape arrived at such a place as well, though not in this world, but the next. He schemes no more; the examination that his companion, Miss McThane, made of the scene at which the Colossus of Blackpool had exploded, annihilating both itself and the closely embracing Prime Minister, convinced us that no atom of he who had steered the lighthouse there remained connected to another. Scape was mercifully vaporized in an instant, suffering little in his translation to the afterlife—or at least I attempted to assure Miss McThane of as much, her grief at his loss being apparent to me then. I had believed the two of them to be more conspiratorially than emotionally bound to each other; at that moment I realized I had been in error about this.

Perhaps in eulogy to the vanished Scape, over the next few days Miss McThane explicated much that had previously baffled me—to wit, why such an individual, so committed to nothing but his own welfare, had sacrificed his very life in bringing about the Iron Lady's destruction. As we had made our own way from the still-smouldering city, she had revealed that his actions in doing so had not greatly taken her by surprise. There had been some alteration in his character, unsuspected by me, of which she had been aware.

In this regard, it is with some satisfaction that I am able to relate that the late Mrs. Fletcher, the secretive, hidden initiator of so many schemes, had yet been cozened by one who she had believed was but a cat's-paw in her own devisings. It had been not to fool me, but to fool *her*, that Scape had maintained his former predatory bearing. When in actuality, other and nobler purposes had prompted his every move, including the operation of the establishment Fex, by which he had gained not only access to the Iron Lady, but her confidence as well.

That which had so thoroughly transformed a rogue to something rather more altruistic, Miss McThane informed me, had been occasioned by Scape's renewed application to himself of that device created by my father, which had enabled him not only to see the Future, but become a creature of those days to come. His doing so had been prompted by nothing grander than the desire to concoct more potentially lucrative schemes, all of his earlier ones having come to naught.

"He got the idea," Miss McThane said to me, "that if he could see even further into the future, he'd know what was really coming down the turnpike, and he'd be able to figure out some way of making a profit from all that. At least that was what he thought."

In the event, however, he glimpsed something else ahead of our kind—and that vision altered him irrevocably. As his companion related to me, through the mechanism of my father's device, Scape had seen a world yet to come, that proceeded not on the powers of either steam or coal, but on some hideous dark substance leaking out of the very bowels of the earth, blackening the oceans, leaving the sea-creatures and birds mired in tarry waste on the sulphurous beaches. Of whatever this diabolical material might consist, in those days of the Future, something occurred that allowed it to continue emerging, like black blood from a black wound. And no-one in that time to come could halt it. Nor did they even desire to.

Understandably, this appalling vision had deeply affected Scape. At first, Miss McThane had thought this glimpse of the Future was really nothing more than a nightmare, a figment of her partner's imagination, than some approaching reality.

"Is such," I had enquired of her, "what you believe now?"

She had replied that she no longer made so confident a dismissal— the change in Scape's every aspect had been so profound. All of his most recent scheming, the whole masquerade of himself and Miss

McThane as the Fex establishment's Duncan MacDuff and Valvienne, their conspiracies with Lord Fusible and the other directors of
Phototrope Limited, even their deceptions practiced upon Mrs.
Fletcher, had been but to lay hold somehow of all the necessary pieces
of the *Vox Universalis* device created by my father. Scape had not
been certain whether or not the whales could be communicated with,
but on the remote chance that it was indeed possible, an overwhelming desire had been formed within him to accomplish exactly that.
He had even achieved some initial success, Miss McThane informed
me, using the pipe organ aboard the Mission's ship upon which the
order's founder, Father Jonah, had been wont to sermonize to the
long-suffering aquatic mammals. What results Scape achieved had
been sufficient to spur him on to even greater exertions to bring the
Vox Universalis into operation, in pursuit of complete and accurate
communication with the immense sea-creatures.

These revelations explicated one minor mystery that remained
from my disagreeable adventures. Miss McThane assured me that it
was very likely one of the whales with which Scape had conversed
that had capsized the boat in the Thames by which I had been rescued from drowning by Evangeline and her father's servants. The
whale, having formed a desire for further discourse with Scape, had
swum up the Thames to find him, fortuitously encountering our
small vessel instead. On the recurring principle that stranger things
had happened, this explanation sufficed for me. But one other item
in this regard still puzzled me.

"What was it," I had enquired of Miss McThane, "of which
Scape had desired to speak to the whales?"

"Don't know," she had somberly replied. "Maybe it was to warn
them. Of all the bad stuff that's going to happen to them someday.
All that black gunk leaking into the ocean, whatever the hell it is. Or
maybe . . ."

Her voice had dwindled away as she spoke to me. "Yes?" I had
prompted.

"Maybe . . ." Miss McThane had turned a melancholy little smile
toward me. "Maybe he just wanted to apologize to them. Who knows?"

Indeed. Of that singular individual, whose machinations had so disrupted my life, nothing is left to impart.

In his absence, my fate and that of his companion became entwined. Fearing the worst, Miss McThane had diverted a portion of the Fex establishment's revenues to a personal cache, all in pounds sterling. Our last errand in the devastated London was to retrieve that money. Having done so, however, she had no further destination in mind. But having also formed some slender affection for me—motivated perhaps more from pity than any stronger emotion—she threw her lot in with mine.

Upon making a return to the Cornish coast, that being a locale both remote from London yet still somewhat familiar to me, we discovered that my former host, the proprietor of the shabby seaside inn where I had once attempted to press forward my own self-destructive resolution, had died from an excess of spleen and alcohol. The deceased innkeeper's heirs were open to the offer of purchase made by myself and Miss McThane. Thus I find myself here, nominally the proprietor of that facility from which I had once anticipated being carried out feet-first and lifeless.

Having launched upon this partnership, which provides a modest sustenance to us, other relations between Miss McThane and myself were eventually initiated, sufficient for the nearby villagers to speak of her as Mrs. Dower. We do not disabuse them of this domestic notion.

Whether she ever thinks of Scape, or dreams of him when I raise my own head from the pillow and gaze upon her sleeping beside me—I do not know. She does not speak of him, or of that world to come. Her silence on those matters is more than acceptable to me.

At this moment, as I reach the bottom of the final sheet of paper upon which I intend to write, she is downstairs in the scullery and kitchen, going about some household task before extinguishing the lanterns and coming up to bed.

I turn my head and gaze out the window at the sea, its presence revealed more by the sounds of its unrelenting motion than anything caught by the eye. I cannot hear them, but I know the whales are deep in those dark waters. And I wonder what they say to each other.

⚜ ABOUT THE AUTHOR ⚜

K. W. JETER is the author of *Morlock Night, Dr. Adder, The Glass Hammer, Noir,* and other dark fantasy/visionary science fiction. In 1987, when discussing *Infernal Devices* to which *Fiendish Schemes* is the direct sequel, he coined the term *steampunk*. A native of California, he currently lives in Ecuador.